Praise for the

Th...

'Intelligent and pacy thriller ... a taut keenly observed tale of revenge, perseverance and the struggle against injustice.' (Paula Hawkins)

'A stunning debut from an exciting new addition to the world of crime fiction.' (Stephen Booth)

Cold Dawn

'Stylish, authoritative crime writing from someone who knows ... vivid and gripping.' (Oliver Harris)

'A gripping and clever thriller in a magnificent setting ... I loved it.' (Sarah Ward)

Cold Summer

'A police procedural so action-packed it reads like a thriller – with a Nepalese twist.' (Dr Andy Martin, *Reacher Said Nothing: Lee Child and the Making of Make Me*)

'Ellson hits the spot with *Cold Summer*. This pacy and intriguing thriller is not to be missed. Pull up the drawbridge and settle in. Castle is back!' (Keith Wright, the Inspector Stark series)

'A gripping series.' (Samantha Brownley, UK Crime Book Club)

Also by James Ellson

The Trail
Cold Dawn
Cold Summer

James Ellson was a police officer for fifteen years, starting in London and finishing as a detective inspector at Moss Side in Manchester. When he left the police he started writing, and his debut novel *The Trail* was published in 2020. Both *The Trail* and *Cold Dawn* were longlisted for the Boardman Tasker Award. *Cold Summer* concludes the Nepal trilogy. *Base Line* is the fourth book in the DCI Castle series.

James is a keen climber and mountaineer, and has visited Nepal many times. He has climbed 6,812-metre Ama Dablam, and soloed the Matterhorn.

He lives in the Peak District with his wife, and manages their smallholding, which includes bees and an orchard.

x.com/jamesellson3
facebook.com/james.ellson.98
jamesellson.com

BASE LINE

James Ellson

Cambium

First edition, 2024

Cambium Press

A CIP record for this book is available from the British Library

ISBN 978-1-7394421-6-3 (paperback)
ISBN 978-1-7394421-7-0 (ebook)

Printed in Great Britain by Clays Ltd, Elcograf S.p.A

1 3 5 7 9 8 6 4 2

For Nick and Max

1

Varroa dotted the inspection board. The tiny orange mites snuck into brood cells just before capping to lay their own eggs, which quickly hatched and fed on the developing pupae. The result was deformed honeybees: stunted abdomens, shrivelled or missing wings. Unchecked, varroa could destroy the colony – and bring down civilisation.

For Rick, beekeeping helped to keep policework in perspective. After counting thirty-nine mites, he brushed them off the sticky board and slotted it back. He opened the top of the hive and laid Apivar strips between the frames in the brood box. An annual treatment kept varroa under control.

In the small gateway of the apiary, a Range Rover with tinted windows parked next to his car.

Rick ignored it. He placed an empty super onto the brood box, and poured a litre of 1:1 sugar solution into a feeder. It was mid-October, the drones were dead, and the worker bees needed to prepare for winter. Some years he'd fed them a dozen times.

A heavy footfall approached.

'I tried phoning.'

Rick fitted the hive roof back into place, cinched down the restraining strap, and hefted two house bricks on top. He removed his gauntlets, unzipped and pushed back his veil.

His boss was upon him. The superintendent wore a diamond-patterned sweater, jeans and wellington boots, and looked as comfortable as a politician at the weekend. Robbo dipped a stick into a pot of chocolate and crunched it down. After careful consideration, held it out.

'Did you miss breakfast?' said Rick, holding up a hand like a traffic rat.

Robbo dipped another stick, licked the chocolate off the end and chewed like a combine harvester.

'The protocol for the special investigations unit, which you agreed to, states you should have your phone on twenty-four seven.'

'It is on.'

Robbo dipped and licked. 'Do we need to amend the protocol?'

Rick listened to his boss chewing, unable to decide whether the reply was more typical of senior management, or of uniform. The former liked nothing better than to tinker with policy and procedures, the latter liked nothing better than to check compliance with every subsection and every subsubsection.

'Have you got a case for us?' Us was almost an exaggeration, but not quite. There were supposed to be four of them in the new unit, five including Mags. Paperwork and brews were shared. The unit wasn't a democracy, but it was egalitarian, in addition to which, he slept in the same bed as Maggie.

Robbo folded the foil cover over the pot, then seemed unsure what to do with it. Finally, he plonked it down on the roof of the hive.

Rick left his boss a few seconds longer to battle alone with whatever it was that required help. A silvery cobweb damp with overnight rain stretched between two of the hives. Bright red mushrooms grew nearby. A robin flew down and surveyed with a critical eye. The apiary was Rick's oceanfront, his mountaintop;

the place where he came to unwind and recalibrate, and forget his night screaming.

'A school minibus has crashed on the ring road. Another fifty metres and it would be South West Manchester's problem.' Robbo shrugged. 'You win some and you lose some. So, it's ours to deal with.'

Rick waited. Road traffic collisions were the remit of uniform – unless there was evidence of, or they were linked to, serious crime . . . a getaway car, a vehicle used to transport a cache of Class A, a clutch of firearms.

He glanced at the horseshoe of silent beehives, austere as a war memorial. Each of the ten hives harboured thirty thousand honeybees hunkered down for the winter. Unlike solitary bees, they didn't hibernate but existed in a revolving football, taking it in turns to be in the middle where it was warmest.

'The driver's new.'

Rick shook his head. 'Is that it? Hardly fits the definition of a special investigation. Your definition, if I remember.'

'It's a bad one,' said Robbo. 'The minibus was carrying a tennis team from Westbury School. Eight boys and a teacher. Plus the driver. Most are in hospital, one's critical.'

'Why wasn't a teacher driving?'

'I knew you'd be interested. The school minibus was being repaired, so they hired one with a driver.'

Questions were already battering Rick. Why was the school minibus being repaired? Why did the school hire a driver? Was the driver new to the school, or to the hire company? Was there any CCTV and mobile phone evidence? There was no point asking Robbo, because he'd either half-know, or not know and invent something. Detectives dealt in often dull but always unassailable facts.

'By bad, you mean serious – and *complex*?'

'Uniform are short staffed. They've also got a warehouse fire and a gang of Albanian shoplifters to deal with. And yes, there are a dozen victims and hundreds of potential witnesses. All I'm asking is that you babysit this for a couple of days, then get back to the cold case you've started.'

The unit's first case had sat unsolved on South Manchester's crime book for almost fourteen years. High-class prostitute Jane Formby also known as A-J or Amy-Jane had last been seen at the Golden Lion hotel, and was suspected of being murdered there, despite her body never being found.

Six weeks earlier, Rick had staged a press conference hoping new witnesses would come forward. The appeal had been picked up by the national media, a clip even being shown on the BBC's evening bulletins. He was slowly working through the responses, as well as revisiting every original witness. The following day he'd planned to meet the original crime scene manager. Not run an incident room for a traffic accident, however grave.

'What about the DS you promised me?' Currently, his new unit only consisted of him and case officer Carmel. Maggie covered intel, but he needed a sergeant to help Kasim with some of the outside enquiries. Especially while the young 'tec was on his FI's course.

'Soon, I promise.'

The word hung in the air, both men knowing its significance. In the middle of the Khetan case, it was Rick who'd promised and had to hope it would be accepted.

'Okay,' he said finally.

He could never say no. He always wanted to know the answer. Who, how, why? In any case, Robbo would at some point remember the final clause in the unit's definition of a special investigation: *(k) or any other crime, or incident, requiring police involvement, at the discretion of a superintendent or more senior rank.*

The two men walked back to the cars in silence. Carrying his equipment alone, Rick imagined his honeybees jostling to keep warm.

At the parking, Rick stashed his gear.

Robbo came over. 'I brought you a coffee.' He handed Rick a takeaway cup.

Rick sipped then drained the lukewarm liquid. He racked his teeth, the coffee stronger than he'd expected.

'Two more things,' said the superintendent. 'One, you need to go and see Emma. Then the chief super's covered if you act otherwise than in the manner you've been trained.'

'You're as vague as a dev nom in interview, Robbo. You mean *you're* covered if I flip out again.'

'Just go and see her.'

'And the second thing?'

'The driver of the minibus used to be police. A colleague of yours.'

'Who?'

'Guess.'

Tired of playing games, Rick crushed the cup and climbed into his car. He'd know soon enough.

Traffic was heavy in the town near the apiary. A succession of small flat roundabouts flummoxed drivers, the result long queues and bad tempers. Rick wondered who the minibus driver was. Someone he knew vaguely, or well. Someone who'd retired, or had left the police early – voluntarily, or not.

Finally, he was clear, and he accelerated along a section of dual carriageway. He tapped Maggie's number on his phone.

Behind him, a burst of sirens.

He glanced in the rearview. A patrol car was fifty metres back, and traffic was making way. Rick postponed the call and pulled into the inside lane.

The patrol car neared. It was a Cheshire unit, and he didn't recognise the two officers. It pulled in behind his car and flashed its headlights.

Rick pulled over. He readied his warrant card, but couldn't stop the gentle wallowing in his stomach. It reminded him of schooldays when he'd just passed his driving test.

The driver stayed in the car, but the passenger climbed out, fitted his flat cap, and approached along the gutter.

Rick wound down the passenger window. 'DCI Rick Castle, South Manchester. I'm heading to a scene.' He showed his warrant card.

'Could you step out of the car, sir.'

Rick was surprised, but he complied. Like accepting gratuities, turning a blind eye for colleagues in the Job was long gone. Patrol officers were equally frightened of mobile phone recording by the public and integrity tests from the internal standards team.

The two of them stood on the pavement, each jockeying for position so they could keep eye contact on the driver of the patrol car.

'I really am on the way to a scene.'

'Be that as it may, DCI Castle.' The Cheshire officer was skinny, plug eared, and mid-career, which was a dangerous combination of resentment and boredom. 'But please let us do our job. We've stopped you because you committed a moving traffic offence, namely not being in proper charge of your vehicle by using your phone. And I can now smell alcohol.'

'No, you can't.' Rick cupped his mouth and checked. His breath smelt of coffee, not alcohol. The strange-tasting coffee from Robbo? A setup didn't make sense – Robbo wanted him to get to the minibus accident asap. Didn't he?

Their disharmony went back to the Khetan case when Rick had blackmailed his boss to let him remove Calix Coniston from prison and take him to Nepal. Rick had only done it for the Job, and – in the end – the tactic had prevailed: Khetan had been lured to the UK and arrested. Despite the result, and the resumption of a working relationship, the distrust and bad feeling had remained. Once, they'd even been friends, and Robbo had given Rick his first nucleus of bees.

The patrol officer beckoned his colleague forward. Traffic slowed as it passed, occupants peering out of the windows.

The driver slouched up. He was a much older man, hadn't bothered with a hat and his fluorescent jacket had no epaulettes. End-of-career. Looking forward to walking the dog and reading the paper all day.

Rick was three ranks senior and tempted to chew them out. The first PC had made a mistake in the law: Rick's phone was secured in a cradle. The second PC looked and acted unprofessional. But Rick was also tempted to see how the stop developed. There was a whiff of unfair play. Horseplay, maybe.

But foul play was also possible, and begged the question.

Why?

'Breath test,' said the first officer. His older colleague pulled out a kit and fitted a tube. He explained the procedure badly and incorrectly.

Rick blew. He *knew* he was under – he hadn't had a beer for three days.

Three giggling schoolchildren walked past. Then an old woman, scowling at Rick as if he'd stolen a charity box.

'All done?' said Rick.

The second officer glanced at the device, and shook his head. 'We're going to search you,' said the younger officer.

'With what grounds? Have you forgotten who I am? That I know the criminal law as well as you?' Much better, he would wager.

'You committed a moving traffic offence. You've tested negative for alcohol. So we now suspect drugs.' The younger man looked at his older colleague. The latter shrugged. 'Your eyes are dilated.'

Rick laughed out loud. He couldn't help himself. The two officers were pre-programmed. But perhaps every member of the public thought that, when grounds for a search seemed dubious. Again, he decided to let the incident play out. A few minutes later to the scene of the minibus wouldn't make any difference.

The driver stood with Rick while the younger officer began searching his car. He'd not bothered or thought to search Rick. Again, it seemed by design. The officer half-heartedly looked in the boot. Moved Rick's scene kit around, turned his wellington boots upside down. He walked round, putting on blue sterile gloves seemingly as an afterthought, and opened the front passenger door.

The young officer searched the door pocket and peered under the seat. He opened the glovebox, and removed the wedge of forensic gloves and exhibit bags. The logbook. A packet of tissues. Maggie's hairbrush.

'What's this?'

The PC held up a package the size of a large box of matches, wrapped in multiple layers of clingfilm.

Rick felt a stab of heat.

'I've never seen it before.'

'I'm arresting you for possession of drugs with intent to supply,' said the PC, pulling out his handcuffs.

'This is a setup.'

'Hands.'

Rick considered his options. He could refuse, demand a senior officer attended the scene, or resist physically, and make them use force. Cause a major incident – and undoubtedly make things worse. Or he could surrender and argue in the custody suite.

2

Ten feet by six, containing a thin blue mat and a prickly blue blanket. Every one identical, like bird boxes.

Rick paced round his cell in the Cheshire custody suite. He tried to ignore the stink of the open WC in the corner, the lewd jeering between the other prisoners, and the sniggered conversations at the custody sergeant's desk. Three times the wicket had popped down, and a sneering face filled the hole. Everyone liked to see a supervisor fall, and the police were no exception.

He sat down opposite a wall dotted with lumps of chewing gum, and graffiti – all obscene, misspelled, and self-deprecatory.

Arrested, booked into custody, searched, rights read, and banged up. He'd been through the rigmarole a thousand times, but always on the home team.

Decisions to make. He'd declined a lawyer, despite the advice he always gave to friends and family: *If in the unlikely situation … always, always request a solicitor.* He'd also declined a Fed Rep and a phone call. He could contact Maggie to stop her worrying, or Robbo to explain why he'd never turned up at the scene of the minibus crash. But the moment he told anyone what had happened, his arrest for P-WITS would become real.

The less people knew about it the better. As it was, he still half-wondered if his arrest was a dream, or a practical joke.

Who wanted to set him up? Several other DCIs including Jack Gibbs at South Manchester would have liked his new job and were irked it hadn't been advertised force wide. Planting drugs, admittedly, the nuclear response. Outside the nick, there was a phonebook of possibilities. Top of the list was William Redman aka The Big Red. The local drugs dealer had been stepping up his operations, and might have been looking to deflect attention. Or get his own back for Rick breaking his nose with a short shield. Or even get some leverage – offer to provide a *volunteer* to admit the subterfuge.

And that was just Redman. The options were endless, but so were the minutes locked in a cell.

Finally, the wicket dropped down. The jailer's unshaven face momentarily appeared, then drew back. Keys rattled in the lock and the door opened.

It was the young PC who'd arrested him. He waved his report book. 'I've written up my notes. I want you to sign your reply to caution. Sir.' The jailer waited in the open doorway, blankly toe-punting the door.

'Any chance of a cigarette?' Rick's tone implied agreement.

The PC turned to the jailer who nodded. Rick stood, and the two men escorted him to the cage, the small outside area accessible only from the custody suite. It was used for prisoners to smoke, and at the same time for arresting and case officers to issue a quiet word of encouragement – or intimidation – prior to interview.

The cage was deserted, the ground strewn with fag butts. It looked out onto the police station's backyard. Dirty police vehicles were parked in lines, and a van was waiting to unload, its lights glazing the scene in blue.

The PC flicked a lighter.

'Have you got a spare cigarette?'

The PC rolled his eyes, took a packet from his shirt pocket, inched one out and tossed it over. Rick held the cigarette to his lips, the PC drew a flame, and Rick puffed for the first time since he'd been a teenager. He turned away and blew smoke through the bars.

'Must be hard,' said the PC, lighting his own cigarette.

'Not easy,' said Rick. Smoking brought unlikely people together. Chief super and cleaner on the fire escape; defence counsel and case officer in the court carpark; accused and accuser. Rick took another faux-puff.

The two of them smoked or pretended to for a minute or so. The van disgorged its prisoner, and three uniforms jumped into a car, and headed out with singing sirens. The young PC stood vacant as a fish, and alongside, Rick calculated enough to populate a Gantt chart.

'So,' said the PC, 'your reply to caution.' Clamping his cigarette in the side of his mouth, he read from his incident report book. 'DCI Castle said, *This is a setup.*'

Rick tapped ash from his cigarette. 'Well, I did say that, but not to caution. You didn't caution me.' The PC reddened. 'Listen, I know you were just doing your job, and I don't blame you. I'll sign your notes as if you did, but just tell me one thing. Who tipped you off?'

The PC shook his head, exhaled. 'I can't tell you, you know that.'

Rick nodded. He hadn't expected to get a name, but the PC had confirmed there was a tip-off. Which was a start. Again he wondered about a jealous colleague. Or Redman.

'Fair enough. Two easier questions, then I'll sign your book. Was it from a registered informant?'

The PC shook his head.

'Am I okay for a phone call?'

The PC nodded.

'Give me your book.' Rick ground out his cigarette, then signed the notebook.

An hour later, a man in a thick pinstriped suit entered Rick's cell. 'Superintendent Warburton, from Standards. I'll be interviewing you shortly. Is it still correct, DCI Castle, you don't want a brief?'

Rick shook his head.

'Pre-interview disclosure, then.' The superintendent handed Rick a sheet of paper and walked out. The door slammed shut.

He stared at the two sentences on the sheet.

Quantity of powder, believed to be cocaine, found in glovebox of DCI Castle's car. Reply following arrest and caution. 'This is a setup.'

He could say nothing, or he could answer some or all of their questions. Saying nothing looked suspicious, despite every solicitor advising it.

The irony of being arrested bit deep. In the course of his duties, he had been obtaining small amounts of cannabis to give to his mum. She mixed it into cakes for Dad, both of them hoping that it would help slow and possibly even reverse Dad's dementia. But apart from his mum no one knew about that – not even Maggie.

And it would have to stop. The cold-bath reality of being arrested – even for something he hadn't done – risked his career. And then what?

An hour later, the cell door opened again. The unshaven jailer looked at Rick as if he was worse than a paedophile or a rapist. If not worse, then maybe a corrupt police officer was at least their equal. Double standards brought down prime ministers and governments. At least, it had used to.

Rick was led past the two sergeants who were arguing over an overtime roster and shown into an interview room. The door closed. He poured a glass of water. He stared at the recording machine, someone else about to press the buttons. It didn't feel real.

Warburton entered and sat down. Put on tortoiseshell glasses, the affectation of a wannabe academic.

'Anything you need, Rick – coffee, a can from the machine?'

The door was shut from the outside. Only one interviewing officer. Warburton was confident and using his first name.

Rick shook his head, wondering if there would now be an attempt at small talk. United weren't playing well. They got that perv in Stretford.

Warburton pressed a button, the machine beeped, and the recording started. The superintendent introduced himself, then pointed at Rick.

For a moment, he thought he'd say nothing. But he thought better about it, he wanted to speak. He loved the thrust and the jab, the parry, the feint, and the killer blow of the interview. Answering questions would be a new experience, but only superficially.

'DCI Rick Castle, special investigations at South Manchester.'

'Would you prefer to be called by your rank?'

'I would.'

'Can you give me your account of what happened?'

Straight in. The water was warm and still. Rick could see the bottom.

'I was stopped by a uniform unit when I was driving my car. The officers said I'd committed the moving traffic offence of using my phone. The arresting officer then said he suspected I was drink-driving. A breath-test showed I was negative, but they persisted in saying I was under the influence. They looked in the car, and after some pretend searching of the boot, switched to the front passenger seat and found your exhibit in the glovebox.'

Warburton placed a photo on the table. 'Is that exhibit SR/1 seized from your vehicle?'

'It's a photo of a similar-looking package.'

Warburton's eyes glinted. 'What is it?'

'I don't know.'

'Where did you get it from?'

'I'd never seen it before the arresting officer found it.'

'What were you going to do with it?'

'Your logic's gone. As I said, I'd not seen it before.'

'Has it come from a house search?'

'I've no idea.'

'From the property store?'

Rick shook his head.

'For the tape.'

Rick smiled. He would have said the same. 'I've no idea.'

Warburton glanced down at his notes. 'How many keys do you have for your car?'

'Two. I keep a spare at home.'

'Does anyone else drive your car, or have access to the second key?'

'No.' Rick thought of Maggie who knew where he kept his spare keys.

'When was the last time your car was cleaned or serviced?'

'The MOT was six months ago. Nothing since.'

'What do you keep in the glovebox?'

'The logbook. Plastic gloves, exhibit bags, tissues.'

'Is there any reason your fingerprints or DNA will be on the packaging in SR/1?'

'They won't be.'

'Will you consent to urine and hair samples for drug analysis?'

'Yes.'

'Finally, I'd like to run through your record of service. You joined Manchester Police in 2006 at the age of twenty-four. You made DI after five years, and during your first night duty, attended incidents where seventeen people died. You took this hard, and have suffered since. You underwent counselling, and still do.'

'Is this relevant?'

'I think so.' The superintendent looked down at his notes. 'Despite this, you made DCI two years later. In 2014 you travelled to Nepal on a missing person enquiry. Although you successfully negotiated the release of two hostages, two more people died along with Brigadier Coniston. In addition, the main suspect, Hant Khetan, escaped. The following year you returned to Nepal with serving prisoner Calix Coniston to attempt to arrest Khetan. Showing spectacular disregard for policy and procedure, you managed to arrest Khetan, but in the process a special constable was shot and wounded. You were subsequently suspended, and demoted to DI. Only a year later, you pursued Hant Khetan one final time. In an O. K. Corral-style shootout, both Khetan and Calix Coniston were killed. Despite further breaches of law and procedure, you were exonerated in the following enquiry, and reinstated to DCI.'

'Your point?'

'My point, DCI Castle, as I'm sure is clear to those listening, is that you have a very flexible attitude to the criminal law, and to Manchester Police policies and procedures. And, extrapolating from your record, it is not so hard to imagine you once again ignoring the law. Even if your aim in so doing, is, in your eyes at least, the pursuit of justice.

'Would you care to comment?'

'No.' Rick regretted in particular the death of Brigadier Coniston and the shooting of his friend, Special Constable Russell Weatherbeater. But arresting major criminals was never straightforward, and both men had appreciated the risks.

Warburton closed his file. 'Is there anything you would like to say?'

'You haven't asked why I would commit the offence of possession with intent to supply. Of course not, because it would weaken your case. So, why would I? Hardly for the money. I'm sure you've done a financial check, and know that my accounts are in credit and there are no suspicious entries. I don't have time to spend what I earn – I'm always at work. So, if not for the money, then as an aid or incentive for some pursuit of justice, as you put it, but where's your evidence?'

Warburton twiddled his thumbs. 'Anything else?

'The arresting officer told me the reason for the stop was a tip-off. Who was the informant?'

The superintendent took off his glasses, folded the arms, and slid them into a leather pouch. 'I can't confirm or deny—'

'You don't know, or you do know and it undermines the allegation?'

'As I said, I can't confirm—'

'Either way, it undermines your case.'

'All done, DCI Castle?'

'Not quite. At best, the traffic stop didn't make sense, and at worst it was illegal. Which is ironic following your earlier speech.'

Warburton said nothing.

'If you have further evidence, put it to me so I can comment. If not, stop the interview and fast-track the packaging. It will be negative, and without corroboration, there's not a prosecutor in the country who will charge me.'

3

Robbo was waiting in the custody suite. He was eating a bag of marshmallows and staring at the fire alarm instructions. He wore a new greatcoat, and his shoes were polished to mirrors.

'Don't say anything,' said the superintendent.

Warburton updated the custody sergeant while Rick's bag of property was retrieved, opened, and handed back. He signed his name and switched on his phone. As he reinserted the belt in his trousers a message from Becky popped up on the screen.

Dad's been accused of groping

Rick pocketed his things, and replied while he waited for the custody paperwork to be completed. *What are 3 Views doing about it?*

The Castle family were having a bad day. Rick's initial thought, disbelief, and then, belief. Dad was becoming – had become – someone else. Who knew what he was thinking, or what he was capable of?

His phoned pinged. *Don't know*

Find out

I'm not one of your trainees

The custody sergeant cleared his throat. 'Back here in three weeks, DCI Castle. No bail conditions.'

Rick nodded, still thinking about the allegation made against

Dad at the care home. The strength of the evidence, whether there was CCTV or any witnesses. Or just another confused and elderly resident.

The jailer escorted Rick and Robbo into the front office. They pushed out through the doors and into the cold air. Rick inhaled deeply, and waited for his boss's pronouncement. Sarcasm and suspension would be normal practice. He even wondered whether Robbo was responsible – belated revenge for blackmailing him about the affair with his PA.

Robbo ate a marshmallow. He studied Rick, and enjoying the moment, ate another one.

Rick grabbed the bag and flung it across the road.

'That was a put-up job, and you know it.'

Robbo smiled. 'I downstreamed the last bit of your interview, quite the show you put on.' He slipped his hands in his coat pockets and walked over to the Range Rover displaying a personal plate.

The car lights flashed and the doors unlocked. Robbo climbed in, and buzzed down the window. 'I trust there's no longer any issue about you taking the minibus crash or going to see Doctor Emma.'

The light was still on in their bedroom, and when Rick pushed open the door, he found Maggie still awake. She was reading a book, which always made him feel guilty. She'd once told him that books took her away, implying her life with a disability was second best – her life with Rick was second best.

Her eye was bruised. A ring of pink shadow, and a dark purple swelling.

'What happened?'

'Turns out you put away the husband of my opposite number.'

'Who?'

Maggie put down her book. 'Simon Turner. He was dealing outside schools and got three years six months for P-WITS. Angela, bless her, is standing by her man. Got me with an elbow.'

Rick frowned.

'What?'

He explained how he'd been stopped in his car, drugs found in the glovebox, and been arrested.

'No!' said Maggie, sitting up.

'Bit of a coincidence with Angela.' He bent to kiss her.

Pondering the Turner case, he hung up his jacket and trousers and cleaned his teeth. It was a spontaneous street arrest, when he'd been driving back from court. Turner had been sitting in his van outside a school, and while Rick had waited at a traffic light, three separate kids had spoken to him. Enough for a stop and search, and bullseye.

He climbed into bed, and Maggie nestled up. He stroked her hair.

'You don't think, Rick?'

'I do.' Turner was connected enough to have an associate plant the drugs while he resided in Strangeways.

'I can't believe it,' said Maggie.

'Neither can I.'

'But Robbo supported you?'

'Sort of. Wants me to investigate a traffic accident.' Rick kept stroking Maggie's hair. 'While I was there, Becky texted about Dad.' He told her about the allegation at the nursing home.

'Is there any evidence?'

'I don't know,' he said, easing out a knot. 'What about you, did you win your basketball?'

'Annihilated them. I scored four baskets and was voted woman of the match.'

Rick squeezed Maggie tighter, then relaxed. He listened to her breathing as it deepened and she began drifting into sleep.

They'd been living there together for a year. The plan was to sell Maggie's flat and his house, which currently lay empty, and buy somewhere bigger and further out. A wheelchair-friendly bungalow with a bit of land, enough for a beehive, possibly near his current place. But work kept getting in the way. The local estate was mixed, especially at the far end, but at least there was parking at the front and a small garden.

He braced her gently again. 'Maggie, I almost forgot, God, I'm sorry. How'd it go at the doctor's?'

She opened her eyes a crack, closed them again. 'Fine, all fine,' she said softly. 'Maybe put the marathon training on hold for a while, but no reason why it shouldn't go swimmingly next time.'

'And last time?'

Maggie wrinkled her nose.

'Tell me.'

'Stress maybe. We – you – have a demanding and—'

'Go on.'

'Well, it's dangerous too. I worry about you.'

Rick held her, listened to the booing and hissing in the shadows. Being a father would make night shifts and long hours trickier. The squads liked officers without attachments, and the chiefs also liked loners, men and women prepared to work 24-7. There was no doubt it would hamper his career.

'Imagine what it would be like,' murmured Maggie, '*not* to have children.'

'You will have children,' said Rick, 'I'm sure of it.' In his head he repeated her sentence in the first-person plural. But she hadn't said that, and it hurt. He wondered, even now, if she wasn't sure about him.

Maggie turned over and fell asleep.

Rick knew sleep would be a while coming, and when it came, he knew it wouldn't be restful. Simon Turner was only one possibility of many.

4

Aeroflot flight AFL 2764 to Manchester, England sat alongside the gate at Sheremetyevo airport. A red pipe snaked from the rear of the plane to a fuel truck, and beneath a wing, the pilot was consulting with an engineer. Soldiers and police officers and security officials stood watching. FSB would be there too.

Inside the plane, Andrei squeezed along an aisle. He carried no hand luggage, but he was a large man. Not overweight, but easily mistaken for a logger or a hockey player. The other passengers avoided eye contact. He reached the row adjacent to the wing and emergency exit. The seats with the extra leg room.

Two men already sat there, one by the aisle, reading a newspaper, and the other at the window, scrolling his phone. The nearest man wore a business suit. The second man, his head shaved, a white t-shirt. Between them, a cup of coffee rested on a tray table.

Andrei leant over and picked up the cup of coffee. He lifted up the table and secured it on the back of the seat in front.

He tasted the coffee, pulled a face.

'*Pozornyy!*'

The man in the suit stood up. Apologising, he shuffled out of the row and headed further up the aisle. The man in the t-shirt continued scrolling his phone.

Andrei cleared his throat.

A burst of pop music played on the phone.

Andrei leant over towards the window. He didn't have exams, but in his view long arms had given him an equal advantage. He poured the coffee into the lap of the skinhead. The man jumped up, swearing and flapping at his crotch. Andrei crushed the cup and let it fall. He jerked his head. The skinhead shuffled out of the row, still patting his wet leg, and Andrei replaced him at the window. The last of the luggage was being loaded. Soon, they'd be in the air and the real fun would begin.

The row heaved.

Kirill had sat down at the end. Some people thought they were twins, and in some ways they were. They looked similar, both had a long reach, and they often knew what the other was thinking. But it was their differences which made them such a good team, Andrei a problem solver and Kirill a finisher. In another life they could have been kitchen fitters or badminton players.

The two of them ignored each other. Kirill flicked the duty-free brochure and Andrei tried to spot their wheelie cases. They had hidden compartments containing more false documents, but other kit would have to be sourced locally.

Finally, the plane juddered down the runway, and took off. It felt like a very pregnant duck, and took ages to climb to a cruising height. The seatbelt sign pinged off, and there was a round of nervous applause.

Andrei beckoned a hostess. She was young and heavily made-up. Her hair was tied up in a bun with a skewer. He smiled but she didn't smile back. He ordered vodka, and a second for the man at the end of the row. The only empty seat on the plane was between them, which meant one passenger was sitting on a jump seat.

The hostess went away, and came back. Andrei reached over

and took a glass. His long arms coming in use again. A little joke with the hostess. He sank the vodka and ordered another. His air hostess now.

Kirill stood up, and forced to stoop, walked towards the toilets. Andrei stared out of the window.

A young girl, only four or five years old, sat down next to him. Her face was freckly and she wore blue-framed glasses. She smiled up at him.

He stared at her.

'*Skazka?*'

She nodded, pushing back the glasses onto her nose. She had a small indentation where they sat.

He swung her up onto his knee, and stifled a grunt of pain. Despite the operation in the field hospital, there was still shrapnel embedded.

Pointing through the window at the clouds, he told her about two brave men flying across the skies to a distant land. They were former soldiers and trained to operate behind enemy lines. Enemies, he explained, are bad people – like Ukrainians. They take the spectacles from little children and crush them in their hands.

Andrei pretended to remove the girl's glasses.

She shrieked.

He ripped open the peanuts and poured them onto his hand. She ate a few, and told him to eat some, too. And to finish the story.

The two big brave men arrived in the distant land and did what they had to. They were chased by their enemies, but after many adventures and much drinking of vodka, they escaped back to Moscow. And there, they were rewarded by Semion with a castle and a forest with herds of deer.

What Andrei didn't say was that if the trip was a success, Semion had promised to pay for another operation on his leg, this time in America. The best surgeons in the world, the best aftercare. No expense spared.

The little girl whispered in his ear. What did they do in the foreign land?

The seat belt sign pinged on. Kirill sat down heavily. Twenty minutes to landing.

'Kristina!'

The girl wriggled down from Andrei's lap, and Kirill shunted his legs into the aisle to let her pass. She pushed the blue glasses back up her nose, and padded off. Watching her go, Andrei wondered how his own daughter, Alyona, would turn out. He would visit her when he got back, take her a present, and talk some sense into her. She was only twelve, lived with her mother and already talking about clothes and makeup.

Clouds shoved past the window. It was Semion's sixtieth birthday at the end of the month and he would also require a gift. What could they get for a billionaire boss who had everything? Who owned a US baseball team, controlled seven per cent of the votes in Michigan, who owned a firework factory in Turkey.

Five minutes to landing. Two presents – on top of everything else.

Kirill threw him the brochure, still open at the puzzle page. '*Nevozmozhno!*'

The plane lurched downwards. Andrei's stomach rolled. He straightened out the brochure. On the front was a huge clock tower under the title *Big Ben*.

The air hostess with her hair in a bun walked past, asking for rubbish. Andrei showed her the clock tower. She told him it was in London, and older than the Kremlin. British people loved it like a pet. Andrei proffered his meal tray. The hostess leant over. If she was playing him, he whispered, he would rip the skewer from her hair and stab her.

The plane clunked down, veered left and right through the puddles, wings shuddering and engines straining like industrial washing machines. Heavy rain beat the fuselage and the runway.

The intercom chimed. 'Local time is ten-twenty in the morning on Wednesday the thirteenth of September. Temperature in Manchester is eleven degrees celsius.'

They collected their baggage separately and waited in different passport queues. Behind the row of booths each with a customs official was an office with one-way mirrors. Andrei popped a couple of painkillers, his leg feeling stiff after the journey.

The official looked up from his passport. He tapped on his keyboard.

Andrei considered a smile. A joke about the weather, about Big Ben. Semion employed only the best, and the passport had been expensive. But the British were bright boys and girls, even the ones in uniform.

'What is the purpose of your visit, sir?'

So polite the British. So calm and measured, despite their dwindling empire and burgeoning debt, and being faced with legions of Chinese hackers, malware creators, and civil rights activists. 'Holiday.'

The official tapped again. A colleague stepped out of the mirrored office, and came forward.

Andrei could fight, take three or four of them down. They wouldn't shoot, not the British, unless he produced a gun or held a knife to someone's throat.

The first official stood up, the second sat down. The first man pushed the passport back. 'Have a good trip, sir.'

Andrei met up with Kirill in the first kiosk. Andrei picked up two mobile phones, and added a bar of chocolate. At the till he asked for a stamp. Kirill came over and set down an identical chocolate bar. Embarrassed, he swapped it for a different one.

Andrei paid, and they wheeled their cases into the centre of the hall.

Hundreds of people milled round them. Drivers waiting with placards, businesspeople, and tourists – like them. As they headed to the taxi queue, Andrei spotted the girl with blue glasses. She waved at him, but he didn't wave back.

5

Rick slotted his car into the layby behind the marked traffic vehicle. Getting arrested already seemed like a bad dream. Only the bail sheet in his wallet confirmed it was real.

He climbed out. Road noise from the nearby M60 was loud as a racetrack, and the wind cut like a flail. The traffic officer stood behind his car, the boot crammed with kit. Three types of fire extinguisher, orange cones, and a spike strip known as a stinger.

'Sergeant Jones?'

The man nodded. His moustache was trimmed, his peaked hat polished, and his trousers creased. The pride in appearance reminded Rick of Brigadier Coniston.

'DCI Castle.'

'From here we can access the closest bridge to the accident.' Jones spoke with a strong Welsh accent. 'Get an aerial view, so to speak.'

Rick followed the sergeant along the road, then down a ginnel beside a plastics manufacturer, huge rolls of sheeting stacked everywhere. A forklift buzzed back and forth.

They reached the footbridge, the road noise intensifying. The bridge consisted of three long metal ramps which zig-zagged up to the walkway, and three similar ramps down on the far side. They started up, their feet clanging on the metal. Through the siderails Rick could see sections of ring road. Three lanes in both directions.

He turned back on himself, started up the second ramp. Flanking the road on the Manchester side were huge grey warehouses, and yards rammed with cars and pallets. The tops of the rolls of plastic were still visible. He turned again, and onto the final ramp. Behind him, Jones had dropped back.

Rick reached the walkway. Two boys wearing dark hoodies stood a third of the way along. They'd climbed up onto a rail, and were peering down at the road. Cars flashed by in both directions. Artics sounded their klaxons as they passed. One of the boys lobbed something down, then the other boy.

Cars hooted. There was the sound of braking. Rick glanced down. Cars in the near three lanes were slowing and changing position.

'Oi!'

The boys jumped down and scarpered.

Rick started chasing, his mind whirring. Had they caused the minibus crash? Few detectives believed in coincidences, or categorised incidents as accidents. There was always an explanation.

He reached the end of the bridge, the boys already two ramps down. If he didn't want to lose them, he had no choice. He climbed up onto the rail, turned round, and climbed over. He dangled from a bar and felt around with his legs for a foothold. He let go with one hand so he was stretched diagonally and longer. Knew he'd only be able to hold on for a second or two.

One.

Two –

His lower foot touched a bar. He let go with his hand and grabbed out in front of him. His hands clutched at wire netting and he drew himself forward.

He hung there, heart pounding. Then jumped the last metre

to the metal. He stood at the top of the lowest ramp. At the bottom, the boys looked round.

'Police!'

They kept running. Beyond them, two BMXs leant against a fence.

Rick climbed onto a rail and repeated the same trick as before, but this time dropped to the ground. He stood up, started running again. Above him, Jones was clomping down the first ramp.

The fence curved round and blocked off a wheeled getaway. One boy threw a blue and white bag over the fence, then the two of them cycled back towards him, one either side of the access road.

Twenty metres, and closing.

Rick flicked out his retractable baton.

'Police. Stop!'

One boy raced, the other slalomed.

They were on him.

He feinted at one boy with the baton but he didn't slow. Rick stepped back, and rammed the baton in the BMX's front wheel. Jumped out of the way.

The bicycle stopped dead.

And the boy somersaulted forward, hitting the ground like a fallen tree.

Rick stood over him. 'You're under arrest.'

The second boy skidded round and stopped. He produced a knife. It was about six inches long, at home in any kitchen drawer.

'Don't even think about it,' shouted Rick. He knew Jones was coming, and hoped the traffic sergeant was using his radio. All he had to do was delay the second boy, give Jones time to arrive. He felt around in his waistband for the CS spray, but it was missing and must have fallen out during the chase. His baton lay a few metres away, caught in the mangled spokes of the bicycle.

Keeping his eyes on the boy – and the knife – he adopted a defensive posture, arms in front of him and slightly curved, ready to be raised to protect his torso.

'Get back!'

Officer safety training advised three tactics in the face of a knife attack. Keep your distance; use PAW – Persuade, Advise, Warn – voice techniques; and prolong the incident. The longer it went on, the more likely the attacker would run away or calm down and would give more time for backup to arrive. If an attack was launched, there was unlikely to be a warning. It would be sudden, frenzied, and your only chance was to deflect the attacker's knife arm away from your vital organs.

'Stabbing a police officer,' shouted Rick, 'would mean ten years in prison. Killing me would mean twenty. You'd leave prison an old man.'

The second boy spat on the ground. He wore cheap plimsolls, an unadorned hoodie. He had colour in his skin and spoke faltering English.

Rick tried a more conciliatory tone. 'Where're you from?'

The boy looked over his shoulder, then slowly let the bicycle drop to the floor. He dummied with the knife.

Rick held his ground, standing over the first boy. There was no way he was giving up his prisoner. The boys might hold a vital clue.

The second boy launched forward. Rick threw up his arms, stepped backwards. He parried left and right. He wheeled round, the boy tracking and slashing with the knife. Rick parried again and again, more in hope than targeted blocks.

Jones jogged into sight, sucking in air like a vacuum cleaner.

The second boy ran back to his bike, lifted it up and pushed off. He swerved around Jones, and cycled away, holding the knife like an ice-cream cone.

Rick looked at his bleeding forearms, the blood dripping onto the ground. He'd not felt the slashes but they were now biting. On the ground the first boy groaned.

Jones lolloped up. The sergeant stood with his hands on his knees, breathing hard. 'Backup and an ambulance are on the way.'

Rick passed Jones his handcuffs and staunched the worst of the bleeding on his arms. The cuts could have been a lot worse, and he knew he'd been lucky.

The sergeant handcuffed the boy, then patted him down. The boy muttered a string of foreign words – no translation needed. Jones shook his head. 'You want to watch it, sir, you'll never get your pension if you carry on like that.'

The ambulance and the police van arrived in convoy. Jones bundled their dazed prisoner into the back of the van while Rick was tended by a young paramedic with dyed blue hair. She cleaned the wounds and applied steristrips. Added a Mr Men plaster.

'Got another call,' shouted the ambulance driver.

The young paramedic climbed aboard, and the ambulance sped away.

Rick walked back to the fence to look for what the boys had jettisoned. His slashed forearms throbbed like beestings. He climbed the fence and dropped down into the scrubby knee-high grass.

He marked out an area the size of a garage, hoping it would guarantee success. Then searched systematically, half-metre strips, up and down. Condoms, tissues, bags of dog shit. Broken bottles, rusty cans. A cucumber.

The blue and white bag. He put on a pair of plastic gloves, and opened it. Inside were a dozen golf balls. He walked back to the van and showed them to Jones.

'Might be our smoking gun.'

The traffic sergeant nodded at the back of the van. 'Need castrating.' He banged on the side door, and the van drove away.

Rick returned with Jones up the series of ramps to the walkway. Wind buffeted as they crossed. The air tasted metallic, the stream of traffic loud and never-ending.

Alongside the road the yards were busy with activity. Vans were loading at the back of a warehouse, and a crane was moving overhead.

'Sure you're okay, sir?'

Rick nodded.

'What do you want to know?'

'All of it.'

'The minibus was heading anticlockwise, and would have turned off at the next junction, which is only a few hundred metres from Bunton Tennis and Football Club, their destination. Travelling, we calculate, at fifty-five to sixty miles per hour. Conditions were fair: the road surface was dry, and it wasn't raining. Slight downward incline. Windy as a *bwlch* in Snowdonia.'

'Traffic?'

'Heavy. Small window when it isn't.'

'And what happened?'

'The minibus suffered a blow-out in the rear nearside. The driver briefly lost control, the minibus slewing left and right. Somehow, he prevented hitting anyone else and drove onto the hard shoulder where he pulled to a stop. You see where the crash barrier's missing.' Jones pointed. 'About halfway along there.'

'Got it.'

'The teacher and some of the boys climbed out and stood around next to the vehicle. Two cars pulled up in front of the minibus to offer assistance. The teacher called 999. And while he was on the phone, a BMW driver rammed the minibus from

32

behind. The minibus swung round, colliding with the teacher and some of the boys, and causing injuries.'

Rick nodded.

'Six boys were injured, three seriously. The latter were taken to St Anne's along with their teacher.'

'Anything strike you as unusual?'

'The total disregard for safety displayed by seventy-five per cent of drivers. The BMW driver's phone was found near his feet. He's been arrested for dangerous driving and is waiting in custody for you.'

'Breathalysed, I assume?'

'Negative.'

'Okay. So traffic offences aside?'

The sergeant looked across at Rick. 'More people die on the roads, boyo, than at the hands of organised crime groups.'

He set off across the walkway.

'Did you examine the minibus?' asked Rick, catching him up.

'It had a flat tyre – flat as a pancake.'

'Is that unusual?'

Jones stopped at the top of the ramps. 'It is. Tyres blow on trucks because they're retreads – that's when you see the rings of rubber on the road. Car tyres can blow if they hit something, but generally they have a puncture and deflate more slowly.'

'Was it lifted by MotorRecovery?'

Jones nodded.

'Witnesses?'

'Not so far. The file's in my car.'

'Accident boards, CCTV?'

'I'll get on them today.'

They clomped back down the ramps, their footsteps echoing. A long day at St Anne's and in the custody suite stretched ahead.

But before that, on the way to the hospital, he'd stop at MotorRecovery and examine the minibus. It was a hire vehicle so the tyres were likely to be new – hence, the lack of tread not the cause of a blowout. Jones had said the tyre was likely to have hit something, but equally, something could have hit the tyre. Which suggested a crime, and until Rick knew for certain, it was an assumption Robbo, Manchester Police, and the public expected him to make.

6

Sitting in his car with the heater turned up high, Rick phoned Maggie. Three missed calls from her, several messages.

'The log says you've been slashed with a knife.'

'It's only superficial,' said Rick, picking at the steristrips. 'Can you find out which neighbourhood team is on days, and tell them to meet me at the hospital to take statements? Update Robbo, tell him I'm on my way to St Anne's, but stopping at MotorRecovery. Then can you watch the CCTV on the backyard for the last week, see if anyone tampers with my car?'

'You think someone inside the nick—'

'I'd like to rule it out.'

'You're sure you're okay?'

'I'm fine, Mags. How's your eye?'

'Sore, looks a lot worse.' Her tone lowered. 'Rick?'

'Yes?'

'I like it in the morning.'

'Noted.'

Rick started the car, turned down the heating, and pulled out of the layby. Three things stood out from the scene. First, the golf ball throwers. Second, the absence of crash barriers at the exact place where the minibus stopped. A less capable driver, and the incident might have been worse. Third, the – very – flat tyre.

The traffic was heavy, and as he stopped-and-started towards MotorRecovery, his mind again turned to his own arrest. Whoever had planted the drugs needed motive, an opportunity, and the wherewithal to do it – either by cloning Rick's keys or breaking into his car without leaving a trace.

The young officer who'd arrested him had confirmed there'd been a tip-off, which suggested the package had only been hidden in the last few days, and apart from his car being parked at the police station or outside Maggie's flat, he'd filled up with petrol, revisited a potential witness in the Formby case, driven to the apiary and Dad's care home.

He switched to motive. Who had done it and why? It wasn't only Simon Turner, Jack Gibbs, and Robbo who held grudges. There were plenty of other people, both inside and outside the police station, who'd like to discredit Rick for a variety of reasons – revenge, disruption, professional jealousy. Doing something about it, though, was a different matter.

The recovery garage consisted of a scruffy parking lot at the front, a barn-sized workshop, and a five-storey carpark. Half the vehicles concerned in crime and serious traffic accidents in Manchester were moved there. Two storeys of the carpark were reserved for crime cases, and Rick hoped the minibus had been taken to one of them.

He parked at the front alongside an array of MotorRecovery tow-trucks, and walked into the open-fronted workshop. Delivery boxes crowded the entrance, and a radio was playing. Behind the boxes, oil drums and tyres stretched down one side. Wheeled crates of tools stood in the middle. An office lurked at the back.

'Mr Castle, what can I do for you?'

Rick turned round. Trevor wore filthy overalls and held a grease gun. He drove the trucks, and according to the crime scene investigators at South Manchester, could impersonate half of the CID.

'Yesterday, you lifted a minibus from the ring road.'

'Up on third.'

'Is Jill here?'

'Examining a Kawasaki 500 on fourth.'

Rick headed up the series of ramps, past gleaming Mercedes and BMWs, two lines of scooters, a van with the back doors open showing a false floor, and onto the third floor. There were mangled cars and motorbikes, the shell of a boat, a caravan without wheels, and halfway along one wall, the minibus from the ring road.

Westbury School was painted in large white letters on the side – on both sides. As usual, Robbo had got his facts wrong. It wasn't a hire vehicle. Deliberately wrong?

The back was dented, the rear window smashed, and the bumper missing. The rear nearside tyre was flat. He walked round. The front nearside wing was gone and the headlight cluster hanging down. Deep gouges ran along the nearside panels. Little damage to the offside.

Rick put on a pair of plastic gloves, and opened the driver's door. There was a bottle of liquid in the door pocket. He opened the lid and sniffed it. It didn't smell, but he set it aside. Despite the negative breath test, driving under the influence was a possibility he couldn't ignore. Common knowledge blowjobs were unreliable. He walked round to the passenger side. Nothing in the door pocket, and only the logbook in the glove compartment.

He climbed out and tugged open the side door. On the floor was a school textbook, *Basic Biology*. Every schoolchild's worst lesson. He would never forget the film on birth control. He checked the seats, and the floor. There was an empty can for tennis balls, two squeezy drink bottles, a mashed packet of biscuits. A handwritten sign, *Tennis Team*, covered in footprints. He assumed it had been displayed in a window, but he'd need to check.

Finally, he considered the flat tyre.

He knelt down. The tread was reasonable. Using his pen torch, he inspected every square centimetre. He lay down and looked at the sections in shadow. Nothing of note. Which left the section he couldn't see – the width touching the ground.

He stood up and walked back down the ramps. No sign of Trevor, or Jill, so he helped himself. He grabbed a cordless impact wrench and a socket set, and spotting a trolley jack, pushed it back up the ramps to the minibus.

He positioned the cup under the jacking point and levered the vehicle up.

'Rick!' Jill's voice.

He looked over his shoulder.

She walked up, tutting. 'You're the most impatient detective I know.'

'Just trying to save you a bit of work.'

'Trevor does the heavy lifting.'

'Boom-boom,' said Rick.

Jill fitted chocks under the three wheels still on the ground. 'I've read the notes.' She nodded at the wheel in the air. 'All yours.'

'It may be nothing.'

Kneeling down, Rick turned the wheel slowly. In the section that had been touching the ground, there was a small but obvious hole half an inch wide. It was clean with no jagged edges.

'Are you thinking what I'm thinking?' said Jill.

Rick nodded. He was excited now. Definitely not an *accident*. He rotated the wheel slowly, but there was no matching hole, which meant there was a chance of finding some useful evidence.

He stood up, fitted a socket in the wrench. Jill took some

photos, and Rick removed the wheel.

'We now need Trevor,' said Jill. She put two fingers in her mouth and whistled. 'He sent me some flowers.'

'Do you like him?'

She nodded.

'Well, then.'

The mechanic appeared.

'Need a wheel breaking.'

Trevor winked at Jill, then fetched a cart. She lined it with brown paper, and with the mechanic pushing the wheel in the cart, they trooped back down to the workshop.

'Used to do this by hand,' said Trevor, hefting the wheel out of the cart. He enjoyed the biceps of an Olympic oarsman. He set the tyre down alongside the breaking machine, and manoeuvred a spade-shaped arm in place. After removing the valve cap, he pressed a pedal, moved the tyre round, and pressed it again. 'Breaking the bead,' he explained. He turned the tyre, repeated the process.

'Can you film this, Jill?'

The CSI opened her carry-bag of equipment and took out a small camcorder. She set it up, and signalled with her thumb.

Trevor then hefted the tyre on top of the machine, fixed it in place, and lowered another machine arm. 'We call this the duck.' He slotted a tyre lever under the duck's head and pressed a different pedal. The tyre rotated and the rim fell away.

'Careful,' said Rick. 'I'm looking for something.'

'We're all looking for something,' said Trevor.

The mechanic lifted the tyre up, replaced the tyre lever against the duck's head, and depressed the foot pedal a second time. The tyre circled and lifted off the rim.

At the same time, a round bronze-coloured object fell out of the tyre, bounced across the machine, and onto the floor. It rolled a short distance and stopped.

Jill stooped down and zoomed in.

'Brilliant!' said Rick, punching the air.

Every detective knew that if you wanted to kill someone, a good way to avoid official scrutiny was to run them over in a car. Hundreds of road traffic collisions happened every day, but few were fully investigated. Even when someone died, the incident was usually handled by traffic officers and only rarely by a senior detective utilising the resources of a murder team.

Only chance uniform had been busy, and Robbo had involved him.

But involved he now was.

Trevor set the tyre down next to the machine. Jill clicked off the recorder and stood up. She put on gloves and dropped the bullet head into an exhibit bag.

Rick inspected the wheel rim. He found what he was looking for: a dent in the rim the same size as the lug of metal. They'd been lucky. A different trajectory, and the bullet would have punctured the tyre and exited in milliseconds. But the metal rim appeared to have taken the force, and the bullet head remained inside.

'Fast-track?'

Rick nodded, although he was tempted to take it to the lab himself. Like a foxhound smelling its quarry for the first time, he surged with adrenalin and would run and run and run, until he dropped. This is what *he* had evolved for.

'While I'm here, Jill, can you have a quick look at my car?' He explained about the drugs package. 'No damage or marks I can see, but can you check for prints?'

'Sure.'

They walked back down to the ground level.

While the CSI worked around his car, opening and closing the windows and doors, and examining the sills and edges with a powerful torch, Rick's phone rang. He stepped further away.

'I hear you've commandeered the neighbourhood team,' said

Robbo. 'They're meant to be targeting the winos and bangers in the parks. Account for forty per cent of our complaints.'

'You promised me a DS.'

'I smell enthusiasm.'

Rick paused a few seconds, building his boss's anticipation. Then told him about the bullet in the tyre. '7.62 is my guess.'

Silence.

Finally:

'Thoughts?'

'Initial hypotheses: A, a random shooter; B, someone with a grudge against the school; C, ditto, but against a particular boy; D, ditto, against the teacher; E, ditto against the driver – who you say I know; F, a mistake.'

'I'll update the chief super and the head teacher; you complete the community impact statement.'

'No, Robbo, I still need to speak to the occupants of the minibus. You do it. And I need neighbourhood.'

'Okay, okay. You can have them, but get on with it. We're already showing our arse on this one.'

Rick pocketed the phone. It was hardly his fault: he'd been arrested for something he hadn't done, held into the night, and asked to investigate a traffic incident with numerous victims and witnesses but no staff. What he really wanted to know was why he'd been assigned in the first place. Robbo had mentioned a previous colleague, and he wondered if his boss knew more than he was saying.

Ten minutes later Jill repacked her trays of kit.

'No damage I can see. Two sets of prints, yours I imagine, and a smaller set.'

'Maggie's probably. They'll be on file.'

'I'll check.'

Rick thanked her, climbed into his car, and headed for the hospital. Still buoyed by finding the bullet.

7

Behind the station, Andrei and Kirill sat on upturned crates in the back of a white van. Through a hole he'd drilled in the rear, Andrei watched the barrier to the carpark. Only their third day in the soggy country, and already they were on it. Semion would be pleased. At least, he wouldn't be displeased. Which always had consequences.

A group of teenagers swept past on skateboards. They wore baseball caps back-to-front, black t-shirts with images of heavy-metal bands, low-slung jeans. The same kids in Moscow.

Police officers in uniform ran out of the station and climbed into two squad cars. The engines were over-revved, the barrier rose, and the cars raced out.

Gradually, the wail receded.

They'd been sitting there for over six hours, alternating thirty minutes of watching, thirty minutes of resting. A steady stream of police vehicles had batted in and out, and from four p.m., there'd been an exodus of civilian cars. He wouldn't be a clock-watcher, but they couldn't risk missing him.

Kirill cracked his knuckles.

'*Ty menia dostal!*'

Andrei's leg throbbed and made him grumpy. He rolled up the trouser-leg and massaged the muscles above and below the grey shadow of the shrapnel. Like a submarine beneath the waves. Caressing the amorphous lump, he cursed the Ukrainian soldiers and the army surgeon who'd bungled the operation.

Kirill opened a bag of crisps. He tossed a few in the air, caught them on his tongue.

Surveillance was cold and boring, but Andrei's partner should have been used to it. Most of the work for Semion was dull, but the occasional minutes of unpredictable trouble and violence made up for it. The same as any job: ninety-nine per cent tedium, one per cent good stuff.

His comrade poured the remains of the crisps into his mouth. Didn't offer.

Andrei looked out. A man and a woman wearing suits exited from the back of the police station. Talking, they walked towards the civilian cars. The man had dark hair. Andrei straightened up and switched to his right eye.

It's him.

Andrei heard Kirill clambering into the front and the van keys jingle.

Ready?

'*Da!*'

The black estate drove to the exit barrier. Andrei made a note of the registration. The barrier rose, and the black estate emerged. Kirill started the van and began to follow. Andrei knelt in the back and occasionally peered out through the windscreen.

The estate car turned right and right again, and stopped at a traffic light. The van pulled up behind. Andrei swore. Already they were too close. The lights turned green, and they continued. Kirill dropped back.

Andrei estimated the house would be no more than twenty miles away, and not less than three miles. To ensure they didn't show out, he planned to break the surveillance into sections.

Today, only two miles, and tomorrow, they'd start where they'd left off.

One mile, said Kirill.

Andrei peeked forward to check. The black estate was there. He crouched again, pain shooting down his leg. Swore softly.

A few minutes later, Kirill pulled off the road and parked up. Andrei looked out. They'd stopped at the Coach and Horses. It was a good place to pick up the black estate again. Kirill had done well, but he wasn't going to tell him. No his *mamochka*.

The following afternoon, they started surveilling in the front carpark of the Coach and Horses. Taking the first shift at the spyhole, Andrei swallowed a couple of painkillers in anticipation.

The carpark was half-full, but by seven, there were only spaces behind the pub. Women in skimpy skirts and shiny tops tottered and tittered towards the bright lights of the front porch. Men in short sleeves with arms like ham-joints sauntered behind. Music seeped through the pub's dirty windows.

Kirill's turn to watch. Andrei moved his crate away and Kirill moved his crate into position. My crate, your crate, like children.

Semion must know someone at the Kremlin.

It's the other way round, said Andrei. Someone at the Kremlin knows him. Told him they don't want any more sanctions from the UK and US.

No polonium, then!

'*Nyet!*'

Nothing which could come back to the Kremlin, or to Gazprov, or to Semion. How many times did he need to repeat it?

Andrei climbed out and went inside the pub. He could have used the piss bottle, but thought he'd have a recce on the off chance of killing a second bird. Exiting the washroom, he saw what he'd hoped to see. Cash changing hands – a thin man with a ponytail, and a second man. Nothing said, death stares aimed at him.

He returned to the van.

Any sign of the car?

Kirill shook his head, they moved crates, and Andrei swapped back to the spyhole. His comrade liked to talk when he was watching, but when it was Andrei's turn, Kirill liked to do word searches in silence.

A black estate approached. It felt like the twentieth of the evening. The registration matched.

'*Da!*'

Kirill stumbled into the cab, started the engine, backed up quickly. Andrei watched the black estate through the spyhole, but when the van had swung round, he switched to looking over Kirill's shoulder.

His partner pulled out onto the four-lane road and followed. Stop-started in the traffic, even at that time. Manchester was as bad as Moscow. They passed chip shops and chicken shops and kebab shops. It started to rain. After two miles, the black estate turned left and right.

They followed, but Andrei felt uneasy. Three miles was enough.

Stop!

Kirill turned into a parade of shops. There was an off-licence with parking where they could start again the next day.

But the black estate didn't drive past, and at ten p.m. the off-licence closed. Andrei drew a finger across his throat, and Kirill drove them back to their cheap hotel.

Fourth day, they parked near the off-licence. Andrei remained in the cab, as if he was waiting for someone. In the back, Kirill ringed words in his magazine. He ate a sausage-roll, and moaned because there was no ketchup.

Cars pulled in and out. Single men, mainly. Four lads in a pickup playing rock music they could hear in the motherland.

Semion must really love his son.

He can't stand him.

A group of younger boys stopped and threw firecrackers. The owner of the off-licence stepped outside his shop and shouted. The boys scarpered.

So what are we doing on this tiny island?

Semion cares about his business and his family name.

The off-licence owner walked over and knocked on the driver's window of the van. He was a fat ugly man with a round head and a bent nose. He'd been in a lot of fights, and didn't care, win or lose.

'Yes?' said Andrei, opening the window a crack.

'You're in the parking space for my customers. Buy something, son, or fuck off.'

Andrei closed the window.

Keep watch, Kirill.

Andrei stepped out of the van, and hobbled over to the door of the off-licence while pulling on a pair of gloves. The cramp in his leg eased. In the window a discount sign flashed above a stack of beer.

A chime sounded when he opened the door. He walked slowly around the deserted shop, past the pyramid of beer cans which must have taken hours to set up, and finally selected two one-litre bottles of the best vodka. He sat them on the counter. The shop owner stared across at him. Andrei peeled off ten-pound notes from a roll and laid them down.

He pocketed his change, stared back.

On the way out he stopped at the stack of beer cans. He squatted down to take an eye-to-can view. He removed two cans from the middle at the bottom –

And the stack came tumbling down.

Outside, he wandered down the road. Kirill knew what would have gone on, they had an understanding when it came to business.

The black estate drove past.

Kirill drove up, and Andrei climbed in.

Okay?

Nodding, Andrei stowed the vodka by his feet.

The road led out of the city and into the suburbs. Everywhere looked the same. They passed three Chinese takeaways, a huge supermarket and a petrol station. The black estate turned into a side road.

'*Nyet*,' said Andrei.

Kirill drove on to the next junction. They waited for five minutes, then went back and turned down the side road. Followed it down, Andrei looking left, Kirill looking right. Kirill turned around and drove slowly back. They kept looking.

Kirill tapped Andrei's arm – the black estate was sitting outside a two-storey block of flats.

They headed back to the city. Andrei grabbed one of the vodka bottles and unscrewed the top.

'*Na Zdorovie!*'

8

A confusion of red, white and green signboards stood outside St Anne's hospital. Obstetrics, Oncology, Outpatients; a dozen carparks. Ambulances waited on yellow cross-hatchings in front of A&E. The huge sliding doors of reception worked back and forth as patients and their relatives filed in and out. A woman in a rabbit costume shook a charity tin.

Rick parked in the bus stop, alongside a police carrier and patrol car. Grabbing Jones' file from the rear seat, he sat and skim-read for a few minutes.

Five boys with minor injuries or shock had been taken home from the scene of the minibus crash. The driver was uninjured and taken back to his base. Three boys, Mont, Simons, and Clare, and the teacher Mr Alderman were conveyed by ambulance to hospital with more serious injuries. Two drivers had stopped at the scene. All twelve would need to be statemented. Also in the file was Jones' scale diagram of the crash site, showing skid marks and the final positions of the two vehicles involved. Missing were details of the ambulance crews and police officers who'd attended.

Rick shuffled the file back together. It didn't take him any further. If the shooter's intended victim was travelling in the minibus – the calibre of the bullet suggested it wasn't a random targeting – why didn't he follow up? Fire additional shots when everyone was waiting around on the hard shoulder?

Maybe, the shooter had followed up but missed his target. Or maybe the shooter had wanted it to seem like an accident and was hoping it wouldn't be thoroughly investigated and the bullet found. By choosing a place without crash barriers, they'd hoped to cause a far worse crash – only the driver's skill had prevented the minibus careering down a steep slope.

His phone rang.

'I've arranged a family meeting at Mum's,' said Becky. 'Tomorrow evening, eight-thirty, to discuss Dad.'

Rick sighed. 'Not sure, I've just picked up a case.'

'Aren't multi-tasking and prioritisation meant to be what you're so good at?'

Rick threw the police logbook on the dashboard and climbed out. She had him. 'I'll be there.'

At reception he pushed a ten-pound note into the woman's tin, noted the location of the café, and set off down a corridor, only then wondering what cause he'd just helped. If it was donkeys, on the way out he'd ask for his money back.

Hubbub from the gaggle of PCs reached him before he rounded the corner and saw them. Sergeant Davison, a quiet serious man with glasses, stood up.

'Sir.'

Behind him, the PCs quietened. Some of them were hardly out of school themselves. One officer was older, wore faint eyeshadow and held his helmet at his side as if it was a family heirloom. Next to him, a young female officer stood with her notebook open and pen poised.

Rick ushered them to a table in the corner. 'I'm DCI Castle. I think you all know the rough circs. Three of the boys and the teacher are here. I will speak to the teacher, and I want you, as directed by Sergeant Davison, to statement the eight boys. Questions?'

'Barton, sir,' said the PC with eyeshadow. His belt bristled with self-bought kit. The police family was not short of eclectics and odd balls. 'Shouldn't they be treated as key and significant?'

'Ideally, yes, Barton. But setting up video interviews will take weeks. At the very least I need first accounts so I can progress the investigation.'

'What about appropriate adults?'

'Yes, parent or guardian. Anything else?'

'Fanning, sir,' said the PC holding her notebook and pen. 'Anything in particular you want us to cover?'

Finally, someone with the potential to become a detective. But he was reluctant to mention anything. If he did, he risked getting statements that missed crucial details he didn't know he didn't know. 'Include everything you think might be helpful to the investigation.'

Fanning made a note.

'Phone me or Sergeant Davison if you have a question or find out something I should know straight away.'

On the way to Angel Ward to speak to the schoolteacher, Rick walked past the coffee shop. Almost every table was full and there was a queue at the counter. The air smelt so strongly of hot chocolate he could almost taste it.

A blond-haired woman at the nearest table stood up and blocked his passage. She wore a tight pink skirt suit and matching high heels. She held a microphone and was tracked by a man shouldering a camera. Before the woman could speak, a man loitering by the drinks machine darted in front of them. He wore a baseball cap and held a Dictaphone.

Rick was forced to stop. He knew all three of them from Manchester's press pack. Oliver worked for the *Manchester News*, and Jackie O'Day was an independent who sold footage to the TV networks.

'Two minutes, Rick?' said Oliver.

Rick glanced theatrically at his watch. Like wild birds, the press needed feeding. Not so much they became lazy, but enough to keep them alive, and in the media's case, hopeful. At the same time remembering, they could always crap on your head.

'It's still very early in the investigation. It was a bad crash. You can quote me.'

'Why have you – a detective chief inspector – been assigned the case?' It was, as usual with Oliver, a good question. 'Is there something you're not telling us?'

The newsman held out his Dictaphone. Jackie O'Day stepped forward and thrust out her microphone. The light on her cameraman's equipment glowed bright red. A hush spread over the customers in the coffee shop, and several stood to see better.

'That's all I've got for now. We'd appreciate the usual help with an appeal for witnesses and dashcam footage.'

'Had the driver of the minibus been drinking?' said Jackie.

Rick stepped around her, dodged the far side of an orderly wheeling a patient, and dived up a set of stairs. At the top, he ran for the lift, and pressed the button for Angel Ward.

Rick knocked twice on room 337, then entered. A nurse ushered him out, asked for identification, and told him to wait.

He sat on a plastic seat and took out a pen, wanting to capture the names floating around in his head. People who might have planted the drugs in his car. The forensic analysis of the packaging would point to his innocence, but was unlikely to yield a suspect, and wouldn't explain *why* he'd been targeted. He jotted down a couple of lists.

Inside the police station
1. DCI Jack Gibbs – *didn't get the special investigations job*
2. PC Downcliff – *I rejected her application to become a detective (3x)*
3. Robbo – *despite bailing me out of custody*
4. Russell Weatherbeater – *one of my best friends, or so I thought, might blame me for being shot in the leg*
5. A n other

Outside the police station
1. An associate of Simon Turner – *the most timely on either list*
2. The Big Red aka William Redman *or one of his soldiers*
3. Starfish, *a Redman soldier, who I stabbed in the hand with a biro*
4. Someone connected to one of my current cases. *The Formby murder was the most high-profile. But it's almost fourteen years old, and I've made no real progress. No suspects, not even any persons of interest.*
5. Any of 20 or so people *whose cases I've investigated or overseen over the last few years and responsible for a long prison sentence*

The nurse came out. 'Ten minutes.'

Rick pocketed the lists and entered the room. Next to the empty bed, a balding man sat in a chair. He wore a hospital dressing gown and slippers.

'DCI Castle from South Manchester.' He showed his badge.

'Graham Alderman.'

'How're you feeling?'

'Headachey, but otherwise not too bad. I got concussion and they want to monitor me for a few days. How's Peter Simons – he looked in a bad way.'

'Still is,' said Rick. 'I'm sorry.'

Outside, a lorry overflowing with hospital waste drove past.

Alderman reached for a glass of water. 'I'm going to get the sack. Worst GCSE results in the department, and now this. Thinking of jumping before I'm pushed.' The teacher sipped the water.

'Are you okay, Graham, for a few questions?'

The teacher put the glass down, and nodded.

'If you can start by telling me what happened – focus on the crash.'

Alderman took a deep breath. 'Driving along on the ring road, me in the front alongside the driver, boys in the back. Middle lane, I think. *Bang.* The tyre goes. We swerve all over, the driver did really well, and somehow we keep going straight, and the driver pulls onto the hard shoulder and stops. Boys start getting out, and suddenly, *wham*, a car piles into the back of us. The minibus spins round, boys are screaming. It's a miracle no one was killed. Then, it's all a bit of a blur. Ambulances, police cars. Hardly seems real. Never been in a crash before.'

'Okay, we'll drill into that in a moment. But, first, can you tell me where you were going?'

'Yes, of course. So then, as well as teaching French, I'm the teacher in charge of tennis at Westbury. The minibus is currently for the sole use of the tennis team. There is – or there was – a handwritten sign in the back saying tennis team. Usually, the boys play at school, but the courts are being re-laid at the moment, so we have to travel to Bunton Tennis and Football Club to practise and play home matches.'

'I was told the minibus was being repaired.'

'No. The courts are being re-laid. The minibus is fine. The tennis team don't usually need it, and I can't drive, so we hired a driver.'

'Got it,' said Rick. 'Any reason why you hired one from

Cosmos Cars?'

'I've used them as a taxi firm, knew their number.'

Rick nodded. 'Go on.' The school tennis courts were being repaired, not the minibus, and they'd hired a driver, not a vehicle.

'Tennis practice takes place on three days a week, Mondays, Wednesdays, and Fridays, straight after school finishes. We leave at three, arrive at the Bunton club at three-thirty, play for ninety minutes, and return to school for parents to collect at five-thirty.'

'Do you always take the same route?'

Alderman frowned. 'Yes, the exact same route. The club is close to the exit just after the place we crashed.'

The teacher offered a bag of grapes to Rick.

He shook his head. 'Tell me about the tennis team.'

'Really nice bunch of boys. Three pairs and two reserves. They all get on pretty well, and they're quite good, win most of their matches. Jack Philipps is the star – he's got a serve like a rocket and is as fit as a sheepdog. At the moment we're training for the Northern Cup, a singles competition, and he should win it.'

'And Westbury?'

'Surely, you can look that up.'

'The stuff I can't.'

'A top-tier independent. Fifteen hundred boys, ten to sixth form. Thirty make it to Oxbridge each year. We produce a lot of accountants, but also a lot of doctors. One or two journalists and scientists.'

'Go on.'

'Interesting staff room, progressive, slightly annoying head teacher.'

'What do you mean?'

'Sands is good, but knows it. And he's not stopping, destined for greater things. A seat in the Lords, maybe. He doesn't like poorly performing teachers or pupils or anything which shows the school in a bad light. Like this crash.'

'Why do you say that?'

'It's messy. Would you want your child to go to a school where the minibus might crash?'

Rick made a couple of notes.

'Okay to keep going?' The teacher nodded, trying not to yawn. To improve recall, Rick divided the incident into three: before the blowout, the crash, and the aftermath. 'Starting this time, from when the tyre blew.'

Alderman described the incident as before, but added that it was Mont, Clare, and Simons who had climbed out and were struck by the minibus when the car hit. It explained why they were the three boys with the worst injuries.

'Before the blowout,' said Rick, 'did you see or hear anything unusual?'

'Like what?'

'A car or a motorbike, a van, whatever, acting strangely.'

'No.'

'What about the driver? You said he did well, but *before* the incident, did he slow down, or take a phone call, or do anything unusual?'

'These are troubling questions. No, I don't think so.'

'Bear with me. Did you see him take anything – medication … or drugs?' Alderman shook his head. 'Did he smell of alcohol?'

'No.'

'Let's turn to the aftermath, from when the minibus was finally at a standstill.'

'It was bedlam. Boys were screaming, drivers honking, and cars screeching as they slowed down. There was the smell of burning rubber and the crunch of broken glass. I tried to phone 999, but gave up and climbed out of the bus to see what I could do for Clare and Mont and Simons. They were in a mess. I was panicking, if you want the truth.'

'What happened then?'

'Two or three drivers stopped to help.'

'Two or three?'

'Two, I think. They started helping the boys out of the bus. Jack Philipps fell over as he got out, and at the time I thought, I hope he'll be okay for the Northern Cup. As if that's important now.'

'Then what?'

'The first police car turned up. An officer with a Welsh accent took charge.'

After a light knock on the door, the nurse entered. 'He needs to rest.'

'Five minutes.'

'Two.' She put a thermometer in Alderman's ear, waited a few seconds, then removed it. She wrote on her clipboard, and went out.

'Have you got any enemies?'

'That's another worrying question.'

'It's just routine. Have you?'

'I wouldn't call him an enemy, but a former pupil probably bears me a grudge. He had a few problems, drinking before school. Drugs. One lesson, he headbutted me and then stormed out. No real reason. Sands expelled him.'

'Name?'

'Wilson. Caspar Wilson. Haven't seen him since that day he assaulted me. Since then, my car's been scratched at school. And once, when I was sitting at traffic lights, a stone hit the windscreen, cracking it so I had to have it replaced.'

'Did you report those incidents?'

'No. There's nothing to connect them to Caspar.'

'I'll still need details. What about the boys in the tennis team: do any of them have enemies?'

'What are you not telling me? I may teach French, but—'

'I can't say anything else at this stage, sorry.' Rick paused. 'Did you hear any other bangs?'

'No.'

'You're sure.'

'Yes.'

The door swung open. 'Time,' said the nurse.

Rick handed Alderman a card. 'Phone me if you think of anything else, however small.'

'One thing's just come back to me. One of the drivers who stopped to help was wearing a fluorescent jacket. I remember thinking, that's a good idea, I should carry one in the minibus.'

Rick nodded. 'Thanks.' He followed the nurse into the corridor.

A trolley pushed by a posse of orderlies thundered past. A doctor with a stethoscope, a trio of nurses, one holding crash pads. Rick caught a glimpse of a head wound. Ripped skin, the end of a bone, blood dripping onto the trolley wheels.

His phone rang.

'Castle.'

'Custody, Sergeant Spoon.'

'Yes, Dennis?'

'I've been told that Tony Rice, the driver of the BMW which crashed into the back of the minibus, is your prisoner, sir?'

'Go on,' said Rick.

'He's approaching his twenty-four hours and kickout time. Already been reviewed twice.'

'Coming.'

Rick jogged alongside the tracks of crimson, took a shortcut through A&E, and exited through the doors marked *Paramedics Only.*

9

South Manchester custody suite was heaving. Three sergeants including Spoon sat at the rostrum, booking in prisoners and issuing sarcastic advice to officers, prisoners and attending support workers, without fear or favour. In the doctor's room, a cleaner was mopping the floor and a heavy stench of vomit and disinfectant trolled the air. A PC sat outside cell 1 on suicide watch.

Rick scanned the whiteboard for his two prisoners. The golf ball lobber, who'd given his name as Bucur, was due a review in two hours; and Tony Rice, who only had fifty-five minutes remaining of the twenty-four-hour limit.

'Ah, DCI Castle,' said Spoon. 'Nice of you to join us. Your new DS has been waiting for you.'

A south-east-Asian woman handed Rick two clipboards with custody sheets. She had large sad-looking eyes and wore an expensive tan jacket. 'Rice doesn't want a solicitor, but the boy needs an appropriate adult, an interpreter, and a brief.'

'The custody suite's blessed trinity,' said Spoon. 'The pair of you'll be here to Christmas.'

Rick flicked the pages of Rice's custody record, noting his reply to caution, and the contents of his wallet. Two cards in particular. The BMW driver had no PNC record, and no warning markers. He'd refused food and been heard crying.

'Get Rice out, Dennis.'

Spoon nodded. 'Or Easter.'

Rick led his new DS into an interview room.

'Is he really called Spoon?'

'His one redeeming feature.'

She cut off a scowl halfway. 'Nhung Guyen, sir. Just arrived at South Manchester. Superintendent Robinson has posted me to your unit until a CID team comes up. You should know I'm on light duties.'

'Why's that?'

'I don't have to say.'

'Are you staying for the interview?' Spoon's sarcasm was contagious.

To her credit, Nhung ignored him. 'I've read the incident log. And I've prepared an interview plan.' She handed it over.

Rick read it. The plan was proficient.

'Okay to lead?'

Nhung nodded.

The door banged open. The custody sergeant loomed while Rice entered. The door banged shut.

Rice was twenty-eight years old. He wore a pale blue shirt, open at the neck, jeans, and cowboy boots which clipped the floor. Rick nodded at the chair opposite him and Nhung. Rice sat down and blew his nose.

Nhung rolled her eyes. Then leant back on her chair and started the recording.

'I wrote a letter saying I'm sorry,' said Rice. He took a folded note from his shirt pocket and set it on the table.

'Nhung,' said Rick.

'Tell us what happened, Mr Rice.'

'I was driving, listening to music, when suddenly a minibus appeared in front of me, I must have been distracted or something. I slammed on the brakes, but couldn't stop and bang,

59

I hit it. I'm very sorry.' He looked like he was going to cry again. 'The minibus slewed round and hit several boys who were standing on the hard shoulder. One or two of them screamed. It was awful. I was stuck in my car for a bit, but when I got out I did what I could to help.'

'How fast were you driving?' said Nhung.

'Seventy, maybe seventy-five.'

'Not ninety-three miles per hour, as calculated from marks on the road, by Sergeant Jones from traffic?'

'What? Maybe for a second or two. I'm sorry, I really am.' He looked down at his lap, and massaged his hands.

'What distracted you, Mr Rice?'

'I don't know. Another car, maybe. I can't remember.'

'Were you using your phone?'

'No.'

'You weren't texting on your phone, causing you to lose control and veer onto the hard shoulder.'

'No,' said Rice, quietly.

Nhung picked up her notes. '*Can't wait babe til we . . .* til we what, Mr Rice?'

'I'm sorry, I really am. We just got engage—'

'Were you texting on your phone causing you to lose control and crash into the minibus?'

'No comment.'

Scowling, Nhung straightened her notes. She turned to Rick. 'Any questions, sir?'

'Just a couple. What do you do for a living, Mr Rice?'

The BMW driver remained silent for a few seconds. 'I don't think that's relevant.' Rick and Nhung waited.

'I'm an actor,' Rice said, finally.

Which explained the RADA membership card in his wallet. Rick changed tack. 'The minibus contained the tennis team from Westbury School.'

'So?'

'Do you know anyone at the school?'

'No.'

'Do you have a grudge against one of the boys, or their teacher?'

'No.'

'Where were you heading on the ring road?'

'For a game of five-a-side football.'

'At Bunton Tennis and Football Club? You have a membership card in your wallet.'

Rice nodded.

'For the tape,' said Rick.

'Yes. Bunton.'

'Which just so happens to be where the Westbury School tennis team are currently practising. They've been going there for a few weeks.'

'Is that right?'

'Just a coincidence?'

Rice shrugged. He'd stopped blowing his nose, stopped sniffing, stopped wringing his hands.

'Previously, Mr Rice, have you had any interaction with the boys?' Rick waited for a few seconds. 'Maybe, they've scratched your car in the carpark. You have – had – a nice new car.'

'I want a solicitor.'

Rick nodded.

'Anything else you want to say?'

'No.' A bead of sweat broke down his forehead.

Rick nodded at Nhung.

'Interview terminated at six-thirteen p.m.'

While Nhung bailed Rice to return to the police station in two weeks, Rick read the custody record for Mihai Bucur. He was a fourteen-year-old Rumanian who spoke little English. Living in care, but frequently absconded. Arrested numerous times. Warning markers included drugs, violence, escaper. In summary, a pain in the arse.

The smell had subsided but a drunk was singing at the top of his voice. The custody sergeants were discussing a camping holiday in Snowdonia and passing round a bargain tin of chocolates. Two PCs were writing their notes while they waited their turn. A different PC sat outside cell 1.

He buzzed out of custody and wandered over to the coffee machine. Checked his phone while he waited. One missed call and a voicemail.

'Rick, it's Elliot Tipper, crime scene manager on the murder of Jane Formby. We were meant to be meeting at the Golden Lion hotel.'

Rick texted an apology. He picked up his coffee, sipping it half-heartedly. Somehow, he'd squeeze the meeting in. Now working as a consultant for the NHS, Elliot had told him he could always get away for half an hour at short notice. A walk-through of the scene and a discussion of the forensics were both outstanding actions in the case review. Forensics, such as they were.

Jane Formby had been reported missing by her mum a week after last being seen at the hotel by a receptionist. Initially, police weren't interested, but three weeks later, without any sightings from friends or family, and no use on her phone or bank accounts, a report was taken, and enquiries initiated. Room 14 at the hotel was identified as having been booked by Formby, and forensically examined. Traces of her blood were found on the carpet, and, together with circumstantial evidence, had been sufficient to start a murder investigation.

Despite the absence of a body, a change in the law in 1954 had made clear that a body was not required for a murder trial. They were rare but averaged five a year. *If a suspect was identified.*

A suspect had not been identified, the victim's body never found, and eighteen months later, the case filed pending new information.

The hotel receptionist, the last person to see the victim, had noticed Jane Formby enter the hotel by the back entrance in company with a man. He was described as white, stocky, at least six feet tall. It wasn't much, but it was something.

Nhung popped her head around the door of custody. 'Ready for you.'

'Do you want a coffee?'

'Don't drink it. Nor tea.'

'Two minutes.'

He phoned Maggie and updated her on Rice and Bucur. One down, one to go. He asked her to research them, and also Caspar Wilson, the Westbury pupil who'd headbutted Alderman. Wondering, as he spoke, whether the texting was Rice's sole concern, or if it was only a side issue. The Bunton club CCTV needed watching, and the staff interviewing. Maggie asked him what he wanted for dinner. When he said pasta, she said they'd had it twice that week already.

Nhung tipped her chair back and clicked the recording machine into action. Swaying forward, she started on the formalities. Rick suddenly remembered he'd been interviewed two days earlier, and *he* was due back on bail in five days' time. He loosened his tie.

They sat in the largest interview room, equipped with a table and six chairs. Five adults might be deemed oppressive, but he had no choice. Unarguably, it would be hot and slow. Alongside the boy sat his solicitor Katherine Halliday-Brown, an appropriate adult from social services, and an interpreter. The woman from social services was plump and red-faced, and spent ten minutes clarifying her role. The interpreter wore a head shawl and had brought a cushion to sit on. Rick knew Halliday-Brown.

And she knew him. There weren't many he didn't know.

The two of them exchanged a glance.

Kickoff.

'Mihai,' said Nhung, 'tell us what happened earlier today.'

The interpreter spoke for three times as long.

Halliday-Brown made a note. She wore a long red skirt, and glasses, which she constantly repositioned.

The boy replied.

'No comment,' said the interpreter.

Halliday-Brown made a dot on her notepad. Like a cricket scorer's dot on a scoresheet. No run, no extra.

'What were you doing, Mihai,' said Nhung, 'on the bridge?'

The interpreter spoke for thirty seconds.

Halliday-Brown made a note.

The boy replied.

'No comment,' said the interpreter.

Halliday-Brown made a dot on her notepad.

'Mihai,' said Nhung, 'what were you doing with the golf balls?'

Interpreter.

Halliday-Brown.

Boy.

'No comment.'

'I think Mihai's hungry,' said Rick. 'Custody record shows he shunned what was offered.'

The interpreter translated.

'Hungry,' said the boy. He motioned to his mouth with a hand.

'Stop the tapes,' said Rick. 'Me, too.'

Halliday-Brown tutted and tried to hide her smile.

Rick told Nhung to show the appropriate adult and the

interpreter to the waiting room. While everyone was collecting their things, Rick slipped Nhung a twenty-pound note and asked her to get a pizza from over the road. The biggest one they had, any topping, but only one pizza. That was the important thing. Her expression suggested he was asking her to make it herself.

Rick remained with the boy and Halliday-Brown. In the pub, he called her H-B. He propped open the door.

H-B put her notebook in her bag, and clipped it shut. She crossed her legs, rearranged her skirt. Mihai motioned to his mouth with his hand.

Rick nodded. He tapped his watch. 'Ten minutes.'

'Okay,' said Mihai.

'You play golf?'

The boy shook his head.

'But you collect golf balls?'

The boy nodded. Confirming Rick's strong suspicion he spoke reasonable English. In his experience, most Rumanian youngsters did.

'Rick!'

'I only want to stop this dangerous game, H-B. I've got an offer for him.' He turned to Mihai. 'Listen, if I offer you fifty pence per golf ball, will you bring them to me at the police station?'

'Two pounds.'

'Fifty p.'

'Okay.'

Nhung returned with a vast pizza box stinking of garlic. Mihai grinned like he was getting away with attempted murder. Perhaps he was. Someone was. Nhung opened the box.

All four of them dug in. The slices were warm, cheesy, greasy.

H-B flashed him a look. She knew what he was up to, but

65

they had an understanding. After a second slice, Rick wiped his mouth.

'Two days ago, Mihai, there was an accident near that bridge in the afternoon. About three-thirty. A car crashed into a minibus. Were you on the bridge at that time?'

The boy took another slice of pizza. Rick pulled out the plug on the recording machine and held it up. The boy glanced at his solicitor.

H-B gave the slightest of nods.

Nhung did a double-take.

'Just before the crash, Mihai, there was a bang. Did you hear it?'

The boy nodded. 'Saw a man on the roof.'

'Can you describe him?'

The boy shook his head.

'White?'

The boy shrugged.

'Will you show us?'

Mihai stuffed in most of the slice and threw the crust in the box. Then nodded.

'Letter?' said H-B.

Rick's turn to nod. He wanted to punch the air.

Nhung fetched back the interpreter and the appropriate adult. Rick and Mihai stuffed the wrappings in the bin.

The interview recommenced.

'Mihai,' said Nhung, 'this is your last chance: what were you doing with a bag of golf balls on the bridge?'

The interpreter translated.

H-B made a note.

The boy spoke.

'No comment,' said the interpreter.

H-B dotted her notebook.

'Mihai,' said Nhung, 'what is the name of the boy you were with on the bridge?'

Translation, no comment.

'Assaulting a police officer is a serious offence, Mihai. Do you understand that?'

Translation, no comment.

'Mihai, if you tell us what happened, it will be better for you at court.'

Translation, no comment.

H-B cleared her throat.

Rick turned to Nhung, and drew a line in the air. He had what he wanted.

Rick waited in the custody suite while Nhung tidied up the paperwork in silence. She was as moody as a teenager.

Outside cell 1, the original PC was back on suicide watch. At the rostrum, the doctor complained to the two custody sergeants about the smell in his room. Dennis offered him a chocolate. Behind him, football played on the TV in the corner.

Rick's new DS deserved an explanation in respect of Mihai. The boy would be charged with affray and assault in respect of the knife attack – no one could be party to an assault on police and not get charged – but Rick would write a letter to the magistrate, explaining the boy had been helpful in an unrelated case. The second offence would be dropped. Throwing items onto a road was dangerous, but hopefully he'd stopped it continuing. It might cost the Job a few quid, but the boy was a potential informant in a hard-to-reach community. A couple of speculative payments from the informant budget were more than justified. Everyone was mollified if not happy, even H-B.

He grabbed a handful of chocolates, and ate them one after the other. He had a new lead on the shooter, a location if not a description.

His phone rang.

'Barton, sir, sorry to call.' He sounded breathless.

'Yes, Barton?' Rick walked over to a corner of the custody suite.

'I took a statement from Paul Chan at his home address. He's bruised his back but is okay.' As he spoke, the PC's voice went up and down. 'But that's not why I'm ringing.'

Rick waited. He remembered what it was like as a PC to speak to the DCI. He'd used to rehearse.

'I'm now at Jack Philipps' address, sir. Talking to his mum. She's just back from a business trip.' Barton stopped, restarted. 'New York, sir. She's a pensions specialist.' Rick's stomach tightened as he listened to Barton's fluster. 'Sorry, sir.' Barton took a deep breath.

'Jack's not here, sir.'

Rick put his hand over his ear to muffle the custody suite, and turned to beckon Nhung. 'Where is he?'

'Mrs Winn – that's Jack's mum – doesn't know, sir. He's been staying with a friend.'

'Text me the address, Barton, I'm leaving the nick right now.'

Rick pocketed the phone. 'Bail Bucur to DS Guyen tomorrow morning, Dennis. Care of social services overnight. We're going.' Neck-jerking at Nhung to follow him, he ran for the about-to-slam-shut custody suite door.

10

A yellow Mini with a *Pemberton Estate Agents* sign on the roof pulled up outside. The driver climbed out, looked up and down, and lit a cigarette. Leaning back against the car, he tried different ways to hold the cigarette, pinched, between his fingers, left hand, right hand. He exhaled quickly, slowly, in clouds. Blew smoke rings.

A teenage girl in a short skirt walked past with a pushchair. Many girls in Moscow looked like her. The young lad from the estate agent said something. She turned, raised a finger, and walked on.

The runty lad waddled a few steps after her in exaggerated imitation. Then went back to leaning on the driver's door.

Andrei took two painkillers and climbed out of the car. Using two vehicles was safer than one. Kirill drove away. Andrei crossed the road, his leg feeling stiff after the wait, and headed for the meet.

The runt stubbed out his cigarette with a cheap black shoe. He wore white socks and a cheap dark suit. A thin black tie, patterned like a slice of carpet. His round face was unshaven and blotchy. He looked eighteen, maybe nineteen. Entrusted with a smart new car, probably against the manager's better judgement.

The runty lad said he was a trainee, and his name was Jason.

They went inside and looked around. Upstairs, first. Three bedrooms and a bathroom. Curtains in each bedroom. Andrei peered out of the window in the largest room.

He could see – just.

It would be better with binoculars.

Jason described the heating system and an economy booster at night. The loft was locked and contained the owner's possessions.

They went downstairs. Jason pointed to the closet. Andrei peered inside. There wasn't a window. *Harasho.*

The kitchen was at the front. Jason opened the oven door, pointed to the fridge and the washing machine. Andrei noted the blinds.

They went into the living room, which ran along the back of the house. A sofa faced a large TV, and opposite were a small table and chairs. A clock ticked. Fir trees and a fence bordered the strip of garden. There was a gate in the fence.

Jason wittered about bank statements and utility bills. The deposit, one month in advance, the contract.

Andrei put a finger to his lips, then pointed to the sofa.

Jason manoeuvred slowly. Andrei wiggled his finger and the trainee plonked down. He seemed redder in the face.

Andrei pulled up a chair and sat, kept his bad leg straight. He'd done a six-week interrogation course. Silence, surprise, slow-time were the takeaways.

'What do you love,' said Andrei, 'most in world?'

'My dog.'

Jason described his dog, how he'd bought it as a puppy, and had increased from short walks to long. He'd built a kennel, but it slept in his room. He'd taught the adult dog to shake hands and play dead. Its favourite food was steak and kidney pie, liked to swim in rivers, watch football on TV. He talked on and on.

Andrei took out a wad of banknotes and laid it on the low table between them.

The trainee stopped talking.

Stared.

The trainee's phone rang. He reached in his jacket and took it out.

Andrei reached over and snatched the phone. He flipped off the cover and dumped the battery on the carpet. Nodded at the money. 'I take house. Need three months.'

Jason looked at Andrei, glanced at the money. Looked again at Andrei. 'It's the twentieth of September now.' His voice was as juddery as a machine gun. 'How about the end of December? Sir.'

Even this English idiot was calling him sir. Andrei nodded. They'd be back in the motherland.

'I'll need three ref—'

Andrei held up his finger. 'You invent false name, sort all paperwork. Keep extra money.'

Jason stared at the bundle of fifty-pound notes. Semion earned more every hour of every day.

'Go on,' said Andrei.

Jason picked up the money, flicked through it. He glanced across, and Andrei nodded. The trainee tucked it in the pocket of his jacket. From another pocket he took out a ring of keys and placed it on the table.

Andrei stood up.

The trainee gathered up his phone.

Andrei leant over and grabbed the trainee's slice of carpet. Yanked him closer.

'You tell no one. Or I teach your dog new trick: *dead*.'

Kirill helped Andrei move the furniture in the bedroom. Company was the only thing that made surveillance bearable, plus sugary snacks and vodka flavours they couldn't get in Moscow. The bulging shelves and breadth of choice still surprised him.

Andrei took the first watch, a chair by the window. He shared a packet of popcorn and together they listed the fifty states in America. A question on the special forces' exam.

Kirill whetted a knife from the kitchen. The sound brought back the sentry post: five of them, no more Christmases. One bad mistake. Andrei rolled up a trouser leg and began to rub his injury.

Half an hour about. Popcorn all gone, still missing two US states. No sign of him or his no-legs pretty woman. Surveillance was as dull as a Crimean housewife.

11

Rick pulled up outside a smart apartment block in the centre of Manchester. A security grille led down to an underground garage and signs warned of surveillance cameras and regular patrols.

'Alright for some, eh, sir?'

At the brightly lit front door, Nhung pressed the buzzer for Mrs Winn's flat. Inside, a banana tree stood in a huge terracotta pot. Becky had given him one as a housewarming present – indestructible, she'd said – but he'd killed it within three months.

'Top floor,' said Barton on the intercom. The door buzzed open.

Rick walked past the lifts and headed up the stairs. It was good for him. He'd already reached the age when he was doing things that were good for him. Nhung didn't follow, showing she could think for herself.

On the top floor, Barton and Nhung were waiting in the hall. More plants stood by the windows.

'She's pretty cross, sir,' whispered Barton. 'Her name's Sandra. She's split up with Jack's dad and has reverted to her maiden name.'

Rick nodded, trying not to breathe too hard.

'Did you walk up, sir? Very impressive, sir.' Barton pointed to the end door which stood ajar.

Rick walked over, glancing at three frames of modern art. Vivid cubes, coiled springs, nonsense clockfaces. Dadaist? He quite liked them.

He pushed open the heavy wooden door to Mrs Winn's flat. The hall was large with a thick burgundy carpet. Gold-coloured walls. A bunch of flowers sat in a vase. Copies of *The New York Times* and the *FT*. A pile of unopened post. No family photos. No photos. No school-age mess. Hearing ice cubes being dropped into a glass, he pushed open a glass door into an adjoining room.

The kitchen.

'Mrs Winn, sir,' said Barton, squeezing past. He turned and held out his hand as if welcoming a guest on stage. 'My DCI.'

'And this is DS Guyen,' said Rick.

'Ma'am.'

Mrs Winn swilled the cubes in her glass. A whisky bottle stood on the central island. High stools were tucked in at one end. 'Where the fuck is he?'

'I'm not sure, but we'll find out.' Only TV detectives made promises. 'It's probably just a mix-up. First, I need to clarify a few details, then we'll get cracking.'

Mrs Winn sank her drink. She was about forty, slim, and her face stretched. Either she worked out, or she ate nothing. Possibly both. She worked in finance, lived in an expensive apartment and was used to getting her own way.

'I understand you've been away, Mrs Winn.'

'Sandra, fuck. You lot, you're all clow—' She poured anther drink.

Rick leant across and took hold of the glass. He walked over to the sink and poured it away. Barton was gobsmacked, Nhung kept her reaction tighter. Amused, if anything.

'We're not clowns, Sandra.' He set the glass down on the draining board. 'We want to find your son as soon as possible and then we'll get out of your life. Sit down and tell us what we need to know.'

'I've told him.' She glared at Barton.

'Tell me.'

Slowly, she pulled out a high stool and sat. Rick glanced around at the immaculate kitchen. Guessed what would be in the fridge: tiny yoghurts, olives, curdled milk.

'I've been in New York on business. I often work away, and Jack stays either with his friend Peter Simons, or with his dad. I understand from PC Burton that Jack's school tennis team has been involved in a traffic accident. Some of the boys were badly injured and taken to hospital. Some including Jack, thank God, were not and were taken home. Well, he's not here.'

Barton stammered. 'If I may, sir?'

Rick nodded.

'Using a phone number from Mrs Winn, I phoned the parents of Peter Simons. They're camped out at St Anne's and have only been home to feed the dog. Jack's definitely not at their house. His stuff is, including his laptop, but not him. He had been staying there since last Friday. I then phoned Jack's dad, Kyle Philipps. He'd seen the accident on the news and had been phoning the school.'

'And he doesn't know where Jack is?' said Rick.

'No, sir.'

'Have you phoned Jack?'

'Yes, sir, of course, sir. Rings out.'

Rick leant back against the sink, speculating on scenarios. Had the shooter followed up? Not another shot, but kidnap. A mix-up was still possible. Likely.

Barton, Nhung, and Sandra were all looking at him.

'Time to get busy.' He looked round the kitchen. A table and chairs stood by the window.

He sat down at the head of the table, and took out a notebook and his phone. Indicated Nhung and Barton to sit down with him. 'Sergeant Guyen, you phone St Anne's and surrounding hospitals; use both his names, and misspellings. Barton, you phone Sergeant Davison and between the two of you, check with everyone who took a statement to see if there's any mention of Jack. Then double-check by phoning all the boys in the team.'

'I can't fucking believe this is happening,' said Sandra.

'Do something,' said Rick. 'Phone his friends not in the tennis team, or any relatives he might have gone to stay with. Has he got a girlfriend?'

She shrugged.

'Has he?' Rick's tone sharp.

Mrs Winn stared at him. 'There's a girl he plays tennis with.'

'What's her name?'

She paused, more for effect than recall.

'Victoria Parsons.'

'Call her – now,' said Rick, making a note.

He phoned Maggie, explained the developing situation, and told her to contact the South Manchester and ambulance control rooms, compile a list of the vehicles that had attended the scene of the crash, and contact all the officers.

'Which bedroom is Jack's?'

Sandra stared at him.

'At the end.'

The room was tidy as the house. No visible clothes, no clutter on the small desk. A row of trainers at the foot of the bed. A shelf of small cups and spoons. The poster every student seemed to have on their wall – a female tennis player lifting her skirt to scratch her bottom. He opened a drawer, looked at a few photos of Jack playing tennis. A couple of a girl. He took them, and a comb with some visible hairs.

In the kitchen he showed the photos to Sandra Winn. 'Is that Victoria Parsons?'

She nodded.

Rick turned to his colleagues. 'Any progress?'

Two shakes of the head.

Strained voices in multiple conversations again filled the kitchen. Barton and Nhung scribbled notes in their pocketbooks. Sandra scrolled her phone with chewed nails. Made phone calls, scraping her hair back as she spoke.

Rick filled a jug of water and dumped it on the table. He found glasses. Poured one for Sandra. He drew a table with three columns in his notebook: *Information source for Jack; Contacted; Notes.*

He looked at his watch.

Phoned Davison. 'Anything on Jack?'

'Not yet, sir.'

After double-checking Barton's instructions, Rick told the neighbourhood sergeant to photocopy all the statements his team had taken, give a set to Maggie, and deliver a set to him at Sandra Winn's flat.

'Can't believe I'm working alongside the DCI,' said Barton, ending a call. His equipment belt sat under his chair like a pet snake.

Nhung tapped another number into her phone. 'Grow up.'

As negative returns for Jack's whereabouts emerged, Rick updated his table. He refilled the water jug. Anything, Rick mouthed at his new sergeant.

She shook her head.

Rick's phone rang.

He snatched it up.

'Most of the crews have gone home,' said Maggie. 'To be definite, we're going to need statements. Tomorrow at best. I've also left messages for the two car drivers who stopped to help.' She paused. Maybe she was thinking about what could have been – and the potential heartache. 'Love you,' she said.

He made a couple of notes on his pad. It wasn't his son, but he was still feeling it. He always did. Nhung shook her head at him. So did Barton. Rick looked at his watch. It wasn't looking good. Soon he was going to have call it. Missing. Not kidnap, not until there was information to support it. But he would have to ask Sandra Winn some difficult questions. Have you got any enemies? Has Kyle? They were successful people, and Sandra at least, intractable. The answer would undoubtedly be yes.

His phone rang.

'What's happening?' said Robbo. 'The control room supervisor just called me.'

'Can't locate one of the boys on the minibus.'

'Cock-up?'

'Time's ticking.'

On the kitchen island, Sandra Winn's phone rang. Rick watched her pick it up, her face tighten even further. Her brows pulled together like a tug-of-war team digging in.

'What the fuck do you mean?' She stood up. 'The police are here.'

'Got to go,' said Rick to his boss.

Sandra handed her phone to Rick.

Nhung ended her call, and waved a hand at Barton to do the same.

'DCI Castle speaking.'

'Kyle Philipps, Jack's father. Jack's fine, he's staying with me now. Sandra is putting me through a nightmare divorce, and, well, I just wanted to make her sweat a little. I'm sure you understand.'

Rick stood up and walked to the window. Looked out at the dark and gloomy city. 'Actually, I don't, Mr Philipps.' He laid a fist on the glass. 'Let me get this right, one hundred per cent: Jack is with you, and he's okay?'

'He is.'

Rick killed the call and spun round. 'Your estranged husband says Jack is with him. I'm not surprised you left him.'

Sandra looked up. 'I didn't tell you that.' She fetched a new glass, poured another whisky. Dropped more ice.

Rick phoned Robbo then Maggie, updated his table and closed his notebook. Barton refitted his belt and looked at himself in a mirror. DS Guyen straightened the chairs and returned the water jug and glasses. They trooped out to the front door.

Mrs Winn followed. She brought her drink, and without speaking, shut the door behind them. DS Guyen opened and closed her mouth. Barton fitted his cap. Rick plunged down the stairs.

He debriefed his colleagues outside by the car. The sky was black and a hidden plane rumbled. A cabriolet stopped in front of the underground garage, and the security grille rolled up. A couple arm-in-arm staggered past.

PC Barton straightened his belt, said it had been a privilege. DS Guyen was silent, her face blank, but Rick could tell that inside she was raging. At things he too had witnessed, and things he guessed he hadn't.

Sergeant Davison turned up with the statements and first accounts. Peter Simons was unable to make any kind of statement due to his injuries. But Davison had first accounts from Clare and Mont, the other two boys in hospital. And statements from the three boys who'd been taken home. Rick already had PC Barton's statement from Paul Chan. Which only left accounts from Jack Philipps and the minibus driver Gary Hamburg. Plus the two drivers who'd stopped.

He sent Nhung with Davison to confirm visually Jack's location and welfare. And he instructed PC Barton to return in the morning to take a statement from Mrs Winn. Nhung could deal with Bucur.

Then he went home to read the paperwork. No kidnap, but he still had a shooter and an unexplained shooting. In the morning, he'd interview Hamburg.

He was still driving when he received a text from Nhung.

Seen Jack. Dad's a dick. A rich dick. See you tomorrow, sir.

12

Following signs for Bottomfield Industrial Estate, Rick turned left and right, jinked through a chicane, turned left and right, bumped over humps. A sandwich cart stood at the entrance to the estate, and Cosmos Cars was the first building. Coaches, minibuses and taxis displaying the company logo were lined up at the side.

Rick parked and sat in the car for a few minutes, reading the statement from Firth Banks. PC Fanning had taken the statement, and it was twice as long as any of her colleagues' efforts. Banks, and maybe other boys, too, had seen the minibus driver Gary Hamburg pouring away a bottle of liquid. Maybe, the blowjob had been faulty.

His phone rang.

'DCI Castle.'

'PC Barton, sir. How are you today, sir?'

First time for everything. 'You got that statement from Jack Philipps?'

'That's why I'm calling, sir. I've just knocked at Mr Philipps. He told me Jack's gone out already. Said he didn't know where he'd gone, would be back in an hour or so. I tried phoning the boy, but it's still going straight to voicemail.'

'Go back in an hour.'

'Yes, sir, thank you, sir.'

Rick climbed out of the car. Wondered if Philipps junior, possibly Philipps senior too, were playing silly buggers.

His phone rang again.

'Sir, it's DS Guyen. Bucur hasn't turned up. I didn't expect him to, if I'm honest.'

Rick doubted his new DS had ever been anything but honest – she was blunt as a knife in an Airbnb – but to be effective, detective work often required a more nuanced approach. 'Circulate him as failing to answer his bail, and let's hope a patrol picks him up. Then go to Bunton Tennis and Football Club and see what you can find out. Staff, incident book, CCTV. We also still need statements from the two drivers who stopped.'

Pocketing the phone, he headed for reception. Robbo had told him he knew the driver, but he didn't recognise the name. At least, he knew a few Garys, but no Hamburgs. Gary Hunter had worked for him a few years previously – notably, on the Khetan case. Near retirement, Hunter had lost interest in the Job, but *he could drive.*

The building was a single-storey industrial unit with large windows at the front. He opened the front door, and turned right to reception. Left was marked *Drivers Only*.

'Police?' said a bulky woman behind the counter. She was wearing a multicoloured hooped top and reading a magazine.

Rick nodded.

'He's through there,' said the receptionist picking up the phone. 'Cosmos Cars.'

Retracing his steps, he pushed open the drivers' door.

The room had the look and feel of a pub. There were sofas, a pool table, and a large TV. In the corner stood a quizzie and a Coke machine. One man sat on a sofa in front of a low table, flicking a tabloid newspaper. He looked up.

'Gary Hunter!'

'Hello, boss.'

They shook hands, Rick both surprised and pleased to see his former colleague. And surprised he was pleased. He wondered how long it would last.

'Sit down,' said Hunter. 'Can I get you anything – coffee, cold drink?'

Rick shook his head. 'No, thanks.' He sat on the opposite sofa, and laid his file next to him.

'You've changed your name, Gary.'

Rick's former DS nodded. 'Only the gaffer here knows my real name. When I left the Job I was served an Osman following intel that Denny K, an armed blagger I put away fifteen years ago, had put my name on a list. But he's only one of many – I put plenty away when I was in the Flying Squad.'

Rick wrote Denny K in his notebook.

Hunter watched him, itching the back of his hands. They were red and puffy, same as before. Rick glanced at the tatty seating, the crude messages chalked below the dartboard, the stained kettle sat on a Formica table. Hunter followed his stare. 'After I retired, I was getting bored at home. There're a few good boys here, and plenty of time to sketch.'

Rick wondered if there was more to it. Debt problems? A motive for a shooter? He would ask Maggie to run a financial check.

'I think I saw you once, with a pushchair.'

'That's my grandson Toby. He's two. If ever you want tips on the best buggy to buy, let me know. Toby's the highlight of my week. Just a shame his dad won't speak to me.'

'Remember chasing Calix Coniston in Nepal?'

Hunter scratched the back of his neck. 'I remember my blisters. We got him, though, and Khetan.' He folded up the newspaper. 'What do you want to know?'

'Is it unusual to be employed as a driver, but without using a company vehicle?'

83

'It is, but it's what the school wanted.'

Rick set down MG11 forms on the table. 'You can write your own statement, but an account now would be helpful.'

'I've had the tennis team contract from the beginning. As usual, I drove to the school in my own car, arriving at three-ish. I checked the school bus, waited for the boys and their teacher Alderman, and then started off. Normal route which I can detail in my MG11. Nothing unusual on way, no crazy drivers or driving. Approaching the exit on the ring road near the Bunton Tennis Club, there was a bang, and the tyre went. The bus sagged down and slewed sideways. My police training kicked in, and although it's only a bus, I managed to correct her, slow down, and stop on the hard shoulder. The boys were getting out, and then some fuckwit piled into the back of us. The bus swung round and the boys who'd climbed out were badly injured. I did what I could until backup arrived.'

Rick made a couple of notes. Then checked the door and lowered his voice. 'Gary, the tyre didn't just blow out. It was shot out. We recovered the bullet from the wheel.'

'You're having a bubble bath.'

'I'm serious. The bang you heard?'

'The tyre blowing, I think. Didn't hear any shots. Suspects?'

'Not yet.'

'Hypotheses?'

'Still developing them. The shooter was targeting the teacher or one of the boys – or you.'

'Me?'

'You mentioned Denny K. One of many you said.'

'Yeah, but up here?'

'Might not have been aimed at you – might have been targeting the school, or even be a mistake.'

'Assuming it wasn't, why choose to do it on the ring road? Why no follow up shot?'

'Maybe there was – but we're yet to find any evidence. The calibre of bullet suggests the shooter knew what he was doing, but it seems a half-job. The best I've come up with is that he wanted it to appear like a traffic accident. Hoped you would lose control of the minibus, maybe career down the bank – it seems a coincidence that it occurred alongside a section with no crash barriers. Hoped we wouldn't find the bullet and it wouldn't be investigated thoroughly.'

Hunter yanked up his trouser leg and scratched his shin.

'Have you had any threats, or in retrospect, has anything happened that now seems strange?'

Hunter shook his head.

'What about other problems?'

'Like what?'

Rick stuck out his chin, shook his head. He thought Hunter would guess he had something, but maybe he wouldn't.

Hunter stood up.

'Sit down.'

'I'm getting a drink.'

'A soft drink?'

'Meaning?'

'Sit.'

Hunter scratched his elbow. Then sat.

'One of the boys saw you emptying a bottle.'

'He's mistaken.'

'Come on. What was in it?'

'I don't know about any bottle.'

Rick see-sawed his head.

The door opened and the big woman from reception waddled in. 'Cheese toasty, Hamburg?'

'Yeah, thanks, Pip,' said Hunter.

The fat woman scowled at Rick, and lumbered off.

He picked up his file, nodded at Hunter, and followed.

'Castle.'

Rick turned, the word confirming that the initial pleasure at seeing one another was spent, their relationship back to being at best functional and at worst fractious.

'There is one thing. Cosmos Cars are having a spat with another hire firm. Cosmic Cars. We've had dogshit through the letterbox and drivers called to duff locations.'

'Have you reported it?'

Hunter shook his head. 'The gaffer ain't a fan.'

Rick nodded slowly. He didn't believe for a moment the spat was a motive for the shooter. The minibus carried the school logo, not the hire company's. Far more likely was Hunter mentioning it as a distraction tactic.

'I'll be in touch.'

Rick sat in his car. Distraction from what? Drink-driving, or something worse? He wondered if Hunter had known about the shooting. He'd been bribed or blackmailed to provide the time and place for something to go down against one of the boys from Westbury or their teacher. Something which didn't go to plan, or only partly.

Hunter, a conspirator to an attempted murder? It was a gloomy thought, his former colleague upending a career of enforcing the law. Police vetting had recently become a hot topic but Hunter had a long and mainly distinguished service. He'd slowed at the end like most officers but when it counted, Rick had trusted him. It made him question his own judgement. Now, his gut was saying one thing, his head another.

He stared through the windscreen at the scruffy building. Paint was peeling, a downpipe was loose.

Hunter was his best lead. The one person in the crash with prior involvement in criminality, albeit from a police perspective. But he still had contacts and the relevant experience.

He phoned PS Davison and told him to post a plain-clothes officer at the school, and one in uniform at the hospital until further notice. He then phoned Maggie and asked her to run a financial on Hunter – aka Hamburg – and to fast-track the drinks bottle he'd found in the driver's door of the minibus. DNA, fingerprints, and an analysis of what remained of the contents.

'Updates?' said Maggie.

'Please.'

'First, the report on the bullet is back from forensics. It's linked to two other shootings in Manchester in the last two years. I'll email you the details.

'Second, Caspar Wilson is living in a halfway house in Bradford. He's got previous for shoplifting and possession, lots of it, a couple for breach of the peace, and one for common assault, but nothing more serious. Has a warning marker for violence.

'Third, Jill phoned to say the prints she lifted from your car are only yours and mine. I'm still working on the backyard CCTV – no one's tampered with it over the last two days.

'Fourth, it's your turn to cook supper.'

'Pasta?'

The call dropped, but his phone rang again.

'Castle.'

'PC Barton, sir.'

'Is Jack back?'

'No, sir. Mr Philipps says he must have gone to see a girlfriend. When I asked for a name he said he wasn't sure. He seemed very vague. Then asked if I'm a hermaphrodite, sir.'

'What?'

'Sir, if I may, sir, I think Mr Philipps is pulling my chain.'

Not your chain, thought Rick. 'Okay, Barton, I'll take it from here.'

'Yes, sir, sorry, sir.'

Rick opened both of the car's front windows and let the cold air blow across him. He would give Philipps father and son until five, then he would visit.

His phone rang again.

'DCI Castle, my name's Trinity, I'm Superintendent Robinson's new PA. You've had the royal summons.' The PA sounded young and feisty.

Rick felt sorry for Lainey, his boss's previous assistant, but after the affair had become public, it was inevitable. Finally, the chief super had acted.

Rick started the car, and drove out of Cosmos Cars. 'Gary Hamburg,' he muttered to himself. Inspired by his former DS's love of beefburgers, not the north German city on the Elbe, which no doubt Hunter had never heard of, yet alone visited.

*

Andrei sat on a chair at the end of the upstairs window. He could see the front door, the front and side windows, the two parking spaces. It was a long way, but okay using binoculars. Runty boy with carpet for tie could sleep easy.

Three rules were all Kirill had to remember. They never entered or exited by the front door, only at the back, via the gate. They never arrived or left together. Some people thought the two of them were brothers, and at a distance, their similar height and build meant they could be mistaken. But no thank you much, Kirill, only Andrei walk with a limp. Third rule, park their vehicles at least a kilometre away, and vary the parking places. Three rules, easy even for Kirill.

Rain hammered like Russian artillery. Water cascaded down roofs and along the road gutters, and a dirty grey mist blocked the sky.

The roads and houses were like a stinking suburb of Smolensk.

Small yards, raggedy front walls, litter in the gutters. Dirty cars sat bumper to bumper. Yards dotted with random artefacts. If everyone died, and a future people examined the yards of South Manchester, they would be very confused. A rusting pinball machine, an eviscerated giant teddy bear, a freezer without a lid, a crate of empty milk bottles, the frame of a motorbike.

Finally, a woman walked by with an umbrella and two big dogs. One had a shit on the wet pavement. The woman ripped a plastic bag from a roll and picked up the shit. He'd tell Kirill – *picked it up*, I say you. The woman walked off with the dogs, the plastic shit bag swinging in her hand. British, crazy people.

The rain eased, and Andrei could hear banging on a door, which was annoying, but not like gunfire ringing in your ears, or a comrade screaming.

A car turned into the road. Not the black estate or the yellow bubble car belonging to his no-legs wife. An old woman drove slowly past, like a Russian peasant on a rusty tractor. She disappeared down the curve of Bowker, past the target. The houses and the cars improved at that end. Their obs point was definitely at the harder end. But Andrei and Kirill could do hard.

Could do concrete, if necessary.

The rain stopped. Kids on bikes appeared from nowhere. They rode down the middle of the road like they owned the place. The same in Moscow: kids were taking over. In some tiny Europe country, the prime minister was in her thirties. Or was it New Zealand? What was wrong with an old white man dictator?

When it was Kirill's turn at the window, Andrei went downstairs. The mission felt like both a long time and a short time. Long time for no happen surveillance. Short time if their mission was to succeed and Andrei rewarded with an operation in America. Very short time because Semion knew where Alyona lived.

Already it was halfway in October, which meant they had a problem.

Castle was still working, still in and out of the police station like a home pigeon. In Russia, a dirty cop would have a quick visit to court and receive a long sentence in a cold, dark place. Breaking rocks, sewing trousers. Castle had a very good record so perhaps he'd been given a second chance. But after that, Andrei felt sure, the detective wouldn't get another one. Not even in pleasant and green land. Which wasn't surprising as it was always raining.

At least patterns were emerging. Castle worked every day, starting early, and finishing late. Castle's wife worked every weekday, and twice a week, played no-legs basketball. Their only visitor, a sweaty woman who'd climbed out of an old red car. Carrying a caddy of cleaning equipment, she walked with a bent back over to Castle's house, unlocked the door and went inside. Two hours later, the washerwoman emerged, even redder in the face, locked the door, pocketed the keys, and drove off in her old car.

A plan sat up and begged like dog.

13

Trinity had a shaved head and rows of earrings. A gleaming push scooter leant against the wall behind her desk.

'This is a police station,' said Rick, nodding at the scooter.

'You lot are the worst.'

'I'm DCI Castle.'

'Thought so.' She looked at him for a few seconds, daring him to argue back. 'You can go in.'

Rick pushed open Robbo's door, wondering if she'd last the week. His boss was sitting at his desk, slurping a milkshake and staring into space.

'How's your new PA?' said Rick, shutting the door.

The superintendent scowled. 'What have you got for me?'

'Three boys from the Westbury tennis team remain in hospital. Peter Simons is now critical.'

Robbo sucked noisily on the milkshake. 'Continue.'

'The bullet recovered from the blown-out tyre is back from forensics – it's linked to two other shootings, which is promising. We have an informant for the scene where the shooter fired from. He's currently AWOL, but we'll find him. Statements or first accounts have been obtained from six of the eight boys on the bus; Simons and Jack Philipps await. Simons for obvious reasons, Jack Philipps should be done soon.'

Robbo swirled the ice cubes in the milkshake. 'Okay.'

'I've interviewed the BMW driver Tony Rice. Turns out he attends the gym at Bunton Tennis and Football Club where the Westbury tennis team is currently practising. He denied anything has gone on, but we're following up. I've also spoken to Graham Alderman, the boys' teacher. And to Gary Hunter, who now works at Cosmos Cars and has changed his name to Gary Hamburg. There are reasons for both to be targeted, Alderman from a pupil he had expelled and who threatened retribution, and Hunter from National Crime Agency nominals he helped convict. Furthermore, it's possible Hunter has drink and/or debt problems, which makes him vulnerable to blackmail or bribery. These are lines of enquiry I'm pursuing.'

'Hypotheses?'

'Unchanged. The incident still could have been a mistake, the shooter randomly firing, or thinking he was targeting someone else. I've not yet spoken to the school, but I intend to. They could also have been the target, and the tennis team the unlucky victims.'

Robbo crushed the cardboard mug and dropped it in the bin. 'Forget the school, I'll update them.'

'I'd like—'

'I said I'd do it.'

'Yes, sir.'

Rick stood up. The last few words were staccato, like the sudden exchange of gunfire on a front line. He glanced at the annex door in the corner of the room. Their relationship had soured, but recently they had been trying to play nice. He walked out.

'*Rick!*'

He walked back.

'Have you been to see Emma?'

'Not yet.'

'*Today.* Even if it's one minute to midnight.'

Rick walked away. Robbo's tetchiness wasn't unusual, but his insistence on dealing with the school was odd. Regardless, he would go and see the head teacher.

He passed the personnel office, and, on impulse, turned back and entered. Four women sat at their desks, one on the phone, the other three typing. A fifth woman stood over the kettle. Radio Two was playing softly.

Rick went over to the woman at the kettle. Gemma was a friend of Maggie's and good value at leaving parties.

'DCI Castle, are you in trouble again? You have the thickest personnel file in the station.'

'If you investigate proper criminals, you get proper complaints. And if you work, rather than hang round the police station, you get a lot of them.'

Gemma nodded. 'Well, after all that hard work, would you like a cup of tea?'

Rick ignored her. 'Do you know where Robbo's son goes to school?'

'I don't.' She turned to the room. 'Mike Robinson's son, where does he go to school?'

There was a shaking of heads. 'Chief super's son is a bit older. He goes to Westbury, I do know that,' said the woman in the corner. A bird feeder was stuck to her window.

'I knew it,' said Rick.

'Knew what?' said Gemma.

Rick shook his head. 'One more thing while I'm here. Can I have a quick look at DS Guyen's personnel file?'

Gemma checked a chart on the wall and opened a filing cabinet, flicked through tens of dividers, and pulled out a file. She passed it over. 'Your new DS.'

Rick opened the file. Nhung's probation was marked by good work reports and exemplary service. She showed a natural aptitude for detective work, her case files were first class, and she could *if she wanted* be empathetic with victims and witnesses. High marks in her sergeant's exam, and transferred to Ashton as a DS. Made a good start, charging a three-handed rape involving nine witnesses under eighteen. Then a redacted sheet, and nothing more except for a recommendation for a move. Finally, a transfer sheet to South Manchester. Light duties proforma. Temporary attachment to Rick's special investigations unit.

Something had happened to Nhung or affecting Nhung, but what, he still had no idea. As her line manager, he thought he should know, but internal politics were often Kafkaesque. He handed the file back to Gemma.

'I owe you a drink at the next do.'

'All of us?' said Gemma.

'All of you,' said Rick, knowing he'd soon be after another favour. He walked out, little the wiser about Nhung, but flushed he'd figured out why Robbo was so keen for Rick to investigate the minibus incident. His boss was brown-nosing the chief super.

On the way to the school, Rick passed Magenta House, and to appease Robbo, he stopped. Twenty minutes max – he set the timer on his watch.

In the old-fashioned lift he slotted the security bar in place, and the metal cage rattled upwards. The air from the lift-shaft was cold and stale. The smell, the rattle, the plunging stomach brought it all back. And made him feel like a psychiatric patient, that there was something wrong with him, that he was about to be sectioned. Every time.

First floor.

He saw the three cots, bloodied and silent. The zoo mobile, bloodied and moving on the breeze from the open window. Martha, Marissa and Mark. They would have been five years old.

Second floor.

Third floor. Feeling like a reprieved bridge jumper, he unhooked the security bar and stepped out.

Emma seemed to be waiting for him. Standing by the door, she wore a black jumper with the motif of a winged horse. He wondered if it had significance. The room was always the same. Emma's white coat hung on the door. Her wheelie chair; the burgeoning spider plant; the two-person couch, uncomfortable as a bus stop. Testing kits were lined up on the shelf.

Rick walked over to the window. He always went over to the window. He passed the framed poster. Swathes of colour, fallen blocks, a bouncing blue ball. In the ball he saw a familiar face. He saw Skye. He wondered how she was. He'd sent her some money on her birthday, but had heard nothing.

Outside, silent people moved up and down the street. He found himself debating if they were real, or part of the setup. A lot of head cases thought they were the only person on the planet, and everyone else was acting. He wasn't special, just thought he was.

'How's Maggie?'

Rick turned. It was a test question. They were all test questions. Maggie was okay.

'Rick?'

'Yes?'

'You have to talk. How are you?'

Rick took a step towards her. He avoided looking at the poster, and tried to keep his mind on the here and now. His psychotherapist. Her question.

'Coming to see you, Emma, brings it all back. I'm fine till I come and see you.'

'You might think you are, Rick.'

'I am. Maybe you should sign me off?'

His psychotherapist didn't answer, but sat down and opened

her notepad. She wrote three lines of tidy script.

Rick wondered if depersonalising her was helpful. To him, not to the process. Once he'd even dreamt about her, and he knew that wasn't. 'But you're not going to do that, are you?'

Still she said nothing.

'It wouldn't be financially sensible, would it?'

'Rick, I don't think you are better. You may be suffering fewer delusions, but I hear you've developed a temper – some people refer to it as *red mist* – and it's affecting your operational judgement.'

Rick's watch started beeping.

He walked to the door. 'I think you're just prolonging things. Well, earn your money. Write your report, write whatever you like. Just know that dragging me back every three months keeps recycling the daydreams. I'll never be free and I think you know that.'

Rick drove slowly through the freshly painted metal gates of Westbury School. He was a detective *ergo* he was bound to be a psych job.

On one side, an immaculate rugby pitch, and on the other, a well-tended shrubbery opened out to reveal a sports hall.

He parked at the front of the main school building, an imposing monolith with twin entrances, a vast gable roof, and a clock tower. A gardener was blowing leaves around the cars, and a gaggle of boys wearing shorts and green jumpers weaved past him. They were chattering like birds, and roughhousing, but the gardener seemed unbothered.

He pulled out the statement taken by PC Fanning and reread what Firth Banks had said about the headmaster's son.

Until recently, the headmaster's son George Sands was in the tennis team. He played third pair with Steven Mont, even though the two reserves were both better. I think Mr Alderman knew this, we all did, but because Sands was the headmaster's son, he was in the team. Until a few weeks ago, that is. Then suddenly, Mr Alderman picked the first reserve Cai Guo to partner Mont. Sands was dropped. And for some reason, maybe he was in a huff, he stopped playing altogether.

What reason?

Rick returned the statement to his file, and climbed out. The young boys and the gardener had disappeared. In their place, a class of sixth formers strolled past. They shouldered sports bags or rucksacks, one or two briefcases. Their voices were low, and serious. At their age, exams were always looming. He was glad it was all behind him.

A huge wooden door stood open, and after striding up the steps, he went inside. The hallway was badly lit and smelt of polish.

A woman stepped out of the shadows. 'Hello, sir, how can I help?' Behind her stood a small desk with a telephone.

'DCI Castle, South Manchester.' Rick showed his badge. 'I have an appointment with the headmaster.'

'Please follow me.'

They walked along the hallway flanked by large framed pictures of previous headmasters. A flurry of boys crossed in front of them. Followed by a gangly teacher wearing a bow tie and tartan trousers.

She stopped, opened a door to a small hallway with coat racks and two further doors, one a closet. She knocked on the second.

'You can go in,' she whispered.

Rick entered a large wood-panelled room. Bookshelves ran around three sides, and in the corner stood a plinth with a marble bust. Windows looked out onto a courtyard, and in front of them stood a shiny desk. A man with black wiry hair sat in a modern leather armchair.

The headmaster stood, and they shook hands. His handshake was featherlight and his breath smelt of mints.

'Where did you go to school, inspector?'

'Chief inspector, sir.' The snip of gardener's shears reached through the windows. 'Not here. Do you have many police officers as alumni?'

The head man's eyes narrowed. 'Not many, I think there was a chief constable once.' He sat down, the chair springs squeaking. 'Please sit. You have an update for me?'

Rick pulled a seat back. 'We have reason to believe the minibus crash was not an accident.'

The headmaster stilled. His eyes darkened. Ramifications for the boys, the school, himself, unfurled in the depths.

He furled it all back. 'Why do you think that?'

'As to method, I can't give you any more detail at the moment. As to motivation, I'm hoping you might be able to tell me. Is there any reason why anyone would want to target the tennis team?'

'I can't think of one, no.'

'Graham Alderman told me you expelled a boy last year.'

'I did, and rightly so. I suppose that could be a motive. Does that make Caspar Wilson a suspect?'

'He's a line of enquiry. What about the school more generally? Does anyone else hold a grudge?'

The headmaster glanced out of the window. On the far side of the courtyard, the gardener shuffled up a ladder, and started climbing.

'Mr Sands?'

The headmaster looked back at Rick. He interlocked his fingers and cleared his throat. 'Chief inspector?'

'I appreciate it's awkward for you, sir, but this is a criminal investigation.'

Still nothing.

Rick stood up and walked over to the sculpture.

Plato, 370 BC.

'*It doesn't matter if the cobblers and the masons fail to do their jobs well. But if the Guardians fail, the democracy will crumble.*'

'Where did you come across that?'

'On my SIO course.'

'City is the wrong translation of *polis*, which actually means republic or state. It's a frequent misquote in policing manuals and on police blogs.'

'Is that right.'

'You believe in policing?'

'I believe in justice, which I think is what Plato is getting at.' Rick turned to face the headmaster. 'The police is an important job, and needs good people.' He walked back to his chair but didn't sit down. 'I understand until recently your son George was in the tennis team?'

'Team selection is in the gift of Mr Alderman.'

'I also understand that George should never have been in the team, both reserves were better. And it was popularly believed that it was your doing he was in the team. Hence, I think it maybe your doing he is *no longer* in the team – and wasn't in the team at the time of the crash. You can see where I am going with this, Mr Sands?'

'Surely, you don't suspect me?'

'No, but I do suspect that you pulled your son from the team for a reason. What is that reason?'

Rick also suspected that Robbo knew, too, which explained his real motivation for asking Rick to investigate in the first place.

The headmaster's face cracked a thin smile. 'I take it you don't know about the letter?'

'What letter?'

'The school received a letter threatening the tennis team. I spoke to Superintendent Robinson about it, and we decided that it was likely to be me they were targeting – I receive a lot of strange mail, mainly as pranks sent by pupils, but also from parents whose boys we reject. I didn't want it disseminated any further, of course, because it would damage the school's reputation.'

'You didn't believe the threat – but you removed your son from the team?'

'I thought if I removed him, I'd remove the threat.'

'Can I see the letter?'

'Superintendent Robinson has it.'

Rick couldn't believe it. A line of enquiry – fingerprints, DNA, handwriting, impressions – suppressed by his boss. Not to mention the deceit.

'Did you take a copy?'

'I didn't.'

'Really?'

'I said, I didn't.'

Rick waited a couple of seconds for his disbelief to ring out.

'What was the nature of the threat?'

'It wasn't made explicit. But in light of your earlier update, I'm now very concerned for the boys' safety.'

'I've posted an officer at the hospital, and with your permission, I'll post one in plain clothes here.'

The headmaster nodded.

On the far side of the courtyard, the gardener folded up his ladder.

'Anything else you think of, Mr Sands, please get in touch.' Rick walked to the door.

'Chief Inspector.'

Rick turned. His head still reeling.

'You're right to believe in what you do. And we *should* encourage some of our boys to join the constabulary.' The headmaster made a note on his jotter. 'Perhaps you would come back some time, and talk to the sixth form?'

Rick managed a nod. The police needed to recruit a cross-section of society, but only one or two with knowledge of Greek philosophers. More important was talking to youth clubs and comprehensives, and winning hearts and minds in parks and on street corners.

14

Rick drove to Bradford with Nhung to speak to Caspar Wilson. The traffic was heavy, and he wondered if he should have stayed in his office, reread all the statements, and harangued Robbo when he returned from a force-wide superintendents' briefing.

'Updates?'

Hands on the steering wheel at ten and two, Nhung shook her head. 'Uniform haven't picked up Bucur or his mate. And the staff I spoke to at the Bunton Tennis and Football Club didn't know anything about an altercation involving any of the boys from Westbury, or Rice. I'll have to go back to speak to the rest. I seized the CCTV and I'm partway through it.'

'What about the two drivers who stopped?'

'Frank Naylor and Trent Watson. Just getting to them . . . no statements yet but spoken to and arranged.'

She scowled. 'I can't make gold out of straw, sir.'

'I didn't say anything.'

'You didn't have to.'

They still had six leads. The letter was the best of them – a clear threat to the tennis team – and needed to be submitted urgently for forensics. The bullet's connection to two other shootings, both unsolved, suggested the gun was a pool weapon. A gun for hire. He needed to speak to the two SIOs for the linked cases. Mihai Bucur, when they got hold of him, might show them the location of the shooter, which might yield something. *Might.* Which left Caspar Wilson, the BMW driver Tony Rice, and Hunter, all speculative lines of enquiry but all offering potential.

Nhung stared through the windscreen. No TV talk, or gossip about other detectives, or sycophantic questions about his career. She wasn't even humming.

Rick pondered *his* arrest. He took out his two lists and worked through the names. He added one more.

Gary Hunter / Hamburg – being leaned on by someone

Sourcing the drugs would be fairly easy for everyone, either by design or by chance. He figured the crux to narrowing the list down was focusing on the mechanics of how the drug was planted. Discounting the unlikely possibility of someone cloning his keys, someone had broken into his car and planted the drugs without leaving a trace, suggesting both premeditation and a degree of criminal sophistication. With the exception of Jack Gibbs, it helped to rule out most people inside the police station. Gibbs' CV included a sergeant's posting heading up the car crime squad and he'd know how to break into cars. One untraceable method would be to use a laptop to bounce a signal from Rick's key fob – in his pocket in the police station or on a coat peg in Maggie's flat – to unlock the car doors. The only way of preventing the crime was to keep car keys in a Faraday box. Rick didn't – he had a crap car – but going forward, he'd bolt that stable door.

Nhung glanced across, but didn't ask. Rick put down his pen, and to break their introversion, told her about his family meeting to discuss Dad, planned for later. He avoided the detail, only that a problem had arisen.

His new sergeant tutted.

'Family means everything to Vietnamese people, sir. We don't need care homes because we all live together. My grandparents live with my parents, and eventually, my parents will live with me. If I had a partner, their parents too.'

They fell silent. Her comments felt like a rebuke. Looking after Dad full time – *or being sacked for the drugs in his car* – would mean he couldn't be a DCI. And if he wasn't a DCI, then who was he? The Job gave him identity, self-worth, absorption. The purpose of life, in his view, was finding a purpose.

And he'd found his.

Sat nav worked its magic, and they pulled into the spacious carpark of an old pub, now the Full Circle halfway house. Rick double-checked the car was locked, and they went inside. He didn't want any more problems.

The bell was answered by a young bearded man holding a paintbrush and wearing yellow-paint-flecked clothes. In the front room, furniture was draped and a stepladder was set out. Two or three residents were larking about with brushes.

Rick showed his badge.

'I'm Jim,' said the man. 'Caspar's upstairs, room four. I looked in our diary for the day before yesterday – he went to Manchester to meet a friend. They're allowed to do that. Builds a bit of trust.'

'What's he like?'

'You people. That would take a week.'

Rick headed up the stairs, followed by Nhung.

Grunge music spilled from room 4. Rick pushed open the door which had fist and boot marks.

The room was dark and stank of sleep and cigarette smoke.

He felt for a light switch.

Caspar sat on the edge of the bed. He wore a green parka with the hood up, and was pulling the hood strings, one way, then the other. His eyes were bloodshot. On the wall opposite were posters of The Cure. The music was heavy with lyrics about prayers and rain.

Rick felt depressed just standing there. He walked over to the iPod and turned it off. He drew the curtains and opened a window. A two-litre bottle of Coke stood by the bed. Nearby, an ashtray of spent roll ups, a green bag of tobacco, torn Rizla packets.

'They said you was coming.'

'DCI Castle, DS Guyen, South Manchester.'

Caspar pulled up his sleeves to reveal rows of silver-coloured bangles and self-harming scars. He grinned like a moron.

But Rick wasn't being fooled so early.

'We're investigating a minibus crash on the ring road. The bus was from your old school.'

'Westbury. Heh-heh.' Caspar's cackle led to a spluttery cough. His teeth were badly stained, and one or two were missing.

'How come you went to Westbury,' said Nhung, 'if you don't mind me asking?'

Rick glanced across at her. She'd asked what he wanted to know, and hadn't waited for him to lead.

Caspar was also surprised, and he pushed back his hood. He tapped his head. 'Got a brain, at least I did have. Heh-heh. Passed the exam, got a scholarship. I was living with foster parents, but they kicked me out when I was expelled.'

'Fairly?' said Rick.

'*C'est la vie.*' Laughing at his joke, Caspar coughed to silence.

'Do you hold a grudge against Mr Alderman?'

'Balders Alders? Nah! Is that what he said?' Caspar cleaned out an ear with a finger, inspected the result, and flicked a bead across the room. 'He was a shit teacher, mind.' He coughed some more. '*Très, très merde.*'

'What did you do in Manchester two days ago?'

He tipped his head to one side, and cleaned his other ear. 'I went to see a man about a dog.'

Nhung jumped in. 'Has he got a name?'

'The dog?' Caspar cackled and coughed.

Rick grabbed the eighteen-year-old and pushed him up against a wall. 'Hands to the sides, legs apart.'

'It's an English expression, Guyen, darling. Means don't be fucking nosy.'

Rick kicked Caspar's legs wider apart. 'Watch your mouth.' He patted him down and checked the pockets of his coat. Found an empty crisps packet, and more Rizla papers. He stepped back. 'Search the room, Nhung, I'll watch him.'

He also watched her. She rifled clothes in a chest of drawers and in a wardrobe. She looked under the bed, but there was nothing except dust balls and a sock. A couple of paperbacks sat on a shelf.

'Nothing,' she said, holding up a packet of razor blades from inside a book.

Rick pocketed them, and they left.

They tramped downstairs, nodded at Jim, who was halfway up the stepladder and painting the ceiling, and went out to the car.

'Waste,' said Nhung across the roof.

'Not for us,' said Rick. 'Even if Caspar does hold a grudge against Alderman, he couldn't shoot straight, yet alone organise a complex hit.'

He waited until Nhung had climbed in and shut the door, then phoned Robbo. When his boss didn't pick up, he left a testy message saying he *must* submit the letter to the lab as a priority.

They drove back to South Manchester in near silence. Rick directed Nhung across the moors. Walls of dark stone and straggly fences stretched for miles. Strange rock formations crested ridgelines, the pale moon already in place.

106

15

'I can't stay long.'

'You never can,' said Becky.

The hall was like the rest of her house: immaculate, and always reminded Rick of a show home. Real people didn't live there.

His phone rang.

'Hang on.' He stepped back outside the front door.

'Sir, it's Esra, family liaison in the Formby case.'

He'd been trying to get hold of her, and he didn't want to pass up the opportunity. Jane Formby's family deserved some attention. As did Jane Formby. 'Thanks for phoning, Esra. When was the last time you made contact?'

'About a year ago. The victim's mother remains hopeful that one day we'll find her daughter. Even if it's only to bury her, at least it'll give her closure and maybe some peace. It was one of my first cases, and I still follow up. Get on alright with her. Jane had a bit of a story, I suppose they all do really. She didn't use drugs and supported financially her sick mother. Her father was dead. She saved most of her money, planning to retire at thirty, and set up a café on Anglesey. She loved the sea, and collected large shells so she could listen to it.' Esra paused. 'Her mother Alison would have phoned me if there's anything, but I will check.'

'Thanks, Esra, it all helps.'

He returned inside.

They were all there, sitting in his sister's beautiful kitchen: Mum; Becky and her husband, dentist and DIY maestro Julian; Maggie and him. There to discuss Dad. Becky made hot drinks in small mugs and Mum opened a tin of homemade biscuits. The kitchen was for cooking *properly* while listening to Radio 4, and eating breakfast. Not for Julian's fancy bite-sized meals, or for family meetings.

'I can't stay long.'

'You already told us,' said Becky.

She suggested Julian could chair because he would have a more objective view, not being family. Rick thought differently.

He sat at the head of the table. A motive for the shooter and the statements from the boys on the minibus churning round his head.

'What's the evidence against Dad?'

Becky scowled. 'Always playing detective.' Until his sister had married, she'd always been his number one fan, but her allegiance had changed, and strengthened, in Rick's view, by the grating nature of her husband. Externally, at least.

'I *am* a detective.'

Maggie pressed his hand and flicked him a look. 'Delicious biscuits, Maureen. Can I have the recipe?' His mum smiled.

'Another resident has complained and it's on CCTV.'

'What're the details, Becky?' said Rick. 'An investigation is about details.' Who had last seen Jack Philipps, and where?

Becky gripped her coffee mug. 'Dad squeezed the bottom of another resident, a woman. In reception.'

'Is *alleged* to have squeezed. We need to watch the CCTV. What about witnesses?'

'I think there's only one, the woman who complained. Is that right, Mum?'

'I made some notes somewhere, when Michael phoned.' She shuffled through a sheaf of envelopes.

'We need a lawyer,' said Julian.

'We don't need a lawyer,' said Rick. 'We need to know what the care home and the victim want to do about it, then assess the strength of evidence.'

'What about Dad?' said Becky. 'They've locked him in his room.'

'I can't find it,' said Mum. Her voice quivered, and she looked like she was going to cry.

Rick couldn't ever remember seeing her crying. He gripped her hand, stopped her shuffling the papers. 'It'll be okay,' he whispered.

He stood up. 'Sorry, I've got to go. I'll go and see Dad, and speak to Michael. Anything else, Maggie can tell me later.' He kissed the top of Maggie's head. Then squeezed the top of his mum's shoulder. 'Great biscuits.'

There were few cars on the road, and twenty minutes later Rick pulled into Kyle Philipps' new estate. A couple of dog-walkers trailed along the shadowed pavements. New cars sat side by side waiting to be stolen.

He rang the bell. Banged on the front door. Philipps' car wasn't on the drive, but could be in the garage. The front rooms were dark, but a faint light emanated through the frosted glass door. Rick banged again.

He stood back.

Waited.

Cautiously, he opened the letterbox and observed. There was no movement or sound. The interior doors were closed.

He banged again. Kyle Philipps was taking the piss. Or was he? Rick climbed over a high and bolted gate, and walked round the back. He peered inside, but couldn't see anything amiss. He returned to the front and knocked on a neighbour's door. Yes, he'd seen Kyle earlier that day. Not Jack, he'd be at school.

Kyle *was* taking the piss, possibly his son too. Rick scribbled a note, posted it through the letterbox, and returned to his car.

He drove away, passing the same ghostly dog-walkers. He wasn't unduly worried: DS Guyen had seen Jack, and the boy's statement was unlikely to take the case much further. Then again, it might. Tomorrow, a statement would be taken from Jack Philipps, even if Rick had to post a uniform unit outside.

*

Andrei waited in the shadows at the back of the Coach and Horses where he'd scored the first time. Their new plan needed more coke, much more, but Semion was a very rich man, so the money wasn't the problem. He felt upbeat. God didn't put man on earth to watch other men.

The pub was busy. Blackboards promised cheap beer and a cover band. Smokers hovered under an awning. Two men as big as Kirill stood by the front door, but the back of the pub and the carpark were unguarded. Dim lights marked the boundary. Andrei massaged his leg, hoping he wouldn't have to trail it far.

He felt peckish, and wondered if Kirill had eaten all the garlic bread. His partner had had his chance yesterday but drawn a blank. So today he had to stay behind. Rule four: one of them always had to stay home. Admittedly, but no say to Kirill, sourcing more coke would have been easier with the two of them.

A rear door of the pub opened, exposing a crack of light and the thin man with the ponytail. Up close he had a narrow face, as if he'd been hit repeatedly with a lump of wood. The runner pulled the door shut, stared out into the carpark, and slipped into the gloom.

Andrei followed.

Reappearing at the front of the pub, the runner scuttled across the four lanes of road. As Andrei dodged the traffic, the runner crossed a worn strip of grass and entered a dark housing estate.

The houses were small, identical, and tightly packed, like bullets in a magazine. Two kids with their hoods up patrolled the opposite pavement. Men sat on deckchairs in front of one ugly pebble-dashed box. Behind them, every window was open, and music blared from a speaker propped on a sill. Andrei felt like a tourist, one who'd been separated from the tour bus and had wandered somewhere he shouldn't. Onto a crumbly cliff-edge, or into the lion enclosure.

The runner turned down a darker side road. TVs flickered in front windows. A man and woman were arguing inside a house with the front door open. Two young girls, one with a ring in her nose, walked past, eating a big packet of crisps and giggling. On a school night. Their parents should be ashamed. Alyona knew the rules, no piercings 'til she was sixteen, and no going out on a school night. The only thing Andrei agreed on with her mother.

The runner darted down a wide alley, along the side of a house. Slipped through a gate, and stopped outside a door. Behind a shuddering fence, a dog scrabbled and whined as if the butcher's boy was calling.

Andrei walked past the alley. Heard a coded knock, glanced across. Kept going. Heard a hatch draw open, the mutter of low voices.

The door was fortified with an external grid of bars. He'd found the right place.

He walked on for a couple of minutes, mentally mapping the route. Figuring the runner would be on his way back to the pub, Andrei turned around and retraced his steps. This tourist wanted to buy a souvenir.

He entered the alley, which led to half a dozen even smaller houses. The stash house was deserted. He walked past, the dog barking and jumping at the fence. The grey squat lump bossed a tiny square of shit-strewn concrete at the back. There was a rear door, also protected by a metal grid. Bars on the windows, dark upstairs.

Inside were civilians, not soldiers. He wasn't a tourist, only felt like a tourist – he'd been lost, but now he was found.

Andrei knocked on the front door. He glanced behind him, looked up and down. The dog chewed the fence. He knocked again.

The hatch opened.

'The fuck you want?'

Andrei held up an envelope of money, twenty times what he'd paid before, and passed it through the hatch. The stash house functioned like an old-fashioned shop – pay first, then the goods prepared and handed over. The hatch closed.

The dog whined, scrabbled against the fence. Andrei flexed his bad leg. The dog pissed. Andrei didn't need coloured ribbons and a dickie bow. He knocked again.

The hatch drew back.

'The fuck you want?'

So it like that.

Andrei walked away. Like a big, stupid American once said, he be back.

*

At home, Maggie wasn't back, and Rick fell asleep rereading the statements taken by the neighbourhood team. Searching out the fine details, what he knew, what he didn't, and how he could fill in the gaps.

When the minibus finally stopped moving, I opened my eyes. Our kit bags were everywhere. Jack made a joke, something like, I hope we can still practise. I climbed out, not believing what had happened. Cars were still zooming past. One man stopped to help. He was wearing a fluorescent jacket.

    Paul Chan

16

The rich smell of comb honey filled the kitchen. A half-drunk mug and a plate with toast crumbs sat on the table. Statement forms propped against the coffee pot. Condensation fogged the windows, still dark outside.

Rick turned the page.

My face was bleeding from flying glass. I grabbed my tennis racquet – I know it was stupid – and climbed out of the bus. Mont was lying on the hard shoulder face down, and sat next to him, Clare was screaming.
    Peter Gibbs

When he'd finished reading, he phoned Robbo, but clicked through to voicemail. He left another brusque message about the letter.

Maggie came into the kitchen. She was dressed for work, and made up. They kissed. She smelt of perfume.

'Julian's a nightmare,' said Maggie. Rick poured her a cup of coffee. 'Becky's so nice.' Maggie took the cup. 'Will you go to Three Views today?'

'Maybe.'

'Your dad's locked in his room!'

Rick shook his papers. 'It's difficult at this stage of a case. Every minute is vital. You know that.'

'Was Kyle Philipps in?'

Rick shook his head.

'What now?'

Rick shrugged. 'I'm about to try him again, camp outside his door if I have to.' He told her about the letter to the school.

'I can't believe it. Robbo always has his own agenda.'

His phone rang.

'Inspector Castle, it's Sandra Winn.' She sounded furious. 'Kyle's just phoned, Jack's not staying with him, and he's not staying with the friend he thought he was with. He doesn't know where he is. He said he was trying to wind me up. Well, it worked!'

Rick stood up.

'I'll be with you in fifteen minutes.'

Outside Kyle Philipps' house, Nhung climbed out of her car, locked it, and climbed into the passenger seat of Rick's.

A dustbin lorry drove into the new estate, followed by two men in reflective overalls. The lorry stopped. The men pulled and pushed and hefted. The back of the lorry rose with two wheelie bins, the lids fell open, the lorry shook, and the bins returned to earth. The beeping and the stench moved down the road.

'Sorry.'

Rick looked across at her. 'You're a DS.'

'Yes, sir. I should have woken him up and spoken to him. I should have confirmed his identity.'

'How?'

'Sir!'

'How?'

'Photo ID. Asked to see his wallet and examined the

contents. Q and A, whatever seemed appropriate.'

Rick climbed out, and slammed the door. Nhung slammed her door harder. They walked up the short drive to a house less than two years old. Manufacturer's instructions were still stuck to the gutters and fence posts.

Kyle Philipps opened the door as they approached, and disappeared inside.

Rick entered and walked through to the kitchen. In uniform he'd attended violent, unpredictable and ridiculous domestic disturbances, and as a fledgling detective had investigated harassment and vindictive, petty crimes. Blinded in the intensity of the moment, people would risk everything – serious injury, losing their children, community shame, imprisonment – just to get one up on their former partner.

'I hate living here,' said Philipps. He was staring out into the garden. Windows from six houses stared back. 'Everyone knows what you're doing.' He turned round. 'She's bleeding me dry.'

'Is Jack here?' said Rick.

'No.'

'Was he ever here?'

'No.'

'Who was here?'

'My other son – Adam. He lives with me.'

'Which friend did you think he was staying with?'

Philipps shrugged.

Nhung walked forward. 'You're under arrest, wasting police time.'

'You must be—'

She clipped on the first handcuff, stepped back and pulled it sharply forward, bending the rigid cuffs up at the same time.

'Agh!'

Nhung clicked the second cuff in place, and pushed Philipps into a chair.

Rick walked over to him. 'When Jack does stay here, which bedroom is his?'

'First on right. Second door is Adam's, one at the end is mine.' Philipps held up the cuffs. 'Can't you tell her to loosen them?'

'You ask her.'

Rick went upstairs to have a look around. In contrast to the room at his mum's house, Jack's bedroom was in normal teenage chaos. Clothes and magazines and schoolbooks on a table, on the bed, and on the floor. Photos of tennis matches covered a noticeboard. He rummaged through the drawers of a desk and opened the wardrobe. Seized a couple more photos, including a headshot of Jack; a toothbrush; an unwashed tennis shirt; an old bank card.

He looked at the photos. Jack was tall, athletic-looking. He had dark hair, like his father. Bright blue eyes. Rick imagined the photo on lampposts, on police briefings, on the news. Bright blue eyes were always an advantage.

The briefing room was in disarray. Chairs higgledy-piggledy, mugs and confectionery wrappers from the previous meeting still on the tabletops.

The neighbourhood team didn't seem to notice. They sat and slouched amongst the mess. Maggie waited at the back, but there was no sign of Robbo.

'Two minutes, sir,' said Nhung.

Rick stood in the corridor, marshalling his thoughts for the missing enquiry. They'd lost almost seventy-two hours.

He went back in. The room was straight, the officers quiet.

'You may be wondering why I'm investigating what appears to be a traffic accident.' He'd wondered it himself to begin with. 'Well, it was no accident. The tyre on the minibus was shot out – we found the bullet in the wheel.'

He waited for the muttering to die away. 'I'm still developing hypotheses as to why. In addition, we now have a missing person. The two things are very likely to be connected, but we don't know for sure, and we don't know how. So, I want a big effort on the following actions.'

'Hear, hear,' said Barton.

Nhung scowled.

'Maggie, I want you to start with the basics. Hospitals and PNC. Then do the enquiries on Jack's phone number. Calls and messages and triangulation. Also financial checks, and social media.'

She nodded.

'DS Guyen, and PC Fanning. We need to nail down the time and location Jack went missing. We know he was in the minibus and at the scene of the crash. But where did he go from there? It's likely he left by ambulance or police car, but we need to confirm this. Who took him and where to? Hopefully, we can then pick up a trail from there.'

They both nodded.

'Who's taking statements from the two drivers who stopped?'

Two hands went up.

'We need these asap. And that leaves everyone else. Barton, I want you to go and sit with Mrs Winn. Find out Jack's medical history, and if he's ever disappeared or run away before. Start contacting his friends and relatives. Get hold of his computer. Sergeant Davison, nominate two of your officers to check the motorway cameras. Also, I want you to organise anniversary checkpoints on the slip road near the crash. Today, and for the next four days between three and six p.m. Stop drivers, let's see if we can get someone who saw the accident. Dashcam footage is what we really want.'

Robbo snuck in through a second door at the back. He was eating from a can of Pringles.

'Good timing, sir,' said Rick. 'Could you do the press briefing, holding back on the gunshot of course?'

'Can't you do it?'

Rick stared at him for a few seconds. His boss hadn't returned his calls, let alone offered an explanation for withholding the letter. 'Better if you do – there might be some awkward questions, and would distract from finding the boy.'

The superintendent nodded as if he'd been asked to dredge a lake, then handed round his Pringles. He should have been a politician – off duty, he already looked like one.

'Okay everyone, go to it.'

The meeting broke up. Rick exited the nearest door, and cut Robbo off at the second.

'Quick word.'

They re-entered the briefing room and waited until it was empty. Rick shut both doors.

'Sands told me about the letter.'

Robbo tipped the crisps into his hand and ate the crumbs. He walked over to the bin, crumpling the can. 'I thought I told you I would liaise with the school.'

'The letter's our best lead and needs to be submitted for forensics.'

The superintendent pushed a chair under a table. 'I was doing Sands a favour. He thought it was only a prank, and didn't want any bad publicity for the school.'

'That was then, this is now . . . a boy's missing, a bullet was fired at the minibus he was travelling in. Surely you realise—'

'Anything else?' said his boss, pushing in another chair.

Something else had gone on between the two men, but what? And the headmaster had put his own son's safety above everyone else's. The cover-up stank.

'Did the letter mention Jack specifically?'

'No.'

'What did it say?'

'The tennis team should stop playing. Or they would be made to stop. You've been warned. Words to that effect.'

'I really need to see—'

'I'll look for it.' His boss walked to the door.

Rick suspected the superintendent knew exactly where the letter was. But if the letter wasn't found, and the only two people who had seen it denied its existence, then it didn't exist. The headmaster's disregard for the safety of the tennis team, and Robbo's suppression of the letter and compromise of an investigation, would all be buried.

'Sir.'

'I said, I'll look for it.' The superintendent opened the door. 'Don't forget, Rick, what I did for you a couple of days ago.' He walked out.

Rick thumped a chair under a table. Either he would have to persuade his boss to *find* the letter, or he would have to look for it himself.

The team busied like honeybees, flitting to and fro on enquiries.

Rick remained in his office, like their queen. Like a grumpy uncle. A nagging aunt, a fussy mother. He was the unreasonable rooster in the hen house, an unpredictable mother-hen. As senior investigating officer, Rick was the cornerstone, the conduit, and the linchpin of the investigation. Everything flowed from him, through him, and back to him. He was the cook, cleaner, and bottle-washer. He was the team's role model and inspiration, their bête noire, and their whipping boy. If the investigation went well, he would praise them. If it flagged, he would encourage, and support, and tear down obstacles. If it failed, the buck stopped with him.

They wouldn't fail. Robbo knew that, and that's why he'd agreed to Rick heading a special investigations unit – to be utilised when the superintendent had a problem.

Rick read through the file. He read every statement and considered his hypotheses. He compiled a table.

Hypothesis	Person of Interest	Target / Victim	Motive?
A	?	n/a	n/a (random)
B	?	Westbury School	?
C	Tony Rice	someone in the minibus	argument?
D	Caspar Wilson	Graham Alderman	revenge?
E	Denny K + others	Gary Hunter (Hamburg)	old score?
F	?	?	mistake
G	(letter)	tennis team	?
H	?	?	?

So many question marks.

He phoned Barton to check on the welfare of Mrs Winn, and DS Guyen to check on her and PC Fanning's progress with statements from the emergency crews. He checked on Maggie, signed the phone and bank applications. They briefly nestled fingers. He visited the checkpoint on the slip road run by PS Davison. He handed out doughnuts and chatted to a couple of PCs, interrogated a couple of drivers, shared a joke with Davison and returned to base.

Nothing of note.

Detective work was like that. Routine, repetitive, ever hopeful.

17

Six hours later, his ad hoc team trooped back into the conference room. Rick had arranged for pizzas and soft drinks at the back. When they were all there, except Robbo, he shut both doors and stood at the front.

'Maggie?'

'Negative, I'm afraid.' She pushed back her hair. 'Jack's not in hospital and not in custody. No movement in his bank account since the weekend when he bought a pair of trainers. No activity on the phone since the time of the crash. He sent a text just before he got on the minibus. Data usage a minute or so before the crash suggests he was using the internet. Triangulation shows his phone at the scene of the crash, and no activity since. Either damaged, or switched off. Still waiting for details of his calls and texts.'

'Sergeant Davison?'

The neighbourhood sergeant put down his slice of pizza. 'Traffic cameras don't cover the scene of the crash. In respect of the anniversary checkpoint, we stood there for three hours as instructed, spoke to one hundred and twenty-five drivers. Quite a few were aware of the crash, and one woman drove past shortly afterwards. She saw the police cars and ambulances. Vinnie Forester's her name.'

Rick raised a thumb. He loved it when a proactive enquiry

yielded a result, even if, ultimately, it made no difference. It showed junior officers what was possible, and encouraged application. 'First account?'

'Yes.' Davison stepped forward, and handed over the action sheet and his notes. 'She doesn't remember much.'

Rick marked them up – Forester would be statemented by a detective. What a witness said they remembered was always less than what they'd seen. 'Same again tomorrow?'

'Yes, sir, three until six.' The sergeant stepped back, rescued his pizza, and sat on a table.

'Barton, how's Mrs Winn?'

'She's better, sir, as you can imagine, having benefited from my company all day, sir.' Barton's face was the colour of beetroot, but his comment produced a laugh.

'Any useful information on Jack?'

'No medical issues. He's not diabetic, doesn't have allergies. He likes gaming online, has over two hundred friends on Facebook, no girlfriend but quite likes Victoria Parsons – his tennis partner. Contacted dozens of relatives and friends. Nothing pertinent, sir. I seized his laptop from Mr and Mrs Simons and dropped it off at the lab. Full notes in my pocketbook.'

'Back with Mrs Winn tomorrow, please.'

'Yes, sir, thank you, sir.'

'Who was taking statements from the two car drivers who stopped?'

Two PCs raised a hand, and one stood up. 'PC Jennings, sir. I spoke to Frank Naylor. Works for a charity, forty-two years old; driving a dark blue Astra. He said the crash happened about a hundred metres in front of him. He stopped and helped some of the boys out of the minibus. Doesn't remember Jack. When the emergency staff arrived, he left his details and drove away. No trace PNC, no intel.'

'Good, thank you. Who else?'

A mature man with a beard stood up. 'I took a statement from Trent Watson. He's forty-five years old, an electrician. He also saw the accident take place in front of him. Recently done a first aid course at work. He stopped and made sure one of the boys – Clare, I think – was breathing. He stemmed the bleeding from a leg wound, and handed over to paramedics when they arrived. Left his details, and went. Like Naylor, doesn't remember Jack, and no trace.'

'Vehicle?'

The PC looked down at his notes. 'Dark blue Ford Focus.'

Rick nodded. 'Nhung?'

'I have to say, sir, there're a few muppets in the Job. Anyway, the three ambulance crews noted who they conveyed to St Anne's in their logbooks. This included the three boys seriously injured, and the teacher Alderman. Plus Paul Chan who was later released. The four police cars who attended the scene, three traffic, one of ours, also have logbooks. The three traffic logs were complete, and showed they transported the minibus driver Gary Hamburg, and the boys Cai Guo and Kirk Walsh back to Westbury School.' DS Guyen scowled. 'The logbook in the patrol car, however, was not completed. PC Fanning and I managed to trace the driver and operator, and confirmed, using photos of Peter Gibbs and Jack Philipps, that they transported Gibbs but not Philipps away from the scene.' Nhung sipped from a can of Coke.

'In summary, sir, everyone is accounted for, except Jack Philipps.'

'Am I right in thinking you only spoke to the crew of the patrol car, and not the crews of the other vehicles?'

'We spoke to one or two of them, but some were off duty or working in different vehicles. We checked their logbooks when that was the case. I have a list.'

'Tomorrow, then, I want you to follow up with PC Fanning, and statement every attending officer, police or ambulance, prompting with a photo of Philipps and asking whether they remember seeing him or transporting him. To double-check.'

'Yes, sir.'

'However, assuming your information holds, Nhung, it means that Jack Philipps was last seen at the scene of the crash, and wasn't conveyed away by police or ambulance or by one of the two drivers who stopped. It's possible he was concussed and wandered away from the scene on foot. The other possibility is…'

Rick's stomach turned. The straightforward traffic collision was proving anything but.

'Someone else drove him away.'

He paused again.

'Someone, we know nothing about.'

*

Andrei loitered again in the carpark's shadows. Stars up there somewhere.

When the runner squeezed out of the Coach and Horses back door, Andrei didn't follow. He popped a couple of painkillers and massaged his leg. The blackboards were offering happy hour. Kirill needed happy hour – he say Andrei, he was fed up playing handmaid.

Fifteen minutes later, the rear door of the pub cracked open, revealing the runner returning – resupplied – in a band of light. A peal of clubby clamour, then dark and quiet. Time for Andrei happy hour.

He crossed the busy road and entered the estate. Retraced his route from the day before. A group of lads surrounded a red car with a tail fin, and a group of girls stood nearby. The car revved, the lads strutted, the girls preened.

Andrei turned down the side road, and after glancing over his shoulder, entered the wide alley. No one was waiting outside the barred door. The dog barked as if the end of the world was nigh.

Andrei lobbed a lump of meat into the shitty square of yard. Russian steak was perhaps what the dog desired, but kebab the only thing on the menu. Barkers, no choosers. The dog slobbered as if it hadn't eaten all day. Andrei slipped the stubby scaffold pole down his sleeve and side-stepped over the fence. Hoping the inbred animal had enjoyed its last supper, he clubbed the dog on the head.

Andrei crept closer to the back door. Voices, music inside.

He didn't have long to wait. A minute or two later, the door opened and an unsuspecting dealer stepped out.

'Killer?'

Andrei hit him with the scaffold. The man's knees sagged and he slumped forward, chinning the concrete.

Andrei slipped off his rucksack, took out a jar containing a petrol-soaked rag. He lit the rag, shoved it into a bag of rockets and catherine wheels and barrages, and hurled the bag through the door. Pulled it to.

An explosion of bangs and whistles and whooshes accompanied by multicoloured lights and flashes rocked the house. No oohs and aahs. He counted to five, yanked open the door, and stepped inside.

Two men lay on the floor, half under a kitchen table, and a third slumped in a chair. Broken glass and banknotes covered the table and the floor. Firework refuse smouldered, ash fluttered around, a smell of burning.

Andrei shoved the back of a chair against the internal door. The seated man, dazed and disbelieving, began to rise. Andrei stepped behind him, and brought the scaffold bar up against his chin. The man spluttered. Andrei pulled harder on the bar. The man's neck was warm, his body growing in weight. Andrei increased the pressure.

The dealer pointed at the ceiling.

Andrei looked up at the white tiles. A couple showed black marks from the fireworks. He yanked the bar up and pushed the now unconscious man away. Looked closer. One of the tiles was dirtier than the rest. He swung the pipe, and the tile disintegrated in a shower of polystyrene shards. Hundreds of plastic bags floated down. He swung again, and again. Half the ceiling collapsed and covered him and the table and the chairs and the three senseless men in a layer of white dust and tiny bags and ten-pound notes. During the snow-like storm, two thuds. The first, like a Chaplin comedy, when something heavy clonked the head of the man who'd pointed at the ceiling. The second, when a foil-wrapped parcel landed on the table.

Andrei shoved the brick-sized package into his rucksack. The handgun was dirty but would clean up. Andrei scooped up some of the money and pocketed the gun as a bonus for his inconvenience. At the door, he turned and surveyed the chaos. So unnecessary. Now they got to get the hoover out of the cupboard.

Outside, he stepped over the dead grey dog and the fence and limped into the darkness. Happy hour was over.

18

The Scent Article Method dog sniffed at Jack's tennis shirt for a few seconds. Max was a white-and-chocolate-spotted Springer Spaniel. Four years old. Cute, playful, and as keen as Rick to get going.

Jack Philipps couldn't have disappeared into thin air. Either he'd wandered off, or he'd been transported somewhere. Voluntarily – or against his will. Kidnap lurked at the edges of Rick's mind like the devil for churchgoers.

The dog set off at a trot, away from the noisy ring road and the scene of the minibus crash. And away from the specialist team who were about to start a fingertip search.

Max slipped down the litter-strewn bank, and without hesitation, padded across the scrubby ground bordering the road. Handler Steve let the retractable lead spool out until the dog was five metres ahead, then followed at a jog.

A fifteen-metre box-cordon of police officers including Rick, DS Guyen, and the neighbourhood team moved with them. Their job was to form a neutral zone around the specialist tracker dog, to protect the public, but more importantly to safeguard the dog. SAM dogs could follow a scent up to a month old, took three years to train, and were worth a quarter of a million pounds each. Having one run over or injured by another dog was to be avoided.

Rick knew he'd been lucky handler Steve had not been booked. There were less than a dozen of the dogs in the country, and Steve had travelled overnight from Cornwall.

But now, he wanted a result.

The dog headed towards a hole in the wire fence. A PC carrying only a radio squeezed through first and jogged on ahead. Steve had said at the briefing that Max wouldn't be distracted by the smell of other humans, and could even track through a shopping centre or a busy street.

Max followed the PC. Then Steve. More PCs bundled through, followed by Rick. He jogged along a ginnel between warehouses. Two men wearing hard hats turned and stared.

The ginnel emerged onto a road where an articulated trailer was being unloaded by a forklift. The driver snapped a photo. Steve held Max back while the box-cordon reformed. Two women with pushchairs stopped and pointed.

They moved off again, Max straining at his leash. The PCs were trying not to smile, trying to remain professional.

Rick could hardly believe Max had picked up Jack's scent. Where had the boy gone, and why? Maybe Jack had hit his head and wandered off, not knowing who he was. Maybe he was lying in a gutter somewhere. Or had been taken in by someone.

The leading PCs reached a junction. A van drove past, the driver slowing and staring. One of the PCs radioed to the two patrol cars that were assisting. Max padded into the junction. The cordon of officers moved with the dog, waiting for an indication. There was no traffic, but lots of parked cars.

Max headed right, and surged ahead. The cordon wheeled round, surged with him. Rick breathed out. The dog still had the scent.

The dog headed onto the far pavement between parked cars, and padded along. Steve followed. Rick followed. Maybe Jack was *compos mentis*. The boy didn't have a regular girlfriend, not one his parents knew about, apart from Victoria Parsons, his mixed doubles tennis partner, but maybe he had a girlfriend – or a boyfriend – they didn't know about. He made a mental note to speak to Parsons himself.

The front side of the cordon reached another junction. It was a busy road, cars streaming both ways. The radio was full of chatter. A patrol car issued a burst of sirens and the traffic stopped. Rick ran forward to the junction.

In both directions, police vehicles blocked the traffic. Max pottered out into the middle of the road. The dog looked up and down, padded across and began to sniff around the base of a postbox. PCs stood watching. People climbed out of their cars. A circus was in town.

But it wasn't a circus. Jack could be injured, or even dead. He could have been kidnapped, could be being tortured or abused. Images from past cases flitted through Rick's head. An Eritrean boy chained to a radiator, lightheaded with hunger and sitting in his own shit; a young Pakistani woman who'd fled an arranged marriage at home, flown to the UK, been tracked down, and repeatedly raped before being beheaded.

Max set off again, past the postbox and along the pavement opposite the way they'd arrived at the junction.

The cordon reformed and ran with him.

'Come on, Max,' whispered Rick. If the dog found Jack, he'd buy it a year's supply of beef bones.

Behind them, the traffic restarted. Max sped up, stopped, retraced his steps. The box-cordon copied the dog, like an absurd open-air pantomime. The dog sniffed a gatepost, took off again. Reached the end of the road. Turned right. To the end of another road. Left.

Max entered a housing estate, an address every officer knew well. Twelve months earlier, there'd been a major disturbance. Public order vans requested from all over the city. The cordon contracted. The road curved round, past shuttered but open shops. A boarded-up pub. A playground daubed with graffiti tags.

Rick began to fear the worst. Jack had a dark side to his life that no one, or almost no one, knew about. Drugs or steroids. Activities or relationships on the dark web. The boy, the victim of a grooming.

The dog headed for a ginnel. Now getting used to its role, the box-cordon merged into a line and followed. PCs ahead, PCs behind. Max and Steve in the middle.

The ginnel jinked left and right, and emerged onto Crenton Road. It climbed steeply, the houses detached and at the end of short drives. Parked cars were more numerous, and newer.

Rick checked his watch. They'd been going for thirty minutes and had covered over a mile. A more-or-less straight line from the scene of the crash. The route didn't seem like an aimless wander, but purposeful. Which meant what? Jack knew where he was going, or was with someone who knew where he, or she, was going?

The dog slowed to a trot. PCs were breathing hard and red in the face.

Max slowed further.

The dog stopped at a gatepost. The wrought iron gate with ornamental spikes lay open. Max inspected the opposite post. The dog raced down the drive to the front door. There was a porch with terracotta pots and hanging baskets.

Max retreated, and sat down to face the door.

It was as if the dog had rung the bell.

Steve turned to Rick. 'Quite a strong indication. Over to you, now.'

Scenarios crashed through Rick's head. Jack had fallen out with his parents, and was staying with a new friend who owned a tennis court. The friend's parents were away, and they were seeing how long before anyone missed them. Or, Jack had wandered there after the crash in a daze and had collapsed in the garden. Or, the boy had been snatched and was chained to a radiator.

He sent two PCs around the back, and radioed the control room for information on the address. He phoned Maggie for intel.

Steve and Max withdrew, and Rick waited at the end of the drive with Nhung.

The downstairs rooms were shielded by blinds. A Japanese sports car stood in front of the garage.

The checks came back: negative.

Rick rang the bell.

'Coming.' A woman's voice.

The door opened. The woman was in her mid-thirties, made up with dark eyelashes, and wearing a beige camelskin coat. 'God! What's happened?'

'DCI Castle, South Manchester,' said Rick. 'We're looking for a missing boy called Jack Philipps.' He held up a photo.

The woman shook her head. 'Well, he's not here.'

Had she been too quick in her denial? Rick glanced at her smart car, her smart house. Many police officers would be discouraged.

The woman took her handbag from the hall table. 'Now, if you'll excuse me, I've got a meeting.'

'We have reason to believe the boy may be here, and we'd like to search the house and garden.'

'No! I told you I've not seen him – and I have a meeting.'

'With respect, ma'am, you said he wasn't here, not you hadn't seen him.' The difference was small, and could have been an innocent mistake, or it could have been a slip. 'Either we can search with your permission, or we can obtain a search warrant.'

The woman slammed the door. 'I'm phoning my solicitor.'

Not a solicitor, but *her* solicitor. The possessive adjective was, in Rick's mind at least, another indicator.

Rick camped at the end of the drive while Nhung went to apply for a search warrant. *Yes, sir, I do know what I'm doing!* Officers remained at the back and sides of the house. Steve walked Max back to their van.

A gaggle of press turned up on foot: Oliver leading, followed by Jackie O'Day tottering on her high heels, and her cameraman. They were held back by uniform, but Rick walked over, intending to give them just enough to keep them useful.

'This looks like fun,' said Jackie.

'Missing children never are,' said Rick. He wasn't being caught out on the six o'clock bulletin. 'However, we're using one of the most highly trained tracking dogs in the country and have a promising lead on Jack Philipps. If we find him, we'll let you know.'

'Is it true, DCI Castle,' said Oliver, 'that you've been arrested for dealing drugs?'

Rick said nothing.

'Why haven't you been suspended?' Alongside Oliver stood O'Day, microphone at full mast, and her cameraman.

Rick kept his face passive despite feeling let down and angry. But Oliver wasn't his friend. In addition, there would come a time, and possibly soon, when he'd need them.

'Switch off the camera,' said Rick.

O'Day nodded at her colleague, and the cameraman swung his equipment down to the ground.

'Give me a break on that, and when this case breaks, I'll have something for you.'

'Even a denial, Rick.'

'Now, if you'll excuse me.'

Rick walked back through police lines. He wondered how the

press knew. An officer leaching information for flattery or cash; a suspect or solicitor ear-wagging in custody or the front office; or someone listening to police radio traffic – the radios were encrypted, but officers occasionally lost them during fights or foot chases. Robbo – to deflect attention from the missing letter.

He looked back at the address indicated by the miracle-working SAM dog. Intel and open-source checks revealed the woman's name was Edith Horton. She was an actress, about D list. Minor parts in soaps, and a couple of British films. She'd once been in trouble for snorting cocaine at an industry dinner. Which could explain her reluctance to let them search inside.

Rick phoned Barton.

'Do you know who Jack's best friend is?'

'Paul Chan, sir. He was also on the minibus.'

'Get another statement from him. Cover Jack's mood over the last few weeks; anything strange or secretive about him; any secrets they shared. Whether he's got any enemies.'

'Yes, sir, will do, sir.'

Next, Rick phoned Robbo. He left a voicemail, asking if he had found the letter. Despite thinking his boss hadn't lost it.

He checked his messages. Five missed calls, one from his mum, three from custody, and one from DC Fashom who was dealing with exhibits at the scene. Also a text from Becky reminding him to visit Three Views – *today!*

His phone rang.

'Sir, it's Dennis in custody. Kyle Phillipps is moaning, and so is our governor. He's been here eighteen hours.'

'About thirty minutes.' In the background, Rick could hear screaming.

His phone rang a second time.

'DC Fashom, sir. We've found a phone, about twenty metres from the road, lying under the edge of a wooden pallet. Screen's cracked, but it belongs to Jack. I phoned PC Barton to check with Mrs Winn. *Play now, work later* sticker on the back.'

Rick booted a stone off the drive. Maybe they wouldn't need Jack's phone.

A patrol car screeched to a halt, and DS Guyen climbed out holding a file. She nodded. Rick wondered if she ever smiled.

19

Fifty minutes later, they'd searched the house, the car, and the garden. They'd checked the loft, the shed, and the greenhouse. They'd found nothing, not even a wrap of cocaine. Edith Horton zoomed away in her sports car, and Rick stood the team down.

Policework was ever thus: a maze of dead ends and disappointments, the occasional glimpses of sunlight, and the hope of a rainbow and a pot of gold, but always the expectation of darkness.

He kicked another stone and climbed into the back of a patrol car. Maybe, Jack's phone would lead to his whereabouts.

*

Castle wife leaving now, said Kirill.

Andrei set the burner phone down on the passenger seat. Castle's wife drove a yellow bubble car and was not difficult to see, but to follow without being noticed needed practice. He was getting plenty. Following Castle to work, following the detective back from work. Following him to hospital, to the school, to an old people's home.

The roads were busy but less so than in Moscow. Less

potholes and trucks, more traffic lights. So many traffic lights.

Which wasn't surprising. Andrei had looked it up: a British man called Knight had invented the traffic light, and in 1868 a set had been installed outside their Parliament. The British had invented everything, the Chinese had copied everything, and the Russians had hacked everything. So who was the smartest, the British, the Chinese, or the Russians?

He phoned Kirill.

The Israelis.

Eh?

They never lost a war.

Andrei followed the yellow bubble car through the traffic to the leisure centre where Castle wife played basketball. He knew the route now, and was able to hang back. He switched on the radio to a rock station, wound the window down, ogled the girls. The sky was grey, black in places. In Manchester, if it wasn't raining, it had either rained recently, or was about to rain at any moment.

She parked in her normal slot, and somehow extracted herself out of the car and into her wheelchair. Andrei felt like clapping. Two women chained up their bicycles, a jogger arrived. She wheeled across to the entrance and disappeared inside.

He estimated he had one hour to obtain her keys, drive back to their house, go inside, and return to the leisure centre, replace her keys. Tight but doable.

The jogger and the cyclists followed her into reception. He climbed out.

The yellow bubble car was spotted with city filth, but the inside was immaculate. The doors were locked. A coat lay on the backseat, but there was no bag or phone or purse. A note on the dash, *No valuables are left in this car overnight, or at any time.* It wasn't surprising: she was married to police.

At reception he bought a ticket for the gym. The girl told

him he didn't look like he needed to lift weights. She was no wrong in both ways. Changing rooms are down the corridor, sir, lockers outside. Thank you. Clutching a bag, he paused at the noticeboard. *Set of dumbbells for sale. Villa with sauna in Portugal.*

She emerged from a female changing room. Rolled over to a locker, stored her things inside, clipped the lock shut. A woman with black frizzy hair buzzed through reception and shouted a greeting. The two women embraced, and moved away down the corridor towards the entrance door to the sports hall.

Andrei entered the male changing room. He stripped down to a t-shirt and shoved his jacket in his bag. Returned to the corridor.

A group of badminton players were arguing. Receptionists busied with a party of children.

Andrei walked over to the lockers and with his back to reception, bent down to the one he'd seen her using. He took out his wires, hid them in his fingers. Two staff in matching leisure centre t-shirts and fake tans walked past. He inserted the wires in the lock, twiddled back and forth. Twenty seconds, thirty seconds, forty seconds. The lock clicked.

'Are you okay there, sir?'

Andrei looked up. One of the staff had walked back. He nodded. The lad walked over to the badminton players, who were still arguing.

The locker was neat, organised, like her car. Like her head, no doubt. He searched, knowing the locker needed to stay that way. Spare clothes, wash kit, towel, but no phone, no purse, no keys. Fuck! He checked again. He unzipped her wash kit – no keys. He glanced around. The badminton players had calmed down and gone to change. Reception were still busy serving customers. Andrei unrolled her towel, rolled it up again, put it back. He checked through her spare clothes a second time. He stopped, popped them in his pocket. Kirill would appreciate the gesture. He wondered how his partner was doing – hoped he was being nice to the lodger. He replaced everything in the locker as he'd found it. The keys weren't there.

He clipped the lock, and limped toward the exit. He'd have to think again – and quickly.

20

Rick went straight to custody. Nhung booked Kyle Philipps out, and in interview room 2, started the recording machine. Rick's shoes were scuffed and his trousers muddy from following the SAM dog. It already felt like a long day.

Their prisoner was unshaven and smelt of stale sweat. He asked whether they'd found Jack, and Nhung told him they hadn't. She went through the formal introductions, and cautioned him.

'I get it,' said Philipps. 'I wasted your time so you're wasting mine.'

Rick stood up. He switched off the machine and sat down again.

'Tell me about Jack.'

Philipps glanced at Nhung, then back at Rick. 'He's obsessed by tennis. Posters on his walls, half a dozen racquets, always practising. Loves to watch old classics like Borg versus McEnroe. He's good, too, could be very good. The Northern Cup is in ten days, and he should win it. Then who knows, maybe he'll get a wild card at Wimbledon. Boris Becker won it at seventeen.'

Nhung whistled softly.

Philipps glared at her.

'And away from tennis?'

'Seems okay with me and Sandra separating. Bickers with his younger brother Adam, less so now they've stopped playing tennis together. Doesn't smoke or do drugs.'

'Where do you think he is?' said Nhung.

'I don't know.'

'You told Sandra you thought he was staying with a friend, then that he wasn't. When I asked you earlier who it was, you just shrugged.'

'I thought that's where he'd be, I still do, but I don't have specific knowledge. I was winding her up.'

'You're winding me up,' said Nhung. 'Where's Adam?'

'With a neighbour.'

'Which one?'

'Number fifty-eight, three doors down.'

Rick glanced at Nhung. She nodded, their working bond beginning to develop. She would speak to Jack's brother after the interview.

He turned back to Philipps. 'Are you worried about Jack?'

'Of course. But not off the scale. He's a boy, he's sensible, and he's lived a fragmented life these last few years. As I said, he's probably with a mate – maybe a new one.'

Rick took a deep breath. 'I need to tell you something, Kyle. We believe the minibus crash wasn't an accident.'

'What?'

'We think someone planned it. Has Jack—'

Philipps stood up. 'Hold on a minute. You think someone's got my son?'

'Sit down, Kyle.'

Philipps sat.

'We don't know if the crash is linked to Jack's disappearance. We think it might be, but have no evidence so far. Has Jack got any enemies?'

'I don't think so, no. Not enemies.'

'What do you do, Mr Philipps?'

'You think this might be about me?'

'It might be.'

'Fuck!' Philipps stood up again and walked around the tiny room. 'Fuck!'

Glancing at Nhung, Rick poured half a glass of water. He held the glass up to Philipps. 'Have you been threatened?'

Philipps took the glass and drank it down in one as if it was something stronger. He sat down. 'No, I haven't.'

Rick waited for Philipps to get his thoughts in order. The unspoken *but* hung in the air between them.

'I'm an adviser.'

'On what?'

'Finance.'

'You're a loan shark?'

Philipps shook his head. 'I give investment advice. I'm not qualified, mind. But it's mainly common sense. I see an opportunity, and tell people about it.' He paused. 'Unfortunately, one of my clients lost a lot of money recently.'

'As a result of your advice?'

Philipps shrugged. 'Maybe.' He sighed. 'I haven't been threatened as such, but I had a brick through the front window.'

'Did you report it?'

'Nah.'

'I'll need to know all the details.'

'I'll think about it.'

'Your son's life might be at risk.'

Philipps glanced over at the silent, unlit recording machine. He looked across at Rick. 'How do I know this isn't an elaborate sting on me?'

Nhung rolled her eyes.

Rick was also surprised. Philipps was on the verge of admitting criminality, and inviting police scrutiny. At the same time, he was downplaying the potential risk to his son.

He stood up.

'Lock him back up, Nhung.'

Driving to Dad's care home, Rick wondered about another press appeal for information on the whereabouts of Jack. The tactic had worked well on the cold case, and his mind flicked over to the murder of prostitute Jane Formby. A-J to her clients.

The Golden Lion hotel, now renamed The Mill, was situated close to the restaurants and clubs of Cotton Street in South Manchester. As the Golden Lion, it had a front and a back entrance. No CCTV, only carefully picked reception staff who were tipped heavily for their discretion. Rooms by the hour. The street CCTV had been wiped because of the delay in starting an investigation.

Collated evidence consisted primarily of testimony, and a morass of forensics from the scene, none of which had yielded a named suspect. Even if the victim's body was found, that was unlikely to change. The original forensics, however, still had potential, and reminded Rick he needed to rearrange with Elliot Tipper, the original crime scene manager.

He'd also hoped the press conference would prompt new witnesses to come forward. Colleagues of Formby no longer seeking obscurity, or wanting justice for their profession. Or punters in the hotel, wanting to atone for their past.

Interest from national media had seemed a good start, and they'd received nineteen pieces of information. One in green handwriting, one on the Moors murders, and seven easily discounted. Which left ten. Three from staff who'd been working in the hotel at the time but hadn't seen anything. Their statements were already on file, but were being revisited to double-check. Rick had spoken to six of the other respondents, visiting four, but they were either confused about the date, or vague to the point of uselessness.

One caller was still outstanding. Philip Clough. One more chance to obtain new and significant information.

Parking outside Three Views, he checked his phone for messages. A text from DC Fashom to say the scene at the ring road was complete, and only Jack's phone thought to be of any value. Another text from Becky, but nothing from Robbo on the letter.

He called Philip Clough and left a voicemail, then went inside.

Michael sat at the front desk. Soul music played quietly from his computer while he puzzled over a form.

'Mr Castle.' He pulled out a file. 'This is the log of the incident.'

Mrs Roberts (room 19) saw Mr Castle (room 6) squeeze the bottom of Miss Clarke (room 23). It took place in an unstaffed reception area. There's CCTV. Reported to me by Mrs Roberts. Signed MJ Howell.

The assistant walked with Rick along the corridor. 'I'm sorry about this, we're just following procedures.' He unlocked the door of room 6, handed Rick the key, and withdrew.

Rick knocked and entered.

The room was hot and airless. Dad stood by the French windows. He stared out with his hand cupped over his brow, like a sailor at sea. Newspaper cuttings were scattered on the floor. A standard lamp lay on its side, and pieces of a broken mug at the foot of a wall.

'Hello, Dad.'

His dad turned. 'I'm in prison!'

'Were you watching the birds?'

'The birds?'

'Out of the window.'

'I'm locked up in here, like a common criminal. Something should be done.'

Rick's phone rang. He walked back to the door.

'Nhung?'

'Sir, there are only twenty-five minutes left on Philipps' clock. No way will the super give an extension for the offence of wasting police time.'

'Has he said anything else?'

'No.'

'Bail him. Grab a DC from the CID office – Woods, he's never doing much – and take Philipps home. Speak to Adam.'

Pocketing the phone, Rick righted the lamp. He put the broken china in the bin, turned down the heating, and opened a window.

'I need to talk to you.'

His dad launched into 'Jerusalem'. 'And did those feet—'

'Dad! Listen, please. Another resident has made an allegation. Said you squeezed a woman's bottom in reception.'

Dad stopped singing. 'Was it that cow from nineteen?'

'Did you touch a woman's bottom?'

A grin spread across his dad's face. 'Might have done.'

'Not on, Dad.'

'Why not? Steffi's my girlfriend.'

Rick closed his eyes. The last thing he wanted to hear. The revelation would break Mum's heart.

'I've got to go, Dad, I'm sorry.'

'Can I go, too?'

'Not yet, Dad.'

At reception, Rick handed back the key. 'Dad says Steffi – Miss Clarke – is his girlfriend.'

Michael threw the key in a drawer. 'The matter's now with head office. You could take him out for a week or two.'

'I'll talk to my sister.' Rick paused. 'But I will need a copy of the CCTV.'

Michael nodded. He tapped keys on his computer.

'What's she like, Miss Clarke?'

'She's very popular – especially with the men.' He tapped again. 'Just emailed you the CCTV.'

*

Andrei waited in the van close to Castle's house. Rubbing his leg, he thought of names for Kirill. Captain Kirill. Killer Kirill. Curly hair Kirill. As Andrei had exited the obs point, his comrade in war and crime had moaned Andrei was having all the fun. He told him to play I-Spy or Twenty Questions.

His phone rang.

She come.

Two minutes later, an old red car drove past. Castle washerwoman was driving.

Andrei followed in the van. This bit he liked. After all the surveillance, this bit was a good bit. Like collecting acorn if you a squirrel, or laying egg if you chicken.

Washerwoman drove rush, rush. She was a bad driver, didn't use her mirrors, and drove close to the kerb. One time, she hit the kerb. At traffic lights, Andrei could hear her music. She did use her mirror: she used it to look at her not very pretty face.

After three miles, the washerwoman parked outside a row of small shops. She heaved out of her car with woman bag, and rush, rush into post office. The card shop next door reminded him he still needed to get presents for Alyona and Semion.

He was a model hoodlum.

He parked on a backstreet behind the shops and climbed out. He could be verbally persuasive, but he was a big man and gestures were preferable. He rolled down his balaclava, flicked his hood up, and limped around the corner. A hoodlum with a drug habit.

The washerwoman exited the post office. She paused to

glance up at the sky, searching maybe for patterns in the clouds, and an idea of her future. He could tell her: it was going to rain, and she was going to meet a tall, dark stranger.

Last look up and down –

He closed on his target. Brandishing a kitchen knife with one gloved hand, he ripped the woman bag from her clutch with the other. Credit where credit due. Sweaty washerwoman did not yield easily. She yanked the bag back towards her. Andrei slashed the strap, pulled harder, and clubbed the washerwoman's face with the back of his knife hand. She staggered, and fell, and even then tried some kind of scissor-kick.

'Coward.'

He running.

Trying to run.

Down the road, side street, backstreet. Not a coward, but no time to argue. After checking no one was following, he ducked down between two cars. He rummaged in the woman bag, found a small black purse and four sets of keys. Washerwoman carried more keys than a prison guard. He posted the bankcards down a drain, pocketed the cash and the keys. He removed his balaclava and his jacket.

Spitter-spatter of rain.

Leaving the washerwoman bag under a car, Andrei hobbled back to the van. A citizen hurrying to avoid getting wet.

*

Rick was pulling into the backyard of South Manchester when his phone rang.

'Castle.'

'It's PC Tyldesley at the hospital. Bad news, sir, Peter Simons has just died. I mean he just passed away. What shall I do, sir?'

'I'm coming.'

Rick reversed, turned, drove fifty yards in first gear and shoved back into the traffic. A murder enquiry meant more scrutiny but more resources. He could investigate more lines of enquiry and quicker.

21

Old sweats and new sweats filled the conference room.

In the middle, sat on the comfortable chairs, DS Martin's CID team. On one side the neighbourhood unit grouped around PS Davison. Robbo stood at the back holding a stick of rock. Near the door, DC Fashom, Maggie, and Nhung.

Rick beckoned his new sergeant over. 'Did you speak to Adam?'

Nhung nodded. 'He doesn't know where his brother is. He's fourteen and a bit scared. Like his dad, he thinks Jack must be with a friend. He can't really envisage anything more serious.'

'Let's hope they're right.'

He turned to face the room, and the hubbub quietened.

'This is now both a murder investigation *and* a missing person enquiry. The bullet causing the minibus to crash and the disappearance of Jack Philipps appear to be connected. We need to work out what connects them. Our priority, however, is to find Jack, and to achieve that, we need to nail down *how* he went missing.'

A detective from Martin's team tipped his chair back, another straightened his trousers. Most of the PCs were annotating the briefing sheet.

'So, I'm pairing you up, one DC with one PC from the

149

neighbourhood team. Each pair is to restatement one of the six boys. Read their first statement, and concentrate, a, on what they saw of Jack at the scene of the crash, and, b, on additional background as to why that boy could be the target for the shooting. Jack, of course, might not have been the intended victim.'

'Don't make an ass out of you and me, eh, sir?' said Barton.

The detectives stared at the red-faced PC with his jumper tucked into his trousers. A couple slow handclapped.

'That's right, Barton. Today, I want you to go and see Mrs Winn again.'

'Yes, sir, thank you, sir.'

'Sergeant Davison, this morning, I want you to use whoever's left to assist DS Guyen in trying to find the two Rumanian boys, especially Mihai Bucur, and if you do, use him to locate the scene of the shooting. This afternoon, I want you to run the roadcheck again.'

One or two of Davison's team groaned. Intermediate sweats. When Rick had been in uniform, he'd have given a finger or two to work with the DCI.

'We need more witnesses at the scene. Jack Philipps did not disappear into thin air. Someone will have seen something, and all we need to do is find them. Clear?'

A chorus of 'Yes, sir.'

Rick turned back to address the room. 'Anyone spare, there are more actions at the back, or see DS Guyen. Questions?'

He waited a few seconds. 'Attention to detail, please.'

The room began to break up, and Rick made a beeline for Robbo.

'We need to do another witness appeal. Can you get some money from the Chamber of Commerce as a reward for information?'

'What about a press conference?'

Rick shook his head. 'They'll want to know what's so special about the boy – and I'm not ready to release the fact of the shooting. But a reward might jog a few memories of people driving past.'

Robbo turned to the door.

'Before you disappear.' Rick lowered his voice. 'We need that letter.'

'I want to find it, I do,' said Robbo. He looked pale, as if he wasn't sleeping. 'I will get you some reward money.'

On impulse, Rick took an action from the slushpile. Every good SIO he'd ever worked under had occasionally taken a green sheet. It helped spread the load, and kept you thinking tactically as well as strategically. *Statement Vinnie Forester.* He checked the back of the form. She was a production assistant at the biscuit factory in Blackville.

Robbo gnawed at the stick of rock like a beaver. The same lettering all the way down.

Rick's message had changed: 'I can't keep quiet much longer. You've got twenty-four hours before I take it up the chain.'

A warm, intoxicating smell of sugar and spices blew through the doorway of the factory's waiting room. Conveyor belts and machines Rick couldn't see clanked and rattled. Voices shouted above the racket. He imagined vats of chocolate and silos of butter, barrels of jam and sacks of multicoloured sprinkles. One or two Oompa-Loompas.

He read a poster for Jekyll and Hyde cakes. The picture showed one cut vertically, revealing the chocolate biscuit topping and doughnut base. *Which Half Do You Eat First?*

A woman wearing a white lab coat, white trousers and a blue hairnet entered the waiting room. She shut the door.

'Mrs Forester,' said Rick.

'Call me Vin, love.'

'Vin, have you got the perfect job?'

She cackled. 'You have, more like. Can you sort my nephew's speeding ticket?' She cackled again, coughed, glanced at the door. 'They'll send you home if you got a cough. With no pay. It's not all hundreds and thousands here.'

Rick gestured at a seat, and they sat down. He had arranged two chairs so they faced into the room, but not quite opposite each other. He wanted them both to stare into space.

'Tell me what you saw, as much detail as you can remember.'

'I was on my way to work, as it happens.'

Rick nodded. The room was warm, dreamy. He wanted it that way. Vin told him she was driving along the ring road. Overhead gantries warned of an accident ahead. She saw the blue lights of emergency vehicles. She hoped she wasn't going to be late for work. She saw a blue school minibus at an angle on the hard shoulder. A nice-looking car behind it not looking so nice. Police vehicles and an ambulance parked behind the nice-looking car. Through the windows of the vehicles, boys wandering about. Two groups of people crowded around what she assumed were injured boys.

Rick was seeing it, too. Her view through the windows of parked vehicles.

'It was all very, very quick.'

'Can you say any more about the two groups around the boys on the floor?'

'I slowed down. Everyone did. Everyone always does. I didn't want to look, but I did. Police cars, police officers. There were more vehicles involved, too. Two more cars, I think, in front of the minibus. Dark coloured. A couple more people. Men, I think. I'm not sure. I'm sorry. I hope they're all okay?'

Rick didn't answer. He wanted her to stay in the zone, didn't want her to think of the consequences, or the families.

He took her through it again.

And again. He sat forward, saw what Vin Forester was seeing. He didn't see – couldn't see – what she wasn't seeing.

And that's what he left with, a question more than an answer. *What was Vinnie Forester not seeing?* That was the key. What was happening that no one had seen? That no one remembered seeing? One moment Jack Philipps was there, and the next he wasn't.

He phoned Maggie on the way back.

'What time did you get into bed?'

'Late, sorry. Picked up a Blackville goodie bag, though.'

'Anything?'

'I don't know. Maybe. Davison checked the overhead cameras on the ring road, but can you see if any speed cams were triggered shortly before or after the crash?'

'Will do. I've finished the CCTV on the backyard for the last week. No one tampers with your car.'

Which suggested it was likely to have been broken into and the drugs planted in the glovebox directly outside Maggie's flat. Which took nerve and planning.

'Thanks. How was basketball training?'

'Just practice at lunchtime so no Angela Turners to be wary of. Forgot my spare underwear, though, which was annoying.'

'The only shopping I like,' said Rick. 'See you later.'

Rick stopped at the apiary. The investigation was whirling around his head, the lines of enquiry, the missing information, the missing links. New information generated every hour, which changed every other piece of information.

He put on wellies, grabbed a tub of sugar solution and his case file, and waded through the damp grass of the apiary. It was cold, but the sky was light and a patch of blue was visible. A shaft of sunlight caught a silver birch tree.

Leaving his case file on the bench, he removed the bricks weighting his hive. He took off the roof and the crown board. The feeder was dry as a desert riverbed. He refilled it from the tub, a couple of sugary slops overflowing down the sides. Bees immediately appeared from below, and entered the feeder. Bathing, or so it seemed to Rick, in the sugary viscous. More bees followed, and soon there were fifty or sixty filling their stomachs.

He replaced the lid and the bricks, knowing he should return tomorrow. A robin flew down and hopped about, only a few feet away.

He sat on the bench and opened the case file. Asked himself the four questions. *What did he know? What were his hypotheses for what happened? What didn't he know, and how could he find out?*

The bullet was linked to two other shootings. The calibre suggested a professional shooter, not an accident or a prank. He'd left messages but still needed to speak to the two SIOs. He made a note. Chewed his pen. He didn't know a location for the shooter, and needed to get hold of Bucur. The target of the shooting could be Alderman, Hunter/Hamburg, Westbury School, or one of the boys. Peter Simons, the boy who'd died? Or it could be a random shot, or a mistake.

He'd not definitively ruled anything out, or in.

The letter to Westbury School was a clear threat, and although not linked to the shooting except by proximate timing, needed to be found and investigated. Priority. How Jack Philipps went missing, and why, were still unknown. Roadchecks and witness appeals were underway. Maybe a different SAM dog. He needed to speak to Jack's parents again, and to Jack's mixed-tennis partner.

Were the three things connected? The shooting and the disappearance of Jack were very likely to be connected. Which meant, more information on Jack might explain the shooting. And vice versa. The letter could be irrelevant, or the start of it.

The possible connection gave him a new hypothesis, G1, the shooting was aimed, directly or indirectly, at Jack Philipps. Obvious, but helped to focus. His priorities were clear: the roadcheck and the witness appeal. Speaking to the mixed partner, and Jack's parents, and finding the letter.

Then there was his own arrest. He was due back on bail the day after tomorrow. The packaging would be negative for his prints and underline his innocence. It was a setup, surely Warburton and the rest of the Standards soreheads and sourpusses would see that. His record was good, not flawless, but good enough. No one could say he didn't give a hundred per cent. And that, he hoped, would be the end of it. When he'd found Jack, he'd revisit the identity of the person responsible, maybe submit an informant tasking.

A red kite was hovering above the copse of trees. He walked over to his hive. A bee flew out. She flew a short loop and returned to the landing board, but fell off onto the grass. He picked her up, and let her crawl over his fingers. She was dozy, and disorientated. They slowed down in winter to conserve energy and rarely left the hive. He made a bridge with his fingers for her to crawl back through the tiny gap in the mouse guard.

Sitting back down on the bench, he read through the statements one final time. Graham Alderman mentioned *two or three* cars had stopped to give assistance, including a man wearing a fluorescent jacket. The Westbury pupil Paul Chan also mentioned seeing a fluorescent jacket. A police officer or a paramedic? But why hadn't they specified?

He prodded his phone.

'Graham, it's Rick Castle, South Manchester. Two quick questions: you said two or three cars stopped to give assistance. Two – or three?'

'I'm not sure. Two, I think. Maybe three. They were all very similar, dark blue or black.'

'So there could have been three?'

'There could have been.'

Rick sighed. 'You also mentioned a fluorescent jacket.'

'Yes.'

'You said you thought it was a good idea for the minibus, but why mention that particular jacket? All the paramedic and police officers would have been wearing them.'

'It was orange. Everyone else was in yellow.'

'Orange! You're sure?'

'One hundred per cent.'

'Can you describe him?'

'Not in any detail. A big man. Tall, stocky. White.'

'Graham, I could kiss you.' Rick stood up. He could see what Vinnie Forester hadn't seen. Three cars – possibly – but definitely a man, a large white man, wearing a fluorescent jacket. A fluorescent *orange* jacket.

Wanting corroboration, Rick made another call.

'Mr Naylor, DCI Castle from South Manchester. Quick question of clarification: when you stopped at the scene of the minibus incident, did you at any point wear a fluorescent jacket?'

'Are you going to tell me that not wearing one is now an offence?'

'No, sir,' said Rick, scuffing the ground with his boot. 'But did you see anyone wearing an orange high-vis jacket?'

Naylor hadn't. He wanted to know what Rick thought about the lack of a speed limit on German autobahns.

Rick phoned Trent Watson and repeated his question. Watson carried high-vis jackets in the car, but he hadn't worn one. Hadn't seen anyone wearing an orange fluorescent. He was positive. No stupid questions. Good luck with the investigation.

Rick pocketed the phone.

He wiped his fingers up the sides of the empty tub, and when they were slathered in the sugary solution, licked them clean.

22

'Police!'

The shout was followed by banging on the front door.

Rick glanced at the clock radio: 5.30 a.m. For a moment, he feared he'd forgotten about an early morning arrest enquiry or a search warrant. But he hadn't. The hammering and hollering repeated. He got up, slipped on a t-shirt and boxers.

Maggie stirred under the duvet. 'Who is it?'

'Our lot.'

Rick opened the door.

Three police officers in plain clothes stood in a semi-circle, more officers behind, and at least one patrol car was parked in the road. They were bleary-eyed and wet-haired from the early start.

'DS Whitaker, sir, Standards. We have a search warrant.' He passed Rick a clear document wallet. He wore a jacket, but no tie. He was young, and eager as a spaniel.

Rick checked the details, his mind racing ahead. It showed his address, had been issued under the Drugs Act, and was in date. There was nothing to find. Another setup? Twice in a week. What the hell?

Maggie rolled up behind him. 'What's happening?'

He explained.

Turned back to Whitaker. 'No way.'

Maggie put a hand on his arm. 'You can't stop them, Rick, you know that. We'll get through this.'

Her use of the plural calmed him, just for a moment.

'You won't find anything.'

He was escorted to the bedroom to dress. Another officer entered and started searching the drawers and cupboards. Rick had seen it a thousand times. He'd never forget this time. He was taken to the lounge, and waited with Maggie. He squeezed her hand, and went to stand by the window.

Outside, the darkness turned greyer and yellowed at the edges. An aeroplane droned across the sky. The bottom of the garden appeared.

Who was responsible? And why? The names on his two lists reappeared like angry bees. Simon Turner, William Redman, Starfish. Jack Gibbs, Gary Hunter. Robbo – a second attempt to distract from the letter?

Turning round, he locked eyes with Maggie. She looked like him: angry, confused, resolute. He winked at her. She didn't wink back. Maybe, she was angry with him. Confused about his involvement, resolute in her own innocence. If she doubted him, then few wouldn't.

He heard a crash from the kitchen.

'I want to have a look.'

The officer detailed to watch them, DC Jordan, shouted to Whitaker. A second officer entered, Jordan explained, and Rick was escorted into the kitchen.

It was a mess. The table had been moved to one side, and the chairs stacked up. The dishwasher stood in their place, its plug trailing. The inside of the door had been unscrewed and the interior gutted to its shell. Metal fittings and screws and tools lay strewn. An officer knelt on his haunches, unscrewing a final panel.

Searching the house to that degree was unusual and would take a week. It suggested Standards were acting on specific information, or trying to make it look like they hadn't by killing time.

He was taken back to the lounge. Maggie looked incensed. Opposite her stood Jordan and Whitaker.

'They want to search my wheelchair, Rick.'

Whitaker stepped forward. 'I appreciate the sensitivity, sir, but we have a drugs warrant. And Jordan here saw you wink at your partner.'

'Are you joking?'

'No, sir.'

Maggie transferred onto the sofa, and shoved the wheelchair hard across the room. Jordan stopped it with her foot. Smirked.

Tools were fetched, and Jordan began deconstructing the chair. The Standards unit was necessary for a corruption-free police service, and necessary to retain public support, but quickly the officers became inured to the process and appeared to revel in the humiliation. Five years in post was too long.

Rick placed a hand on Maggie's shoulder. She gave it a squeeze.

He paced up and down. A wheel already lay on the carpet. Then the second. Followed by the seat, and the lining of the seat.

He stared out of the window. More names on the lists came back to him. PC Downcliff – no, not twice. Someone connected to one of his old cases? One of his new ones? The historic murder of Jane Formby, or the minibus crash. The disappearance of Jack Philipps.

'Sir, I think you should see this.'

Rick turned. They were the words he feared.

When he'd moved in, Maggie said he could keep some of his stuff in her spare room. She'd thrown away her student notes, sold some of her old racing equipment and taken some clothes to a charity shop. He'd installed a decent chair, a pedestal of drawers, and with the help of a local decorator, a pull-down screen with a large map of Manchester. Underneath the map, a wall of mugshots. Homework on the Redman OCG, and against the rules.

Instead, Whitaker escorted him to the bathroom. It was often the last room to be searched because it took the least time, but not that morning. A detective wearing gloves and holding a camera knelt by the bath panel. Whitaker pointed to one end.

'You see the retaining screws, well, two are missing their protective covers and if you look closely, you can see signs of recent use.'

Rick see-sawed his head. 'You really think if I was trying to hide something, I'd hide it under the bath? Remove the screw head covers, and not bother to replace them? I've done a searching course, I know the best places to find stuff, hence the best places to hide stuff. And under the bath isn't one of them.'

'Stand back, please, sir.'

Rick retreated to the doorway.

The detective placed the camera in the bath, and unscrewed the side panel. He clicked on a pen torch and looked under the bath. He leant in and pulled out an oblong, well-wrapped package. He checked with the torch. Then took photos.

'Sir,' said Whitaker, 'I'm arresting you for possession of drugs with intent to supply.' He trotted out the caution and looked at his watch.

Rick slapped the doorframe, the noise like a gunshot.

He walked back to the lounge, Whitaker on his heels. Maggie looked at him blankly, as if he was a stranger, or she'd once known him but a long time ago.

'Any reply?' said Whitaker.

'No comment.' No fucking comment.

*

At North Manchester police station, Rick sat on a bench and waited to be booked in. The layout was the same as South Manchester, the same number of cells and interview rooms, the same bored jailer, the same overweight custody sergeants. The Rolling Stones blared from the radio, but they were wrong. It was no Ruby Tuesday.

An arrested police officer, a DCI no less, was a star billing. Uniform carriers wandered into custody, wandered out again. He was good with faces. Wouldn't forget.

Closed his eyes, pondered.

He'd not seen any damage to a door or a window, and unless he'd missed it, meant it was another professional job. Maybe he or Maggie had had their keys cloned. Not his keys, they were always in his trouser pocket, he never left them in his bag or jacket on the back of a chair. Never. Maggie's keys – when she played basketball, or at work? She hung her bag on the back of her wheelchair. But suspecting someone they worked with still seemed a bit extreme – even Robbo. Rick agreed with Maggie that the superintendent usually had his own agenda. Maybe one of the police station cleaners? Maybe *their* cleaner?

His turn at the counter.

Name, address, employment ha-ha. He was searched, offered his rights. He declined, except for the phone call. The jailer escorted him to the phone.

'Maggie, it's me. I'm sorry, but I can promise you—'

'You don't have to. Stinks worse than the Stockport sewage works.'

'Thank you, and I will prove it. I've been wondering, what do you do with your keys when you play basketball?'

'I've got a zipped pouch on my sport chair. I always take my valuables.'

'But at work you hang your bag on the back of your everyday chair?'

'I do. You think someone in the police station has taken my keys, and what, copied them?'

'Maybe, I'm just working it through. Can you phone Tara, get her to forensicate the flat? I'm not hopeful, but she might get something.'

'Anything else?'

'Phone Tricia, see if she's lost our keys. She's the only other person who's got a set.'

The jailer loomed.

'Got to go, Mags.'

The interview room smelt like the back of a cupboard. As airless, too. Rick poured a beaker of water and hurled it against the wall. He reflected again on Robbo's agenda, and finally came up with a plan.

The door opened, and Superintendent Warburton sat down. He observed the wet patch, but didn't comment.

'We meet again.'

Rick said nothing.

Tapes, introductions, caution.

'So?'

'I don't know anything about the package. I've never seen it before. It's a setup, same as last time. Someone's got it in for me.'

'Who?'

'I've got some ideas.'

Warburton pushed over paper and pen, and Rick wrote down his list of suspects outside the police station. The names inside might be leaked. Even by Standards.

'The same person each time, or a different one?'

'The same seems very likely.'

Warburton put on his tortoiseshell glasses and glanced down at his notes. Rick stared at the drying patch on the wall.

'Why're you so sure it's a setup?' said the superintendent.

'Aren't you? A week ago when I was arrested, you didn't even do a house search. Because you didn't really think I was dealing. But today, you do think that. It's not as if I'm a long-term surveillance target of your department. You've received some information, and you've jerked like a knee joint.'

Warburton took off his glasses. 'Are you suggesting we shouldn't act if we receive information regarding a senior police officer?'

'Find some corroboration! Otherwise, you're going to dance the can-can to phone calls from every do-gooder and do-badder in Manchester.'

Rick stood up and walked to the door.

'Where do you think you're going?'

'Back to my cell.'

He opened the door and walked out, the superintendent blustering commands and fumbling with tapes and paperwork until the door slammed shut.

An hour later the cell door opened and Robbo entered. He was eating sweets from a paper bag. The cell door clanked shut.

'God, these places stink.' The superintendent proffered the bag. 'They're chocolate mice.' Rick shook his head.

'Twice in a week?' said his boss.

Rick remained seated, Robbo standing opposite. Not enough room to stand up and argue, yet alone fight. 'Did you tell anyone you were going to assign me to the minibus crash?'

Robbo plucked out a mouse. 'I may have discussed it with the chief super.'

'Anyone else?'

'No.'

'On a secure line?'

The tips of Robbo's ears turned red. 'He was in a rush and I caught him in the station office.'

'Public side?'

His boss nodded.

'Fuck, Robbo! We need to pull the tapes, see who else was there.'

'You think someone's trying to get you removed from the Philipps investigation?'

'It's one possibility. Someone's setting me up – that's a definite, and I think you know that.' The timing for the Philipps case was tight but worked. Shortly after the crash, Robbo wanted an SIO, an unusual decision, so he checked it with the chief super. He was overheard, and a few whispers later, someone wasn't happy and planting drugs in Rick's car, and when that didn't work, their flat.

Robbo ate another chocolate.

'You might be right,' he said slowly. Not as if he was unsure, but as if he was thinking through the implications of saying so.

'Get me out of here, sir, let me keep investigating.'

Robbo held up a mouse. 'Believe me, that's what I want. And I want to find the boy *toute suite*. But getting you out is not that simple this time.'

'I think it is,' said Rick. He stood, walked to the door and leant back against it. 'I've sat in this stinking cell a long time today, pondering, amongst other things, the missing letter. Your son will be the right age to sit the Westbury School entrance exam next year, and I think you've *lost* the letter as a favour to the headmaster in order that he looks positively upon that application. I think the two of you have an implicit or explicit deal.'

His boss twiddled the mouse between thumb and forefinger. Dropped it into the paper bag and tossed the bag on the bunk. He looked yellow.

'You don't have to confirm or deny. All I'm asking is that you get me bail and back onto the enquiry.'

'Guard!' shouted Robbo, walking to the door.

Rick barred the exit. He needed other things, too. He needed the letter, and the sources of information leading to his car and house being searched.

His boss pulled up.

They eyeballed. They needed each other, they both knew that.

'What's going on, Robbo?'

'I can't tell you, Rick. Just find the boy.'

The cell door grated open, and the superintendent squeezed out.

Rick decapitated the last mouse and ate the pieces. He screwed up the paper bag and punted it at the ceiling.

After twelve hours in custody, Rick was bailed and given a lift home. The evening was dreary and vehicle lights blurred like speeded-up film. The young constable driving gabbled about betting on horse racing. Rick closed his eyes and dozed. He'd lost another day.

23

Or maybe not.

When he walked in, Maggie was on the phone.

Tricia, she mouthed.

Rick only heard one side but it was enough. Their cleaner had been robbed outside a post office and her handbag containing a spare set of their front door keys had been stolen. The suspect was a tall, white male. *Big.*

Maggie wrote on the back of an envelope, handed it over.

OIC, DC Carver.

Entering the phone number on his mobile, Rick walked into the kitchen.

'Ben Carver.'

Rick explained he was South Manchester's DCI and Tricia's employer. Didn't mention the messy details.

'Not got a lot if I'm honest, sir. CCTV from the post office doesn't show the incident or the suspect. No witnesses, only a vague description. It doesn't sound like one of our regulars – too big, but victims tend to overestimate. We've done some house-to-house, left some leaflets. We might get something.'

'Accent?'

'Didn't speak. Not a word, so she says.'

Maybe Tricia's attacker had, maybe he hadn't. At knife- or

gunpoint, the five senses were extremely unreliable.

Rick washed his face in the sink and poured a glass of orange juice from the fridge. He felt dirty and his teeth furry after a day in the cells.

Breaking into his car was one thing, but breaking into their flat was another. The former a punch, a salvo, a sending off. The latter a beating, an invasion, a lifetime ban. Together they were a declaration of war.

The drugs had been planted in his car and their flat on two separate occasions. The perpetrator would not have wanted to be seen, yet alone disturbed. It was possible his car had been interfered with at night. But unlikely the person responsible would have entered the flat overnight. Which meant the perp or the person controlling them could have been watching Maggie's flat. From a vehicle, in which case it would be long gone. Or from another house.

House-to-house wasn't a bad idea. It was possible a neighbour would remember something unusual, and he had a couple of hours before people went to bed.

In his office he powered up his computer. Adjusted a street map so it was centred on the flat and a mile in diameter. The printer whirred.

Bowker Crescent was a curved road with access at both ends. Their block of eight flats was roughly halfway round. Bowker Crescent led to Birch Road, which connected with the main road. Driving to or from the flat, Rick had no option but to use the first half of Birch Road. Which suggested an observation point would be sited in the first half of Birch, or in Bowker Crescent with a view of Maggie's flat. About eighty properties in total.

He tapped out a short letter to post through letterboxes where there was no reply at the door. Printed eighty. Devised a chart to record his door-knocking.

In the hall he put on a jacket and kissed the top of Maggie's head.

She put a hand over the phone.

'Tricia's in bits.'

'Tell her I'm sorry, Mags. Did Tara get anything?'

'No damage on doors or windows, not surprising as it looks like they had Tricia's keys. She got prints, but thinks they're ours. Will let us know.'

'I'm heading out to knock on a few doors.'

Maggie nodded, and Rick kissed her again.

Outside, he walked across the pavement and stood in the middle of the road. Turned three hundred and sixty degrees. Someone had been watching them and was possibly *still* watching. The top end of Bowker and all of Birch was full of short rentals and sublets. Emergency and social services were frequent visitors.

He started at the flat next door.

Pat answered. The television was on in the background, and she looked embarrassed. A sleep line marked her face.

'We've been having a few problems in the last couple of weeks, damage to our cars, unpleasant stuff through the letterbox. I'm their target, so nothing for you to be worried about. But I was wondering if you'd seen anything or anyone unusual?'

Stifling a yawn, Pat shook her head. 'Don't think so.'

Behind her, a quiz show squawked.

'Is Frank here?'

'Still at work, but I'll ask him.' She yawned again.

He left Pat to the TV and marked up his chart. He knocked on the two flats at the back but there was no answer, and he posted letters. No success on the first floor either, although he hadn't expected any – one resident worked late shifts as a courier, one was on holiday, and two stewardesses worked long-haul and were never at home.

He moved on to the adjacent house. Again there was no reply and he posted another letter. Same with the second house.

The third house was opened by a heavy man in shorts and a t-shirt. Warm fetid air cascaded out. Rick stepped back, showed his badge, explained why he'd knocked.

'Not seen anyone, mate.' The man stepped back inside, and shut the door.

He rang more doorbells, posted more proformas, updated his chart. A young woman just home from work and playing pop music for the benefit of everyone in the suburb told him she hadn't seen anyone. She was vague about her neighbours, saying she didn't know their names, or when she'd last seen them. As to anyone else in the road, no idea. Two doors along, the front window revealed half a dozen children watching TV in a chaotic room of toys and furniture. Eventually a woman wearing an enormous white t-shirt came to the front door. She hardly knew who was present in her house, what with five kids and some of their friends. Asked him to arrest her for something, take her away.

In his first set of nights as a DI – the week he'd dealt with seventeen deaths and been headlined in the *Manchester Evening News* as 'Manchester's Deathcop'; a week he'd never forgotten – he'd been called to a body in a bath, an old man who'd been dead for three months, despite living in a communal block with a shared entrance.

A rental van drove past, two men in the front. Rick didn't recognise them or the name of the rental company. The passenger leant forward and glanced at him in the wing-mirror. Rick wrote down the registration plate.

He rang another doorbell. A young couple came to the door, children tugging at their legs, the man with a baby in his arms. Could he get someone to deal with the damp above the kitchen? Rick looked up a number for them on his phone before walking away. South Manchester social services had recently discovered two illegal migrants staying in the back room of a vulnerable adult. They'd followed him home and moved in.

House-to-house was never any different. Annoying, frustrating, depressing in equal measures. But could, at any moment, yield the vital clue. A witness, or footage from private CCTV, doorbell cams, dashcams.

He knocked again, showed his badge to a hunchbacked old woman, and explained why he was calling.

Wearing only a thin gown, she told him her name was Sheila and she was eighty-nine. She knew he was a dibble – she'd seen him on the news asking for witnesses to the crash of the Westbury School minibus. Her husband Paul had died ten years earlier in a motorbike accident. He was a light sleeper, and would have seen something, she was sure. Her daughter called round every other day, and she would ask her. He stepped inside and hastily made her a cup of tea and some toast.

An orange light caught the top of the trees in the park as he jogged back down the path. The temperature was dropping.

There was no reply at the next two houses, and after delivering more letters, he turned into Birch Road. Occupants could still watch from their windows, and note when Rick drove home, or departed again in the morning.

Darkness fell and the evening unspooled. Teas and dinners were eaten and washed up. Kids claimed they'd finished their homework, messaged on phones, gamed online, watched TV. Alcohol was drunk, soap operas watched, cannabis smoked. Teenagers complained about going to bed. Arguments started, flared, petered out.

Rick kept going. He reached the junction with Ashmead Drive, crossed the road and worked back down Birch. The terraces were smaller, their occupants reluctant to open the door. Downstairs windows were barred. Residents peered out from behind blinds, some remained suspicious even when he showed his badge, or *because* he had. A few gave him the finger, some opened the door on a chain, others not at all. Don't know anything or anyone, keep ourselves to ourselves. There were exceptions – Sheila, a handful of others.

Rick reflected on the major enquiries that made the TV news. Murderers, terrorists, rapists lived in the midst of communities who were oblivious, thought they were harmless, or in some cases were upstanding members of society . . . *we had no clue he was a bombmaker . . . he always said hello . . . no idea he ran a porn empire from his bedroom . . . he cut my grass for years . . . can't believe he hacked into the Australian defence ministry . . .*

Rick returned to Bowker Crescent, and worked his way along the opposite side to earlier. Knocking, explaining, delivering, marking up his chart.

A big man walking towards him on the pavement crossed the road.

To avoid Rick? He didn't recognise him, at least not at that distance. Rick pretended he was looking for an address on one of his handouts. He walked over. A pair of binoculars hung around the man's neck. Rick stepped onto the pavement. Military binoculars.

'Excuse me.'

'What?'

The man stopped under a streetlight.

Rick showed his badge.

'So?'

'You fit the description to a couple of recent break-ins. Turn around and put your hands on the wall.'

'You and whose army?'

Rick stepped back, took out his phone, and called the control room. Requested a backup unit to assist with a stop. His pulse ramped up. His baton and handcuffs sat on his belt, partially hidden by his jacket. Equipment could calm, or exacerbate.

'What are the binoculars for?'

'Birdwatching.' A waft of alcohol.

'Really.'

A siren sounded in the distance.

The man shook his head.

'Keep your hands where I can see them.'

'Fuck off.'

The man advanced, Rick stepped back, whipped out his baton. He held it by his leg, his other hand directly out in front of him. 'Stay where you are.'

'You lot are a fucking joke.'

'Just doing my job. What's your name?'

'Friends now?'

The patrol car hit the end of the road, gunned towards them. Reassuring to know the system worked. The double-crewed unit screeched to a halt, killed the sirens, left the blues flashing. Two constables jumped out.

One PC ran towards Rick, the other positioned himself at right angles. The four of them making an L shape. Both officers drew their batons and held them in the same defensive position as Rick.

'Thanks for coming,' said Rick. 'Stop and search not playing ball. Not seen a weapon.' He turned back to the man. 'We'll try again. Turn around and put your hands on the wall.'

Scowling, the man turned, slowly put his hands on the brickwork.

'Legs apart.'

'Do you enjoy this?'

Rick holstered his baton, and patted the man down. There was a wallet in one trouser pocket, keys in another. No weapons, no possessions apart from the binoculars.

'You can turn round – slowly. I need you to show me the keys.'

The man delved into his pocket, pulled out a keyring, and threw it on the ground.

Not the keys to Maggie's flat. Rick left them on the pavement.

'Name?'

'Morgan. Nick Morgan.'

'If you show my colleagues here some id, you'll be on your way a lot quicker.'

The man thrust a hand in –

'Slow-ly.'

He threw the wallet on the ground. 'Fill your boots.'

The PC next to Rick picked it up and walked back to the patrol car.

'So, Nick, the binoculars?'

'Just got 'em. I was showing 'em to a mate. I'm a grunt.'

Rick nodded.

'We did look at a few birds as it happens. His place backs onto the park.'

'It's dark.'

'Had a few Sherberts, didn't we.'

The officer returned from the patrol car. 'He checks out. No trace PNC. I phoned his barracks and they said Lance Corporal Morgan is on a week's leave, due back Monday. Intel shows one domestic at his home address. Control room called, girlfriend was expecting him home hours ago.'

Rick turned to Morgan. 'Smile for the camera.' He took a photo.

'Are you allowed to do that?'

'Either that or keep you hours while I get my witness here.' He was ninety-nine per cent sure Morgan had nothing to do with the break-in, but showing a photo to Tricia would give him an additional half per cent.

'You can go. Thanks for your time.'

'At least in my job, you get to shoot people you don't like.'

Morgan strode away. At least in mine, thought Rick, I don't.

He thanked the two officers, and after a burst of sirens, they drove away.

Nine-thirty. Too late to continue; he'd almost finished a first round, although a lot of houses would need revisiting.

In the dim light of Maggie's porch, his pulse calmed down, and he sketched a map and totted up the results. Ninety-six properties fitted his hypothesis. He'd spoken to at least one person at forty-one of them, but twenty-five would need a revisit to catch the other residents, or information on visitors. Letters delivered to the remainder.

Inside, he took off his shoes and hung up his coat.

Maggie came out of the living room. She'd cleared up but the furniture, their things – photos, plants, books – were still out of place.

'How'd it go?'

Rick shook his head. 'Wrote down a reg on a hire van, stopped and searched one man, dropped a lot of letters. Might get lucky.'

'Pasta? I know it's your favourite.'

He sat at the kitchen table with a beer, watched Maggie bustling. The van-hire company was closed. She brought the bowl over, sat with him.

They talked it through. Tomorrow, she'd phone a home security company, get the locks changed and an alarm fitted. They both needed to vary their routes to and from work, possibly go in together for a bit. Maggie could get a lift to basketball with a friend. They needed to move house – and soon.

Rick finished his beer and washed up.

He'd go again tomorrow.

House - to - house

DCI Rick Castle

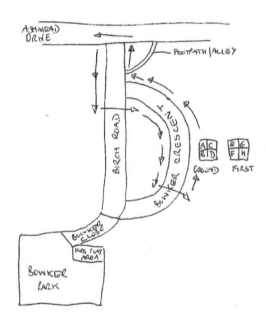

24

Rick slowed as he drove past the press camped outside Westbury School, raised a hand at the uniform constable, and sped up the slope. He didn't have an appointment, but he needed to make up time.

The morning meeting had been a washout: half the neighbourhood team were at court, and no new information. The only bright spot, the enthusiasm of the detective-uniform teams to re-statement the Westbury boys following Rick's update on the fluorescent jacket. The orange jacket was key. The jacket *and* the letter.

Rick entered the school through a side-door. Bypassing reception he headed directly to the headmaster's office. A woman escorting a boy in tears was halfway down the corridor. The smell of wood polish hung thickly.

He entered the annexe and knocked on the main door of the study.

'Come!'

The deep, rich voice echoed. Expecting, Rick imagined, a recalcitrant boy, or a poorly performing teacher. Alderman, maybe.

He opened the door, closed it behind him.

Sands stood in a corner, stirring an ornate silver-coloured teapot.

'Tea, or would you prefer coffee?'

Rick was in a rush, but needed to seem as if he wasn't. 'Tea's fine.'

Sands finally poured. He brought two cups towards his desk and handed one to Rick. 'Do sit down.'

Rick remained standing. '*Patet omnibus veritas* is your school motto.'

The headteacher sat down. After sipping his tea, he placed the cup back on the saucer. 'Truth lies open to all.'

'A little ironic don't you think, Mr Sands?'

Rick walked over to the window, and looked out over the empty courtyard. There were four access doors, one in each corner. Classrooms ran over three storeys. Directly opposite, nine lessons were taking place and in each room a teacher stood at the front of a class of twenty boys. Rick felt like James Stewart in *Rear Window*. Maggie had made him watch it.

He turned round.

'As you know, Jack Philipps is still missing. We've made some progress, but I need to see the letter you received. Superintendent Robinson says he can't find it. You told me you didn't keep a copy. I'm not sure I believe either of you.'

'Is that so?'

Rick bumped his empty cup and saucer onto Sands' desk. There was almost no liquid in a teacup.

A buzzer sounded. Moments later, the courtyard was full of running boys, dozens of them, haring from one door to another.

'Why did you wait a week to report the letter?'

'I told you,' said the head, above the hurly-burly outside, 'I thought it was a prank.'

'Yet you removed your son from the tennis team.'

'What do you want, Mr Castle?'

'I want the truth!' Rick waited for the clamour outside to diminish. 'One of your pupils has died. Another is missing.'

A door slammed on the deserted courtyard. Books sat forgotten on a bench.

'Well?'

'I have every confidence.'

There was a tentative knock on the door, and a high-pitched voice announced Class 2L were outside.

'One minute!' shouted Sands.

The head stood and walked slowly to the door. He pushed shut a filing cabinet. 'The Westbury family appreciates your efforts. You, and your team. A week after I received the letter, one of our gardeners was robbed on the school grounds. To use your lexicon, the timing appears suspect. His name's Dick Masters. The gardeners and maintenance people work out of a garage around the back.'

'I can't believe you're only telling me now.'

'I have the school's reputation to think of.'

The head opened the door and boys in green jumpers clutching thin yellow books flooded in.

At the back of the school, there was a knee-high sign next to a sprawling holly tree.

Maintenance (No Boys Past This Point)

Snaking through birch trees, a wide stone path led to a double garage with its concertina doors wide open. The garage was crammed with equipment. Mowing machines, white-line markers, fence poles, dustbins of netting, and partitioned spaces for tools.

A man carrying a strimmer appeared down the side of the garage. He wore a red and black lumberjack shirt. Rick explained he was looking for Dick Masters.

The man nodded at the garage. 'Dick!'

Rick entered. Towards the back a lawnmower lay on its side like a beached turtle. A gardener in green waterproofs was working at a bench. Rick walked closer. The man was filing the lawnmower blade held in a vice.

'Dick Masters?'

'Aye.'

The gardener stopped filing and looked up. Revealed a fading bruise under his left eye.

Rick showed his badge. 'South Manchester. Mr Sands told me you were robbed on the school grounds.'

'Did he now?'

Masters continued working. One-way strokes. Tiny grey shards flecked the vice and the work bench.

'Nice job,' said Rick. 'You should teach the boys here.'

Masters put the tool down. 'And take away the job that my son – and my son's son – is destined for?'

'Can you tell me what happened, Mr Masters?'

He leant back against the bench. 'I was in the garden at the front of the school, trimming the hedges, when this man started wheeling away my barrow. I shouted and went over. And he hit me, with my own bloody trowel. Knocked me out. When I came to, my money and cards had gone.'

'Did you report it?'

'To the school, but not to you lot. Sands told me not to. Didn't want any negative publicity. The missing boy has changed that. Poor sod.'

'You didn't think this might be connected in some way?'

'Nope.'

'What was taken?'

'About twenty-five pounds. My debit and credit cards.'

'Can you describe him?'

'Big. Tall. Taller than me. Six one, six two, maybe.'

'White?'

'Aye.'

Two men entered the garage, nodded at Masters, and took

down a three-tier ladder kept along the rafters. They looked Rick up and down as they carried it away. He wondered if he'd come across them.

'Do you think it was caught by the school's CCTV?'

Masters shook his head. 'Sands is getting some more installed.'

'Did anyone else see him?'

'None of the gardeners.'

'Would you recognise him again?'

'Maybe.'

Rick took out his wallet. 'We have a compensation scheme for victims.' He handed Masters twenty-five pounds.

The gardener took the money without comment. Tucked it away inside his waterproofs.

'One thing. He stole my jacket and barrow.'

Rick wanted to punch the air. It was always worth doing that little bit extra. Praising a witness's child, stroking a pet, changing a light bulb, or having a word with a noisy neighbour. In Masters' case, giving a straightforward bribe.

'Stole?'

'Well, he moved the barrow, stole my jacket mind. Left the barrow round by the pitches, near the tennis courts. Now, why would he do that?'

Rick sat in his car. Why indeed? Because the thief was planning to target someone in the tennis team? A school gardener was an unlikely target for a robbery, especially one on school premises. He phoned Nhung and asked her to grab a couple of people and drive up to the school. Help him speak to the other gardeners and the rest of the school staff. Sands could read out a notice in the next day's assembly. The least he could do.

The school clock struck midday. He just had time to get a sandwich and call in at the jewellers.

His phone rang.

'Nhung?'

'Elliot Tipper,' said the retired crime scene manager. 'Is now any good?'

Rick phoned Nhung a second time, briefed her on what he wanted. Lunch and the jewellers would have to wait.

Elliot was waiting for him in the hotel's reception.

'Sorry about before.'

'I remember what it's like, Rick.' They shook hands. 'You should get a job as a consultant. Set your own rates, knock off when you feel like it.' Elliot was freckly, round faced, cheery. Rick warmed to him straight away.

'Looks nothing like the Golden Lion,' said Elliot.

The hotel had been sold, refurbished, and rebranded as The Mill. Now targeting tourists, the front doors were flanked by glossy-leaved pot plants and window boxes. Inside, the large reception area was furnished with leather sofas. The theme was the industrial revolution, Manchester's brief period as world leader. Sepia photographs showed textile mills and the machines that drove their new prosperity. The spinning jenny, the water frame, the spinning mule.

Rick obtained the room key, and they walked up the stairs. The corridors and décor were gloomier and more cramped than the reception area. Usual tourist hotel tricks. Rick unlocked the door of room 114, the old 14.

'Totally different now, of course,' said Elliot, following him inside. 'Layout, light fittings, everything. You've seen the pictures. It looked like a normal hotel room, but a lot, lot seedier than it does now. Reds and golds, drapes, cushions, low lighting.'

Rick let his mind drift back. The file photo showed Jane Formby wearing a red dress. He imagined the sordid scene. The awkward introductions and the contrived conversation. Or maybe Formby was good at her job, and put her client at ease.

The stocky, tall man. But somewhere down the line, it had gone wrong. Her client had got angry, something she'd said or done, or not done. Or maybe it was him. He'd not performed. Maybe he'd been drinking or was on drugs. He had a temper. Lashed out. Used too much force. She wasn't big. Five foot six and slim as a model. Rick doubted a weapon had been used. Doubted it was premeditated. The incident was on the spur. He'd hurt her badly, too badly, so he'd killed her. Suffocated her, maybe. Easier to dispose of the body than risk her reporting a serious assault. Or so it had seemed. But now the client-turned-killer had the body to dispose of.

'Can you talk me through the forensics?'

'Sure. There was no obvious scene, remember this was three weeks on. But we did what we could. As you might expect, apart from traces of the victim's blood on the carpet, we recovered numerous sets of fingerprints and DNA. We matched and eliminated about half. The remaining sets of prints and DNA profiles we circulated on PNC.'

Rick nodded. A suspect would be identified only if they were arrested for another offence, their fingerprints and DNA taken, and a PNC record started. The new record would be checked against outstanding cases, and a match highlighted. Setting off flashing lights and a phone call to the officer in the case. The arrested person might be blameless, a previous hotel guest, or might be Formby's killer.

'Anything else?'

'Not really. We didn't recover any of her clothing, or her phone or bag. And the duvet cover was missing. The room wasn't cleaned until the morning, there wasn't a booking after Formby's. The hotel cleaner told us she didn't think anything of the missing bedding – she'd experienced far stranger things cleaning at the hotel.'

Rick stood for a moment in the ensuite bathroom, imagined

Jane getting ready. He walked over to the window. The room was at the back of the hotel. A narrow side road led to Cotton Street with its night life. A monkey puzzle tree stood on the corner. He wondered if Jane had looked out. Looked wistfully along the road to the peculiar tree and bright lights at the end, pictured the café she was saving toward.

They returned down a back flight of stairs. The rear door was a fire exit, but fourteen years ago, it had been a second entrance. The last place Jane had been seen. Rick pushed through the door and walked down the steps to the side road. Elliot followed.

'What were your thoughts on what happened to her body?'

'Either took it with him, had a vehicle parked up, or dumped it nearby. Lots of building work was going on in Manchester at the time. Sites were everywhere, boarded up or fenced off. Maybe they pushed open a fence and dumped her body in a hole. Got lucky.'

One person could have carried her down the stairs and out of the hotel. But two people would have made it easier and less risky. One to fetch a car, then to act as lookout. Then again, no one had mentioned two people. He looked down the road towards the flashing lights of entertainment venues, wondering if Jane had been buried somewhere in the Peak District, or whether her body was far nearer, under one of the buildings in front of him.

Rick bought a sandwich and ate it walking the half-kilometre to the jewellery shop. He rang the bell. Trays of rings and watches lined the window. Silverware to mark birthdays, anniversaries, special occasions. Trinkets to help men get out of situations, get into situations.

The door buzzed open. He'd previously attended after an armed robbery and shots discharged in the ceiling.

Manager Nathan appeared from the back. 'Hello, Chief

Inspector.' It was only six months, but Nathan's hair was greyer. His wife had stopped working in the shop.

'I said you'd see me again.'

Rick examined a dozen or so. He had no idea as to their worth or technical attributes, but wanted to choose one that spoke to him. He chose. It was different. Maggie was different.

'I can give you a discount,' said Nathan.

Rick shook his head. A discount would detract, would suggest imperfection. Maggie was perfect. He paid, slipped the box into his pocket, and walked back to his car.

A parking attendant was standing by the windscreen and tapping on her machine. She was built like a cement bollard.

'There's a police logbook on the dash.'

'So?'

'I'm in the middle of a murder enquiry.'

'I'm in the middle of a parking ticket.'

Rick waited until she'd finished, climbed into the car and drove away. One day, probably quite soon, she'd need the police, and they'd come running. The Job was like that.

The afternoon meeting was disappointing. Nhung hadn't found any more witnesses to the robbery of Dick Masters at the school, and none of the schoolboys in the minibus, Paul Chan included, remembered a fluorescent orange jacket. The boy thought the jacket he'd seen was yellow.

Rick returned to his office and went through every piece of information again. Maggie came to see him.

'We've had another call on the cold case. His name's Philip Clough.'

Rick nodded at her. Remembered his feelings as he looked at the trays in the jeweller's. The box sat in his coat pocket on the back of the door – within touching distance of Maggie.

'I'm going home. I'll cook something. I've already been home once to have the locks changed.' She pushed a set of keys across his desk. 'These are yours. He's coming back to fit an alarm.'

'You might want to vary your route, Mags. I'll be home in a bit.'

Rick listened to her moving down the corridor. He phoned Clough and left several messages. He wondered about Jack, where he was, and how he was doing. He worked until two a.m. and drove home wanting to drive back.

25

Rick went back in early. He sat in an interview room so no one could find him and worked through the list of witnesses. He reread all the first accounts, the telephone notes, and the statements. There was one person they'd spoken to soon after Jack had gone missing, but not followed up with a statement. He was about to put that right, and at eight he returned to his own office.

Three people were waiting for him: Barton, Nhung, and Sergeant Davison. A willing team, although he wouldn't want to get stuck in a lift with any of them.

Superintendent Robinson walked in. But if there was a choice.

'I'll come back,' said Barton and Davison together.

'Okay,' said Rick. 'Nhung, can you meet me in the yard in ten?' Scowling, she tramped away in the wake of her two colleagues.

Robbo closed the door.

'Have you read the redacted sheet in her personnel record?'

'Let's just say, I know of it.' Robbo walked over to the window, and glanced out. He turned. 'Bad news, I'm afraid. Chief super's not happy. The day after tomorrow, this is going to the murder team.'

186

'What? Give me a few more days. At least until we've got the forensic results from Jack's phone.' He paused. 'Of course, there's also the missing letter. Does the chief super know about that?'

'He only cares what headquarters are saying, and this month, after a succession of anti-police headlines in the media, it's corruption and discreditable conduct. So, it's not the investigation he's bothered about, it's you – and being arrested twice in a week. And when the murder team take it, you're confined to the station.'

'You are joking.'

Robbo held up his hands. 'Don't shoot the messenger.'

'I've been set up. Twice. Surely you don't disagree?'

Robbo was silent for a few seconds. He still looked liverish. One of the few times recently Rick had seen him when he wasn't eating. Something was eating *him*.

'I don't.'

'What couldn't you tell me in the cell at North Manchester?'

Robbo sighed, shook his head. 'I want to find Jack as much as you, believe me. Let's hope his phone tells us something.'

Rick grabbed his jacket. Shooting would be too painless. He opened the door. 'I'm going out – while I still can.'

Rick drove, and beside him, Nhung sat with her hands under her thighs. The early morning traffic was heavy, and bad-tempered.

At a traffic light, he pulled a file from the back. 'Read this, notes from our original call to Victoria Parsons, Jack's mixed-tennis partner.'

She read the sheet of paper in less than thirty seconds – and that was the problem.

Inside the Parsons' house, they were shown to the sitting room. It had been tidied and vacuumed, the strands of carpet lying in one direction. Photos of tennis players and a small gold-coloured cup stood on a shelf. They stayed standing, Rick deliberately declining coffee.

Mrs Parsons returned with her daughter. She shooed out a loitering younger son in school uniform, and shut the door.

Victoria Parsons sat on the sofa. She was toned, and athletic-looking, and like her brother, wore school uniform. Fancy shoes with a buckle.

Mrs Parsons sat next to her, and Rick and Nhung sat opposite.

'I've been so worried,' said Victoria.

'Do you know where Jack is?' said Rick. 'He's not been seen since.'

The teenager shook her head. 'I told the officer that on the phone.' She looked at the floor.

Nhung shuffled forward on her chair. 'It's really important, Victoria, if you know anything.'

A breakfast radio show played in another room. A chair squeaked across the floor. Heavy footsteps pounded up the stairs.

Victoria shook her head.

'How often do you play with him?' said Rick.

'Once every couple of weeks. He won't get better practising with me, he knows that, but we do play. It's good for my game, especially return of serve. Matches, too, of course.'

Rick nodded. 'Is there any reason why Jack might want to run away – is he worried about anything?'

Victoria glanced at her mother, then back at Rick. 'He's worried about his exams, and also about the Northern Cup. It's a prestigious tournament and he's got a good chance to win it. Only one serious threat – he reckons, anyway. Some Russian boy.'

Rick paused, then tried another tack. 'Do you see Jack outside of tennis?'

The schoolgirl didn't reply for a few seconds. Which was enough to discount anything she then said. 'Not really.'

'Could I get that coffee, Mrs Parsons?' said Rick.

Victoria's mother rose, and went out. Rick eyeballed Nhung

and nodded at the door. His DS closed it, and sat back down. Footsteps thumped back down the stairs.

'Were you more than tennis partners?' said Nhung.

Victoria shook her head. Her eyes were watery. Nhung took out a packet of tissues and handed one across. The girl dabbed at her eyes.

'Did Jack want to be?'

Victoria nodded.

In the next room the radio had been switched off, and muted voices punched back and forth.

'You need to tell us, it's important.'

Victoria looked up. 'You mustn't tell my mum.'

'All we want, Victoria, is to find Jack.'

'Promise.'

Nhung looked at Rick.

'We promise, Victoria,' said Rick, making eye contact. There were caveats and exceptions, but it wasn't the time.

'We got pretty high playing tournaments together. Some big matches. A couple of weeks ago we won in Chester. It was all weekend and we stayed in a hotel. My mum was there, too, but I had a separate room. Jack's good-looking.' She glanced round at the door, as if her mother was outside listening. 'We shared a bath, experimented a bit. But—'

'But what?'

'He asked me out. I said no.' She paused. 'I like him – a lot – but I'm not ready to play Mr and Mrs.'

'Is there anywhere you think he might go?'

'Possibly back to the hotel in Chester. My room was number sixteen. It was an old hotel and had a corner bath. Other than that, I don't know. I've been half-expecting him to come here.'

'A couple of days ago we used a dog to track Jack from the site of the minibus crash. About a mile away, the dog stopped and indicated in Crenton Road. Do you know if Jack's ever been there?'

'My aunt lives on Crenton, she's got MS and Jack sometimes mows her lawn.'

Rick was amazed. Max the SAM dog had very nearly found a needle in a haystack.

The door opened and Mrs Parsons entered with a tray. Victoria tucked her skirt tighter under her legs. Nhung stood to help. Rick asked if he could see Victoria's phone.

'Of course,' said Mrs Parsons.

'Mum!'

'Just the messages from Jack,' said Rick. 'It would be really helpful.' He took the cup of coffee, sipped it, and set it down. 'Thanks.'

Victoria passed over her phone. 'Jacks is what I call him.'

The phone had a pink surround and stickers of pop bands on the back. The huge screen made Rick's phone look last century. He scrolled through the social media messages to and from Jacks. Arrangements for the Chester tournament, a couple of intimate ones during the Saturday. More on Sunday, a photo of Jack holding a trophy. The last message was twenty minutes before the crash, from Jacks.

I think I love you.

They returned to Crenton Road, and three doors up from the D-list actress Edith Horton, parked outside the house of Victoria's aunt. She opened the door, invited them inside. It felt too easy, and Rick feared another dead end. Victoria's aunt knew Jack well, had watched him play in a local tournament with Victoria, but hadn't seen him for a month or so, when he'd last cut her lawn. They were welcome to look around. They did, then left.

Max the SAM dog had somehow picked up a trail for the boy and tracked him to Crenton Road. Trying again with a second dog made sense.

It felt like they were getting closer, but feelings counted for nothing.

Back at the station, Rick climbed the stairs to the sixth floor to speak to the chief super about the missing letter. Informing on his immediate boss didn't come easily, but without a hot lead, it was the right thing to do – a boy's life was at stake.

The hall was deserted. Neither Trinity, nor the chief super's PA, sat at their desks. He knocked on the chief super's door but there was no reply. He checked Trinity's desk diary. There was a finance meeting in the conference room from eleven-thirty to two. Lunch provided – to ensure Robbo's attendance.

The corridor was empty. He tried his boss's door, but it was locked.

At Trinity's desk, he slipped a hand over the top of the drawer pedestal and felt around. His fingers touched a key.

He unlocked Robbo's door, checked the corridor, opened it. He stepped inside and shut the door quietly behind him.

The police was a strictly hierarchical organisation – in the issuing of commands, in pay, and even in room sizes. The office was double the size of an inspector's, fifty per cent larger than a chief inspector's. And there was an annexe. Rick surveyed the room as if he was executing a search warrant. There was the desk and pedestal, the bookcase, and cabinets. The double locker, a riot helmet sitting on top. Finally, three filing cabinets in the corner.

Would Robbo keep the letter in his desk, or hide it away?

Rick checked through the trays on his desk, and opened the drawers. The bottom drawer was locked, the key not obvious. He walked over to the filing cabinets and opened a drawer, heavy with documents. There were three more below. Searching all twelve for a letter would take hours. He pushed it back.

He glanced through the bookcase and the cabinet. Binders of know-how documents and policy files.

Voices outside.

Rick stilled. A bead of sweat dropped from his armpit. He could hide in the annexe, or front it out. He was waiting for the superintendent. And if it was Robbo? No different.

The voices moved away.

Rick didn't have long. He needed to be smarter. His boss would know it would be Rick trying to find the letter, so he tried to think like his boss. Where would Robbo think Rick wouldn't look? In Rick's personnel file? In the first aid kit, pinned to the wall by the door?

Where would Rick look? In unusual, difficult-to-access places. Which meant Rick wouldn't look in obvious places. A good hiding place is in full view, or so the search training team liked to say. In the seat of the chair? In the light fitting?

He reached down the riot helmet, and checked inside. It was empty except for a pair of earplugs.

There was a knock on the door.

'Sir?' called a young voice.

More knocking. 'Sir?'

A conversation outside.

Rick stepped into the annexe, and pushed the door to.

He sensed the room door open, and someone – maybe two people – enter the room.

'What if he comes back? The door's not locked.' Rick recognised the voice, a young PC on a uniform team. The name would come to him.

'So what if he does. Just say we're waiting for him.'

The second voice Rick also recognised – PC Vanders. He was older, slapdash, and thought the Job owed him both a living and an easy life. People like him were dangerous on a uniform team, but the problem was where else to put him. Not in the station office, not in a specialist unit. The property office needed propriety, and the jailer was recorded on

CCTV for the entire shift. So Vanders remained on a team.

'We should go.'

The two men fell silent. Rick could hear footsteps, and paperwork being rustled. He thought they were skimming the superintendent's desk.

Rick eased down onto the lid of the WC. The annexe was similar to an ensuite: basin, WC, shower. A cupboard below the basin.

Laughing sounded in the main office.

'How do I look?' said Vanders. If there was a reply, it was non-verbal. 'At ease, PC Hennessey,' said Vanders, impersonating the superintendent. 'Don't bring me problems, bring me solutions.'

Hennessey, yes, thought Rick. He was only recently out of his probation, but he showed promise, and, only two weeks before, had arrested a daytime burglar after some decent Q and A. Rick bent forward and peered through the keyhole in the annexe door.

'Bring me cakes, more like,' said Hennessey.

Through the keyhole, Rick could see the middle third of the room. Vanders was wearing Robbo's flat hat and strutting about.

Hennessey looked uneasy. 'Come on, let's go.'

Vanders climbed down. 'We should leave our mark.'

Rick considered opening the annexe door and confronting the PCs. The problem was explaining his own presence. Looking for an overtime code? Robbo wouldn't believe any story. Rick stayed where he was.

The two PCs discussed leaving their mark. Pissing in a coffee cup, swapping pictures around. They settled on wiping the whiteboard clean.

Vanders' radio beeped with a personal call. The PC whispered into the handset fixed to his chest. He nodded at Hennessey, and the two of them went out. The office door slammed shut.

Rick poured a glass of water. He felt embarrassed to work for an organisation which employed people like them. Vanders was leading Hennessey astray, but had probably been led astray himself. A strong individual would push back. And what about Rick? He was also committing a disciplinary offence, although only to find the letter and progress the investigation.

He rinsed the glass and set it back on the basin.

He squatted down and opened the cupboard. An envelope marked *Mister Sand, Head Teacher, Westbury School* was propped up between toilet rolls.

Hidden in the annexe, in full view.

26

Rick placed the exhibit bag containing the envelope on his desk. The school's full address including postcode was correct. A first-class stamp, no legible postmark. He turned the bag over. The back was clear. He put on gloves and pulled out the letter.

Mister Sand
Tennis teem STOP play big match strait way
Or BIG problem and make stop
You warning

The paper and envelope were thick, and good quality. A school pupil taking them from a parent? Hotel stationery? The poor English suggested the author wasn't British. But equally could be a pupil trying to disguise himself, or someone else doing the same.

Stop playing in big matches, but not playing altogether. What were big matches? Important ones, against major schools, or did the writer mean tournaments? Jack had the Northern Cup coming up – and Victoria Parsons had mentioned Jack as only having one main threat. A Russian boy, she'd said, which if somehow connected, would fit with the broken English.

Rick took photos. He needed the letter and envelope

examined for prints and DNA and impressions. He could take them to a different police station to wrongfoot Robbo, or hope his boss wouldn't intervene once they were in the system.

He jogged down the stairs to the basement and along the corridor to the CSI's office. Desks for five staff, and an adjoining storeroom, it was dingy as a dungeon.

Tara sat at a desk stacked with trays and books and lit by an Anglepoise. She was staring at a computer. Her eyes were ringed with indentations, and a towel was drying over the door.

'I heard you're swimming five k?'

'For Cancer UK.' She passed up a clipboard. She smelt of chlorine.

Rick signed his name, and an amount which was proportionate to the hierarchy of police pay. He didn't break all the rules.

'I've checked the prints from Maggie's flat – only hers and yours. Sorry.'

'Unlikely whoever set me up didn't think to wear gloves. What about Jack's phone?'

'Still waiting.'

'Got something else for you.' He set the exhibit bag down on her desk.

'You need it yesterday?'

Rick nodded. 'Everything you can think of.' He went to the door, and turned back. 'I'll double my sponsorship if you can get it back tomorrow.'

He walked out. Maybe he did.

Back in his office, Rick waded through the results of the press appeal for witnesses to the minibus crash. He kept thinking about the letter. The same time tomorrow, thanks to Tara and the DNA or fingerprint database, he might have a named suspect.

There had been thirty-three calls. Twenty-three about

something else, knowing the phone would be answered. Seven about a different crash. Two had heard about the school minibus, but hadn't seen it. One had driven past and seen the emergency vehicles.

Rick pulled out the contact form. Joe Stransby, twenty-eight years old, worked at HBW tool hire. *Very interested in the reward*, Davison had scrawled at the bottom of the form.

His phone buzzed, and a text from Becky flashed up. *Dad's still locked in his room. What are you doing about it?*

Okay, okay.

Rick logged into the Police National Computer and looked up Michael J Howell, the assistant at Dad's care home. Guessed at his age. A third of UK males over thirty had a criminal record. He might get something. Seven pages of possible matches. He switched to the intelligence database and tried again. A stop and search form three years earlier – negative – yielded the care assistant's date of birth. He tried the PNC a second time.

Michael J Howell aka Michael Mason, previous for employee theft, false accounting. Served a year in Strangeways.

Nhung appeared in the doorway. She wore a grey mackintosh like a detective in the seventies. 'Not feeling too good, sir. But I'm meant to be taking the statement from the lad at HBW Tools.'

'What's wrong?'

'Things.'

'Okay. I'll do it.'

'Thanks.' She smiled for the first time Rick could remember. He didn't deserve it. He was tempted by the Stransby action. The witness could have seen Jack get into a car, could have noted the registration. It could lead to finding Jack and arresting the suspect tonight. He thought the same about every action. Every detective, he imagined, did.

He drove to HBW.

Rain slanted down and passing vehicles threw up spurts of dirty water onto the windscreen. The city was cold and grey. Car lights and streetlights fuzzy in the gloom. Pedestrians hurried, bent like coastal trees.

HBW Tools occupied a railway arch, the door cut into the wooden frontage. A train with misted windows rattled across the top. He parked and climbed out, flipped up his collar, and banged on the door.

He looked around, hammered again. Another train clattered overhead.

A petrol station glowered at the end of the road. Rain dripped from its roof and slicks of spilt fuel lay on the forecourt. A tiny fish and chip van stood opposite. The shop was already barred, and Rick approached the night window.

The young cashier wore bulbous headphones and jigged up and down. No man, he had no idea.

Rick walked over to the chip van. He laid down a ten-pound note. People could smell police in Manchester, the way people could smell money in London.

'The lads in HBW Tools?'

The woman in the van wore a blond wig, and a tight t-shirt under a duvet jacket. She held the banknote up to the light and snapped it tight. She winked at him.

'Try the Six Bells.'

Rick walked. He was already wet. He turned up his collar, avoided the worst of the puddles. Detectives pounded the pavements, trod the tarmac, wore away their shoe leather and blistered their feet.

He crossed a road, water swirling along the gutters and sliding into the drains. He turned right, and ducked into a wide alley. The Six Bells squeezed in at the end. Rotten air spilt through the front windows. A low hum of drunkenness and conspiracy.

He pushed open the door.

It was low-ceilinged and dark. Silence fell, as if they knew he was coming. He turned down his collar and walked toward the bar.

'I'm looking for Joe Stransby. Works at HBW Tools. He's just a witness.'

The barman was drying a glass. He had a ponytail and rows of earrings. He set down the glass and flicked the cloth over his shoulder. 'Drink?' He took down a bottle and poured a measure. 'On the house.'

Rick rarely drank the hard stuff. But the deal was clear: he wasn't going to get any information unless he did. He tipped it down his throat, the whisky burning like petrol. His eyes felt alight.

'Another,' said the barman. 'For the road.' He filled the glass.

Rick drank a second time. Already, his feet felt warmer. 'I'm going.'

'Matchbox Tavern,' said the barman.

Rick walked out of the pub. The alley was bathed in yellow from a streetlight. Rain swirled. He felt he should light a cigarette. He would try one more place. Stransby could hold the vital piece of information.

He headed back down the alley, back to the main road, turned right. A couple holding onto each other for support staggered past. A rough sleeper slumped in a doorway. The sleeping bag was dark blue from the rain. He walked through a tunnel of scaffolding, past a bus stop where an old man was sheltering with his dog.

His phone rang.

'Where *are* you?' said Maggie.

'I'll be home soon.' Rain spattered his face as he held the phone. 'Did you get through to the hotel in Chester?'

'Jack's not there. And I've got the report on his laptop. I've read through it, there's nothing obvious.'

'Shouldn't be too long, now.'

He pocketed his phone and resumed walking. His socks were wet. She knew the deal. Perhaps she'd say no; he hadn't considered that scenario. He turned down a side street and reached the Tavern. Blackboards with rain-streaked chalk menus lay on the ground. A bench was chained to a metal post.

Inside, it was warm and busy with punters. His clothes steamed.

He asked his question.

'Who wants to know?' said the landlord. He was bald and fat. His face red, pockmarked, and soggy as the weather.

'Who do you think,' said Rick.

'John O'Fucking Groats.'

'You'll need us one day. Everyone does.'

Rick walked out. Behind him, a barrage of jeers and catcalls and spit.

Outside, he took off his jacket. He wiped off the patches of gob. He would speak to the licensing sergeant and request a review. They would make a formal complaint to the brewery. And on New Year's Eve, they would shut the pub down at four in the afternoon.

Rick sat down on the sofa with Maggie, who was watching a film. The lights were dim, and the room was warm. There was a chink in the curtains and shadows moved outside.

The screen flickered.

Jack Philipps could be dead, decomposing in a ditch or encased in cement or buried under four feet of earth. He could have been taken miles away, abroad even, or he could be sitting or lying somewhere within Manchester. In one of the million houses or flats. He couldn't knock them all, couldn't interview every resident. He should have made the team work late. They could have knocked more house-to-house near the crash site.

Obtained and investigated a fixture list for the school tennis team. Identified and spoken to Jack's rival for the Northern Cup. Tried a second SAM dog. Conducted surveillance on the BMW driver and Hunter the minibus driver. Trawled the backstreets for the golf-ball thrower Bucur. Followed Jack's father. Found and analysed more CCTV footage near the crash site. Conducted more phone enquiries on Jack's parents, on the BMW driver, on Hunter. On everyone. Enquiries were limited only by imagination and resources. He had the imagination. He shouldn't be sitting down.

He stood up.

'Where are you going?' said Maggie. She aimed the remote at the television. The screen stopped flickering and there was quiet.

'I thought I'd give Philip Clough another call. The outstanding respondent to my appeal on the Formby murder.' Jack was the priority, but if he could, he wanted to keep pushing the cold case along.

'Isn't it too late? It's bedtime.' She paused. 'Do you think you should go and see Emma?'

Rick was only half-listening. He'd phone Clough, and then comb through the file on the minibus crash and Jack's disappearance. Write out the next day's priority actions. Revisit HBW. Track down Jack's rival. Chase the forensics on Jack's phone and the letter.

'Rick,' said Maggie, shaking his arm. 'You came in after ten, soaking wet and stinking of booze. A child could look after themself better.'

'I keep thinking about Jack. He might be hurt, might be hurting, might be being hurt, I can't just sit here.'

Maggie held his hand. 'You can't do this with every victim, every family member, every case.'

'You knew it would be like this, Mags.'

'Long hours, yes, and some introspection, but not exclusively.'

'Anyway, I've already been to see Emma.'

'You walked out.'

'How do you know?'

'She phoned me. It's against their code of practice, but she figured it might be the only way to get you to engage – not just sit there – and maybe save your career. Maybe, save you,' Maggie added quietly.

'Her words or yours?'

'A mixture, but please, Rick, do it for me.' She looked at him.

He felt the force of aeons of evolution which had moulded his genes. He wanted this woman to bear his children, wanted this woman to love him. He would do anything for her, say anything to her.

'Okay.'

'You'll go?'

'Yes.'

But not any time soon.

He pulled his hand away and stood up. He walked into the kitchen, phoned Philip Clough, left another message. Despite the passage of time, it might make a difference. It just might.

He unlocked the garden door with the new keys and stepped outside. It was cold and still. The rain had stopped, but he could hear dripping, and smell the dampness. He could smell rotting leaves. He could hear a couple arguing, a dog barking, a car accelerating.

He looked toward the orange glow of the city. Jack was out there somewhere. He had to be.

27

Robbo was waiting in Rick's office. The superintendent sat in his chair, swivelled to face the window.

'Shut the door, Rick.'

He shut the door. Wondered if Robbo had a covert camera in his own office, and knew Rick had found the letter.

His boss turned to face him.

'The letter's turned up,' said Rick, trying to control his sarcasm. 'I've submitted it for forensics.'

'What about the chain of evidence?'

'If it leads to Jack, it won't matter.'

The superintendent stood up. He still looked peaky. Maybe, thought Rick, he'd started a peculiar new diet. Suddenly he wondered whether Robbo was also being targeted – blackmailed – and couldn't tell Rick for fear of the consequences.

'You're off the case.'

'What? You said the day after—'

'I said, a murder team are taking it; DCI Walsh will be here at nine. And I'm sorry, Rick, but you're suspended.'

'Come on, Robbo! There's no corroboration – you *know* both allegations are rubbish. Someone's got it in for me.'

'Be that as it may. The press and social media are in a frenzy, and the chief super's folded to pressure from headquarters. I did my best.'

'What if I confront the chief super with the letter you hid in your office?'

'He might ask why you haven't done so already. He might dig out your history. He might say enough is enough. Trust me, I'll get you reinstated.'

'Trust!'

Rick chucked his warrant card on the desk. If he'd been an American cop he would have thrown his gun, too. And maybe he wouldn't have checked it was unloaded.

He drove back to HBW Tools and parked alongside moss-covered railway sleepers. The petrol station was in darkness, the chip van gone. Above the line of arches, trainline wires and stanchions trellised the gunmetal sky.

The only place with a sign of life was the central arch: the wooden frontage of HBW stood propped open and a grey pickup parked outside. Remaining in his car, Rick phoned Philip Clough one more time.

'Hello.' A man's voice.

Rick said a silent thank you to the power above – the sun. He was one hundred per cent certain there was no form of benevolent god.

'Mr Clough, it's DCI Rick Castle from South Manchester. You got in touch after seeing the press conference.'

'It's not actually me you need to speak to, it's my father William Clough. He's Canadian, but he's over here for a couple of weeks.'

Nothing was straightforward, nothing. Even an indifferent god was doubtful.

'December 1st, 2003, there was a problem with his flight to the UK. He ended up in Manchester and stayed at the Golden Lion hotel.'

Rick gripped the phone. 'What did he see?'

'Nothing. At least, he's never said so. But I thought you might want to speak to him anyway?'

Rick released his grip. There was still a chance Clough's father had seen or heard something. He wrote down a phone number for Philip's daughter Suzie, who lived in Manchester. William Clough was visiting his granddaughter for a few days.

He rang her, but there was no reply and he left yet another message. God might be forgiven yet.

Rick climbed out of his car and walked into the arch housing HBW. The cavernous space was badly lit and smelt of petrol and cannabis. The walls were grey-green with damp grime.

'Anyone here?'

His voice echoed.

He walked forward, dodging patches of oil, and past a wire cage full of equipment. Lawnmowers, chainsaws, hedgetrimmers, strimmers, rotavators. Machines he didn't know the names for, or purpose of. They looked torturous – at both ends.

A hooded man entered the cage on the far side and threw a blanket over a quadbike. A second man unlocked the cage at the front, and the first man wheeled the bike forward. Neither looked at Rick.

He let it go. He'd mention it to Maggie and she could enter it on the system. Half of Manchester, Rick sometimes thought, was breaking the law.

At the back was a large square workbench. Boxed compartments along the walls, each with a tool and a label attached with brown string. A man was replacing the till roll on a cash register. He wore a padded jacket, work trousers with pockets, scuffed boots. He was about twenty.

'I need to speak to Joe Stransby.'

The young man poked around inside the slot for the till roll with a biro. He pushed the new roll in, and clipped the hatch shut.

'That's me.'

'You phoned about the minibus crash.'

'Is there definitely a reward?'

Rick nodded. The Chamber of Commerce had come good. 'A thousand pounds. What did you see?'

'How do I know you're going to give me the money?'

'Because I'm police.'

'Exactly.'

'I came here last night, after you'd closed. Looked for you in the Six Bells and the Matchbox Tavern.'

'I heard.'

Stransby fingered a battered desk diary. He turned a page and reapplied the rubber band. He ran a stained finger down the page.

'If your information leads to us finding the boy, you'll get the reward.' Rick took out his notebook. 'What did you see?'

'It's on my dashcam.'

Rick remained expressionless, but inside he was grinning like a fool. If Stransby was telling the truth, and if the dashcam showed something – a glimpse of Jack – he'd hire every machine in the place.

Stransby took a phone out of his knee pocket. 'I downloaded it.' He rested the phone sideways against a socket set on the bench. A T-shaped crack split the large screen. The mechanic prodded and scrolled.

The footage started: vehicles driving along the motorway. Rick bent for a better view. There was an obstruction ahead, cars slowing. Brake lights. Hazard lights. Police vehicles and an ambulance. The minibus loomed up, slewed sideways. The BMW sat on the hard shoulder, its front buckled.

Come on, Rick intoned in silence.

After the minibus, three dark-coloured vehicles had stopped on the hard shoulder. A large white man wearing an orange fluorescent stood near the far vehicle. With a boy.

Then the scene was gone: vehicles were accelerating, and gaps appearing between them.

'Rewind,' said Rick.

Stransby pressed, and played.

The three dark-coloured vehicles. The tall white man in the orange fluorescent. The boy was also tall, and had dark hair. The boy was Jack Philipps.

Without doubt, the murder investigation now included a kidnap. Who by, and why? And why had there been no demands?

Rick watched the video clip a third and a fourth time. He strained for recognition on the man, for a detail of the car. The number plate was obscured, the footage grainy.

'Can you send it to me?' said Rick.

'What about the reward?'

'You'll get it if we find the boy.'

'Nah, I want it now.'

Rick took hold of Stransby's phone. 'Well, I'm seizing this. It's evidence of a serious crime.'

The two men who'd removed the quadbike appeared. Sleeves of tattoos. Rick recognised Johnson, recently released from prison for a daytime robbery on a bookmaker. Stamped the dog of a customer to death.

'Phone,' said Stransby.

Normally, Rick would call for backup, but having been suspended, that option was not without complication. Three to one, the reverse of the odds, according to the brigadier, an army unit liked before they attacked. The police preferred five to one.

But on any count, he was outnumbered. Another investigator working solo would headbutt and elbow strike his way to the car. Another would turn the garden sprayer on the nearest shelf into a flamethrower by detaching and reattaching a pipe, and escape in a whirlwind of fire and confusion. Another would lean back on his office chair to release a huge fart, having sent a pair of slow horses.

The three men advanced in a loose semi-circle, almost as if they knew he'd been severed from his backup.

'Johnson,' said Rick. 'Isn't your younger brother Toby Johnson? And isn't he returning on bail in a week or two for shoplifting?' Reading the daily custody summaries occasionally yielded a crop.

'And what if he is?'

'First time offence, low value. Get him to admit the offence and write a letter of apology to the chemist. And I'll sort an NFA.'

Johnson grunted. 'Your call, Joe. Toby's a little toe-rag.'

'Look, Joe,' said Rick. 'Forward me the footage, and keep your phone. Believe me, this is a new and crucial piece of information. I'll make sure you get your money.' He'd have paid the reward himself, but there was a principle at stake. He was reaffirming the rules of engagement for the next generation.

The mechanic glanced at his two mates, then at Rick.

Finally, he nodded.

Rick tossed him the phone and the mechanic forwarded him the footage. He checked it worked, and resisting whooping and hollering, resisting breaking into a run, walked out to his car. Technical would be able to clean it up. Facial recognition might be a possibility, reading the number plate even. An obscure detail on the car or the suspect.

Outside, a second car was parking alongside the railway sleepers. There was a surfeit of aerials on the roof. Two men climbed out wearing suits, but no ties. One held a statement binder.

'What are *you* doing here?' said the driver.

Rick unlocked his car, and climbed in. He started the engine and pulled onto the road, his head flowing with sarcastic quips about his chainsaw needing a service. He buzzed down the window. 'Jack's been kidnapped. Best you tell DCI Walsh a-sap.'

28

Andrei sat at the window. It was mid-morning, and for the second day in a row, Castle's car was still parked at home. His no-leg wife's car too. Once or twice, he'd seen the detective staring out of the front window. Watching the weather, like everyone else in the wet country.

What Andrei couldn't understand was why, when two days earlier, he'd watched police take him away in handcuffs.

Castle wasn't locked up in what the British called prison – three meals a day and a range of welfare counsellors – but he wasn't working at the police station as normal. The detective was at home and swimming around the rooms like a goldfish. Two drug offences would be enough for a trial, and despite the glacial British law system, Castle ought to be discredited and jailed. His cases abandoned. Even wonder detective Castle couldn't get a third chance.

So why was he at home?

Andrei realised he was biting his fingernails. It made him think of his daughter Alyona. Willpower, he'd told her, and eliminating the problems in your life. When she'd asked what he meant, he'd shown her some self-defence moves, and for balance, a few for attack. He wondered what she was doing. At school, probably. Or avoiding her mother. If he was at home more, she said she wanted to come and live with him. But Andrei wasn't sure if she was only saying that, and it saddened him. Not much did, except Alyona growing up – and meeting people. The world was a dangerous place.

The front door opened and Castle walked outside. The sky was light as a bedsheet. The calm before a storm.

Andrei stood up. His leg hurt like it happened last week.

The detective half-turned, called inside. The sun has appeared, he might be saying, the one time in Manchester year.

Castle's wife rolled down the ramp. The detective disappeared inside and returned with a kitchen chair and a collapsible table. He uncollapsed the table. Went inside again and returned carrying two mugs. Sat down alongside her.

They peered up into the sky, looked around. Then they got to talking, quiet, serious. Maybe he'd do a lipreading course when he got back.

He was biting his fingernails again. No tell Alyona.

If Castle had been given a third chance, he couldn't get a fourth. Maybe they should change tactic and use something more effective. Not polonium, but a new poison. Before they'd left for wetland, rumours had been swirling in an old soldiers' bar about new untraceable poisons being manufactured. If it was untraceable, it couldn't come back to the Kremlin, or to Semion, or to him and Kirill.

Castle brought a large pan out from the house and set it on the table. He made a phone call. Then he set to work with a knife over the pan. Andrei used binoculars. No idea what the detective was doing, but it wasn't police. His no-legs wife was looking around, staring up at the sun as if it had a smiley face.

They started to argue, like married couples the world over. Marriage was not so much a rollercoaster as a down escalator, and at the bottom, some people fell off with a bump. Castle fetched more paraphernalia from the house. Soon there was more stuff outside the house than inside.

Andrei stamped on the ceiling – changeover time. The sofa was back downstairs; Kirill was driving him as crazy as a dog with two heads. Kept complaining about preparing three meals a day. Like working in a café, he said.

Kirill always took his time. Always collected a drink from the fridge and some snacks before plodding upstairs. Always used the bathroom, before finally appearing as if he was the lead tip-toer at Bolshoi.

I add minutes on, like football.

Why no show me red card?

Andrei kept watching.

Castle made another phone call. He put a small pan inside the big pan. Detective wife was watching, asking questions, like she was interested.

No trust? said Kirill.

'*Nyet*,' said Andrei, glancing at his partner. He would have one last look, then go for painkiller and much needed bathroom.

Castle wife was pointing in his direction.

Andrei shrank back.

They see us.

What?

Castle wife pointing this way.

You panic?

I no panic.

You voice say panic. Kirill crept over to the window.

Andrei pushed him back.

I thought you want me look?

'*Nyet*!'

Andrei edged back to the window. The blind was down, and no one should have been able to see inside. But maybe there'd been a reflection. He looked out again. Castle wife sat alone, the front door open.

What happen?

Andrei neck-jerked at the window and Kirill crept alongside him.

You panic.

I no panic.

They waited at the window, like a married couple. Kirill was woman. Put cream on his feet.

A minute later, Castle returned with binoculars. Not as good as Andrei's pair. The detective had taken out Hant Khetan, once cited as the replacement to Osama Bin Laden. He was bound to have a sixth sense. He looked over in their direction.

Keep still. He look us.

The detective observed for thirty seconds, handed the glasses to his wife. She looked, he looked again. They chatted like best of friends now. Castle took out his phone.

He make phone call.

I can see!

Red card.

No have two.

Castle wife passed back the glasses. The detective finished the phone call, observed again through the inferior binoculars, then they both went inside. Took the pans and hundreds of equipment with them.

Now what?

We wait, said Andrei.

They watched, waited, no panic.

Thirty minutes later, Castle's wife emerged and rolled over to her car. She did an amazing procedure to get into the driving seat and stow the wheelchair beside her. Respect to strong lady. Castle was lucky to have a strong lady.

The detective followed soon after, climbed into his car, and drove away as if he was competing in grand prix.

Excitement over, Kirill could surveil, and Andrei stepped

away from the window. But already Kirill was not watching. His comrade had put his foot on a chair and was rolling up a trouser leg. A knife was strapped to his ankle.

We should kill him now, end all this and go home.

His partner was always the same: pig-headed, mulish, dogged, always erring on the violent side of any action. He'd been like that at the sentry post.

But maybe this time, he was right.

*

Beginning to feel like a goldfish, Rick wandered from room to room. He wondered what actions the SIO of the murder team DCI Walsh was prioritising. It was ten-thirty in the morning and felt wrong to be at home. Maggie wanted him to show her how to make beeswax from old frames. She'd swapped her shift to the afternoon, thinking he'd have some spare time.

He watched the dashcam footage over and over, in the vague hope if he studied it long enough, he might see something. Nhung was on the way to technical with a copy. If they were able to enhance the image enough to read a registration plate, it could lead directly to Jack, but even if it didn't, a car hired using false details, or a stolen car, or even stolen plates might be enough to find the boy indirectly.

'We can do the messy stuff outside the front door,' said Maggie. 'Sun's meant to come out this morning.'

Her thinking was flawed. Dashcam aside, if he couldn't make headway finding Jack, he could work on the cold case murder, and also try to prove his own innocence. Either of which could keep a whole team busy. Still, she had taken the morning off to spend time with him, so maybe he could multitask.

The drugs in his car and in their flat had been planted, suggesting the use of an informant – and confirmed by the young PC who'd arrested him for being unfit to drive. An informant would have a name and a phone number. Either, they would have a criminal record and be a covert human intelligence source, or they wouldn't, and be the subject of a protected docket. In both cases, their personal data would be confidential and safeguarded by the informant handling system.

There were four handling systems in Manchester, north, east, south, and west, each run by a controller with the rank of at least DCI.

It was possible Robbo would be able to obtain the information, but even if he could, would be unlikely to do so. However, the controller for the south was DCI Ian Holcroft. Rick and Ian had been on the same DCI's course. Ian was bright, argumentative, and could do a great impression of Winston Churchill.

Maggie opened the front door. Rick got the hint: he carried out a small table and chair. She made coffee and he fetched the large pan and a super of unusable frames stored on top of the kitchen cupboards. He set the pan on the table, the super on the ground.

'Need to make a call, first.' He went back inside, scrolled through his phone contacts, and selected Holcroft.

He waited three or four rings.

'Holcroft.'

'We shall fight on the beaches—'

'Rick!'

'Ian, long time.'

He explained he'd been set up and what he wanted, the phone number used by the informant for the drugs in his car, and if different the source of the information for the search of Maggie's flat.

'I heard you'd been arrested, Rick, and I'm sorry, but you shouldn't be contacting me.'

'Listen, Ian—'

But he'd gone.

Rick went back outside. When Maggie left for work, he'd go and see Ian, talk to him face to face.

He picked up the first frame, knocked off the bottom bars with a hammer, and crumbled the grey friable honeycomb into the pan. He scraped the wooden frame clean with a knife and set it aside. Passing Maggie a knife, he reached for the next frame.

His phone rang. Too soon for technical. Ian, having changed his mind? An update on the boy? If it was Walsh, it would be bad news.

'It's Alison Formby, Mr Castle, Jane's mother. Esra told me about the press conference. I hoped you might have something.' Rick could hear her laboured breathing. 'I haven't got long left.'

'Even if we do find Jane, Mrs Formby, it's very unlikely she'll be—'

'I just want to lay her to rest properly. To find some peace before I go.'

Rick put the phone down.

'That was—'

'I know,' said Maggie. She placed a hand on his arm. She did know. She was police, understood how his cases affected him, energised him, subsumed him, and would, he hoped, understand on all the other cases which would follow.

They deconstructed more frames. He fetched an electric ring and plugged it into an extension cable. He hefted the pan onto the ring, and added water. The pan boiled, and they left it to cool. They talked about Mrs Formby, about Jane Formby, about Jack. Maggie let him talk, and then let him fall silent.

Jane Formby hired a room at the Golden Lion once or twice a week, usually for two hours, occasionally six. Fourteen years ago, 1st December, she'd booked room 14 for two hours. Although she'd been seen by a receptionist to enter the hotel, no member of the hotel staff or any guest had seen her leave. And the victim had not been seen again.

Twenty-nine people who'd been present at the hotel had given accounts to police. No one remembered seeing Jane Formby, or a tall, white male, or didn't want to admit they had. Twenty-one were unwilling to go to court.

Rick's recent press conference had generated nineteen pieces of information, eighteen of which had been disappointing. William Clough was his last hope.

'Need to make another call.'

Maggie nodded. 'It's nice out here. Being with you.' She drank some coffee. Rick wondered what she was really thinking. Making the best of things, or hoping one day he would change, mellow like an old station officer. Maybe over time, Maggie thought she could change him.

He phoned Suzie Clough to make an appointment with her grandfather, and left another voicemail.

Beeswax the colour of custard solidified in the bottom of the pan. Rick removed the waste layer, and Maggie broke up the still-impure beeswax into pieces and put them into a muslin bag. Rick placed this in a second small saucepan inside the large pan of boiling water. The beeswax melted a second time and dripped through the muslin into the saucepan. While it was still a hot liquid, he poured it into an old ice-cream tub.

'We could give blocks as presents, or make candles or lip balm, or add almond oil and make a waterproof boot polish.'

Maggie sat back.

'Oh my God! I've just seen someone climb in through a window.'

'Where?'

She pointed. 'Side of the house, the one with twin satellite dishes. Upstairs window. White man, buzzcut, definitely saw him.'

Rick looked where Maggie was pointing. He couldn't see anyone. He went inside for his binoculars. He couldn't find them. Work bag. Office. Cupboards. Drawers. Kitchen. In the fruit bowl.

He ran back out. Trained the binoculars on the house with twin satellites, on the side window.

'Anything?' Maggie shook her head. 'No, me neither. You're sure?'

'Yes!'

He passed Maggie the binoculars, and phoned the control room. She observed for a few seconds, passed them back.

'No vehicles in the drive, I can't see a van on the road. Oh, no, wait. There's a second guy, or might be the first guy. Carrying a ladder from the back. Young boy with him. He's carrying a bird box. Maggie!'

'Sorree.'

He kissed her on the nose. Phoned the control room and stood them down. Kissed Maggie again.

Still in his hand, the phone rang.

'Suzie Clough,' Rick whispered to Maggie. He waited for Suzie to say her grandfather wasn't well, or had returned to London, or Canada. Instead, they arranged to meet at the university, and as he pocketed the phone he felt the familiar knot in his stomach. William Clough could be the case-breaker.

29

When Maggie went to work, Rick drove to Knutsford. It was a forty-five-minute drive from South Manchester, over an hour at peak times. But, Ian argued, he was less likely to be recognised and harassed there.

Fingers of low sunlight reached through the houses as Rick parked under a spreading oak. Ian lived in a detached house with a double garage. A basketball hoop protruded from the fascia and a Smart car sat on the drive. An empty hanging basket hung in the porch.

Rick eased his seat back and waited. A jogger with red trainers ran past. The streetlights came on. The jogger ran back.

Ian arrived, swinging his car into the drive on the far side of the oak tree.

Rick climbed out. He walked across the grass under the thick branches as Ian manoeuvred around. Rick held up a hand in greeting.

Ian got out of his car.

'You shouldn't have come here, Rick.' He walked towards his house. Behind him, his car's central locking beeped and lights flashed.

Rick followed him to the porch.

'I've been framed.'

The front door opened and a woman with long brown hair stood on the threshold. She held a small child in her arms, and another one stood at her side. 'He's been here ages, Ian.'

'Can I come in?' said Rick. 'Just five minutes, no one will know.'

'Go inside, Jan,' said Ian.

The woman retreated with the children.

Ian pulled the door shut. 'Not here, Rick.' His voice was whispered, strained. 'Christ!' He glanced over his shoulder, looked up and down.

'If you won't help me, Ian, no one will.'

'I'm sorry, Rick.'

'You once said, Ian, you would do anything for me.' Rick paused. 'I wrote most of your final assessment, five thousand words on policing modern society. And you passed, made DCI.' Rick pushed the hanging basket, which squeaked back and forth. 'I might start shouting, or throw something.' He picked up a small pot plant, passed it from hand to hand.

'Please, Rick.' Ian's voice was now faintly whiny. Holcroft feared losing his job, but Rick had lost his. They'd been good friends on the DCI's course, studying together and having the occasional beer.

Rick lobbed the pot plant onto the lawn. The impact caused the terracotta to break, the black humus spilling out and the plant roots lying exposed and vulnerable. It wasn't his finest moment but he was getting desperate – and Ian owed him.

'For God's sake,' said Ian. 'Alright. But I can't access anything here. It's all at work – on a standalone.'

'I'll follow you.'

'Now?'

'Now.'

Ian shook his head and took a deep breath. Shouted, 'Going out.'

Rick shoved the hanging basket and walked back to his car. As the two of them drove away in convoy, the basket was still screeching.

Rick waited in his car at the back of the Manchester Police operations building in Stretford. He sank down in his seat, and watched the minutes tick by on the clock. He cracked the window, needing some more air, even the grimy gases Manchester could offer.

He phoned Maggie.

'Any progress on Jack?'

'I've been reassigned.'

Rick told her where he was and who he was waiting for.

'Aren't you – and me by association – in enough trouble already?'

'I've got to try and prove it's a setup, Mags. I can't just sit at home.' He paused. 'Speaking theoretically, *if* I get a phone number from Ian, will you push it through the system?'

'No!'

Rick slid the phone onto the dash. He wondered if her answer would have been any different if they'd been married. He suspected not.

The passenger door opened.

Ian climbed in, and passed Rick a paper towel from the men's. Opening it out, he found a phone number.

'Only one?'

'Same number, both times. Memorise it.' The informant controller waited a few seconds, then held out a hand.

Rick passed it back.

Ian ripped off the corner showing the phone number and put it in his mouth. He swallowed. Climbed out.

'Thanks,' said Rick. If their situations had been reversed, he would have helped Ian. Sometimes, you had to break the rules to fight for justice, and when you did, you needed your friends to stick by you. Making difficult decisions had been a topic on their DCI's course.

The door slammed.

Only one phone number. The *same* number had been used for both of the calls setting him up.

Rick phoned Maggie again. Across the road, two men were loading a freezer into a van. She didn't answer so he texted. The van drove away, revealing a shop window with a closing-down sale banner.

His phoned beeped.

I told you, no

Paradoxically, he loved her more for it.

He tried Nhung.

'Hello, sir.'

'Can technical do anything with the dashcam?'

'They'll do their best – usual story – but didn't want me to wait. Been busy though: finally lifted Bucur, and his mate. Booked them in, then took Bucur to the bridge near the crash. Asked him to show me where he'd seen the man on the roof. After a bit of pissing about, he seemed fairly sure. However, despite a thorough search, we couldn't find a casing. Couple of fag butts, but old. Do you want me to submit them?'

'You'd better ask DCI Walsh.'

'Bucur had a bag of golf balls for you. Twenty-seven, so you owe me £13.50.'

'What have you done with them?'

'The balls?'

'No! Bucur and co.'

'Charged them with affray and assault, as discussed.'

'Well done.' Not charging Bucur, despite the boy assisting police, would send the wrong message, and endanger officers in the future.

'Nhung?'

'Yes, sir?'

Rick explained he needed a phone number interrogating, which might help prove his innocence.

There was a pause.

'You don't have to, Nhung.' He could – would – find someone else. Nhung still had a long career ahead of her.

'Send it across, sir.'

'Thanks,' said Rick. He typed the number he'd obtained from Ian. Pressed send. Opposite, a man in a lumberjack shirt wheeled out a fridge.

Nhung phoned back. 'Forgot to say, Tara wants a word. But don't phone her at work.'

'Okay.'

'Sir?'

'Yes, Nhung?'

'Good luck, sir.'

The car phone rang. *Louise, CPS.*

They spoke briefly, and Rick agreed. Maggie was working the late shift, and he owed Louise dinner. Just possible she'd know something.

He drove to the Taverna in Lightfields and parked around the back. Louise climbed out of her car.

'I wasn't sure you'd come.'

He was already wishing he hadn't. The CPS senior counsel wore a black sequinned dress and carried a tiny silver handbag. Her legs were encased in shiny tights and glowed like street-lights. Over the top and making a point, and he knew she knew he knew.

They sat in a cubicle at the back, Rick tucked into a corner. The wash of garlic when the kitchen door opened like a salty breeze at the coast. They ordered garlic bread and a bottle of cold white wine. He ate a piece. No law against smelling of garlic. He'd told Maggie he was working late. Not to wait up. He *was* working. A friendly ear in the CPS was always useful. A wet tongue in the ear *from* a friendly CPS not so.

Rick picked up a menu. 'This is on me.'

'For future service?' The queen of double entendre raised a plucked eyebrow. She finished her glass of wine and poured another.

'For your help in sorting out the Carmichaels' file.'

'What about Barney Williams?'

Rick nodded. 'For that, too. You can have a dessert.'

Louise smiled. She finished her wine. 'What kind of dessert?' She raised another eyebrow.

The waiter wandered over.

Rick waited for Louise to order. If he was the perfect gentleman, he wouldn't be there. The waiter scribbled on a pad, and walked away. Rick drank some water. 'You might have heard I've been suspended.'

'I've heard lots of things.' Louise poured more wine.

Rick ate an olive, glanced at the door. He spat the stone into his hand, set it down. Ate another.

'Don't you want to know what else I've heard?'

Rick leant forward. 'Do you know who's set me up?'

'I don't know who.'

'Maybe you could ask around. You know people.'

She laughed. 'Maybe you've forgotten, I work for the Crown Prosecution Service, I prosecute the naughty rascals.'

'You used to do defence. Represented William Redman if I'm not mistaken.' There wasn't much in South Manchester The Big Red didn't know about.

Louise drank more wine, topped up her glass. 'For you, Rick, I'll ask around.' She stared at him.

'What?'

'Don't you find being with Maggie a bit—' She paused, her wine glass held aloft as she searched for a word.

'A bit what?'

'A bit restrictive?'

Louise could be useful, could be fun. But she drank too much, leered too much. He stood up, threw too much money on the table, and walked out.

30

Rick found a note from Maggie on the breakfast table. Plus a recipe for making furniture polish using the beeswax they'd rendered.

1 part beeswax
3 parts olive oil

a) Finely chop beeswax
b) Melt in a double boiler
c) Add the olive oil
d) Pour into a jar and leave to cool and solidify

Happy polishing!

Rick screwed up the piece of paper. He texted Nhung, telling her to phone technical for an update on the dashcam as soon as they were open. He sent a follow up, asking about the phone number he'd squeezed out of Ian. He sent a third to Suzie Clough, reminding her of their meeting at lunchtime.

He made coffee in his car mug, a honey sandwich, and headed out to find Tara. Making furniture polish, he was not.

*

The cavernous L-shaped hall had an arched and windowed roof like a railway terminus. It was light and cool, and the voices of spectators echoed. Steam rose from the baby and toddlers' pool, and the smell of chlorine and dampness hung in the air.

In the foot of the L was the diving pool, boards at one, five, and ten metres. The main pool was fifty metres in length and divided into lanes. In the medium lane, swimmers thrashed up and down, but in the fast lane they glided like dolphins.

Rick sat near the exits to the changing rooms. Troughs of chlorine water were a compulsory barrier, in his memory always freezing cold and harbouring a used plaster and a fag butt. He wondered if Tara was a thrasher or a glider.

He checked on a swimmer in a black bathing costume approaching the exits. She took off her plain white cap and tossed out her hair. Not Tara. He sipped his coffee. There were worse places to be on assignment.

Another woman approached the exits. She stopped to pick up a towel from a bench. She removed her cap, and long black hair tumbled out. Rick raised a hand and stepped down the tiered seating to the front. Drying her hair, the crime scene investigator walked over. Her face was pink from the swim.

'Drink?' said Rick, glancing at his watch.

'Hot chocolate, thanks.' She jogged down the tunnel to the changing room.

Rick bought her drink, two pastries and a packet of sweets at the coffee shop in reception. He sat at a table in the corner, tapping the glass top with a fingernail. The early-morning swimmers bustled in and out, some clutching cycle helmets, one eating a banana. After he'd spoken to Tara, he'd have another crack at the house-to-house around Maggie's flat.

Tara sat down, her face still glowing.

She adjusted the wrapping on the cinnamon bun and took a bite. 'Sorry, starving.' She took the lid off the hot chocolate and stirred in extra sugar. 'A couple of results have come back,' she said between mouthfuls of pastry.

'And?'

'I found a couple of fingerprints on the threatening letter sent to Westbury School. Unfortunately, there's no match on the database. I also got a partial lift from Jack Philipps' phone. Again, no match on the database.' Tara shoved in the last of her pastry, wiped her lips with the serviette.

Rick's bun still sat untouched. He'd been hoping for better news.

'But the thing is, they're from the same person.'

Rick clenched a fist. It meant the kidnapping of Jack Philipps was linked to the letter, and suggested Jack's disappearance was a planned operation.

'Can you push it out?'

Tara raised a thumb.

He passed his pastry over to her, and stood up. The CSI could approach Europol, maybe even the Americans, with the fingerprint.

Invigorated by the information, if not by exercise, Rick set out on a second circuit of the house-to-house. Working at a different time of day, he hoped to catch different people at home, and walking in the opposite direction, hoped to see things he hadn't seen before.

No one answered his knocking at the first three houses. He posted more proformas, marked up his sheet and continued.

An Asian boy in shorts and a grubby t-shirt opened the door at the next house. He was only four or five, but looked at Rick suspiciously.

'Who are you?'

'I'm a policeman.'

The boy ran off, but returned a few moments later with a

man and two more children. Rick showed his old badge and explained why he was calling. Handed out sweets.

The man shook his head.

Rick walked on.

He mulled the new information from Tara. Kidnapping Jack could mean the target was Jack, or more likely, one of his parents. But why send the threatening letter? It pointed to Jack being the sole target. Jack was a public schoolboy, a hormonal tennis ace. It was possible the boy had become involved in something on the dark web, or the grey area alongside: bitcoins, day trading, an investment scam. But financial checks had been negative, and there was nothing on his laptop. Drugs was a possibility, or maybe steroids.

The inconsistency with the letter was that it didn't mention Jack specifically – only the tennis team in general.

He needed a new set of hypotheses, his originals all discounted bar one. G1a, Jack had been kidnapped for money. G1b, Jack had been kidnapped as leverage to make someone do something. G1c, Jack had been kidnapped as revenge.

An estate agent's board had been erected at the front of the next house. It hadn't been there the day before, and it made him think. None of the houses he'd visited were noticeably empty of furniture, but they could be awaiting sale or letting. He phoned the estate agent.

The Rabbetts' receptionist was helpful, and checked their list of rental properties. There were none in Bowker Crescent or Birch Road. She gave him the names of three other local firms. He sat on the garden wall at the front and phoned each one. None had a property to let which fell in his house-to-house parameters.

At the alley leading to Ashmead Drive, he decided on a detour. He walked down the path to the main road, then walked back. It afforded partial views of back gardens and houses on

Ashmead, Birch Road, and Bowker Crescent. Garden fences and hedges were mainly inaccessible except by climbing, but three properties had gates. All three were secured with oldish padlocks, and all three showed signs of occasional use.

He reached Sheila's house. He walked her wheelie bin back to her lean-to and refixed the bungee to stop it blowing over.

A shoe hit the front window.

Rick peered inside. The old woman was already shuffling out of the room.

The door opened. Sheila was only wearing one shoe. 'I thought – well, it doesn't matter what I thought. Do you want to come in?'

Rick helped put her shoe back on. It was more of a slipper, a furry boot without laces.

'Did you ask your daughter?'

'Forgot. You don't want to get old. Forget to breathe, eventually.' She pointed at her phone on the table next to her. 'Number's on the pad.'

The large old-fashioned phone was connected to the lamp so when the phone rang, the light flashed. He pressed the buttons for Sheila's daughter. There was no answer and he left a message.

'What about lunch?' said Rick.

'What about it?'

Rick nosed around the kitchen, and found a small loaf, butter and jam. He fixed a sandwich, cut off the crusts, and cut it into squares. Chewing on the crusts, he left it on the table next to Sheila who'd fallen asleep with her mouth open.

There was no answer at the next door, but the one after was opened by a builder in overalls.

'You're not going to make a habit of this, are you?'

'You said you'd ask your brother.'

Rick could smell cannabis and hear two women laughing. Knife handles protruded from behind a gold-framed mirror.

The builder stepped outside, pulling the door to. 'Yeah, I asked him, said he'd seen something. He was coming back late, about midnight, some big guy dressed in black.'

'Did he see where he went?'

The builder shook his head.

'Where did he see him – exactly?'

'Top end, near Birch. Where all the immigrants and scummers live. But he weren't a freeloader, that's why he remembered. Like a commando he said, big but limping a bit.'

'Did he say when?'

'Week, ten days ago.'

'If he sees—'

'That's your lot, Mr Policeman.' Behind him, more laughing.

Rick walked away. It wasn't the golden ticket, but it was something. He checked his watch – enough time to visit Dad before meeting Suzie Clough and her grandfather at Manchester University.

Rick walked into the reception at Three Views. The smell of boiled vegetables leached down a corridor. Michael sat at the desk, tapping on the computer. A radio sat behind him on a shelf, and a DJ was talking about a new film shot in Manchester.

'There's a female resident in one of the end rooms,' said Rick, 'who's knocking on the window and flashing at passersby.' If it was Steffi Clarke, it would make things simpler.

'That'll be Josephine.'

Michael walked round from behind the desk. 'I'll go and see her. You okay here for a minute?'

Rick nodded, and Michael walked up the corridor. He waited until the care assistant was at the first set of fire doors.

'Michael.'

'Yes, Mr Castle?'

'The video file you emailed me was blank. Do you mind if I have a look?' He nodded at the computer.

'Go ahead. In a folder marked *Monitoring*.' The care assistant pushed through the doors.

Rick sat down on the desk chair, glancing at a mug with Snoopy asleep on top of his kennel. He touched the mouse and the screen woke. The *Monitoring* folder was in the top right corner. He double-clicked it, found the video file for the date in question, double-clicked, chose the last option.

A message flashed up on the screen: *Are you sure?*

He clicked yes. Then found, and deleted, Michael's email to Rick. Finally, deleted it from the deleted folder.

Stuck to the edge of the screen was a yellow post-it with the day's menu. *Pasta Bolognese, fruit salad.* He glanced again at Michael's mug. Snoopy would be uncomfortable on top of the kennel. Why had the dog not hauled the mattress out of his kennel and lain on that? Rick thumbed the papers propped up against the computer and pulled out a hardback notebook marked, *Patient Notes, Confidential.* An elastic kept it shut.

Rick glanced at the fire doors but there was no sign of the care assistant. He slipped off the elastic. The notebook was the A–Z type. He turned to the letter C. Canning, Carter, Castle, Clarke. *Stephanie Clarke, next of kin, Paul Clarke (son) who lives in South Africa. Stephanie has a history of seducing other residents, often in an inappropriate way. The problems arising from this behaviour have led to her staying in a succession of care homes in the last five years.*

Rick hoped his dad had had some fun. Not his fault he couldn't remember, but the consequences painful to those who could.

He turned back a page. *Roger Castle, next of kin, Maureen Castle. Two children, Rick Castle and Rebecca Williams. Roger is suffering from early onset Alzheimer's. Very little short-term memory.* ** *Note* ** *Rick Castle works for Manchester Police, Detective Chief Inspector – will NEVER take no for an answer.*

The fire doors banged shut. Rick closed the book, snapped the elastic back in place, and stood up.

Michael walked behind the desk.

Rick lowered his voice. 'I was wondering if you could move Stephanie Clarke to your sister care home, Grand View.'

'I could ask, but I don't really have the authority.'

'Sit down, Michael.'

The care assistant sat down.

'Does your employer know your history? Your alias of Michael Mason?'

Michael looked away. He screwed up the post-it with the lunch menu and threw it in the refuse bin.

'I didn't think so. I could make a fuss. Tell your employer, and ask them to check the accounts here.'

'I've changed.'

Rick hoped he had – Michael was a kind, thoughtful care assistant. 'Move Stephanie Clarke to Grand View, and I'll probably forget all about it.' He wouldn't, and he would check. Rehabilitation of offenders was statistically unlikely, but possible.

'What about the CCTV?'

'Gone. There's no complaint from the victim, so all that remains is one person's word against another.'

Michael J Howell aka Michael Mason nodded slowly.

'I'll go and tell Dad he'll be allowed out in a day or two.' Rick walked away, down the corridor towards Dad's room. Everyone had a history. Everyone.

31

The Manchester University canteen was as busy as a marathon drinks station. Students queued at the tills in noisy abandon. The specials board offered burger and chips, and apple pie and cream. The juice bar was leaking onto the floor. New Order played on university radio from overhead speakers. In the middle of the room a man was doing a headstand on a table and playing the recorder. The fire exit was propped open, and two women with multiple piercings were selling tickets. Cool air wafted inside the room. The mood was upbeat, slightly unhinged: anything might happen.

'Detective Castle?'

Rick nodded.

A small young woman with long red hair and a wicked smile stood in front of him. Behind her, an old man with a walking stick.

'This is Grandpa Bill.'

Rick shook the man's hand. It was white, cold, liver-spotted. He wore a thick black coat and a black hat. 'Thank you for agreeing to meet me, sir.' The old man nodded, seemed about to say something, but coughed into a handkerchief.

Rick looked around for a table. A group were standing up in the corner, pushing and shoving like loons. It brought back good memories. Carefree days, interesting discussions, laughing till his stomach muscles ached.

He walked over, and cleared it of food wrappers and soft-drinks bottles. 'If you don't mind getting us something to eat, Suzie, I can talk to Bill.' He held up a twenty-pound note.

She grinned as if he'd requested a squirrel sandwich.

Rick helped her grandfather stash his walking stick. The old man sat down heavily, coughed into his handkerchief. The next table of students looked across.

'Mr Clough—'

'Call me Bill.'

'Bill. Are you okay?'

The old man nodded.

'Why were you staying in the Golden Lion hotel, sir?' It was a test for competence. Rick wanted to check the old man could remember without being prompted by his relations.

'Christmas. I came for Christmas.' Bill coughed, glanced at Rick and scowled. 'Staying with my son and his wife in south London, Battersea. But there was a problem at Heathrow and my plane was diverted to Manchester.'

His granddaughter returned. She passed around sandwiches and cups of coffee, and sat down. Opened a plastic packet for her grandfather.

The old man sipped his coffee. 'As I was saying, I landed in Manchester. The only place I could find to stay was the Golden Lion hotel. Maybe, it was a scam by the taxi driver. Ridiculously expensive.'

'It's a prostitutes' hotel, Bill. Rooms rented by the hour.'

'What? I didn't know that. I left very early the next day. Caught a new flight to London.'

'Bill, I'm investigating the murder of a woman who was last seen in the Golden Lion on 1st December, 2003. She was staying in room fourteen. Her body still hasn't been found, but we think she was murdered that night – in the hotel.'

'She was a—'

'She was.'

'I wasn't—'

'No. Do you remember what room you had?'

'Twelve.'

Rick's throat was dry. He drank some coffee. 'I'm sorry to have to tell you this, Bill, but you were in the room next door.'

Suzie gripped her grandfather's arm. 'That's awful.'

'I didn't see anything,' said the old man. 'I don't remember seeing anyone, except for the woman on reception.'

Rick stayed quiet. The old man had put himself back there, in the next room, on the first night of December in 2003.

A student on the next table backed out his chair, jogging their table and spilling their drinks. The moment ruined.

The student shrugged, and slouched away. Rick shoved the chair back under the adjacent table, sat back down.

'I did hear a bit of a kerfuffle in the next room. Woke me up in fact. The whole place was noisy, compared to what I'm used to at home in Canada. The street noise, I mean. Cars, people shouting late into the night.'

Suzie poured sugar into her coffee. Rick felt he could hear the individual grains falling into the water. The swish of the spoon, one way, then the other.

'A kerfuffle?'

'I did finally get to sleep, then people in the next room woke me up again. Must have been about four or five by then. Because I was thinking I would get up at six, and head straight to the airport.'

'Was the noise from different rooms, or the same room?'

'Same room. Room fourteen. I checked when I left, I was thinking about complaining. I didn't hear a woman, though. I heard two men arguing, and that was it. Hushed tones, but arguing, and moving stuff around. I thought at the time they were packing, and leaving even earlier than me.'

Rick felt a squeeze in his neck.

'What did they say, Grandpa?'

'That was the thing,' said her grandfather. 'I don't know. They were speaking in a foreign language. Russian, I think.'

'What makes you say that?' said Rick. The second time in a week he'd heard the word *Russian*.

'Films, maybe. Or the news.'

'I know it's a long time ago, but can you remember any specific words?'

'*Nyet*, that means no, I think. Quite a lot of *nyet*. A few times, one or other said *da*. That's yes.'

'Anything else?'

Shaking his head, the old man coughed into his handkerchief. 'Wait. There was one word they did keep using. Struck me as odd at the time. It sounded like an English word, but an everyday one. Any. Eeney. Easter. Eating. No, none of them. It might come to me. As I said, they used it a few times.'

'How many?'

'Five, six, I don't know. I wasn't counting.'

'This could be important.'

Suzie waved her hand to indicate Rick to go slowly. He was going slowly!

'E-e-e. Eejit. That's Irish! I want to say elephant, but it wasn't elephant. Maybe two e's.'

'Maybe if I take him for a stroll?' said Suzie.

Rick shook his head. He wanted to keep Bill in the moment. The old man had closed his eyes and was muttering to himself.

'E-e-e-e-eager. That's it! Eager. The word they said five or six times. I remember now, I couldn't understand what they were so eager about in the middle of the night, but I wanted to be asleep, and I wasn't thinking straight, and it can't have been an English word.'

'But sounded like eager?'

'I'm not sure. I mean, I'm sure that's the word I've been trying to remember.'

'Okay, well done, Bill, well done.' Rick wasn't certain what it meant, if anything, but the old man had tried. 'Bill, one more thing. You say you heard two men talking, arguing – was that both times you were woken up?'

The old man thought for a moment. 'No. Only the second time. The first time I just heard people moving, moving furniture maybe.'

'How long for – both times?'

'I don't know. I was trying to sleep. Five, ten minutes the first time, longer the second. They kept on arguing.'

Rick remembered being in the hotel room with Elliot Tipper, the crime scene manager. His hypothesis was developing. The suspect had panicked, had called a friend. They'd argued, and together they'd moved the body. But where?

'If you remember anything else.'

'Of course.'

'And you definitely didn't see them?'

'Nope. As I said.'

'Did you see anything odd when you left the hotel so early?'

'No. Not really.'

'What do you mean, not really?'

'It was annoying more than anything. I called a cab, but it couldn't get near the hotel because of a line of trucks queued up. Big trees on the back of them. So I was hanging around, worrying I was going to miss my rearranged flight.'

Rick pulled out a file. 'You okay to make a statement?'

'Sure thing, cowboy.' The old man glanced at the next table. 'Still a bit peckish, though.'

At the counter, Rick bought three plates of apple pie and cream. If Bill Clough wanted a whisky chaser, he only had to say the word. Just not cowboy.

Pupils streamed through the gates of Tower Girls School. The younger pupils ran around, screeching and giggling. Like birds of prey, cars swooped alongside, hovered, and sped away with protesting offspring. Most of the older pupils walked away quickly, but some hung in the shadows. A clutch of them grouped around a boy on a scooter, three or four stood behind a blue car with darkened windows. They removed their ties, lit cigarettes.

Rick surveilled for Victoria Parsons. He felt like a drug pusher, at best a voyeur. One day he might be waiting for his own daughter. A younger version of Maggie?

There was no sign of her. The blue car wheelspun away, and at the top of the road U-turned, and drove back with hip-hop playing at full volume.

A new wave of girls poured out of the gates.

Twice in a week, he'd come across a Russian connection for his cases. Victoria Parsons had said the main tennis opponent of Jack Philipps was possibly Russian, and now Bill Clough thought the men in Jane Formby's room were speaking Russian. It was also possible they'd killed her. What, if anything, did Jack and Formby have in common?

He drew two overlapping circles in his notebook. He titled one, *Jack,* and one, *Formby.* Then populated them with everything he knew. *Tennis, Westbury School, seventeen years old. High-class prostitute, twenty-five, studying business as a mature student.* The area in the middle remained blank – they had nothing in common. They were as unlike as salt and pepper, but like salt and pepper, they were connected.

He looked around again for Victoria.

A second scooter turned up and parked alongside the first.

The rider took off his helmet, and Rick recognised Boyle, a development nominal. Burglary, drugs, on bail for a stabbing.

Both Jack Philipps and Jane Formby were white. Both were victims of crime. He wrote the commonalities in the overlap of the circles.

He surveyed the last trickle of girls leaving school.

Could the same people be responsible for the murder of Formby and the kidnap of Jack? It seemed unlikely. Perhaps they both had dabbled in the dark web, fallen to a bitcoin scam. He was getting carried away. He drew a mountain and a molehill. The Russian connection was tiny. Insignificant.

But it was still a connection and itched like a bee sting.

Spotting Jack's tennis partner, he climbed out and started to cross the road.

'Victoria!'

She backed away.

'Get away from me! Stalker!'

Rick stopped in the middle of the road, looked around. She was talking to him. A car bore down, and Rick jogged back to the pavement.

Victoria was surrounded by girls, one of them making an obscene sign in his direction.

Rick returned to his car and drove away. He wasn't sure what had just gone on. Maybe one day he'd understand the angst and capriciousness of teenage girls.

His phone rang.

'It's Victoria.'

'Are you okay?'

'Sorry about that, Mr Castle, but girls talk. And no way could I be seen with an old man.'

Maybe he should have shaved. 'I need to speak to you.'

'There's a carpet shop on the main road, meet me in the carpark round the back.'

Two minutes later, Rick parked next to a vast skip overflowing with carpet offcuts and scraps of underlay. The shop had been extended at the back, and a sign promised regular security patrols. He doubted it.

Victoria Parsons appeared around the side. She was alone. Carrying a rucksack, headphones plugged.

Rick climbed out of his car, and leant back against the driver's door.

'Have you found Jack?' said Victoria, removing her earplugs.

Rick shook his head.

'Have you found his—'

'No, nothing like that. I wanted to ask you something. The opponent of Jack you mentioned, his main rival in the north of England, you thought he might be Russian?'

She nodded. 'His family are super-rich – oil, I think Jack said. Always has lots of racquets and amazing kit.'

'Do you know his name?'

'Vol… Volk…'

'Volkov?'

'Something like that.'

Rick vaguely thought he'd heard of an oligarch called Volkov, but knew it was a very common Russian surname.

'Can I drive you home?' He nodded at the overfull skip. 'You can cover yourself in bits of carpet.'

Victoria walked round to the passenger door. 'Someone knows you're police.' She opened the door. 'So you don't count.'

After dropping Victoria Parsons at home, Rick drove round the corner and parked up. He sat his laptop on the passenger seat and typed Volkov and Russian oligarch into the search engine.

Rick whistled.

Semion Volkov ran a huge energy company with links to the Russian mafia and the Kremlin. Numerous hits, even a Wikipedia entry. There were newspaper articles, websites for the Volkov companies, stock market valuations. Like anyone else, he started with Wikipedia.

The photograph showed a dark-haired man in an open-necked shirt. He looked surprisingly young. Volkov had been educated at Harrow. Married four times, two children. His daughter was an accountant who worked for the family business. His son Igor also worked for Volkov, his role undefined. Volkov's personal fortune was estimated at five billion US dollars.

He tried the PNC. There might be intel but behind a more secure firewall. He emailed a check to General Registry. Knew it would take a day or two.

He tabbed back to the internet and searched again.

He found a grandson.

Whistled again.

Rurik Volkov was Igor's only son, Semion's only grandson. He was a keen tennis player, attended school in England. Rick clicked on the link for Igor Volkov.

A Swedish newspaper report filled the screen. From the *Stockholm Times* ten years previously.

State prosecutors want to question thirty-year-old Igor Volkov, son of the billionaire Russian Semion Volkov, about an allegation of serious sexual assault on a Swedish woman aged nineteen. However, they fear Igor Volkov has returned to Russia, and will never face justice due to the lack of an extradition treaty.

Rick whistled a few bars of the theme tune to *The Great Escape*.

As far as he knew, Russia did not extradite its citizens anywhere. His brain went into overdrive. His cold case involved a murder, possibly a rape. His new witness William Clough had heard Russian voices. Fourteen years earlier, Igor Volkov would have been twenty-six.

He took a screenshot and emailed it to Maggie. Asked her to try contacting the Swedish OIC as a matter of urgency.

It was possible Igor Volkov was responsible for the murder of Jane Formby. And it might explain why someone was trying so hard to get him suspended. Someone with deep pockets, or the son of someone with deep pockets.

He felt cold.

But what had Jack Philipps and the tennis team got to do with it? Tennis rivalry between the two schoolboys seemed too trivial. Then again, billionaires thought they ruled the world, and increasingly, they were right.

His phone rang. Nhung's name on the screen.

'Dashcam?'

'Not yet. Telecoms, though, on the number you gave me. It's a burner phone. Mainly calls to another burner phone. Only three other calls, the first three weeks ago, the second ten days ago to Manchester Police drugs information line, and the third, again to our drugs line, the day before you were arrested at home. You know about the second and third, the calls to police regarding the drugs in your car and home.'

'The same informant for both my arrests. What about the first call?'

'A bit odd. It's a shop in a backstreet near Piccadilly. Serious Games they're called. Model soldiers, board games, puzzles. I thought everybody was online now, but apparently not. No website, no social media presence. I had to phone them up.'

'Did you say who you were?'

'I didn't, sir.'

'Thanks, Nhung. I'll go and see them.'

Rick shut the laptop and started the car. He weaved through the backroads of the suburb, veered into the traffic on the ring road and headed for Piccadilly, wishing he had a blue light to stick on the roof.

32

Glass fragments from the boarded-up door of Serious Games lay on the pavement.

Rick entered, an old-fashioned bell tinkling. The shop was badly lit and smelt of dust. In front of him a large glass cabinet contained a world war two scene: a battered and bombed French street with a café-tabac on the corner. Halfway along stood a roadblock secured by half a dozen Resistance fighters. Approaching were German half-tracks and infantrymen, the painted soldiers a centimetre high.

He walked further into the shop. A black cat ran up and nestled against his leg. The nearest shelf held boxes of scale models – aircraft, tanks, personnel carriers. At the back was the cash desk and above it shelves of jigsaw puzzles. A 2,000-piece Eiffel Tower, a fruit bowl, the Norfolk coast. Five thousand pieces to make a plate of baked beans. Next to the till and a box of Star Wars stickers, a game of chess was underway.

A man about sixty appeared from a doorway behind the desk. He wore a brown bucket hat and a green cardigan with holes in the elbows. Hands in grey fingerless gloves clutched a cup of tea. Through the doorway, steep wooden stairs led to the first floor.

'DCI Castle.'

Rick showed his old badge, and explained he was investigating a murder and searching for a kidnapped boy.

The man set the mug down on the desk, spilling the tea. Faffed around with a tissue.

Someone tapped down the stairs.

A woman appeared. She was of a similar age to the man and her hair was turning grey. She tutted at the mess, and disappeared for a few seconds before returning with a cloth.

After wiping up, she looked across at Rick. 'How can help?' Her first language not English, her accent eastern European. Russian?

As Rick explained for a second time, the man studied the chessboard, picked up a rook and set it down again.

'The phone call was three weeks ago today,' said Rick. 'At two-thirty in the afternoon.'

The woman shook her head.

Rick glanced back over his shoulder. 'What happened to the door?'

The woman muttered to herself. Then opened a large desk diary and flicked back to the relevant date. 'Ah!' she said, pointing to the sole entry for the day, a name underlined and circled. Even upside down, Rick could read *Mr Smith*. It was hardly original.

'Remember now. I spoke on phone and he come shop later in week. Shut door very hard when go.'

Rick glanced up for a camera but couldn't see one. 'What did he want?'

'Jigsaw Big Ben. He ask it on phone, and I tell him we have. Very popular tourist. He come shop a few days later and buy. He was big man. Not want change.'

Rick's disappointment over the lack of CCTV was compounded by the cash payment. One step forward, two-thirds of a step back.

'Can you describe him?'

'Big.'

Next to her, the man screeched. It sounded painful, part bat, part parrot. He remained fixated on the chessboard.

On impulse, Rick picked up a white castle and moved it two spaces forward.

The man considered fleetingly, then moved a rook diagonally, knocking over a white pawn.

'It's my name,' said Rick.

'Nikolai not stupid,' said the woman.

Rick recalibrated. He'd mentioned his name once, yet both of the old couple had remembered it. 'This line of enquiry is really important in our investigation. You say he was big, but—'

Nikolai screeched again.

'Apology,' said the woman.

'I get it,' said Rick. He studied the chessboard and to unblock his queen, moved forward a pawn. As soon as his hand retracted, Nikolai moved his knight and knocked over Rick's rook.

'Was he English? I mean, did he speak with an accent?' He looked across at the woman, wanting to judge the truthfulness of her reply.

'Not English. Perhaps Russian. Perhaps Belarusian.'

Rick moved a pawn on the chessboard like an automaton, as he thought through the coincidences and possible connections. The implications, if she was telling the truth, and if she wasn't. He wondered again about the broken door. In his experience, old women made the best liars. He remembered Mrs Grieve lying for Calix Coniston on a train.

'Do you think you've still got the banknotes the big man paid with?' Most transactions were by card so again he was hopeful.

The woman shook her head. 'I go—'

Her husband screeched.

Rick took Nikolai's knight with his queen. His fingers had hardly uncoiled when Nikolai removed Rick's queen with his own. He didn't care, just needed to last a couple more moves.

'I go bank every week.'

Rick moved another pawn.

Nikolai moved his queen. 'Check.'

Rick ignored him. Nikolai was an eastern European name, and the old couple had eastern European accents, possibly Russian.

He walked behind the cash desk, and pushed past them. Ducked into the doorway and ran up the stairs, his feet punching the wooden boards. He emerged into a dark and drab hallway. Four doors were part-closed.

'Jack?'

Voices sounded at the bottom of the stairs.

Rick opened a door. A dark green bathroom, smelling strongly of pine. On the wall hung an intricate pattern of stitching: a love heart connected the names Nikolai and Iva. He checked the cupboard. Rain was striking the windows.

He backtracked, chose another door. Shouted for Jack again. Yanking it, he entered a room filled with boxes. Behind them, a single bed with the blanket thrown back. The bottom sheet felt warm. He checked under the bed, and behind the door.

Two rooms to go. He opened a third door. There was a small table and two scratched metal chairs. A lamp, books. More boxes. A window was open, the pane cracked. It was raining hard.

Final door. He was losing hope.

He pushed it open, entered. Another bedroom: single bed, covers thrown back. An old chest of drawers, a dark brown and buckled wardrobe. A heap of women's shoes. Drawn curtains, the smell of sleep. Rick switched on the light, drew the curtains. The rain was hammering. He checked the few person-sized spaces.

No Jack, no sign of Jack.

He returned downstairs.

'I thought I heard something.'

Screeching, the old man nodded at the chessboard.

Rick toppled the white king.

He took out his phone, and scrolled through the images until he found the best one from Stransby's dashcam footage. He held it up to the old woman. 'Is that him, Iva?'

She shrugged. 'Maybe.'

He had another thought. '*What* did he say?'

The old woman sat down on a chair. 'He say it was birthday present. Friend is sixty.'

Rick checked Semion Volkov's entry on Wikipedia. The Russian oligarch would be sixty in a few months.

Rick righted the white king. He moved the white queen, a white rook, and both castles. 'Checkmate.' He'd long ago stopped playing by the rulebook.

He drove home. Raining cats and dogs. Vehicles moved slowly through flooded sections of road and left wakes like boats. Soaked pedestrians hurried over crossings and sheltered in bus stops and shop doorways. Slicks of filthy water overflowed the gutters. A pub was flooded and sandbags were being filled. The war spirit.

The man who'd abducted Jack Philipps looked like the man who'd phoned and visited Serious Games and purchased a puzzle of Big Ben; the phone number used to phone Serious Games was the same number used to phone the police information line and give false drugs information regarding Rick – *twice*. The same fingerprints on Jack's phone and the threatening letter connected the kidnapping to the shooting at the minibus. Fourteen years earlier, the witness William Clough had heard Russian voices in the adjacent hotel room.

He wondered if it was *all* connected: the cold case murder of Jane Formby, the planting of the drugs, and the kidnapping of Jack Philipps. Semion Volkov behind it all. The Russian billionaire had the money, the power, the antecedents. His son Igor had previous for serious sexual assault in Sweden. His grandson Rurik was a tennis rival of Jack Philipps.

Rick's reopening of the cold case gave a motive to Volkov to discredit Rick, and have the case return to obscurity.

But why kidnap Jack Philipps? Could a tennis competition really be the explanation? Hypothesis G1d: Jack had been kidnapped to incapacitate him.

Experience told him it could. Gangs killed for the slightest of slights: a facial expression, bad mouthing, talking to the gang's girl. Russian mafia wouldn't think twice.

He'd connected the dots. But connecting the dots didn't bring Rick any closer to catching the people responsible. A two- or three-man Russian cell, he guessed, sent by Volkov to the UK. Or to finding Jack.

Connecting the three cases gave one significant advantage: a lead on any one of them would help solve them all.

But he still needed a breakthrough.

A mile from Maggie's flat, Rick stopped at a pedestrian crossing. He'd braked in plenty of time, but the car behind had been close, and he checked his rearview. The car was still close, really close. He eased forward another metre, but the car behind kept coming –

And *bang*.

The car behind collided.

Rick's car bounced forward and back and stopped for a second time. The impact speed was minimal, and he doubted there was any damage. Nevertheless, he climbed out to check who the idiot was behind him. An early lesson as a probationer – road traffic offence, think crime – still stuck.

As he squeezed the door shut, a van drove alongside and stopped in the centre of the road, half in his lane, half in the oncoming. A second idiot.

The side door opened, and a man jumped out.

'Get in.'

Accent? One thing for certain, Rick wasn't getting in. He considered his options: run, fight, or argue.

He shoved the man back and ran.

Helter-skelter, between the two vehicles. The van's passenger door flew open –

Knocking Rick to the ground.

The man behind was on him like a rabid dog.

Rick thrashed out.

A second man arrived to assist. Rick kept thrashing, one fist colliding with a jaw, one knee with a crotch.

Sensing movement behind him, Rick jerked his head to try to see. Around to the left, to the right. To the left.

The world went dark.

33

Let's chop off a couple of the boy's fingers and go home. He can't play tennis if he can't hold the racquet.

Patience, said Andrei.

Kirill leant down and plucked his knife from the strap around his calf. Started cleaning his fingernails. He glanced at Andrei, and knowing he was being watched, set two of his fingers on the edge of the table and pretended to saw with the knife.

Andrei poured more vodka into their glasses and took his over to the kitchen window. The grass was wet with moisture, the trees were dripping. Britain was drowning. He stared into the colourless liquid. Thought of previous operations when they'd been in the special forces, and since they'd left. Kirill would never change. Andrei rubbed his aching leg, and for a few seconds was back at the sentry post. Watching Kirill climb the tower, waiting for his signal, entering the bunker . . . shooting the sleeping men.

It's job done, said Kirill. Castle will be disgraced – the British prefer investigating state impropriety than misdemeanours by their people. Jack Philipps can be injured so he can't play, we've even got a birthday present for Semion. We no have to wait until the Northern Cup has finished. Let's go home.

Andrei emptied his glass into the sink. A change of plan was always to be expected, and although they'd made the backup work, it was far from ideal. The root problem was Semion's insistence on two missions. It confused things. Former soldiers were no different to soldiers in preferring one clear mission. Then again, only himself to blame for a third mission, and making things even worse.

He turned around.

'*Nyet.*' Semion didn't want the boy to be assaulted. He made that clear. The Kremlin made it clear to him. Assaults and serious injuries attract too much attention.

What about the boys who were injured in the minibus, and the boy who died? That was our intention for Philipps. And it was headline news.

'*Avariya.*' Accident.

Eh?

The minibus had a puncture, stopped suddenly, and a car driver piled into the back. We cannot be blamed – by the British, by the Kremlin, or by Semion.

Andrei turned back to the window. He preferred shoot 'em up operations, the enemy easily defined, in and out quickly. He stared at the dripping trees, the washed-out sky. He could hear Kirill's heavy breathing and the steady knocking from the closet in the hall.

The boy was a problem.

Castle another problem.

Kirill a third.

*

Rick came to.

Water was being splashed on his face.

He sat up, rubbed away the loose drops. He was at the base of a tree, and his hands were secured with plasticuffs. The type used

251

by specialist police units, the military, and the intelligence service. His shoes were missing. Pine trees all around. It was cold, and gloomy. His neck was stiff and his wrists sore. He moved his head from side to side and up and down.

The man who'd poured the water stepped forward and sawed through the plasticuffs with a serrated penknife. The pieces fell to the ground. He wore jeans and a stained sweatshirt. Trainers. Looked like he'd been rooting around in the bins outside a charity shop. He proffered the bottle.

Rick drank, handed it back. The skin where the plasticuffs had gripped was puffy and red. He flexed and loosened his fingers.

The man retreated to a line of three vehicles and two small groups of people. Mostly men, but there was one woman. Rick could smell their cigarette smoke, and hear faint voices.

The cars and the van were parked in a turning circle at the end of a rough track in the middle of a wood. Tree stumps flanked the track. Two lines of deep ruts requiring four-wheel drive led further into the wood.

Four men and the woman formed a raggedy circle around the nearest car, an old dark blue Mondeo. One wore a green anorak with toggles, the others wore greys and browns. They looked unremarkable. Almost invisible on a station platform, or in a café, or walking down a street. Which was the point. Two men stood a little further away. They weren't talking, and gave the impression they'd run out of things to say. Or maybe they hadn't said much in the first place. The older man wore a V-neck sweater and glasses, and looked like an academic. His colleague, the only person who looked official, wore a thick pinstriped suit, as if he was a broker.

Rick stood up, stretched.

Sat on a tree stump.

He felt tired, but had no idea whether that was from being

knocked out, or the distance they'd travelled, or both. They could be in the National Forest, or in Scotland. Red marks on some of the trees indicated they were to be kept alive, or they were to be felled.

The academic and the broker walked towards him, and the others stopped talking and turned to watch. Intelligence officer and murder team inspector.

'You can call me Harry,' said the former. 'And this is DCI Fraser Walsh from murder team seven. He picked up the minibus job.'

Chewing gum as furiously as a losing football manager, the pinstriped man stepped forward. He was used to being in charge.

But Harry was in charge, and Rick addressed the older man.

'You could have asked to meet.'

Walsh made a regurgitating noise.

Harry grinned as if he was attending a summer garden party. 'How can I put this generously – you have a reputation for thinking for yourself.'

Rick took it as a compliment. He knew why they were meeting in a wood – no one could be listening, and no one could be watching.

'And you're a pain in the arse,' said Walsh. The detective looked like a broker but chewed and spoke like a football fan.

Harry said nothing for a couple of seconds. He and Walsh wouldn't share a beer if they were the last ones standing. Which might be useful to know.

'Apologies,' said Harry. 'You're here, Rick, because your search at registry for Semion Volkov raised a red flag with us.' Harry spoke carefully, his voice soft. 'I need you to tell me why you're interested.'

Rick glanced at the onlookers, and down the track. He'd once watched a TV programme about woods. How the side of the tree the lichen grew indicated north – or was it south? The type of lichen revealed the latitude.

'I haven't got it all yet.'

'Tell us what you do have.'

'I think Semion Volkov the Russian oligarch is connected to the minibus crash and kidnap of Jack Philipps; also to the historic murder of Jane Formby; *and* to my arrest for possession of drugs. The drugs were planted to derail my investigation of Formby's murder.'

Rick expanded on the detail, and when he'd finished, Harry turned to Walsh.

'Sounds a bit fantastical to me.'

'The Russians have their own style,' said Harry, 'blunt but effective.' He turned back to Rick. 'Where's the dashcam footage?'

Rick felt in his pockets. His phone, keys and wallet were missing. 'With technical.' He glanced at Walsh, who was unwrapping another piece of gum, and back at Harry. 'What can you tell me? Tell us?'

'You're currently suspended, so not much.' He turned to Walsh. 'Keep me updated, Fraser.'

Walsh chewed furiously.

'Rick, you'll be staying indoors, but let me know immediately if our Russian visitors call you out to play.'

Rick nodded.

'And just to be clear to both of you, we need to find the boy, apprehend our visitors, and neutralise the threat to national security.' Harry glanced at Walsh, then back at Rick. 'We're all on the same team, but national security takes priority over the investigation of criminal offences. Are we agreed, gentlemen?'

'Agreed,' said Walsh.

'Agreed,' said Rick. He wasn't crossing his fingers, but he certainly wasn't going to be staying indoors, literally or metaphorically.

'Okay, Fraser, to give Rick a lift home?'

Walsh nodded.

'No hard feelings, I hope, Rick.' Harry extended a gloved hand. Rick shook, thinking the veiled hand reflected the entire meeting.

Harry turned to his colleagues and drew a circle in the air. One of them brought over Rick's shoes, and the others climbed into the van. He and Harry climbed into the Mondeo, and the vehicles trundled away down the track.

The second car manoeuvred closer.

Rick laced up his shoes.

Walsh climbed in and the passenger window buzzed down.

'Sorry, Rick, stuff on the back seat.'

Walsh dropped Rick's keys on the ground, the window pulled up, and the car bumped away down the track.

'Fuck you, Fraser.'

Rick ran after it, stooping to pick up a clod of muddy peat and hurl it at the back windscreen. It thumped home and slid down until it came to rest on the windscreen wiper.

The car increased speed, Rick fell back, the car rounded a corner and disappeared. He drew up. Had no idea how far it was to the nearest road, how far the road was from Manchester.

Silence came surprisingly quickly.

Then hidden birds. Another time, he might enjoy the solitude. But Jack was in danger, and despite Harry and Fraser's efforts, every minute might count.

Loosening his tie, he set off again, and jogged for a few minutes. At least they'd left him his shoes. Pale sunlight filtered through the canopy, and the temperature was dropping.

He slowed to a fast walk, his city shoes slipping on the wet ground. He still couldn't hear traffic or see telegraph poles. He could hear only birds and the occasional aeroplane, see only pine trees.

The track reached a junction and the trailer of a lorry stacked with denuded tree-trunks. But no signpost. Rick was thirsty, hungry, tired. He was concerned for Jack and hoped Walsh was top of the league for investigative ability.

He heard the grumble of a lorry. He headed uphill, towards the sound. The track crested a rise, and headed down again. Still no sign of a road or a house. The track widened and drainage channels appeared at the sides. It crossed a river, and curled upwards on the far side.

At the new crest of the track, he saw the road. A timber lorry and trailer were disappearing around a bend.

He hurried on. At the road, it was fifty-fifty as to which direction to head. He chose uphill, making it easier for vehicles to see him and stop.

No vehicles passed. He wondered if Harry had spoken to Robbo, and leaving him in the middle of nowhere was a joint enterprise. As soon as he got home, he would have a third sweep at the house-to-house. The only lead which didn't require access to the police station.

He looked up and down, strained his ears.

No signpost, no vehicles.

He reached the top of the hill. The road curved round, straightened, and after half a mile, reached a straggle of houses and farms.

He sped up.

A man was smoking outside the first house. It was the end of a line of terraces abutting the road, their downpipes pasted with reflective yellow chevrons. The front door was ajar and pop music drifted out.

'Where am I?' said Rick.

'Costa Rica,' said the man. He was young, wearing a t-shirt and baggy trousers. He was tapping his bare foot against the doorjamb.

'Really.'

The man glanced at Rick's filthy shoes and trousers. Raised an eyebrow.

'Are you high?' said Rick. Sometimes he wondered if he was the only person who wasn't.

The man threw down the end of his cigarette. 'You're in Rookpit, part of the black peak. Next valley over calls us Armpit. Affectionately, like.'

'I need a lift.'

'Where?'

'Manchester.'

'Have you escaped from somewhere?'

Rick feinted with a shoulder.

The man flinched. 'Ha, ha.' He lit another cigarette. 'It's like you've come down from space.'

'I'll pay you.'

The man turned and went inside. Closed the door.

Rick sat on the doorstep. He was exhausted. He heard water gush into a drain in the road. Opposite was a small community hall with a child's picture of a rainbow in the window. Another timber lorry strained past. A Scottish flag was draped at the back of the driver's cab.

Behind the row of terraces a car started. Conked out. Restarted.

The Costa Rica joker?

A small grey car emerged from the far end of the terraces and drove towards Rick. It stopped alongside him and the passenger door was pushed open. The seat was crowded with rubbish, the footwell full of clobber. The man still wore nothing on his feet.

They set off, the direction Rick had arrived.

'Why are you doing this?' he said, after a few minutes.

'I'm a writer,' said the driver, 'and you're manna from heaven.'

34

Rick unlocked the front door and stepped over a padded envelope on the doormat. He found some cash in a drawer and returned outside to pay his driver. The writer honked and the small grey car drove away.

In the kitchen he emptied the envelope on the table, his wallet and mobile tumbling out. He powered up the phone. Drank a glass of water while it beeped with arriving messages. A text from Maggie, *Where are you?* Two voicemails. The first from a woman who said she was Sheila's daughter. Neighbour Sheila? A second from Robbo, telling him to call.

He'd do better than that: he'd pay him a visit.

Parked up behind the police station, Rick could see the barrier to the backyard in his rearview mirror. Half the marked bays were occupied, including Robbo's. The black Range Rover gleamed, and as usual, sat positioned for a quick getaway.

Rick eased his seat back.

He texted Maggie. *Tell you later. X*

A builder's van parked nearby, and two men climbed out. One tossed an apple core in the gutter and the other brushed down his dusty trousers. They walked off. Opposite, the backyard barrier rose to let a CSI van drive out. The barrier clanged back down.

Three-thirty, the end of the school day.

The back door of the police station opened, and Robbo stepped outside. He was wearing his tunic and his hat and carrying a briefcase. He always looked the part.

Rick started the engine.

The barrier to the backyard rose and the superintendent drove out. He'd put on dark glasses and his alloys spun anti-clockwise like a kingpin's. He drove quickly to the end of the road, and the main drag.

Rick manoeuvred to exit the carpark.

Robbo turned right.

Rick accelerated hard, slowed at the main road, and pulled out sharply. He was three cars back. It was possible Robbo would clock him, but unlikely. His boss wouldn't be expecting a tail, and in any case, would only mean he'd have to argue his case sooner rather than later.

Robbo drove to the ring road, turned clockwise, and drove for twenty minutes. He took the Vale exit, the start of the footballer belt. After five minutes, he turned into a private road. The carriageway narrowed and there was an empty sentry box for a security guard.

Rick stopped at the road entrance. He wondered if Robbo was visiting. The grand houses and drives too much for a police officer's salary, even a senior rank. If his boss wasn't a visitor, it begged the question of affordability.

The superintendent turned into a driveway, the gates opening automatically. Rick parked nearby and returned on foot. After checking up and down, he climbed over the gates.

In front of him stood a new and enormous house. A metallic silver convertible sat on the expanse of drive. There was a separate double garage with accommodation overhead. He rang the bell but there was no answer. A lawnmower hummed behind the buildings, so he walked around the side to the back.

The garden stretched as far as he could see. Close to the house, there was a large pond covered with wire, then well-kept rolling lawns and some tall trees. At the far end, a sit-on mower was working back and forth.

Robbo was sitting at a glass table on the patio. French doors stood open behind him. His hat and briefcase were on the table, alongside a tumbler with a slug of oak-coloured liquid.

Rick stepped onto the patio. Big brown-black fish swam across the pond, silent and ponderous as submarines.

'What are they?'

'Coi carp,' said Robbo. 'The heron's being a bloody nuisance.'

'Is he.'

'She,' said his boss.

Rick had learnt more about his boss in the previous five minutes than in his years at South Manchester. He'd occasionally pondered the top-of-the-range car, but assumed it was on finance. He wondered how Robbo afforded such a lifestyle. The superintendent had inherited money or won the premium bonds – or he was on the take.

'Drink?'

Rick shook his head.

'I think I've connected all the dots, and I'd like to be reinstated. Find Jack, and nail some people up.'

'Tut, tut, Rick. We don't do that any longer.'

'I'm going out.' Janice's voice, through the double doors.

Robbo glanced towards the house but didn't speak. Moments later a door slammed, and a car engine started. There was a short pause, then the throaty roar of heavy acceleration.

The superintendent picked up his drink and put it down again.

'Walk with me.'

They circumnavigated the pond, the heavy coffin-like fish remaining in the shadows.

As he had with Harry and Walsh, Rick explained the connections he'd made, and the likelihood of a Russian cell operating in Manchester at the command of Semion Volkov. Minibus/kidnapping, cold case, subjugation of Rick, all linked.

Robbo stopped at a tap at the edge of the pond. He attached a hosepipe, turned on the tap, and began to top up the water.

'So, you think a Russian cell entered the UK to kidnap a British boy so a Russian boy could win a tennis tournament?'

'No,' said Rick. 'I think they entered the UK because I started re-investigating the cold case, and they planted drugs in my car and in our flat to make it go away. And while they were here, they got involved in something else.'

'A kidnap in order that Volkov's grandson Rurik can win a tennis tournament?' Robbo moved the hose from left to right. The fish had disappeared. 'Have you been eating mushrooms in the woods?'

Rick wondered how much his boss knew about the visit from MI5. Surely Robbo hadn't sanctioned the false imprisonment and leaving him in the middle of a forest?

'It's complicated.'

'Is it,' said his boss. He turned to point the hose at Rick, pushed a finger over the end and sprayed.

'Oi,' said Rick stepping back.

'Don't follow me home again.'

Robbo removed his finger and the water flopped onto the lawn. He pointed it back at the pond.

'Did you sanction MI5?'

Robbo moved the hose from side to side and up and down. 'The spooks have their ways of doing things.'

'But did you know? Walsh was also there.'

'Only after the event.'

His boss threw the hosepipe down. 'Am I right in thinking, one, the fingerprints only connect the letter sent to Westbury

School with Jack's phone, so there's no direct link between the minibus crash and the kidnap, and two, the drugs found in your car and in your flat are connected only by witness description to the historic Formby murder?'

Rick nodded, surprised by the detailed analysis. His boss was usually hazier than sea fog.

'There's the jigsaw puzzle of Big Ben, and the Russian accents. They connect all three: cold case, drugs plant, and minibus/kidnapping.'

'Fanciful, I already told you.'

Rick glanced across at the big house, at the three storeys plus an attic. Seven, eight bedrooms? On one side of the patio there was a circular wall of seating and an elaborate barbeque. Overhead an awning pulled out from the house. The plot covered several acres, and a gardener was employed. Enquiries into Robbo's finances would take a week or two, time he didn't have. And not being officially at work would make it harder.

He took a deep breath. He'd blackmailed Robbo before, threatening to expose an affair with his PA. But he'd told himself he wouldn't do it again. Yet here he was.

'How do you—' he said, waving an arm at the house and grounds.

'Afford all this?' said Robbo. The superintendent scowled and feinted at Rick with the hosepipe. 'I wondered how long it would take before you went down that route. Well, it's a non-starter. I married in. Janice's family own a string of chemist shops and have done very well. Sorry to disappoint.'

'You risked it all for Lainey?'

'Money isn't everything.'

Rick stared into the murky pool. Water was a deceptive medium, objects seeming to change shape as they entered.

'There's still something you're not telling me. What is it?'

Robbo threw down the hose.

'You're halfway there – yes, I want my son to go to Westbury. It's a great school and Alex would be able to do whatever he wants in life. I can accept, though, that he must first pass an entrance exam.' He sighed. 'Janice, however, will not. Alex has fallen behind at his current school, and she blames my affair for unsettling him.'

'Does she know about the letter?'

'No. But it seemed a golden opportunity to ensure Alex attends Westbury, and go some way to appeasing her.'

'You risked another boy's life. A boy not too dissimilar in age to your own son.'

'I can't lose Janice a second time.'

'What about this place?' Rick pointed again at the house.

'I like all the trappings, I won't deny that. But when you come down to it, it's love, affection, call it what you will. I'm not so far from retirement and I want to live out my days with her. If you marry Maggie, you'll see . . . you'll do things for her, things maybe you shouldn't.'

Robbo bent down to turn off the hose.

He straightened.

'Look, Rick, you're currently suspended from duty. Give everything you've got to Walsh and his murder team, and leave them to it. If you have been set up as it strongly appears, then you'll be reinstated.'

The superintendent walked back to the table, downed what remained of his drink.

'I used to be like you, Rick, when I joined the Job. Blazing a trail through the darkness, pissing off a lot of connected people, feeling the heat.'

'And?'

'I got tired.' Robbo picked the ice-cube out of his glass and dropped it in his mouth. He crunched it down. 'Doctor Emma told me you walked out at Magenta House.'

Rick made a face.

'That's what I thought. Hand over to Walsh, then go back to see her. Engage with the counselling process and I'll chase up getting you reinstated.'

Rick walked away. If Maggie's distaste for Robbo hadn't been so entrenched, he would have thought it was a conspiracy between the two of them.

'How about that drink now?' his boss called after him.

35

The clacking of the old-fashioned lift brought the memories back: Skye's mother Pearl and her co-joyriders; the headmaster; the old woman in the fire. The brigadier, Calix Coniston, Hant Khetan. Rick wondered if he should have met Emma at a different venue, a park or a café.

The door of room 341 opened, and the equivalent of Winston's 101 stood on the threshold. Emma wore a black one-piece dress tied around the middle. She always wore black. Meetings with her were like acting in old silent films.

'Hello, Rick.'

'Hello, Emma.' It wasn't much but it seemed a lot. The brigadier was climbing onto the handrail. Calix pointing the gun. The blood-spattered zoo mobile hung down from the ceiling.

Avoiding the window, Rick sat. He inspected the spider plant, scanned the bookshelf, the carpet. He forced his eyes up.

'How's Maggie?'

The test question. Maggie was okay. She was very okay. He was thinking of popping the question. Worried she might say no.

'Rick?'

He looked up.

'We're not prolonging things, Rick, or going through the

motions. Last time when I said you had a temper, you didn't let me finish. Yes, you have a temper, but it's more of a fervour, almost like a religious zeal. And that's what I want to talk *with* you about, and if we don't, then your career in the Job is in jeopardy.'

'O-kay,' said Rick. Emma had grabbed his attention. Saying the word was like opening a secret door.

'Assume I know everything.' Emma nodded, eager to get going, just as he was when interviewing a suspect. Everyone had their own sandpit.

'I thought,' said Rick, 'that with Khetan and Coniston both gone – both *dead* – the problems would all stop. The flashbacks, the visions, the nightmares have decreased. But –' He paused. 'But new problems have arisen.' He paused again. 'I've developed an anger and it's started spilling out. Not all the time, but as a means to getting the job done.'

'Good,' said Emma.

'Really?'

The psychotherapist nodded. 'Khetan is responsible for some of your issues, but only in part. The fundamental reason, Rick, goes back further into your past, to all the deaths and dead bodies you've seen and investigated.'

Rick glanced at the spider plant. He'd read somewhere they were meant to combat the harmful effects of a computer.

'It's why I came to see you originally. The seventeen deaths in my first week of nights after my promotion to DI.'

Emma nodded slowly. 'I know you'll never forget that week.'

He wouldn't. He could name every person who had died. Friday night, Percy Shenton, the old man who'd been found lying in his bath, dead for three months. The five joyriders, Pearl Peters-Green, Trevor Peters-Green, Marcus Howe, Denzil Young, and Alex Bent-White, who'd crashed into a bus stop on the Saturday night, killing Sanda and Torin Toma. Head teacher

Craig McLachlin who'd hanged himself in his garage on the Sunday night. Monday had been the only clear night, the only break in the blackness, the only night the worms had gone hungry. Tuesday, the banker Stein Weber had shot his three babies Martha, Mark and Marissa, murdered his wife Alexi, and turned the shotgun on himself. Wednesday, Chinese siblings Xiang and Min Zhou, who'd jumped off a tower-block in Salford. Maisie Power who'd died in a fire in an old people's home on Rick's final night. Seventeen people.

Rick had been known ever since as the Manchester deathcop.

Emma recrossed her legs. 'Listen to me, Rick. The Coniston missing person enquiry and the subsequent two-year hunt for Hant Khetan, and especially the feelings of guilt they generated, exacerbated your mental distress. This initially presented as delusions of one form or another, but more recently as frustration at the Job, and occasionally develops into physical violence or the willingness to put yourself at serious risk. Both of which are unacceptable to your senior management.'

Rick glanced at the still-fresh scars on his wrists. 'Is that what this is about?'

'This is about you, Rick.'

Emma glanced at her notes, before continuing. 'You've made some progress, but the assaulting of a suspect with a riot shield and stabbing an interrogee with a biro were a step back during your last case, and your knife wounds during this one are signs there's still work to be done.'

'A lot of other cops would have done the same.'

'Not many. Perhaps not any. You're still suffering.'

'You think so?'

'That's my professional opinion, yes. Whether you realise it or not.'

'How do you even know about those incidents? They all went under the radar.'

'I have my sources, just like you do.'

Rick's brain raced. Maggie knew about the latest incident, but not the other two. Unless Hunter had told her – his sergeant had once accused Rick of becoming Robocop.

'I don't think it's saying too much if I say I have three sources. They all share the aim of you resuming your resilience, and fighting crime in a legal manner.'

There was a lot to compute. The two aims were fudged but the three prime suspects were clear, and one took him by surprise.

'Can we rewind a bit? You're saying my actions are the results of all the deaths I've witnessed?'

'I am. And they were triggered by that first week of seventeen; in fact, even the number can set you off.'

'You're right. I see it everywhere. When Skye was in hospital, she was in Ward 17. And one of the crucial exhibits proving Barney Williams was lying, windscreen glass in a pair of trainers, was exhibit KA/17. And going further back, I even remember one of the trekkers I interviewed on my first trip to Nepal – he had Asperger's – saying he had seventeen more places on the map beginning with G to list before he could speak to me.'

'Exactly,' said Emma. 'The impact of that week was then perpetuated by the dozens of suspicious deaths, murders, shootings and stabbings you've attended and spent hours thinking about since.'

'And, or so you're saying, is making me behave in certain ways?'

'In simple terms, you've seen a lot of bad things, a lot of *evil*, and you feel like you've got to get your own back – on behalf of *good*.'

'Really.'

'You once said to me that safeguarding Skye's welfare is your deal with the devil. If she's alright, then you're alright. Well, here you are again, trying to make right all of Manchester's wrongs.'

'I'm a police officer!'

'Yes, but you can't work miracles. You have to work within the rules, and there are some things you can't fix. And you can't work twenty-four seven.'

Emma took a form from a drawer and laid it on her pad. 'Your boss Superintendent Robinson has signed you off for a period of extended treatment. Twelve sessions to start with, one a fortnight.'

'No way.'

'He said you'd say no, but he won't have you at work unless you agree.'

'I'm not having time away from work.'

'I knew you'd say that. And it's so important you get treated asap, I argued him round. I told him the police would be vulnerable in a civil claim if they didn't support you, didn't get you the right treatment.'

'Such as?'

'Mainly CBT – Cognitive Behavioural Therapy, as we have been doing, or at least trying to do. Discussing your feelings and emotions, and understanding they are different to the events per se. But I'll also suggest coping strategies: time away with Maggie; not working on your rest days; walks in the country. The Japanese call them *shinrin yoku* – literally, tree bathing.'

'Have I got a choice?'

'You've dedicated your life to the Job, Rick, to improving society, and it's only fair the Job and society look after you.'

Descending in the lift, Rick felt like he'd gone ten rounds with a heavyweight. The last thing he needed was a long walk in the country. Screw them all, Emma, Robbo, and Harry. He'd done what his boss had wanted by going to see Emma. He'd given everything to Walsh's murder team. Now he was going to do what *he* wanted: finish the house-to-house. Find the Russians' observation point. Find Jack.

*

Commotion downstairs.

A door banged. Kirill swore. *Thumps* in the hall.

Andrei pulled on his balaclava. Limped to the side of the bed, yanked open the drawer and took out the handgun he'd confiscated from the stash house. Shoving it in his jacket pocket, he headed to the top of the stairs.

He could hear more swearing from Kirill, and his comrade's heavy breathing. A muffled gasp from a second person.

Hand gripping the gun and with his back against the wall, Andrei climbed slowly down.

Turning the corner at halfway, he could see into the hall. The closet door was open, and Kirill was struggling with the boy. The boy's legs and arms were untied, and he was trying to crawl away. Kirill was hanging onto the boy's legs, and swearing, breathing hard, and mother of Sundays, half-smiling.

Andrei battered down the remaining stairs, oblivious to the pain. He took out the gun, stepped alongside Kirill, and pistol-whipped the boy.

The boy crumpled. Down, and out.

Sorry, said Kirill.

Andrei took a half-swing at his comrade. If he'd told him once, he'd told him a hundred times, there must always be two of us when untying the boy so he can eat or take a shit.

Kirill held up his hands in surrender.

Andrei turned up the sound on the television. At least his comrade was wearing his balaclava and had remembered to close the kitchen blinds.

He hauled the shoeless boy up by his armpits, and dragged him into the kitchen. Kirill fetched the chair from the closet, and Andrei dumped the boy down. Kirill retied the boy's legs to the chair legs, retied the boy's hands and arms, and strapped the boy's torso to the back of the chair. He fitted the long strip of cloth they were using as a gag across the boy's mouth and around his head, pulled it tight, and tied it off. He held up the drawstring hood.

Andrei shook his head. He threw a glass of water in the boy's face. It diluted the line of blood under his eye from the strike with the gun. Unlike Kirill, the boy would learn.

The boy came to. His face was pale and his eyes glassy. Already he appeared older.

Behind him, Kirill stepped closer.

The boy's neck twisted left and right, his glassy eyes at their limits.

'If promise quiet,' said Andrei, 'I remove gag.'

Jack nodded.

Kirill untied the knot and whipped away the strip of cloth.

The boy breathed deeply. He hyperventilated. Andrei threw another glass of water over him. The boy started crying, and deteriorated into gasping and gurgling. Eventually, he calmed down.

Andrei helped him sip some water.

'Hungry?'

The boy quivered his head. He looked over his shoulders. 'Who are you?' the boy sniffed. 'What do you want?'

'No questions, we say already.'

'My dad's got no money, and my mum doesn't have enough for this.' The boy jerked his head from side to side.

The boy wasn't as spineless as Andrei had thought. Maybe he did have some of the famed English spunk in the face of impossible odds.

'Not about money. In week time, we let you go. Back to your *mamochka*, back to your girl.'

'I don't have a girlfriend.'

'Pretty boy like you have girl, for sure.'

As if Andrei had asked, Kirill stepped forward and twirled a lock of Jack's hair. The two men had an understanding, cemented over years of clandestine operations in the special forces. It had only gone badly wrong once.

The boy bucked in the chair, and laughing, Kirill let go.

Andrei clicked his fingers. 'But try escape again, we cut off some your fingers. You able live normally, but end of tennis.'

'One week?' said Jack.

Andrei nodded.

'I'll miss the Northern Cup.'

Andrei's careful argument had been lost in the boy's egotistical dreams.

The two Russian men stepped forward. They had an understanding. Kirill untied the boy's arms. Andrei grabbed the boy's left hand and twisted it behind him, at the same time putting an arm around the boy's head and securing a lock. Kirill grabbed Jack's right hand. He reached down and extracted his knife. The boy jerked and squirmed.

In the great USSR, order and compliance had been maintained across the fifteen socialist republics not only by violence but also by the threat of violence. The guiding principles were surprise and arbitrariness. The brutal murders, the night-time killings, the town-square executions were occasionally the result of one citizen informing on another, but more often were purely random. Addresses chosen at whim, names taken from utility records, faces plucked from a crowd.

Kirill yanked the boy's right hand forward to reach the table. Leaving the index finger extended, he folded Jack's thumb and other fingers back. He pressed down on Jack's hand and wrist so the boy couldn't move. Kirill placed the knife between the second and third knuckles on Jack's index finger.

The two men had an understanding. The threat of violence, the threat of random violence, was enough. Andrei began to release his hold of the boy. Their point was made. If the boy caused them a problem, his tennis-playing days were over.

Kirill pressed down with the knife to take up the slack, pressed down harder, sawed back and forth, and through.

The boy screamed.

And the end of the finger severed.

Lay bleeding like a cocktail sausage on a plate in the officer's mess.

Boy hysterical, the lack of the gag compounding Kirill's impulsive and unilateral action. His boredom and his bloodlust. The exact same at the sentry post.

36

Standing at the kitchen window, Rick phoned Sheila's daughter. He hoped her message concerned his house-to-house enquiry, and not a speeding ticket.

One day he'd dig a small pond, a water feature. Good for attracting birds and insects. Good for the bees.

'Hello?'

After explaining to Jan why he was calling, he asked if she'd seen anything unusual.

'I haven't. I did hear one thing though, a while back. I was in the hairdresser's when someone mentioned number one Bowker Crescent was going to be re-let. I was worried about migrants so I've been watching. But I've not seen anyone and no board's gone up.'

'How did the person in the hairdresser's know?'

'They're looking for somewhere.'

'Do you know their name?'

'I don't.'

'What about the letting agency?'

'Sorry.'

'Hairdresser's?'

'Shirley's.'

Rick was already walking out of the kitchen. He'd knocked twice at 1 Bowker without an answer.

Cursing himself, he dug out his house-to-house notes and flicked through the replies. Number 3 Bowker – the occupant had seen a man next door a couple of times. Never said anything. Thought they were a shift-worker, as they came and went at irregular times. Never seen a vehicle. TV too loud. There were twenty-five or thirty not dissimilar responses.

An enquiry at Shirley's to ascertain the name of the letting agency would be protracted. Starting over simpler. He'd already considered properties being let by estate agents, and he'd spoken to Rabbetts and three other local firms. But he'd left it there. Not exhaustively bottomed the lead.

He searched the internet for local estate agents, and came up with a list of eleven. *Eleven!* He ticked the four firms he'd already contacted, and started phoning. Wondered if there were more than eleven. An internet search was far from infallible. Maybe he would have to visit Shirley's.

The fifth agency was Pemberton. The man on the lettings desk told him to hold. Rick waited, picking at his fingernails. Cursed himself again. An investigative fundamental: to exhaust all enquiries. To think about grey areas. Different search engines, multiple sources, brainstorming.

'Yes,' said the lettings man. 'Number one Bowker Crescent has recently become one of ours. But it was taken straight away, and we never put a board out. One of our junior staff – Jason Schupp – dealt with it. Three-month rental, about halfway through. John Player is the name of the tenant. Is there a problem, Inspector?'

The name rang an immediate alarm bell. 'I've knocked several times. Can you get Schupp to meet me on Ashmead Drive, and tell him to bring the spare keys?'

'Have you got a warrant?'

'Isn't a routine inspection part of your tenancy agreement? I don't need a formal search.'

Rick put on his harness holding his baton and handcuffs. He grabbed a banana, slipped on his jacket, and headed out.

The roads were quiet after the rush for work and school, but he ate self-consciously, wondering if a Russian cell was watching him walk past. On Ashmead, he sat on a wall in the shadow of a tree dropping big brown leaves and waited for Schupp. He wondered what he was going to find. The Russians' observation point? A member or members of the Russian cell? With or without a trussed Jack? The boy's decomposing body? A grumpy shift-worker trying to sleep?

He sent a message to Nhung, giving the address for his enquiry. Leaves floated down and blew along the pavement. Schupp was taking his time.

Nhung texted. *Leaving South Manchester now.* Rick imagined her enthusiasm. But he didn't want a drinking partner – he wanted a sergeant who would turn out even when he was suspended. A DS like Hunter.

A yellow Mini with a *Pemberton Estate Agency* sign on the roof pulled up. A spotty teenager wearing a dark suit and white socks climbed out. A cigarette was clamped in his mouth and smoke billowed out as he slammed the door.

The boy looked up and down. He took the cigarette out of his mouth, put it back, and tucked his shirt into his trousers.

Rick stepped out of the shadows.

The boy swayed back in exaggerated surprise. He threw the cigarette butt down and scraped it to shreds. He straightened up.

'Jason Schupp?' said Rick, flashing his badge. 'DCI Rick Castle. Do you remember the tenants at one Bowker?'

'Vaguely.'

Rick waited. Another leaf floated down. Schupp would be vague about what he'd eaten for breakfast, his date of birth, whether or not he smoked.

Schupp shrugged. 'I only met one of them. Mr Player was his

name.' The trainee took out another cigarette. He flicked a plastic lighter several times, his fingers juddery.

'John Player?'

'Yes.'

'As in the cigarette company?'

'I s'pose.'

'What's the story, Jason?'

The boy looked at Rick. He pocketed his cigarette and cheap lighter. He shrugged, toed a stone on the pavement.

'This is what's going to happen,' said Rick. 'You're going to give me the key to the property and your car keys. You're then going to wait here in your car.'

'You've got no—'

Rick grabbed Schupp's collar, shoved him back against the wall.

'Keys!'

Schupp handed them over.

'Wait in the car.'

Pocketing both sets of keys, Rick walked along Ashmead toward the alley leading back towards Birch. Behind him, the driver's door on the Mini slammed. He stopped at the entrance and texted the information on Pemberton's letting at 1 Bowker to Maggie for verification. Within seconds, the app showed she was typing a reply.

Are you working?

Got a lead on Jack

At 1 Bowker???

Rick plunged down the alley. A well-worn path led behind half a dozen houses, but only a couple with access. The gate corresponding to 1 Bowker was locked. He hauled himself up, and dropped down the other side. Glanced at the house, but there seemed to be no reaction inside. He squatted down and inspected the bottom of the gate. A mark was clear where it opened and closed, and there was no overgrowing grass. Someone was using it.

He walked down the garden path, glancing from window to window. Shadows flared and shrank.

He reached the back door, and peered inside.

The door led to the living room which ran along the back of the house. There was no sign of anyone or of recent occupation. No magazines, or newspapers. There were pictures and a bookcase, but they looked like fittings, not a tenant's possessions.

He walked around to the front. The window blinds were down. No junk mail poked out of the letterbox. He pushed it open, but the opening was protected by stiff hairs and he couldn't see. He remembered forcing his questionnaire through. The wheelie bin was empty.

Rick glanced up at the windows and next door. He looked up and down the road. No one seemed to be taking any notice. No sign of Nhung.

He returned to the back of the house, pulled on a pair of forensic gloves, and unlocked the door.

Stepped inside.

A fridge was buzzing.

He padded across the room and into the hallway. He stopped and listened again. Still nothing but the fridge.

He quickly checked the downstairs rooms. In the kitchen there was no dirty crockery, or meal preparations. No paperwork or shopping bags. No clothes or shoes. White goods, cupboards, but no stuff. The closet smelt of paint.

He jogged upstairs and looked in each room. Three bedrooms, and a bathroom. No one, and on cursory examination, no clothes, and no toiletries.

The house was not just empty, but clean. Very clean. Too clean?

He returned downstairs, and searched again more slowly.

The kitchen cupboards were half-full of crockery and utensils. Many were empty. There were no tins or dry goods. The bin was empty. The fridge-freezer was empty. Once he'd found a human head in a freezer. Every time he took out a bag of peas or a salmon fillet, he still saw the victim's bloated face.

The tenants would win a prize for cleaning up. He bent and sniffed a surface in the kitchen. It smelt of bleach. He stood on a chair and looked along the top of the cupboards. They were clear, and even they had been wiped.

He returned to the closet and opened the door. Again, he smelt the whiff of new paint. The walls and the woodwork had recently been painted. What, he wondered, had happened that required covering up?

He pushed the door back and forth in contemplation.

Externally, there were screw holes at the top of the door and on the frame, and at the bottom. Bolts would be one explanation.

To lock someone in?

Jack?

Surely, they – whoever they were – hadn't brought Jack to their OP. It was only half a kilometre from Maggie's flat, and the risk unnecessary. The operatives were either super confident or forced to compromise. Their plan gone awry. The botched minibus *accident*.

Rick crouched down. The floor was beige tile. He examined the grouting between the squares. He examined the corners. They were dark. Dirt, or blood? He looked behind the sink pipe, and behind the WC. Checked inside the cistern. Staring at the newly painted walls, he ran his hand across them, wondering what had taken place to necessitate repainting.

The closet would be a very small room for an assault.

But didn't have windows.

TV too loud.

Rick imagined Jack sitting on the floor. Scared, bored. Not

knowing if or when he would be harmed. If or when he would be freed. Where was the boy now?

He sat on the floor, his back against the door, the same way he imagined Jack might have sat. What would he have done?

Marked the walls in boredom, or in protest.

Left a message?

He fetched a couple of knives from the kitchen and set to work. He didn't need to find much, just something to convince Robbo. Something to convince himself.

He scraped a wall. The new paint clogged the knife and he kept wiping the blade clean. It was a tricky task to get right: press too hard, and he removed the layer below, too lightly and he would be there until Christmas.

Slowly, he cleared a patch one metre square. Nothing. He worked a similar patch above.

His phone rang.

'I shouldn't be doing this.'

'Course you should, Mags. A boy's life is at stake.'

Maggie took a deep breath. 'The documents relating to the Player tenancy are bogus. They relate to other tenancies and the countersignature by the Pemberton manager is false. Schupp's going to be fired.'

'Thanks.'

'One Bowker, I can't believe it. Have you found anything?'

'Still looking.'

Rick started on a different wall. Perhaps Jack had never been in the house. He scraped all the way along the wall, half a metre up. There was no message, no hint of a drawing or inscription.

He decided to have another word with Schupp, then come back.

Schupp was dozing with his head slumped. A cigarette smouldered on the dash.

Rick banged on the window.

The boy climbed out and lit another cigarette.

'Tell me about John Player.'

'Eh?'

'The tenant.'

'Like what?'

'What did he look like?'

Schupp shrugged. 'Bigger than me.'

'His documents are false. In fact, I don't think he ever attended the Pemberton office, and only you met him.'

Schupp waggled his cigarette.

Rick stepped forward and plucked it out of the boy's mouth. 'Stop messing me around, Jason. I need you to tell me what happened when you met the man who you assigned the name John Player.'

Schupp squeezed back against the car door.

Rick held the end of the cigarette close to Schupp's cheek. Cross-eyed, the boy looked down his nose at the flaring cigarette.

Rick moved it close enough for a wisp of smoke to rise. The smell of singed cheek hairs immediate.

'A boy younger than you might die, Jason.' Rick grabbed Schupp's hand and stabbed it with the cigarette. 'Tell me the truth, dammit!'

Schupp shrieked.

'Alright. Fuck! I made the name up.'

Rick let go of Schupp's hand, stepped back and flicked the cigarette away. The teenager spat on his hand and hopped around, swearing. Rick wondered whether Emma was right, whether he was suffering from red mist.

'Talk to me, or I can do your other hand.'

Schupp stopped hopping around, gripped his hand, and spoke between gritted teeth. 'I only met him once. Ahhh! Fuck, this hurts.'

'Keep going.'

'He paid me double what was due. I booked in half, and kept half. All I had to do was sort the paperwork.'

'Or what?'

'Kill my dog, beat the crap out of me. He was a big mother.'

'Describe him.'

'He was . . . big, heavy, like a bouncer. I didn't want to annoy him. He wasn't English, spoke with an accent.'

'What kind of accent?'

Another shrug. 'Russian?' Schupp rubbed his hand. 'Are you going to tell Mr Pemberton?'

'You should look for a different job,' said Rick. 'Maybe in a cigarette factory.'

He tossed Schupp his car key.

'Run your hand under a tap, put some antiseptic on it.'

A car pulled up and hooted.

Nhung.

'Am I too late?'

'Perfect timing,' said Rick.

He climbed in and directed her the short distance to 1 Bowker. Leaving her to call up a crime scene investigator, he returned inside.

He now knew he should find something. Something objective to put to Robbo, not simply conjecture and speculation. Police officers, even uniform, liked evidence – facts.

In the closet he re-examined the areas he'd stripped of paint, but he still couldn't find anything. He needed a CSI to complete what he'd started. There had to be a reason for the paint job.

Upstairs, he walked from room to room observing, then returned back down, and looked again in the kitchen. He felt behind the drawers, stood on a chair, and checked the tops of the cupboards.

He stood in the living room, slowly wheeling round. The

bookcase was a landlord's fitting. There was a cupboard, and four rows of books. At the top was a thin shelf, too thin for books.

A cardboard box sat on the shelf.

He looked closer.

A 1,000-piece jigsaw puzzle of Big Ben.

His stomach heaved.

He took some photos, then ran out to Nhung who was waiting in the car. He needed to get the jigsaw puzzle to the lab as a priority submission, and the house forensically examined and searched as soon as possible. Fingerprint impressions and DNA profiles could be compared against the forensics from the Golden Lion, and would show whether the Russians, if that's who they were, had been involved in the Formby murder. Forensics might also confirm Jack's presence, and a systematic search provide leads as to his whereabouts. He was coming, Jack, he was coming.

37

Andrei and Kirill sat in room 132 at an airport hotel and glared at each other. The boy was tied up in the bathroom. Andrei had given him ibuprofen and told him if he made any noise there would be consequences. Told him it would soon be over.

For the boy but not for them.

Andrei crushed a Coke can and hurled it at the wall. Bad enough that they'd forgotten the jigsaw puzzle in the rushed exit from the obs point in Bowker Crescent. Semion would just have to make do with duty free, like every other fat man with manicured hands. But worse, much worse, was Kirill sawing off the boy's finger. No man was bigger than the mission, an operational principle of Russian special forces. Something he and Kirill had believed in since they were eighteen.

He picked up the crushed can, pretended to throw it at Kirill.

Impassive, his comrade sat on the other bed, carefully removing the label from a vodka bottle with his knife. He *could* be careful – could be patient, could think things through – but most of the time, he didn't bother.

Kirill was hairy as a gorilla and had to shave twice for military dinners. Following the sentry post operation – six months after, to allow for Andrei's leg to heal, and his discharge and pension to be sorted out – there'd been a ceremony *and* a dinner. They'd both received medals, but only Andrei ordered to leave.

He'd been lucky to get a job with Semion, unlucky to be assigned to his son Igor, a hothead like Kirill. Almost immediately, he'd been involved in another debacle.

Kirill exited a few years later, after another mistake, another rash decision, not that he told it like that.

The operation to take out the sentry post couldn't be reimagined because Andrei had taken part, had led the two-man team. They'd parachuted into a Belarus forest, hidden their chutes in a barn, and speed-marched ten kilometres back to the Russian border. The thinking was that the border guards wouldn't be expecting an attack from behind.

But the sentry post operation had gone wrong.

Andrei and Kirill had moved up to the final RV, a small footbridge by a water channel. They'd climbed down into the channel and allowed themselves to be carried towards the sentry post. Their intel was for a twelve-man unit, working sixteen-hour shifts. Eight men on duty: two at the post itself and two teams of three patrolling north and south.

At the Belarusian sentry post, a tower built over a bunker, Andrei had created a distraction while Kirill climbed the structure and shot the two guards using a pistol fitted with a silencer. Andrei had entered the bunker and shot the sleeping men. Young men, conscripts, sleeping like babies, then unconscious as stillborns.

Except that Kirill had not killed both sentries. One he'd shot in the kneecap and pushed down the ladder, intending, or so he said, to extract intel. At the foot of the ladder, the sentry had removed a pistol from his boot and shot Andrei in the leg. Only then had Kirill shot the sentry dead.

A while later an informer brought the converts forward. Fifteen men, women, and children, entering Russia and working for the motherland. Two of the men and two of the women were specialist computer hackers.

The operation had been deemed a success: six dead, four heroes transferred to the motherland, one injury. A relative success if it was your leg.

Drink? said Kirill, turning to face Andrei, and raising the vodka bottle.

Andrei shook his head. Kirill was becoming a bigger problem.

His comrade took a swig and waved the now pristine bottle. Shards of white paper surrounded him like sawdust.

I think we should kill him. Kirill took another swig from the bottle.

You know plan, said Andrei. We wait with the boy until after the Northern Cup, then fly home. Just a few more days. Then Semion happy, and we get paid.

And Alyona wouldn't be hurt.

Castle is on us. I feel it. We should kill the boy and scooch up to the northern escape route. Wait for boat. Safer than waiting at airport like sombrero-wearing '*khuylos*'!

Andrei jumped up. He snatched the bottle from Kirill and limped back to the chair. The pain from his leg was getting worse. He snapped out a handful of pills and swallowed them with a mouthful of vodka.

We shouldn't even be at the airport. We should be far away, but as usual you screwed up. Too impulsive, same at the sentry post.

Kirill nodded slowly. He'd drunk too much. I'm sorry about your leg, Andrei. Sorry I didn't kill the sentry first time. I say sorry fifteen years. You might not think, but every time I see you hobble, I hurt, too.

Really.

Kirill nodded. You more than brother to me. You twin.

Words, Andrei thought, were cheap.

*

Half an hour later, Andrei drove out of the hotel carpark. One thing might appease Semion, and keep them out of a self-dug hole in Khimki Forest. Might even keep Kirill – Andrei's new twin brother – and him in the Volkov family's employ. Andrei had never witnessed a soft side to their boss, but with an injured hostage likely to attract the attention of the Kremlin, buying a special jigsaw puzzle for his sixtieth birthday was their only hope.

*

'You've got to be patient, Rick,' said Maggie. 'The murder team are flat out on it. MI5 have been appraised. Standards have been updated. I don't often say this, but Robbo's right. Leave finding Jack to Walsh's team.'

They were at home, in the kitchen. Mention of his boss made Rick reflect on what he might end up one day doing for Maggie, assuming . . . he'd hidden the ring in a sock stuffed into its partner sock, and pushed to the back of his underwear drawer.

'Rick, are you listening?'

He was and he wasn't.

He sent messages to Nhung and Tara asking for a copy of the exhibits seized from 1 Bowker, and the items sent to the lab for forensic analysis. He sent another one to Tara asking her to chase the fingerprint comparisons against those from the Golden Lion hotel.

The million-dollar question was what the Russian cell was going to do with Jack. Three possibilities: take Jack with them, kill him, or let the boy go when they had what they wanted. The third begged the question, what did they want? There had been no ransom demand.

They went out. Maggie packed Rick's car, and Rick drove after checking his phone. Still no messages. Robbo hadn't mentioned Schupp, which was one thing.

At the apiary, the working party had been busy. A new padlock secured the gate, the grass had been scythed for the winter and the paths had been topped up with wood chipping.

Maggie fitted her prosthetics, and they suited up. She hated them, caused her days of pain afterwards. She was only doing it for him, trying to distract him, help him relax. He didn't want to be distracted, didn't want to relax. Still, he loved her for it.

Maggie set to work, Rick checked his phone. Still nothing.

His hive – *their* hive – showed no sign of activity, but if they stopped moving, they could hear the hum of the bees inside. Maggie prepared the smoker, and puffed a cloud of smoke in his direction to show she was ready.

Rick removed the varroa inspection board and showed it to her. They took it in turns to count the orange mites. They agreed on twenty-five, but the count wasn't as bad as it seemed, because he'd not visited for a few days. Maggie brushed the board clean and slotted it back.

She blew a puff of smoke through the hive entrance.

Rick lifted off the roof and set it down. The feeding tray was still half-full, which meant the bees thought they'd taken down enough sugar solution. He removed the feeder and prised off the crown board. A few bees emerged to see what was happening. Maggie issued another puff of smoke and most disappeared back down amongst the frames. Rick gathered the spent pieces of the strong-smelling varroa treatment, and put them in a bag for disposal.

'The whiff of this stuff reminds me of creosoting fences when I was a boy. Dad paid me fifty pence an hour.'

Maggie smiled through her veil.

He hoped the image was a good omen. At some point in the future, he would be going down on one knee.

His phone rang.

'Yes, Tara?'

'Search team took the sink and waste pipe apart,' said the CSI. 'And the first submissions confirm Jack's DNA.'

'Brilliant. Anything else?'

'There are hundreds of exhibits already, but nothing spectacular – apart from the puzzle. The clean-up job was really good. Everything stinks of bleach. But they're still going. Will take another day or two.'

He pocketed the phone.

Maggie had opened a new packet of Apivar and was laying out the strips across the frames. He helped her replace the crown board and the roof. Then pulled over the pink polystyrene cladding which fitted over the hive during the winter to keep off the worst of the weather. Not pretty, but effective.

Maggie grabbed the screwdriver and a handful of long screws. Rick pulled and pushed the cladding into position. He fitted a plank of insulation across the front of the hive and Maggie twisted the screws through the side pieces and into the front plank. It would stay in place in a gale, but the bees could still access the hive.

They grabbed their equipment and retreated to the bench. Rick would have to return once more to remove the varroa strips, but otherwise that was it for beekeeping until the spring.

'We just have to hope now.'

'That they have enough stores, and the queen survives.'

'And a badger doesn't knock over the hive, and thieves don't steal the colony.'

Maggie slapped his arm. 'You've got a one-tracked mind.'

She wasn't wrong. But it was true, there was nothing people didn't steal: silverware from churches, copper from telegraph lines, plants from the gardens of stately homes, sand from beaches. Children from minibuses.

He wondered about Jack. Scared, alone, and possibly worse. Much worse. There was nothing else he could do. It was so –ing frustrating.

Maggie produced a bottle of water, and they passed it back and forth. Rick pulled out a cereal bar and snapped it in half. Sharing it was going to be symbolic, but he wasn't hungry. He gave both pieces to Maggie.

Listening to her chewing, he stared out at the hives.

'I'm glad you went to see Emma.'

Rick nodded, knowing he'd had little choice. 'Do you agree we should move, we can't stay at Bowker. We need somewhere bigger, somewhere with a proper garden.'

'We?'

He took hold of Maggie's hand, and massaged her fingers the way she liked it. She closed her eyes, and Rick stole another look at his phone.

Still nothing, despite being all over the news. Jack's photograph and a request for information or sightings of him and a tall, white man with a Russian accent. Probably two men. They'd need food. Or maybe they were getting it delivered. Maybe the Russians had killed Jack and left the country.

Maggie put her head on his shoulder.

Dad had told him how he'd asked Mum. Not asked her. One day when she was visiting overnight with a girlfriend, he'd driven to her parents' house, and taken his prospective father-in-law – Rick's grandfather – to the local pub. Dad had bought him a pint of Old Grenadier and asked *him* if he could marry Mum. Which seemed ludicrous. *Was* ludicrous.

'Penny for them,' said Maggie, opening her eyes.

'Mm?'

Next to him on the bench, his phone rang.

He grabbed it up, glancing at Maggie. The number was familiar. But it wasn't Nhung or Tara. It was the Serious Games puzzle shop.

'DCI Castle.'

'Man here now. In shop, wants – not joke – same puzzle Big Ben.'

'Tell him . . . tell him it's in your stockroom. Drop the puzzle so you have to pick up all the pieces. Or tell him you can't find it. Tell him anything, just keep him talking. I'm coming.'

'I ask him wait.'

'A boy's life depends on it. I'll be there as quick as I can.' He ended the call. 'I've got to go, Mags. It's—'

'The puzzle shop, I got the gist. Do you want me to call Robbo, get you some backup?'

Rick was walking away, backwards. 'Surveillance and entry teams. And go in, Mags, get on a computer.'

He turned and started running.

Adrenalin coursed through him as he vaulted the gate, ran to his car. Hypothesis G1d: Jack had been kidnapped so Rurik Volkov could win the Northern Cup.

38

Rick drove as fast as he could, overtaking, pushing into the front of queues, advancing through red traffic lights.

The Russian would be unlikely to fold in interview so would need following for as long as it took to find Jack. Or was about to leave the country. It was possible he'd arrived at the shop on foot, but unlikely. More likely he'd need tailing in a vehicle. Either way, surveillance would be difficult by himself. Maggie was calling for backup, but he needed people quickly, people who'd do what he told them.

He made a phone call.

Which was eventually answered. 'Hamburg.'

'I need an extra pair of eyes on a surveillance job, Gary. Right now, central Manchester, shop called Serious Games.'

'And my cock's a kipper.'

Dialling tone.

Rick's former DS may have changed jobs and names but had lost none of his charm.

Vehicles slowed to a standstill at a temporary set of lights. Two men on the back of a lorry were shovelling grit into a dumper truck.

Rick phoned his friend and special constable, Russell Weatherbeater, who was guaranteed to turn out. He listened to the recorded message.

'I'm in Nepal, likely to be a few days before I get back to you.' Rick had forgotten the mountaineer was away – he'd taken Velvet to Annapurna Base Camp to celebrate her twenty-first birthday. According to Maggie who regularly checked up, he'd stopped hitting his young girlfriend.

He tried Nhung.

When his current DS answered, he told her what he needed. She sucked in a breath. 'I'm on a course today as it happens – there was a cancellation. An introduction to HOLMES. I want to apply to a murder team.'

'I'll write you up,' said Rick.

'And you won't if I don't come?'

Rick lifted his phone from the cradle and slammed it back down. He wasn't asking for blood.

The vehicles in front of him started moving. A learner driver two in front kangarooed forward. The lights turned orange, the learner braked hard. The lights turned red. The men shovelling grit stopped for a breather.

Rick thumped the steering wheel. Then called the shop.

'Please phone again, we deal customer.' Iva's voice was loud, strained, knowing. 'I drop puzzle,' she said, under her breath. 'Pieces everywhere. He not happy.'

'Well done,' whispered Rick. He was. Or would be if they found Jack alive and unharmed.

Cars streamed past in the opposite direction, and the men in hard hats resumed shovelling. Grit skitter-scattered on the road. The lights turned green and the learner driver engaged first gear.

He phoned Sergeant Davison.

'Yes, sir?'

Rick explained, at the same time alternating between first and second gear behind the learner.

'The thing is, sir, we're on a day off. I can make a couple of phone calls. But I'll have to advise people, there might be consequences.'

'I'll sort it.'

The learner indicated left, and Rick saw his chance. He swung out into the opposing lane, floored the accelerator and swung back – just before a recycling lorry thundered past, horn blaring.

His phone rang.

'Robbo's taken it up the chain,' said Maggie. 'Teams are being called in and someone will phone you shortly. I'm in a minicab on the way to the nick.'

Five minutes, he estimated before he arrived at Serious Games. He needed surveillance support now. The suspect could leave the shop at any moment.

Rick pictured the interior. Iva and Nikolai and the Russian scrabbling around on the floor picking up pieces of jigsaw. The Russian swearing at Iva's cackhandedness and her refusal to accept notes greater than ten pounds. The cat padding around the chaos, the tiny second world war soldiers looking on.

Two minutes.

He readied himself. Following a suspect was difficult alone, and near impossible if the Russian was looking for a tail.

One minute.

A courier riding a tricycle pulling a trailer of vegetables wobbled away from the kerb to miss a pothole. Rick swerved to avoid a collision. He'd reached Main Road with restaurants and shops. Serious Games was on a side street.

He checked his phone.

Just him, then.

He parked on a meter and threw a *Broken down* sign on the dash. He put on a pair of no-prescription tinted glasses and climbed out. Bundles of free newspapers were piled higgledy-piggledy on the pavement. He was wearing jeans and a fleece top. He grabbed a bundle, the papers blending him into the background.

Pedestrians, mainly shoppers and students, streamed along the pavements. The road thick with traffic. It all helped.

He turned down the side street, immediately zeroing in on the front door of the puzzle shop. Parked cars on both sides, but no moving vehicles and fewer pedestrians.

As he watched, the door opened and a tall white man stepped out. The Russian was carrying a bright yellow Serious Games plastic bag, the size and shape of a jigsaw puzzle. Rick wanted to shout out: It's him! The suspect he'd seen on Stransby's dashcam footage. The man, or one of them, who was holding Jack prisoner. Who'd been setting Rick up.

He stepped into a doorway. Plonked the newspapers down and sat, removing himself from the easiest field of vision for the suspect.

Like an advanced driver anticipating the way a car would turn by the angle of its front wheels, he watched the yellow plastic bag. Avoided the risk of eye contact.

The bag moved in his direction.

The Russian man walked with a limp, but surprisingly quickly. He would be furious, and maybe careless because of his temper. The bag remained on the same pavement as Rick, was heading for Rick.

Fifty metres.

The Russian had to cross.

He wasn't crossing.

Rick ripped out a newspaper, opened it wide, slouched down in the doorway and covered his face as if he was dozing.

Ten seconds to run a hundred metres. One minute to walk it. Thirty seconds for fifty metres. One thousand, two thousand . . .

. . . thirty thousand.

Rick held his breath, counted ten more.

Slowly, he lowered the newspaper.

The Russian had crossed over and was at the corner, turning into the main drag.

Rick's phone sounded.

'Yes.'

'It's Gary, I'm two minutes from the shop, where do you want me?'

Rick could have kissed him. Cockney charm, bloody-mindedness, but solidity when it counted. 'Target heading south on Main Road,' said Rick, standing and walking to the corner. 'He's carrying a bright yellow plastic bag. Walks with a limp. I'll send you a photo. As soon as you see him, you've got the eyes.'

At the corner, Rick spotted the Russian ploughing down the pavement, the other pedestrians getting out of his way. Rick crossed the road, and followed.

His phoned beeped.

Message from Hunter: *Got eyes*

Rick stopped, U-turned, and hurried back to his car, past a betting shop with cardboard footballers in the window. Two people were ten times better than one, but surveillance would still be difficult unless the Russian did anything but walk from A to B.

He reached his car, climbed in, and started the engine. Waited. He checked his phone. Nothing.

He pulled up the map app, zoomed in, and familiarised himself with the street names and geography where the Russian was heading. There was a park five hundred metres away, a couple of hotels, residential areas, and carparks.

Three long-haired students walked by, pushing and laughing. They wore black shirts with logos of bands he'd never heard of.

He drummed on the steering wheel. Stared up at a huge poster of an Olympic swimmer advertising the local leisure centre.

His phone rang.

'Gary?'

'Nhung, sir. Against my better judgement, but I'm near the shop. I'm driving.'

Rick was touched by her loyalty. He would have said so but feared it would backfire. She took praise the same way as criticism – it was unnecessary, and messy.

'Target is on the move, heading south on Main. You've seen the dashcam footage of him; he's carrying a bright yellow plastic bag, and he's limping. Gary has eyes.'

'Hamburg?'

'Hunter.'

She tutted.

Rick checked the map. 'Wait, Nhung, at the junction of Main and Parsons.'

His phone beeped with a message from Hunter/Hamburg: *Still Main*

Rick stared at the map. He couldn't believe it. Both Gary and Nhung had turned out. Together, the three of them had a chance of following the Russian undetected. Of finding Jack.

He phoned Hunter. 'My new DS, Nhung, is on the plot. At Parsons, let her take over.' He rang off, phoned Nhung to tell her the same.

A window cleaner carrying a ladder walked past.

Hunter phoned. 'Target's turned right, right, right on Stafford.'

Rick checked the map.

Offices, a multistorey, then residential.

He told Hunter to keep following. Relayed it to Nhung. Police radios, he thought, would have made things easier. He entered the line of traffic and headed towards Stafford Street.

Text from Hunter: *Disappeared into multistorey got him!*

Rick phoned him. 'We need to keep following, hope he'll lead us to Jack. Can't rely on him telling us.' He phoned Nhung and relayed.

Rick turned into Green Street, one block up from Stafford, and manoeuvred his car back into a space. He couldn't get any closer, not on foot, and not in his car. The Russian would recognise him, so he would have to remain in the background, and trust Gary and Nhung to do the follow.

He phoned them both, told Hunter to retreat to Main Street as soon as Nhung had eyes on the multistorey exit.

'Come on, come on.' He wondered if Nhung would be able to identify the Russian from the photo. The yellow plastic bag would no longer act as a flag. He could park closer, but risk showing out. He could walk closer, but the risk remained.

His phone rang. 'Target out, out, out,' shouted Nhung. 'Driving an unmarked white van.'

'You're sure it's him?'

'I think so.'

'Go with it.' Surveillance allowed no time for decision making, only decisions. On a normal job, a footie would have confirmed. But Rick had no footies, and only two cars in addition to his control car.

'White van, P-Papa L-Lima One Seven J-Juliet I-Indigo G-Golf. Looks like a hire. Heading back to Main Street.'

Rick texted Hunter with the registration, then Maggie.

The lack of communication was going to break the job. He climbed out of his car, clicked the locks, and ran down the pavement to Main. At the corner, he turned and sprinted south towards Stafford. Phoned as he ran.

'Gary, pick me up.'

His former DS grunted into the phone.

Rick slowed to a walk and hugged the building line. Fifty metres ahead of him, he saw a small white van pull out of Stafford. He bent to his shoelaces, and glanced up. The van turned the other way. He stood and continued. A moment later, he recognised Nhung's car stop at the junction and turn to follow the van.

Rick ran past a pet shop, the soiled, defeated smell spilling across the pavement and reminding him of the custody suite.

A car peeled off the oncoming traffic, and glided into the kerb. A familiar face at the wheel. Rick climbed into the passenger seat.

'Like old times, boss.'

Hunter U-turned, and set off down Main.

Rick phoned Nhung. He explained he was riding with Hunter/Hamburg, and he would try keeping the line open and on speaker. She told him their target was heading south.

'Still there?'

'Yes,' said Nhung. 'Still south. Passing the Babs'n'Tots superstore now.'

Hunter drove steadily. He was tapping on the wheel, frequently checking the mirrors, moving out to the centre line, so he could see further forward.

Rick looked at the map and tried to think like the Russian. As soon as he'd achieved what he'd come for, he'd want to get home. Which meant, fifty-fifty, he was heading for somewhere near the airport.

Maggie phoned, and Rick switched calls. 'It is a hire vehicle,' said Maggie. 'No Fuss rentals on Wellington. Hired to a Mr John Smith. Eight-week term, due back in ten days. They're emailing me copies of the docs.'

'What about surveillance support?'

'Robbo said they'll phone you direct.'

Rick's phone beeped with another call.

'Castle.'

'Sergeant Davison, sir. I could only get hold of two of my officers – Barton and Fanning. They're with me now and we're en route to you.'

'Head for the Stockport junction of the ring road. We're following the target – he's in a white van ending Juliet Indigo Golf.' Rick paused. 'Thanks for turning out.'

'Barton's got a question, though.'

'I was wondering, sir, as we're technically off duty, are we allowed to carry our officer safety equipment?'

'Have you brought it, Barton?'

'Yes, sir – baton, cuffs, CS.'

'Good, you might need it. And you're not off duty: you're engaged in a spontaneous operation to save the life of a kidnap victim. Got it?'

'Yes, sir.'

Rick ended the call, reverted to the open line with Nhung.

'Numpty,' said Hunter.

'He'll learn,' said Rick. Then louder: 'Nhung, how're you doing?'

'Still got eyes. Still heading south. I'm about three cars back, looks like the target's heading for the ring road.'

'Keep going, if he takes the ring road, we'll take over, and you can drop back.'

'Okay.'

Hunter weaved left and right in his lane. He hadn't changed, always liked to be at the knifepoint. So did Rick, every police officer did. Which explained why the neighbourhood officers and Nhung had turned up. They didn't want to miss out.

'Is she any good?'

'No worse than my last DS.'

'I can hear you,' said Nhung on the speaker.

They passed a school with young children running around in the playground.

'Ring road,' shouted Nhung.

Rick nodded at Hunter, who changed down a gear. 'When we pass you, drop back,' said Rick.

Hunter squeezed through a set of lights, and drove onto the ring road. Rick updated Davison and Maggie. He was nervous, butterflies in his stomach. Still, after eleven years in the Job and countless operations.

The ring road was busy.

Hunter accelerated and moved into the central lane. He drove fast, but not fast enough to attract attention. They both scanned forwards.

'There she is,' said Rick. 'The grey Kia.'

Hunter closed on Nhung's car.

'And there he is,' said Rick.

The target vehicle was five cars up, in the nearside lane. Between it and Nhung were a dark blue van, and four cars. Hunter overtook Nhung, and steered back into the inside lane. Rick resisted any sign of recognition.

'Good job, Nhung,' he said on the phone. 'Stay about half a mile back, and wait 'til I call again.' He dropped the call and phoned Davison, explaining he should also follow west along the ring road.

'Airport?' said Hunter.

'Maybe.'

They continued in silence. Without the radio or conversation, the road noise sounded louder than usual. They passed a sewage works, the stink washing through the car.

'Still got him?' said Rick. His view was blocked by the blue van.

'Uh-huh.'

Brakelights loomed ahead. Rick felt his stomach tighten. Hunter pulled into the central lane, moved up alongside the blue van.

Vehicles were slowing in all three lanes. The target van swerved onto the hard shoulder and kept going. The three lanes of traffic slowed almost to a standstill.

Hunter pushed back into the slow lane, and finally edged onto the hard shoulder.

'Boss?'

'Go.'

Hunter followed the target van up the hard shoulder. A couple of cars hooted in umbrage.

Rick phoned Davison. 'We've shown out, you need to take over from us as soon as possible. Use the hard shoulder.' He ended the call. If they'd waited in the lines of stalled traffic, they would have lost the target. A risk either way. The crux of policework, he'd often thought, was decision making under pressure. The crux of senior management was selling those decisions.

Hunter let the target van move further ahead, but there was nothing between the two vehicles. Rick began to feel uneasy.

The van turned off at the first opportunity. The airport junction. At the roundabout, it took the first exit.

'Sail on past.'

'You sure?'

'Don't start second-guessing me now.'

The target van drove away, and Hunter drove past as instructed. Took the second exit.

Rick phoned Davison. 'Take the airport junction, then the first exit, quick as you can. You should catch him. Let us know. We're taking a detour, but should be back behind you within a few minutes.' He phoned Nhung. 'Airport junction, use the hard shoulder when you hit traffic. Davison's trying to regain eyes.'

Hunter sped up, until the car started juddering, then slowed a fraction. Neither of them spoke. Hunter scratched his neck. They reached the next junction, turned off, curled around another roundabout and drove back.

Rick felt sick. Come on. Come on.

He phoned Davison.

'Just pulled off the ring road.'

'Keep the line open.'

'Yes, sir.'

They reached the first roundabout, and took it at speed. Rick held onto the roof handle and braced as they curved round.

'Got him,' said Davison on the phone. 'White van J-I-G.'

'Yes!' shouted Rick. 'But not too close.'

'We're three cars back.'

'Okay, hang on there.' Rick phoned Nhung. 'Where are you?'

'Behind you.'

A car flashed its lights behind them. Rick raised a hand.

'Terminal Two,' shouted Davison. Excitement filled his voice.

Traffic was heavy and slow. They passed a series of huge duty-free posters.

'Taken a side road. Palmerston. Heading for the hotels, I shouldn't wonder.'

Hunter shook his head, a faint smile appearing and disappearing. He scratched an ear. He'd seen everything, heard everything, good and bad and the bloody obvious.

'Yes, yes, yes,' shouted Davison. 'He's turned into the carpark of the Chequered Flag hotel.'

'Don't follow,' said Rick, 'I repeat, do not turn in.' Despite being in plain clothes, the three uniform officers would stand out like foxes in a hen coop. He phoned Nhung. 'You're on. Target is at the Chequered Flag. Keep the line open.'

Hunter turned into Palmerston and dawdled like a kerb-crawler. After a kilometre he pulled into a petrol station and parked in the air and water bay. A woman in pilot's uniform was filling her car.

Nhung drove past.

Rick checked the map: the hotel was a kilometre further down.

He could feel his heart pounding.

'Okay, I'm at the hotel,' said Nhung on the phone. 'I'm going to park up.'

Hunter winked.

As excited as he ever got.

'Target's out of the van . . . and into the hotel.'

Rick nodded at his former DS, who pulled out of the petrol station. Gunned down the road.

After a kilometre, Hunter slowed and turned into the carpark of the Chequered Flag. *Cheapest hotel within walking distance of the airport.* Walking distance if you were a hungry wolf, maybe. The carpark was packed with vehicles, and busy with people and their luggage. Two boys were kicking a football between the cars.

Rick balled his fist: they were about to rescue Jack.

Surely.

39

'DS Allen, team three, central ops. Where do you want us, sir?'

'What have you got?'

'Seven double crewed units, plus two bikes, a couple of footies, but the operators from the cars can double up.'

'Target's gone to ground in the Chequered Flag at the airport. Plot up on the hotel road entrance. I take it you've seen an image?'

'A copy of the dashcam but we'll need verbal confirmation from you.'

'What about entry teams?'

'Mounting up as we speak. Where do you want them?'

'Somewhere close. I haven't got a radio, so all comms via my phone. What's your ETA?'

'Ten to fifteen.'

Rick phoned Davison. 'Park up in the petrol station, Paul. Wait for my call. Try and look inconspicuous.'

'With Barton?'

Enough said.

Rick switched calls. 'Nhung?'

'Room 132. Ground floor corner, booked two days ago in the name of John Smith. Paid cash. Two big men – white, foreign accents, good English. No sign of a boy. All clear, if you want to enter through reception.'

Rick felt a stab of disappointment. But the information didn't mean Jack wasn't in the hotel, far from it. He grabbed a kitbag from the boot of the car, and together with Hunter, walked past a line of dead conifer trees to the door of the hotel. Fag butts littered the concrete pavers.

Inside:

Cheap prints of chequered flags and racing cars lined the lobby. The reception was at the back, and rooms led off both sides. To the left a seating area, to the right a noisy cafeteria.

Nhung loitered at reception, and the two of them walked over.

'He's coming back,' whispered Nhung, nodding behind them.

'Take him?' said Hunter.

'Not until we confirm Jack's here,' said Rick. 'Now get out of here, both of you.'

Rick pushed through a door marked *Private*. Entered an office with desks along one wall and a series of computer terminals. There were charts on the opposite wall and a whiteboard in the corner. The sole occupant looked over from a computer.

'Can I help you?'

Rick put a finger to his lips. Whispered, 'Police.' Showed his much abused old badge.

The man glanced at the warrant card, nodded. 'Tom Brennen, I'm the manager.' He was about thirty, wore a white short-sleeved shirt, and had a bulging stye under one eye. 'What's happening?'

Rick's phone beeped with a text.

He's gone into the café

'Two men have kidnapped a schoolboy and are hiding in room 132,' said Rick, dumping his kitbag. 'One of them has just walked into reception.'

The hotel manager raised his eyebrows.

Rick's phone beeped a second time.

He's buying some food

'Is there an empty room close to 132?'

Tom Brennen tapped on his keyboard, touched his weeping eye. He shook his head. 'We're almost full.'

At the till. Sarnies, Pringles, choc bars, 6 cans of soft drinks, bananas, 1 apple

Two people or three? Fruit?

'Should I be worried for the hotel guests, and for my staff?'

'Our suspects have their target, so not directly.'

Brennen nodded. 'That's a relief.'

'Is there CCTV along the corridors?'

The hotel manager shook his head. 'Front doors, reception, and in the carpark.'

'What about at the back?'

Brennen shook his head.

Rick wrote down an email address. 'Whatever you've got, can you send the last week's footage to my colleague Maggie?' He wasn't hopeful. If Jack was in room 132, then it was unlikely he'd entered, conscious or otherwise, through the hotel's front entrance.

'Have you got a spare camera?'

'I think so.' Brennen walked over to a cupboard.

Ten days earlier, the Russian cell had shot out the minibus tyre, so a firearm was a possibility. Unlikely they'd still have the same weapon, but possible they had a second one, a handgun for emergencies. The Russians might be holding the schoolboy elsewhere, or there might be a second cell. If they did make a run for it, the hotel would shortly be surrounded. The crux was confirming Jack's presence in the hotel – at which point the armed entry teams could engage and neutralise. Any operational plan would involve getting eyes on the suspects – and Rick was the officer on the ground. A cleaner or odd jobs – the suspects knew Rick, so Hunter? – could glance through the windows, but the blinds were likely to be drawn.

'Tom, is there an adjoining room with a communal door?' Maybe he could listen for Jack's voice, or even look through a keyhole.

Still searching the cupboard, Brennen shook his head. 'Not that one.'

'What about spyholes in the doors?'

'Found it.' The hotel manager turned around holding a box. 'Yes, every room.'

The door opened, and Hunter walked in, past a red button for the fire alarm protected by a plastic cover. Which set Rick thinking.

'Suspect's gone back to his room.'

Rick turned to Brennen. 'Gary's a colleague.' He led Hunter over to a corner.

'Nhung's watching the carpark, boss. What're you planning?'

'To wait.' The Russians couldn't remain in room 132 forever. But if Jack was being held somewhere else, the delay might be critical. 'Wait 'til they make a move, and while we do, bring in some technical.' Drill a hole and insert a listening device or an endoscope camera. Although, obtaining the kit along with authorisation to use it would take time.

'So we just sit here?'

'Maggie's checking the CCTV footage, and Tom's going to show me where to install a spare CCTV camera at the end of their corridor.'

'So *I* just sit here?'

'Phone Maggie, ask her to request ears and eyes, I'll only be a few minutes.'

On the way, Rick commandeered a cleaning trolley. There was a small risk he would coincide with a suspect leaving the room, but the significant advantage it gave, made it justifiable.

The corridor containing rooms 121 to 140 was deserted.

'At the end,' whispered Brennen, fingering his stye.

Rick manoeuvred the trolley and used a box of soaps to conceal the camera.

A lock clicked and a door opened.

Voices.

But not Russian.

The two of them snuck away, and returned to Brennen's office. Hunter had rolled up a trouser-leg and was scratching his calf.

Rick phoned Maggie and asked if she'd spotted Jack on the CCTV. She told him she'd requested the technical kit and had co-opted two more analysts, but they'd only just started.

He called DS Allen.

'All plotted up, sir. It's on you.'

Hunter started pacing. Brennen offered him a cigarette, then a brew, pointed at the kettle and the biscuit tin.

Rick pondered a worst-case scenario – they needed to get Jack out quickly. Setting off the fire alarm wouldn't guarantee the Russians would leave the room. And even if Hunter knocked on the door, pretending to be hotel staff ensuring compliance, they might not answer. Gary could open it with a master key, but it might spook them. Still, it was an option. He picked up the tin and emptied out the contents. Asked Brennen if he could borrow his lighter. He balled a few sheets of paper from the printer and tucked them inside the tin. A bee smoker with bellows would have been better, but it would do.

Emma was wrong about red mist. Rick was calm, and rational. He discussed the backup plan with Hunter.

Looked at the clock, then at his watch. He wondered if Jack was hurting. With hostages, every minute could count. Every second. How long was he going to wait for Maggie to check the CCTV?

He phoned her.

'About ten per cent watched. So far, nothing.'

'Technical?'

'Travelling time from ops.'

Rick pocketed the phone. Had another thought. 'Tom, do you have an incident book?'

The hotel manager nodded, pointed. Rick took the binder from the top of a filing cabinet and set it down on the desk. Flicked to the most recent entries, and worked down.

7.10 a.m. Sink still not draining properly in 140.

7.55 a.m. Kettle missing from 136.

9.15 a.m. Blood on carpet near fire exit end of corridor, 121–140. Needs deep clean.

Rick wasn't waiting another millisecond. He hit the red fire alarm button, and a dissonant belling began.

40

Rick scanned the CCTV of the hotel's carpark as guests began to gather in the muster area. Couples, family groups, a youth team in matching tracksuits. They milled around, marshalled by hotel staff in fluorescent tabards. He checked the adjacent monitor, showing feed from the CCTV camera concealed in the cleaning trolley. The corridor was busy with people leaving their rooms, but there was no movement from 132.

His phone rang.

'Superintendent Montgomery. Gold commander as of two minutes ago. What the fuck's happening?'

Rick explained about the blood on the carpet. 'I suggest you move the entry teams up to their final RV, sir, but tell them to stay put until I've confirmed Jack's whereabouts. If I can't locate him, I'll call you back.'

Montgomery sucked in a breath.

'Gives us the best chance of safeguarding Jack.'

The gold commander exhaled.

'Alright.'

Rick pocketed the phone.

The fire alarm kept ringing.

'I should get out there,' said Brennen, handing Rick a key fob. 'That's a master. Good luck.' Touching his eye, the hotel manager walked out.

In the distance, a fire engine klaxon.

Hunter rooted around in a few drawers, eventually found a tie. He tied a knot, loosened it, scratched his neck.

'Ready?' said Rick.

The fire engine's clamouring strengthened. More people had filed into the carpark, and the corridor with room 132 was deserted.

Rick wondered if his former DS was thinking about Weatherbeater, and they were both silent for a moment, Rick replaying the scene in Aldershot two years before.

'If you don't fancy it—'

'Course I fancy it. Done enough supermarket and bingo pickups.'

A fire engine arrived in the carpark, and a stocky woman climbed down from the cab. Nhung walked over to meet her.

Still there was no movement from 132.

Rick pulled his body armour from the kitbag. 'Wear that.'

'Ain't bulletproof.'

Ballistic would have been too heavy or too awkward. 'You don't have to do this, Gary.'

'Yes, I do.'

Hunter slipped off his jacket and slipped on the armour. He adjusted the Velcro straps and put his jacket back on. Buttoned it up. Rick picked up the biscuit tin, and with Hunter following, walked out into the lobby.

A couple of guests hurried past, debating whether there was a real fire or it was only a drill. Through a window, fire-fighters were uncoiling a hose. A hotel employee was calling out names and marking a clipboard.

Rick led off towards the corridor with room 132. He pushed open the double doors, passing the strategically placed cleaning trolley, and walked down the corridor. His ears rang from the alarm.

They'd agreed a series of hand signals: key card held up meant Jack was in the room; key card held flat, the room was empty; key card down, no sign of Jack but someone else was in the room.

Outside room 132, Hunter glanced over his shoulder.

Rick held up a thumb. Holding the cylindrical biscuit tin sideways, he lit the scrunched paper with Brennen's lighter and waited until white puffs billowed around the corridor. He bent down and pointed the tin under the door.

He heard a man's voice from inside.

One voice, or more than one? Rick's pulse notched up, as if he was preparing to open a beehive and take the year's honey crop.

He unlocked the door of room 130 with the master key, handed it to Hunter, then slipped inside, ensuring the door squeezed shut without a sound. He set the biscuit tin down, and looked out through the spyhole.

Hunter banged on the door of 132.

'Anyone in there?' Rick's former DS banged again. 'There's a fire. Mr Smith? You're not accounted for.' Hunter waited for a couple of seconds, but there was no response, and he inserted the master key card into the slot.

As he did so, the door opened.

'Mr Smith?' said Hunter. Through the spyhole of 130 Rick could see his former colleague trying to look into the room.

'Yes?'

'There's a fire, you need to come with me to the muster zone. Is there anyone else in the room?'

'Eh?'

Hunter pointed into the room. 'Anyone else in there?'

Rick couldn't hear a reply.

'You're sure?'

The man stepped into the corridor. He sniffed, looked up and down. He wasn't the Russian man they'd followed from the puzzle shop. Rick hadn't seen him before. He was as big as a bear with the demeanour of someone woken from hibernation.

The man stared at Hunter, sniffed again. Finally, he pulled the door shut behind him. 'No big fire?' His accent was Slavic – Russian, if Rick had to guess. The Russian man he'd followed from the puzzle shop, the man on the dashcam footage at the minibus crash, could be still in the room. Guarding Jack?

'Big enough,' said Hunter. 'Come on.' He turned towards the fire exit, the big man following.

Rick observed Hunter's hands, but they were empty. His former colleague had left the key card in the door.

FFS, Hunter.

The former DS shoved open the fire exit, the noise from the carpark increasing. He stopped, swore, and returned to the door of 132. He retrieved the key card, showed it to the bearlike man, then jogged the three or four metres back, holding the card flat.

Which meant the room was empty.

The first Russian man was somewhere else in the hotel or had snuck away – maybe via the fire exit while Rick was setting up the camera in the corridor – and Jack wasn't in the room. The boy was being held elsewhere; Rick's fear realised. But all was not lost. The fire alarm would finish, the bearlike Russian would return to his room unawares, and Rick could resume surveillance via the hidden CCTV camera. Superintendent Montgomery would ensure the Russians were followed to a new location – hopefully where Jack was being held – or arrested if they tried to leave the country.

The fire door slammed shut, leaving the corridor deserted.

Rick set the tin down and went out into the corridor. Entering 132 was an opportunity not to be spurned. A quick look round and a dirty search might provide the clue to locate Jack.

He slotted the master key in the slot outside 132. The lock

clicked, and Rick pushed open the door.

A man shouted in a foreign language. It was a question, rhetorical. The accent was Russian, the intonation surprise and annoyance. The shouter, the man Rick had followed from the puzzle shop, was standing near the foot of the double bed. Then moving towards Rick at speed.

For a moment Rick thought of Brigadier Coniston and one of his favourite sayings. *No plan survives first contact with the enemy.*

But only a moment.

The Russian reached the doorway. Threw a punch. Rick jerked the door back, deflecting the man's arm. The Russian's fist connected with the door and slewed across his body. He said something in Russian. Rick pulled the door back and thrust it forward again, slamming into the Russian a second time. The man swayed backwards. Rick stepped forward and stamped down on the man's shin. More Russian. The man grabbed all around, one hand grasping a kettle in an alcove. He hurled it at Rick. Then a succession of mugs.

Rick raised an arm and deflected the kettle which crashed to the floor. The first mug smashed behind him, the second caught him under the eye. The pain sharp, then nothing. He drew his baton and flicked it out.

Officer safety training instructors always emphasised that in a real situation, there would be no time to think. So techniques had to be instinctive. Breathing they said was essential.

'Get back!'

The Russian straightened, roared, and charged forward. Rick stepped back into the corridor, ready to jump aside at the last moment. But the Russian's momentum was checked by his belt catching on the door handle. His trousers twisted round, pulling his body sideways and off-balance. Rick moved forward and struck the Russian man on his upper arm, then his thigh. His baton felt like a flyswat.

The Russian yanked his belt back and forth, screaming in annoyance.

The fire alarm continued to bleat.

Rick wellied the Russian again, arm and leg. He sensed the man weakening. He struck him again, hard as he could.

'Down.'

Finally, the man freed his belt from the door handle, and sank to his knees.

'Lie down.'

Slowly, the man fell on to his hands and collapsed to the floor.

'You're under arrest – for kidnapping Jack Philipps, on suspicion of murdering Jane Formby, and for perverting the course of justice.'

The man looked back into the room as if his explanation was there. The yellow plastic bag from Serious Games lay on a bed. The TV was flickering and tinny voices added to the clamour. But there was no sign of the boy.

'Jack!' shouted Rick.

Unable to discern an answer above the clacking alarm, he holstered his baton and took out his cuffs. Stepped forward. The man lashed out with his feet, catching Rick in the shin. Rick retreated, swapping back to his baton. He would knock the man unconscious if there was no other way.

The Russian got to his knees, stood up, and staggered back into the room, clutching at the hairdryer bracket on the wall. The bracket ripped away, the dryer falling out and bouncing across the carpet.

Rick followed, stopping to open the door of the ensuite. He glanced inside but couldn't see the boy. Where was he?

The Russian knew.

Might be persuaded to share.

Baton raised to strike, Rick advanced further into the room. Shattered mugs and a broken lamp littered the floor. A tray of food sat next to the burbling TV. The Russian had collapsed on the nearest single bed, the linen bunched and bloodstained. Jack's blood? The man was hauling himself towards the headboard. Clothing lay on the second bed, but nothing Rick recognised as belonging to Jack. The blinds were drawn.

'Where's the boy?'

The Russian ignored him. He'd reached the end of the bed and bent towards the drawers. Pulled out a handgun.

Rick hurled his baton. One chance at the adults only coconut shy. The baton struck the Russian's wrist and the gun fell from his grip. Lay halfway between the two men.

They both dived for it. The Russian marginally quicker, his hand clutching at the weapon. Rick landed heavily on his back, his opponent crying out with the jolt. Rick grabbed at the Russian's hand gripping the gun. With his other hand he flailed around for a weapon. He felt broken china, a flex. He yanked on the flex. The Russian bucked around, trying to free himself. They wrestled for control over the gun, both grunting with effort. The Russian jerked his arm back and forth. Rick couldn't hold on. He let go, hauled on the flex. The Russian threw Rick back, half-sat up. Rick's hand felt the short stem of the lamp. He gripped, lifted, swung, and smashed the heavy square base down on the Russian's face.

The Russian sagged back and the gun fell from his grip. His head struck the protruding bedside drawer.

Rick grabbed the gun. He pointed it at the Russian, prodded his leg. The man didn't move. Rick stuffed the gun down the back of his waistband. On his knees, searched for his dropped handcuffs amongst the chaos. He found them. He handcuffed the Russian's hands in a front stack and tied his legs with the flex of the lamp. Every police officer should carry one.

Picked up his baton, tightened his grip.

He could simply beat the Russian until he revealed where the

317

boy was. But the big man might not yield for hours. Rick could bargain. Or he could apply a different kind of pressure. He looked around the room, unsure how long he'd have. Lamp, pillows, kettle, hairdryer. An arsenal of torture with only a little imagination.

A helicopter flew overhead. He had two or three minutes, maybe less.

He crawled to the foot of the bed, put his baton down, picked up the kettle. It was empty. He grabbed the hairdryer and turned it on. Heat pumped out.

A grunt made him turn.

The Russian's eyelids flickered, half in, half out of consciousness.

Rick switched on the hairdryer. Pointed it at the Russian, scalding air pumping out and wafting over.

The Russian looked at Rick, glanced at the hairdryer. They stared at each other, an old soldier with a war wound, Rick speculated, and a detective who was feeling older every second. Both would be sore in the morning, might wish they'd done things differently. Using the hairdryer might be counter-productive, the smarter move not to use it.

Rick turned off the hairdryer, threw it down. He sank back against the wall. His eye hurt, his shoulder hurt. Everything hurt.

'Where's Jack?'

The Russian stared at Rick, kept staring. Finally, he nodded at the ensuite. 'He . . . okay.'

'Jack!'

There was no reply.

Dark figures appeared in the doorway. They wore helmets and padded uniforms, pointed firearms.

'Try the bathroom,' shouted Rick.

The entry team glided into the room, gave short, sharp instructions. Rick did as he was told. Lay on the floor and held out his hands.

'Lad's in here,' shouted one of the entry team. Their leader spoke into a lapel mike.

Rick lay still. His head felt like a football, his ear was throbbing and his eye closing up.

'Needs a paramedic but he's okay.'

Rick closed his eyes. Other people were now in charge. He felt as if he could sleep for a week, possibly forever. He wondered if that was what it would feel like at the end: he could sleep forever and *wanted* to sleep forever.

41

Rick staggered out of the fire exit and along the side of the hotel, stopping to lean on the metal benches. Everything ached. He was hoping for another few minutes with the Russian he'd arrested, but beforehand, he needed a sitrep.

An ambulance exited the carpark with sirens and flashing lights. A second stood with its back doors open. Two police vans waited in the drop-off and pick-up zone outside the hotel reception. A driver sat in each van, and at the rear, an armed officer stood guard.

Seeing Rick, Hunter broke away from talking to Nhung and a uniform inspector.

Behind them, the hotel carpark was in noisy disarray. A dozen police vehicles and tens of plain clothes and uniformed officers, some carrying weapons. Rubberneckers were held back at the road entrance, and a large group of hotel guests contained behind a line of police tape. A line of unmarked dark blue vans with multiple aerials and reinforced bumpers stood in the centre. The side doors were open and armed officers were stowing weapons and kit.

'You okay?' said Hunter.

Rick nodded. One out of ten, but not mortally injured. 'What about Jack?'

'On way to hospital. He's lost a finger but he's going to be fine.'

'Second suspect?'

'Nicked. They're both in the back of a van, and the armed convoy are getting ready to take them away. You, Rick, need to get seen by a paramedic.'

'Later.'

Rick stumbled over to the marked police vans. An update on Jack's injuries and confirmation of the second arrest were all he'd wanted, and he might not get another chance.

He knocked on the passenger door of the nearest van. The blue lights were rotating and flickered across his face. Recognising Rick, the driver unlocked the door.

He climbed in and looked into the back – across the jump seats and storage racks to the cage. Inside, the Russian he'd arrested.

'Two minutes.'

Rick climbed over the seat and into the back. Ducking down, he stepped past the racks of equipment. The cage was a small prison cell, one-and-a-half metres high and one metre square, made of reinforced plastic. Thin gaps for air at the top and bottom and a band of breathing holes at mid-height.

Sitting on the plastic seat was the Russian, handcuffed in the front stack position and wearing a police-issue boilersuit. A bloody bandage wrapped around his head.

Rick banged on the plastic. 'You cut off his finger.'

No response.

He banged again. 'You mutilated him.'

The Russian looked slowly across. 'I no touch boy.'

'One of you did.' It didn't matter – joint enterprise would cover both. 'What about the prostitute Jane Formby? Killed at the Golden Lion hotel in Manchester fourteen years ago.'

'No me.'

'Was it Igor?'

The half-smile disappeared, replaced by a frown of miscomprehension.

'Igor – Semion Volkov's son. That's why you're in Manchester, yes? To stop it being investigated?' Rick tried again. 'How long have you worked for Semion Volkov, and for his son Igor?'

The Russian frowned again. 'E–ager?'

Bill Clough had told Rick he'd heard the word eager several times in the next room. And the Russian in the cage had frowned each time Rick had said the name of the Russian oligarch's son. Each time Rick had *pronounced* his name I-gore. If E-ager was the correct Russian pronunciation, it placed Igor Volkov at the scene of the murder of Jane Formby. The Swedish historic allegation showed his propensity.

But it took him no further with the involvement of the two Russians sitting in the van cages. Minders or otherwise henchmen employed by the Volkovs. Had they worked for the Volkov family for fourteen years? Was either of them the man arguing with Igor Volkov in room 14, as overheard by Bill Clough?

'Sir, I've got to go,' shouted the driver, 'the armed escort is waiting.'

'Thirty seconds,' said Rick, standing up.

'If you didn't kill her, recovering her body might help prove that.' Killers varied, but some liked to take souvenirs, others liked to boast about it. Maybe one of the Russians had heard where Jane Formby was buried – maybe one of them had *helped* bury her – or maybe they hadn't, but until Rick knew otherwise, he was surmising they did.

'Sir, the sergeant's going ballistic on the radio.'

'Ten seconds.'

'The prostitute's mother is dying and wants to bury her daughter – and find some peace – before it's too late.'

The Russian rubbed his leg.

Rick remembered he walked with a limp, and changed tack. 'You need an operation on that leg? Well, I might be able to sort something – but only if you help me.'

He banged on the plastic.

His prisoner looked up, for the first time meeting Rick's stare. In the Russian's eyes, pain – or hope? They'd shared a moment of reflection in the hotel room. Both were foot soldiers for a cause.

'Sergeant's coming over.'

'Go for God's sake.'

'To be continued at South Manchester,' said Rick. He banged a final time on the cage, and backed up to the front seats, the van already moving.

'Hit all the bloody potholes.'

'Yes, sir!'

Rick pulled open the side door and leapt out, slamming it behind him. The Russian's hopeful stare was a tiny green shoot, but he needed more material to work with. He needed both men's antecedents, and their history with the Volkovs. Needed Maggie to chase the Swedish police for their case file on Igor Volkov. He needed to compare both Russians' DNA and fingerprint profiles against the ones recorded from the Golden Lion. A match would place one of them at the murder scene, together with Igor Volkov, fourteen years ago.

He got to his feet, brushed himself down.

The van lurched forward to join the line of waiting vehicles. At point, a police car containing three armed officers, then two vans each holding a prisoner and an unmarked van belonging to the entry team, and bringing up the rear, another police car with armed officers. Blue lights flickered atop the liveried vehicles. Sirens wailed from the lead car as it pulled onto the road. The convoy followed in a whirl of blue and two-tones.

As it disappeared from view, a minicab with a Cosmos Cars sign on the roof pulled into the hotel entrance. The driver hooted.

'You don't change, boss,' said Hunter, walking up. 'I'd best get off. Perk of my new job never to have to wait long for a cab.'

'Haven't you missed it?'

'I'd be a Dunlop tyre if I said I ain't.'

His former DS waved a hand, and scratching the back of his neck, walked toward the waiting cab.

Clutching her daybook, his new DS appeared. 'I'll give you a lift back to the nick, sir, or home, or wherever.'

Rick followed Nhung to the CID pool car, and sat heavily in the passenger seat. His cheek was swelling, and he was losing vision in one eye. He closed both of them.

'Sir, a couple of things.'

'Yes, Nhung?'

'From Monday, I'll no longer be restricted to light duties.'

Rick nodded, and wished he hadn't. 'That's good news.'

'I messed up confirming Jack was at his dad's place.'

'No one's perfect.'

'Do you want to know why I'm on light duties?'

Rick forced his eyes open, looked across at Nhung. 'I think I figured.'

'You did?'

'I pulled your personnel file and saw you had a sheet redacted. That's unusual and suggests counterterrorism or undercover work. My guess, considering your ethnicity, is that you were asked to consider being a UC, maybe even recruited, but you didn't like it.'

Nhung nodded. 'They wanted me to spy on my own people.' She looked around again. 'I flipped out, and they decided to give me a fresh start. You're the only person who's interested in my potential as a detective.'

'I'm glad it's working out. What's the other thing?'

'I've been offered a place in the CID office – to replace DS Harris when he leaves on promotion.'

Rick was disappointed but not surprised. Nhung thought for herself, a competency he admired. If she decided to leave his team, she would be a useful ally in the main office. 'I'd be sad to see you go.'

Nhung started the engine.

At the same time, a second convoy turned into the entrance of the hotel, the first a high spec Range Rover with tinted windows, the second a blue Mondeo, the third a dark saloon. The driver's window of the Range Rover buzzed down, a PC raised the police tape, and the three cars entered the carpark.

'Better wait, Nhung, see what they want.'

Harry climbed out of the Mondeo, and Walsh out of the pool car. Chewing gum, the DCI nodded at Harry. The gesture not returned. Robbo eased his feet down to the tarmac from the Range Rover. He put on his flat hat, checked his reflection in the window, and followed the other two towards the hotel.

Rick pushed open the door of the pool car and hauled himself out. He leant back against the bodywork and waited.

The three men changed course.

The intelligence officer the first to speak. 'Heard you had a little operation going on.'

'Rick,' said South Manchester's superintendent, walking alongside Harry. The three men appeared in front of Rick like a mirage of Shakespeare's witches. He could almost smell burning.

'Sir.'

'Well done. I'll be putting you forward for both an investigative commendation and an award for bravery.'

'Am I still—'

'All gone away.'

Robbo handed back to Rick his warrant card. It showed the

correct rank and the current chief constable. All Rick wanted was to be allowed to run South Manchester's special investigations unit, but he suspected there was a sting coming.

'Yeah,' said Walsh, 'nice one – worth a new bit of gum.' He spat out a lump, unwrapped a new piece.

'Where are the two Russians?' said Harry.

'Custody at South Manchester.'

'They were meant to be held here.' The intelligence officer glanced at Robbo but didn't comment. He turned back to Walsh and Rick. 'Priorities, gentlemen, like I said last time. We'll look after them for a bit, do the debrief; then DCI Walsh can interview for the kidnap; and finally DCI Castle, now happily reinstated, for the cold case murder.'

Walsh nodded, chewing gum as if it was necessary for respiration.

Robbo pulled out his phone. 'I'll sort it, Harry.' He turned to Rick. 'Go home and recover. Start again next week.'

Rick no longer felt tired. He folded back down into the passenger seat and yanked the door of the pool car shut. Waiting three or four weeks before he got another crack at the Russian might be too long for Mrs Formby. The wheel would turn: MI6 would no doubt be briefed, and international players including the US might become involved. He might not even get a chance to try to offset his feelings of guilt for not preventing Jack's injury by finding some peace for Mrs Formby.

Unless.

'South Manchester, Nhung, pedal to the metal!'

42

Nhung sat close to the steering wheel which wasn't the police method, but she drove hard and without hesitation. And she said nothing which suited Rick, silently urging her to drive faster and hardly noticing his throbbing eye.

The barrier rose and Nhung sped into South Manchester's backyard. PCs loitered. The yard lights full glare. Patrol vehicles were lined up against one wall, and outside the van dock stood the two police vans.

Rick breathed a sigh of relief. They were in time.

He jumped out, ran over. The cages in the back were empty, and there was no one in the cabs. He thought again. Wondered why neither van was parked inside the dock, and the dock locked down.

'Custody,' shouted Rick in Nhung's direction.

He banged the code into the keypad for the door into the nick. Hauled it open, and jogged down the corridor. Banged two more codes, hauled two more doors.

Custody.

Heaving. When was it not. Smelling of cannabis and microwave food. Shouting, swearing, jeering.

He ran up to the sergeants' high counter. Two of them, both going grey – almost as he looked. Fat as bakers. An open tin of chocolates on their desk.

He scanned the whiteboard above them. *Winslow, Off Weap. Thomas, D&D. Komsky, Murder.* He read down to the bottom, including the juvenile cells. His stomach throbbed in company with his eye. Maybe they hadn't been written up on the board yet.

'The two bodies from the Chequered Flag?'

The sergeant shook his head. 'I know nothing.' Comedy accent. His colleague laughed.

Rick slammed the desk.

'Sir?'

'Van drivers?'

They shook their heads.

Rick retraced his steps, and bumped into Nhung in the corridor.

'I'm going to try the canteen.'

He ran up the stairs and along the corridor, following another microwave reek. He walked into the canteen. At the corner table half a dozen PCs were playing cards. He recognised the van driver.

The PC glanced up.

'A minute of your time.'

The room fell silent and the PC put down his cards. Walked over.

'Where are the prisoners?'

'Superintendent Robinson phoned. He told me and Alec, the other driver, to release them to MI5. A few minutes later, three cars turned up in the backyard. They hardly said a word. Hustled the two Russians out of the vans and into their cars. I asked the officer in charge to sign my notebook.' The PC delved into his pocket and pulled it out. He opened it at the rubber band, and passed it over.

'It's signed Donald Duck.'

A spit of laughter from the cardplayers.

Then silence.

'Are you saying?' said the van driver.

Rick walked out, leaving the PC to stew. He walked back down the corridor, climbed another set of stairs, and retreated to his office. What had Hunter once said? Rick never gave up, never took no as an answer.

Nhung entered.

'Tea?'

'No. Yes. Sorry.' She didn't even drink it.

Nhung switched the kettle on. Rick updated her.

'What now?'

'They'll be held by the intelligence service for a couple of weeks and *debriefed*. Service euphemism for interrogation – everything they've ever seen, heard, or done. MI6 are likely to contact the US, possibly the Russians. Maybe they'll be persuaded to switch sides, and sent back; but hopefully they'll be passed onto the murder team to be interviewed and prosecuted. Our historic investigation of the murder of Jane Formby is last in line. Might take a month or more. Might never happen.'

'By which point—'

'Mrs Formby is likely to have died.'

Nhung handed him a mug of tea. 'Is that it for now, then?'

Rick nodded. 'The good news is Jack's okay. Go home, Nhung. Make your decision, and I'll see you Monday – or not.'

She nodded, walked over to the door. 'You should go home too, sir.'

Rick set down the mug. He probably should. But like a honeybee when the sun was shining, he couldn't stop himself. The two Russians had been watching Maggie's flat. *Had spied on him and Maggie, had followed them around*. It wasn't just for Mrs Formby, it was personal. He wanted to point the finger.

Intelligence service and counterterrorism prisoners were usually held in super-secure custody suites, and there were four sets he knew about across the north-west. Almost definitely several he didn't know about. Choosing one to visit would be a lottery with half the tickets missing, and even if he was lucky, he might not even be able to confirm the two Russians' residence. He could try online or by phone, but security protocols were tight and effective.

If there was a weakness, it would be personnel – and there were three angles and a wild card he could try. Ian Holcroft; Maggie's former sapper colleague Duncan; and a vague contact at the airport.

He started with Ian.

His mobile rang out, so he tried his home phone number.

A sharp intake of breath. Then a pause.

Swapping Churchill quotes on the DCI's course seemed a long time ago. Rick explained what he wanted.

'And what makes you think I'll know where they're being taken?'

'You're an informant controller. Part of your job remit is to attend all north-west strategy meetings. You know people who'll know.'

Rick sensed the mouthpiece being covered. He heard muffled, strained voices, and a door being slammed. Then:

'Not this time, Rick.'

A ringing tone.

Rick banged the handset down onto the base. Shoved the whole contraption off the desk. He picked it up, jabbed numbers for his wild card.

Three rings and the line was cut. He tried again. Straight to the honeyed tones of Louise Nottingham, senior counsel at Sunlight House. *Please leave a message.* He wasn't surprised she wasn't accepting his calls having walked out of the Taverna.

He tried Maggie. Strike two.

'It's been on the news. You got them.'

'Yes and no. MI5 have whisked them away.'

'No, Rick.'

'I haven't even asked yet.'

'You want me to contact Duncan, see if he's heard anything.'

'Well?'

Duncan was six, not five; Legoland, not Box 500. But there was a chance he might know something. 'Could you?'

'I can't – not again. I contacted him during the Khetan case.'

'Last time, Mags.'

There was silence for a few seconds. Neither of them believed it.

'You shouldn't be asking, and he shouldn't be telling. He'd be putting his job at six at risk.'

'Please, Mags.'

He could make his case – he was trying to help a dying mother who'd spent over a decade grieving – but it wasn't the full story, and she'd know.

'Okay.'

'You'll ask him?'

'Yes.'

'Can you also chase the Swedes? Their case file, background knowledge etcetera might give us something.'

'Will do. I have got one result, though. Tara phoned me when she couldn't get hold of you. Preliminary results from her forensic exam of one Bowker have yielded a hit. A DNA profile from a hair found on a front bedroom curtain has matched one of the profiles from the Golden Lion. You'll be able to confirm soon enough but—'

'One of the Russians was at the scene of the murder of Jane Formby.'

'Did she compare the fingerprint which linked Jack's phone and the letter to the unidentified sets of prints recovered from the hotel?'

'She did, but there wasn't a match.'

Maybe he'd worn gloves. It didn't matter – Rick could now put one of them and, circumstantially at least, Igor Volkov at the scene. The two Russians arrested at the Chequered Flag could have entered the UK without a problem if they hadn't – so far – got a criminal record on the PNC.

'We've almost got them. Don't forget the Swedes – or Duncan.'

He placed the handset back down. He knew Maggie well and wanted to know her even better. But he already knew her well enough to know she would chase the Swedish police but not her former colleague.

Although he now had the information to challenge one of the Russians, he still needed to establish which one, and find out where they'd been taken.

Strike three: his little black book.

Not previous girlfriends, for which entries wouldn't fill a page, but the names and phone numbers for people he'd met on his senior investigating officer course. There had been a lot of emphasis given to new SIOs establishing a network of contacts not only within the police, but across the public services of the north-west. The emergency services, hospitals, prisons, Manchester Cathedral, the Sikh Temple, Khizra Mosque, the border force, customs, some government departments. Plus a busload of specialists, including an ecologist, a farrier, a vet, an entomologist, a cave diver; even a lepidopterist and a pedologist. The course had lasted three weeks, and every day there had been networking opportunities. Some officers had gained ten pounds in cakes and beer; Rick had filled his little black book.

He pulled it out, turned the pages. Most people he'd never spoken to, but hoped, in his moment of need, they would still have the same phone number.

DS Pam Stevens. She worked at the national crime agency, had worked there for twenty years. Intelligence coordinator. Not much she didn't know about how all the myriad arms of the police, security services, and the military worked together.

He dialled.

One ring.

'Pam's phone.'

'Is she there? Tell her, DCI Castle, South Manchester.'

Thirty seconds . . . a minute . . . two minutes.

'Rick, this is unexpected. Work or –'

The memory made him smile. One or two entries in his little black book covered both bases. 'Work.'

'Thought so. Seen you on the news. Nice job, sir.'

'It's not over.'

Rick explained for the third time.

Pam didn't say yes, but she didn't say no. Which meant he would just have to wait. The reason honeybees were such effective pollinators was due to the waggle dance, the way they told each other the direction and distance to the best sources of pollen and nectar. He knew that, but still he was tempted to drive to a secure custody centre on the off chance.

43

Rick overslept, took a long shower. In the kitchen he checked his phone, then read the note from Maggie.

I've taken tomorrow off, figured you'd be out of it today.
Love you.
Mags X

He poured a bowl of muesli. He checked his phone again for a message from Pam. He didn't want a message. If she had anything, it would be a phone call. He checked for missed calls but there weren't any.

There wasn't any milk either.

He hoped the Russians didn't have milk, didn't have any breakfast. He hoped they were being questioned with thumbscrews. It was *him* they'd followed. *Maggie's* flat that had been broken into. It was *their* privacy that had been invaded. Not Walsh's, not Robbo's, not Harry's.

He phoned Maggie.

'Feeling better?'

'A bit. I was wondering—'

'About Duncan?'

'About the Swedish file.'

'Nothing.'

'I can't wait any longer, or for the intelligence service to feed us their scraps. Let's do it ourselves . . . we've got a DNA profile for one Russian, images for both, proximate dates of birth, and know they work for Semion Volkov. One of them it seems for at least fourteen years. You could contact Euro- and Interpol.'

'That's what a half-rate intelligence analyst would have already done.'

'Sorry!'

'As soon as you got the dashcam photo I sent out the requests for intel, and this morning I've updated them with the image of the second man and the DNA profile.' She paused. 'Rick?'

'Yes?'

'There's no milk.'

He checked his phone for messages and missed calls. He phoned the hospital to check on Jack Philipps. The boy was recovering from an operation, and wanted to know when he could start playing tennis. Rick phoned both Jack's parents, and differences temporarily forgotten, left messages of condolences and support.

The doorbell rang.

Pam?

A man with tattooed arms and wearing an apron of tools stood on the doorstep. The rep from the security company, scheduled to install an alarm, a Faraday box, hinge bolts on the front door, and CCTV. He got busy.

Rick walked to a local shop for some milk. He checked his phone on the way there and on the way back. The Russians he hoped were still on the rack. Being slowly stretched, or waterboarded, or subjected to hours of heavy metal – or psalms. Whatever.

The installer finished. Bolting the door after the horse had bolted wasn't cheap. Three cups of tea and a bill with four figures.

Rick tidied up.

His phone rang. At last.

'Is that DCI Castle?' A woman's voice, but not Pam's. 'I'm ringing from Greenacres care home, we specialise in respite care. Alison Formby is one of our residents and thinks she saw you on some breaking news on the TV. Is that possible?'

'It is.'

'She's been telling me what happened to her daughter.' Rick could hear the woman sniffing. 'A terrible business.' She took a deep breath. 'The thing is, Alison hasn't got much longer. A week maybe. If there is any good news. We don't get much of that here.'

Rick sat on the cleaning caddy. He sent his mum a message, wondered about visiting Dad.

Maggie came home from work. He told her about the call from Greenacres. He showed her how the alarm worked, and the app for the CCTV. She said it felt like they were the ones now in prison. Yes, he'd bought milk. But the alarm installer had drunk half.

She produced two slim files from her workbag.

Rick shut up.

'The Swedish police called. Superintendent Fager, then an inspector, was officer in the case for the rape committed by Igor Volkov. Spoke perfect English and knew all about the Volkovs. He had a list of associates and hangers-on and has managed – one of his team, I think – to identify our two suspects.'

Rick read the notes standing up.

Andrei Petrov, forty-five years old. Former Russian special forces. Has been employed by the Volkov family for fifteen years; bodyguard mainly, suspected of occasional special ops as per his skillset. Walks with a limp, a gunshot injury from his military career, and the reason he left. Estranged from his wife. Believed to have a young daughter.

Kirill Zalinski, forty-three years old. The image was similar, in fact they looked like brothers. The biography was also similar – former special forces, currently in the employ of the Volkovs, but only for ten years. No family history.

Only Petrov had been working for the Volkovs at the time of Jane Formby's murder – which meant it was Andrei Petrov's DNA profile recovered from the hotel room at the Golden Lion and matched with the scene at 1 Bowker.

'What about Igor Volkov – does his DNA on file match a profile recovered from the hotel?'

'Still chasing it up with Fager. There's some red tape.'

Rick nodded, his mind still whirring.

'What now?'

'Wait my turn for an interview.' If he got to sit across a table from Andrei Petrov, hopefully sooner rather than later, it gave him a few more cards to play with. He'd already dangled an operation in a western hospital.

They ordered a takeaway. Rick kept checking his phone, but didn't tell Maggie about his call to Pam Stevens.

'It'll be weeks, won't it?'

'Probably.'

He put the phone in his pocket and checked for a message from Pam in the kitchen and in the bathroom. Debriefing should be slow, but might be fast. The longer the two Russians were in the UK, the harder it would be to repatriate them without public disquiet. A good thing, but not for Mrs Formby and locating her daughter's body.

No messages overnight, or waiting when he woke.

In the bathroom, he phoned Pam. It went to voicemail and he left a message.

Maggie was unimpressed. 'Was that your fancy woman?'

'*You* are my fancy woman.'

They discussed the day. Visiting Jack at hospital. Lunch –

'Somewhere nice,' said Maggie – a visit to Three Views to see Dad, and then a quiz night with Maggie's basketball team. Rick pulled a face.

Maggie pulled one back.

Nothing from Pam.

First, a haircut. Maggie insisted, or she'd cut it herself. As good as married already, Rick sat next to Steven Forest who'd robbed the petrol station with a bread knife he'd stolen from the supermarket next door. Three years, just out.

Maggie was waiting outside.

'Is that?'

Rick nodded.

His phone rang.

'DCI Castle.'

Maggie pretended to punch him in the stomach.

'It's Pam. They're at West Kington.'

Rick balled his fist. He knew it, having been there once to collect a prisoner. It was a super-secure suite, but not a secret one. Located alongside an industrial estate.

'Two front row tickets for the show at the Palace coming your way.' They weren't a bribe, but a thank you. Not from the bottom of his heart, but anticipating the next time.

'With you?'

'Afraid not.'

Rick pocketed his phone. 'The Russians are in Merseyside. I'm going.'

'The debrief's over?' Maggie frowned.

'I've got a chance to have five minutes with Petrov.' He kissed her on the lips. 'You okay to get a cab home? Love you. Enjoy the quizzie.'

'Rick?'

He was already pulling away. 'Last time,' said Maggie, 'we go anywhere together in one vehicle.'

44

Armed police officers sat behind bulletproof glass in the sentry box at West Kington. Rick picked up the yellow gate phone.

'DCI Rick Castle, South Manchester.' He held his badge up to the camera. Hoped he wouldn't be needing his old one for a while.

There was a pause. 'You haven't got an appointment.'

'Tell Harry, it's me.'

'Harry who?'

Hunter would have appreciated the knock-knock absurdity. 'He's in charge of the two from Manchester Airport.'

'Wait there.'

Behind the sentry box enclosure of barbed wire, another fence, topped with razor wire and CCTV cameras, and behind that a squat building the size of a football pitch. The walls and roof were capable of withstanding mortar shells. Most of it was underground.

Quarter of an hour later, an officer holding a Heckler and Koch rifle emerged from the sentry box. The outer gate trundled aside.

Rick drove into the wire enclosure, and the gate closed behind him.

'Unlock your doors and open the boot.'

The officer checked the backseat and peered into the boot. A second officer appeared, a Glock pistol holstered on his leg. He checked underneath Rick's car with a pole mirror.

'Okay,' said the first man. 'Park in bay sixty-three and report to reception.'

The inner gate slid open and Rick drove inside. He parked, walked over to reception, and showed his badge to another camera.

After a short delay, the door buzzed open.

'Here to see Harry.'

'Who's Harry?'

This again. 'Overseeing the two arrested in Manchester.'

'But no appointment?'

'No.'

'I can make an enquiry.'

'I'll wait.'

A door clicked open. 'Walk through there.'

Rick opened the door into a room at the side. An airport X-ray cubicle stood in a corner. Two officers walked through from reception.

'Shoes, belt, laces, personal items.' The officer held out a plastic tray.

Rick took off his shoes, removed the laces and his belt. Emptied his pockets, and deposited everything in the tray. He held up his arms while one of them patted him down. After the man nodded, Rick walked into the X-ray cubicle. The door swung round, a light turned green, the door swung back, and he stepped out. The officer handed him a pair of plimsolls and the door at the end clicked open.

'Wait in there.'

Rick walked in, and the door locked behind him.

There was a chair, and a window at the top of a wall. It was barred and not even Oliver Twist could have squeezed through.

He sat down and waited. He'd been locked up more times in the last fortnight than a South Manchester dev nom.

After twenty minutes he stopped looking at his watch. It would be what it would be.

The door buzzed open.

Harry stood on the threshold, eating a sandwich from a brown paper bag.

'Did you get lost?'

'I'd like five minutes with Andrei Petrov. I think he might know where the body of Jane Formby is, the victim of my cold case.'

'Petrov?' said Harry, raising his eyebrows.

Rick nodded. 'I've now got a match on a DNA profile that puts him in the hotel room where she was murdered.'

'You have been busy.'

'Her mother's not got long to live.'

'How long?' Harry took another bite of the sandwich.

'Days.'

Harry kept chewing, scrunching his nose as if he wasn't really enjoying the sandwich, or talking to Rick, or both.

'Petrov sat on my chair. He ate my porridge.'

'I thought it was about the Formbys?'

'It's about both.'

The door behind Harry started beeping. He nodded, took a step back. 'Wait here.' He stepped forward again. 'Want the other sandwich? Never got on with tuna.'

Rick wasn't hungry but he took it. The two of them were bonding.

The sandwich was long since eaten, the paper bag made into an aeroplane; unfolded, blown up and popped; balled and booted around the room. Was he going to be shown back to reception? Dumped in another wood?

The door buzzed open.

Rick recognised the woman he'd seen in the pinewood. Dumpy with straight, unfussy hair, she reminded him of a school crossing patrol. He felt her staring analysis. Indicating for him to follow, she clicked through another door, and down a corridor to a lift. Buzzing in the background. They descended two storeys in the lift. The control panel was coded. A camera watched from a ceiling corner. They exited the lift, passed through another locked door, down another silent corridor. No signs on the walls or doors, as if it was wartime.

'Wait in here.'

The door shut and the lock clicked. Progress, or so he hoped.

He'd been left in an interview room, but a big one. Big enough to swing a cat, or a person dressed as a cat. The size of four at South Manchester. In the centre were a table and two chairs. A half-height metal cabinet stood on one side. A blanket sat on top. Cameras occupied ceiling corners, and covering half a wall, a black observation screen.

More waiting.

Missed his paper bag. Regretted not asking the school crossing patrol for some water. He wasn't a prisoner, but he was being treated like one. He was beginning to feel like Joseph K.

The door clicked open and Andrei Petrov was escorted into the room by a uniformed police officer. Two armed officers stood by the door. The first man handed Rick two bottles of water, then removed Petrov's handcuffs. The three officers withdrew and the door shut.

'Fifteen minutes,' said Harry on a hidden speaker.

Rick sat down, pointed at a chair.

Petrov rubbed his wrists and looked around slowly. The Russian pulled out the remaining chair and sat down with his legs stretched out. Instinctively, he felt for his leg, but stopped himself and retracted his hand.

Rick unscrewed the top of a bottle and drank deeply. He screwed it back. Tossed the second bottle to Petrov.

The Russian set it on the table. Leant back in his chair and focussed on a spot on the wall behind Rick. Textbook.

Petrov kept his focus. Two minutes. Three.

The Russian glanced at Rick, looked away again. It was almost impossible not to. The human condition was to engage. To help. To love, and be loved.

Long way to go.

'Your English, Andrei, is very good, yes?'

There was no reply, no change of posture or gaze.

'You've been spying on me, Andrei. Me and my girlfriend. You planted drugs in my car, and you planted drugs in my house. You *broke into* my house – *our* house. Upset my girlfriend, terrified my family.'

The Russian's eyes didn't flicker.

'Fourteen years ago, Jane Formby was murdered at the Golden Lion hotel. Evidence puts Igor Volkov, your boss, in that room at the same time. Your DNA profile has recently been identified, and I now know you were also there. You told me in the back of the police van at the airport you didn't kill her, but leaving that aside for the moment, what did you and Igor do with her body?'

Petrov didn't move, yet alone speak.

'As I told you earlier, Mrs Formby hasn't got long to live. A day or two. So I ask you, please, tell me where her daughter is.'

Unmoving and unmoved, the Russian remained a picture-like student of the opposite wall.

'Ask yourself, Andrei, what have the Volkovs done for you? They sent you here knowing there was a strong risk you might be prosecuted for the very crime they were trying to cover up. They haven't helped you get medical treatment for your injury. They don't care about you. You're not family, you're disposable.'

343

Still there was no reaction.

Rick stood, thumped his chair under the table and against the injured leg of Petrov. The Russian gritted his teeth. He'd been a soldier in the special forces, knew how to endure pain and hardship. But Rick had made his point. 'You need an operation on that leg, and we might be able to help you get one – *if* you help us.'

The Russian remained as lifeless as a shop dummy.

So much for a carrot.

Time for a stick.

'Imagine, Andrei, if it was *your* daughter?'

Like a marksman adjusting his aim, Petrov shifted, bringing his intense gaze to focus on Rick.

Rick stared back, knowing he now had the Russian's attention. 'I know you have a daughter, Andrei. A young one. That must be nice, but at the same time it must be worrying for you. The mischief she can get up to. Talking to strangers, getting lost, running away.' Rick paused for effect. 'The Volkovs, Andrei, as you well know, are *very* unpredictable people. As is the Kremlin.'

'Castle,' said Harry from the hidden speakers. Loudly, and sounding strained, very unHarry.

Rick had got to him, too.

Inference was one thing, execution another. But saying it was easy. Saying it so he believed it. Saying it to someone whose employers and state actors would do that sort of thing, someone who would believe it might happen.

'We could send them a message, Andrei, tell them you've cooperated with the British security services.'

The door buzzed open and two men in plain clothes entered. Standing by the door, the two armed officers.

'This way, sir.'

'Think about it, Andrei.'

'Sir?'

'You were a soldier, Andrei. Do the honourable thing.'

The two men secured Rick's arms and shoulders, and forced him towards the door. Only in the corridor did he stop struggling. A third man led back towards the lift. Rick had no choice but to follow.

In the X-ray room next to reception, Rick's possessions were returned. He put on his belt and tied up his shoes. Pocketed his effects.

Walked out into the carpark.

Harry appeared like Banquo's ghost, and followed Rick to his car.

'Next time, I'll ask for an interview plan.'

Rick climbed in, cracked the window. Harry stood alongside, as if he was about to wave goodbye to a troublesome son.

'There is a small chance, Rick, however, a very small chance, that it worked. Petrov just told us they dumped Jane Formby's body in a hole dug for a new tree, near the back of the hotel.'

45

Rick found Mrs Formby in a chair, looking out from her room across the Peak District national park. Greenacres care home was set on a hillside at its western edge. Curlews could be heard in the summer, and white hares spotted in the winter. It specialised in palliative care, and had been chosen by Alison Formby to spend her last few weeks.

He introduced himself, and as he brought up a chair, could see her tensing.

'We've found her.'

Mrs Formby grabbed his wrist, her eyes glassy. She dabbed at them with a tissue. 'I'm sorry.'

Rick shook his head. 'No, I'm sorry it's taken this long.' He poured her a glass of water and glanced out at the moor. A bird of prey was riding the thermals.

'There's binoculars at reception.'

He nodded, half-smiled.

'We received information she'd been buried close to the hotel, in the hole prepared for a new tree. After a specialist sniffer dog gave us an indication, we dug up a monkey puzzle tree. And that's where we found her, wrapped in a duvet cover. I'm so sorry.'

She took his hand, her fingers icy cold.

'Would you like a cup of tea?'

Mrs Formby shook her head. They sat holding hands for a few minutes, staring out at the national park. The black peat, the dying bracken, the pink-edged sky.

The tree they'd dug up had been an unusual part of Manchester's tree planting programme. One of six trees imported from Chile. Bill Clough had seen them when he'd exited the hotel. Rick had spoken to a partner in the design company who'd worked on the project. The trees were already semi-mature and bespoke pits had been prepared to allow for future growth, and to ensure there was no disruption to foundations or utilities. Each tree pit was lined with rubbery crates, not unlike, Rick thought, the hexagonal cell structure made by honeybees. Jane's body had been shoved under a layer of crates. Igor Volkov and Andrei Petrov had got lucky, Elliot Tipper had been right.

'Thank you,' whispered Mrs Formby.

'It'll take a little while, but as soon as we can release her body, we will.'

She gripped his wrist. 'And you'll get them?'

'I'll do my very best.'

As Rick drove away, he pondered how difficult it would be. Her daughter's body might give a cause of death but was unlikely to yield any forensic evidence, despite what he'd told Andrei Petrov. There was nothing much left except the skeleton and a tiny rag of duvet. Thanks to Swedish Superintendent Fager, Volkov's DNA, like Petrov's, had been confirmed as one of the previously unidentified profiles recovered from the Golden Lion. Which meant Rick could now place both Igor Volkov *and* Andrei Petrov in Formby's hotel room. However, charges might not receive CPS approval unless they made admissions in interview. Even arresting Igor Volkov would be difficult.

But Igor was a hotspur and might one day travel to a country with an extradition treaty with the UK. There was circumstantial evidence from Bill Clough about what he'd heard, and maybe the pathologist would work wonders. Maybe too, another strand of evidence would turn up. If he knocked on enough doors, spoke to enough people.

Another bird of prey soared high above the park, above the dark green fields, above the pale browns and russets of the moor and the black rocks of the gritstone edges.

46

The Pavilion Racquets Club stood on the outskirts of Harrogate, a prosperous northern town with attractive buildings, little crime, and one of the five Royal Horticultural Society gardens. The Club and the RHS garden shared a boundary, and the occasional tennis ball was found in the orchards. The finals of the Northern Cup were played there every year, and this year for the first time, were delayed by a month.

Rick glanced at the tournament programme. 'Do you think he's going to win?'

'Of course he is,' said Maggie.

The match was poised at one set all, and the players were having a drinks break. Jack drank from his bottle, swilled, and spat like a professional. He bounced his bandaged right hand on the racquet strings. He was lucky to be left-handed, he'd told the media. A self-effacing answer which had splashed across the newspapers.

Rick and Maggie sat at the front at one end, and when an ace was served towards them, they felt the impact of the ball crashing into the barrier. The speed and the power and the vibrations were surprising and helped build the occasion. Although, it was already big enough. Rick's jacket pocket bulged, his head awash with rehearsed words. He'd probably practised too much, but he wanted Maggie to know it was something he'd been thinking about for a long time – he didn't only have policework running around his head.

'Time, gentlemen.'

At the far end, Jack threw a ball high in the air, jumped, and at the same time extended his arm holding his racquet, his shirt pulling to reveal a slash of pale midriff, and boom. The ball whizzed over the net, striking the line of the service box.

His opponent hit the ball back. Jack flung himself across the base line, and backhanded, sent it diagonally over the net. But the ball had too much force and landed out. The crowd of five hundred, swelled by the media interest, fell silent. Maggie scowled.

Rick wondered how Andrei Petrov and Kirill Zalinski were faring. Still staring at a spot on the wall? They faced either a long prison sentence in the UK, or being returned home to be debriefed by the Kremlin and/or tortured by Volkov in the outbuildings of one of his luxurious dachas for a job not even half-done. A job undone, and made worse. Volkov's son Igor was now wanted by Manchester Police for the murder of Jane Formby.

Jack served again, the ball slamming into the barrier for an ace. Maggie squeezed Rick's hand. Tomorrow, he thought, they could visit the RHS garden, wander round the flowerbeds, the vegetable plots, the orchards, have a bite to eat, and drive slowly home, ready for work on Monday.

How to lure a suspect from a country without an extradition treaty with the UK had been Rick's obsession midway through the Khetan case, and he already had ideas for Igor Volkov. Offering specialist medical treatment in the UK, or finding – and *turning* – a Russian associate, or dangling an opportunity – diamonds or drugs or a sophisticated weapon, maybe something to make Igor's father proud.

In front of him the tennis was stop and start, violent for a few seconds, fifteen at most, then calm as snooker. Three games each, according to the scoreboard.

Maggie shook Rick's arm. Her skin was glowing, her face animated. She rolled her programme into a tube and bellowed: 'Come on Jack!'

Four all, five all.

As the players tired, the rallies lengthened and the tennis became more varied – sprints to the net, lobs, drop shots, sliced backhands.

'Six games all,' said the umpire, 'tiebreak.'

The players strode to the side of the court, and sat on the green plastic chairs. Jack wrapped a towel around his head. His opponent unzipped a banana.

Peering out from under the towel, Jack looked over in their direction. Rick raised a thumb and the boy raised a fist. They raised their fists together. The boy was recovering well, both physically and mentally – he was going to be okay.

Maggie squeezed his arm. Rick nodded.

The winner would play again in the afternoon, against Rurik Volkov. Semion's grandson had been invited to South Manchester and interviewed under caution, but had denied knowing anything more than rudimentary details of his grandfather's business or employees. And nothing about his father's time in the country over a decade earlier.

Play resumed, and Rick clapped a thundering passing shot. Come on, Jack, he found himself shouting.

A refreshments area set up among the courts had been cordoned off with fluttering white tape. Instead of a spreadeagled body and numbered yellow markers, there were twenty red-and-white umbrellas. Maggie queued for a table, and Rick went for drinks.

After switching his phone to silent, he returned from the bar with a bottle of champagne and bowls of strawberries and cream.

'Wow!' said Maggie. 'What will you do if he wins the final?'

Rick had closed his eyes signing the receipt. But it was something he was only going to do once.

He smiled as he set the bowls down, his heart pumping like a volcano. He felt hot as a volcano. He grabbed the bottle from the ice bucket and unpicked the foil. It all felt right. End of case. Decent weather. Maggie looked happy. He felt relaxed, at least as much as he ever did. A moment he would be proud to share with Mum and Dad and Becky. And Maggie, again and again. He twisted the cork –

And let it fly.

Maggie grabbed his wrist. Maybe she knew.

He poured two glasses, the champagne bubbling and lightly popping. He set down the bottle. Felt in his pocket for the small box. Still there. He went down on one knee.

'Maggie.'

She looked across at him, her face suddenly pale and serious.

'Will you marry me?'

There was a pause. Maybe she was thinking about the lost weekends, the late evenings and the all-nighters, his blood-soaked cuffs and his suits smelling of post-mortems. His purple-edged dreams day and night, his hot sweats and shivers, his meetings with Emma. But Maggie had stuff, too. Helmand, losing her legs, being deserted by her first husband, issues at work.

'I will.'

Rick closed his eyes. He felt lightheaded.

They drank the champagne, fed each other spoonfuls of strawberries and cream. Made each other laugh with impressions of people at work. The ring fitted and Maggie kept holding up her finger and grinning. They took selfies and asked a waitress to take one of the happy couple. Smiling, attractive people milled around them, and in the background, there was the whack of tennis balls and occasional burst of applause.

'Small world.'

The voice was familiar, and for a moment Rick hoped it was his subconscious playing with him. The morning too perfect.

He didn't look up. Maggie glanced across at him. Her right hand surreptitiously covered her left fingers, and in that moment, if it was possible, Rick loved her even more.

'Are you celebrating?' Robbo wore jeans, and a dark polo neck jumper which made him look pregnant.

Rick craned his head upwards. 'Thought we'd support Jack after what he's been through.'

'My thoughts exactly.' The superintendent looked at the bottle of champagne and the glasses, the remaining strawberries. 'In fact, it's lucky I spotted you: the control room are trying to get hold of you.'

'He's unavailable,' said Maggie. She tried to wink at Rick, sandbagging her face.

The two of them inhaled the moment.

Robbo glanced at her, then back at Rick. 'The protocol for the special investigations unit, which you agreed to, Rick, states you should have your phone on twenty-four seven.'

'It is on.'

Robbo leant over and plucked one of the few remaining strawberries out of the bowl. He dipped it in the cream and popped it in his mouth.

'Do I need to advertise?' he said, still chewing.

'No,' said Rick, quietly. It was typical Robbo, more answer than question. Line manager aside, leading his new unit was a privileged role, not just one he was suited for, but one he liked. 'Excuse me.'

Avoiding Maggie's stare, he stood up and walked away. He ducked under the tape and stood by a tennis court with four players warming up. 'It's DCI Castle.' In front of him, two balls were being bashed up and down.

'Two hours,' said Rick, 'depending on traffic.'

With the crash and thump of rubber balls echoing around, he weaved his way back through the crowd. Maggie would understand.

Lexicon

Russian	English
avariya	accident
da	yes
harasho	good
khuylo	dickhead
Na Zdorovie!	Cheers!
nyet	no
nevozmozhno	impossible
mamochka	mum
skazka	story
Ty menia dostal!	Don't do that!

Acknowledgements

I would like to thank my wonderful editors Eve Seymour and Mary Chesshyre. Also, the brilliant cover designer Mark Ecob, and Andrew Chapman (Prepare to Publish) for typesetting and all-round publishing expertise. Thanks to Oleg Makarov for checking the Russian.

As always, I would like to thank my wife Sarah for her endless support.

If you enjoyed Base Line, *please take a few moments to write a review. Thank you!*

You can sign up to James's mailing list at jamesellson.com

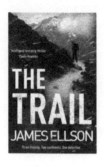

The Trail

The first book in the DCI Castle series.

**Longlisted for the Boardman Tasker Award
for mountain literature.**

A missing person enquiry leads Manchester DCI Rick Castle to Nepal.

Manchester. DCI Rick Castle is inspecting his bees when his
boss phones. A minor cannabis dealer has been reported
missing. His father's a war hero.
Rick flies to Nepal, and heads up the trail. Through villages of
staring children and fluttering prayer-flags. Brilliant blue skies,
and snow-capped mountains.
He finds a dead body.
Then a second.
Nothing in this world was ever straightforward. Nothing.
Finally, he puts himself in the firing line, and has a decision to
make. Is it the right one? The moral one?

Three missing. Two continents. One detective.

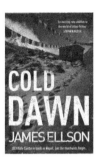

Cold Dawn

The second book in the DCI Castle series.

**Longlisted for the Boardman Tasker Award
for mountain literature.**

Against the rules, Manchester DCI Rick Castle removes a
prisoner from Strangeways and returns to Nepal.
His aim: to bring to justice his nemesis Hant Khetan, rumoured
to be the next Osama Bin Laden.
When the prisoner escapes, Rick and his small team must search
for him along the paths of the Everest foothills.
Trekking in the shadow of snow-capped mountains and
through earthquake-flattened villages,
Rick becomes increasingly desperate.
If they can't find him, Rick can't even begin . . .

DCI Rick Castle is back in Nepal. Let the manhunts begin.

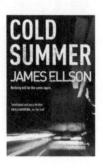

Cold Summer

The third book in the DCI Castle series, and the final part of the Nepal trilogy.

A race against time as DCI Castle hunts for two wanted suspects before they kill each other.

Manchester, England, the European migration crisis rampant…
On the site of a disused supermarket, the hidden compartment
of an articulated lorry is being unloaded. At the same time,
a prisoner escapes from Strangeways.
Are the two things connected?
DI Rick Castle, recently demoted but inspirational,
starts to investigate . . .

Nothing will be the same again.

− AGLE